Farley

JOURNEYMEN OF STONE - BOOK ONE
C. J. MILBRANDT

OLEXI

Journeymen of Stone, Book 1
Farley
Illustrated Edition

Copyright © 2023 by C. J. Milbrandt | CJMilbrandt.com
ISBN: 978-1-63123-091-2

Cover Illustrator: Hannah Lavender | hannahlavender.com
Interior Illustrations: Lindslee Goleman
Jacket Design: Elza Kinde | bumblebess.com

Also available in audio! Narrated by Travis Baldree

"Tread lightly lest the silence catch you unawares."

table of contents

Farley

PROLOGUE

In Open Territory

"*This*," Aurelius complained. "With all the unparalleled grandeur of the Pred capital before you, I still can't believe this is the one place you wanted to go."

"Yep!" Farley assured, ducking under a low-hanging branch.

"You're only complaining because it's such a long walk," teased Hadwin.

"Are you calling my fitness into question?" Aurelius arched a challenging brow at his third son. "You've never once bested me in Open Territory."

"Ulric has," grumbled Hadwin.

"Oh, aye. Ulric *has* distinguished himself, and I couldn't be prouder. But we're speaking of *your* chances. Were you planning to challenge me while we're here?"

"As if that wasn't your plan all along."

"Nay! I planned to pit you against Aggie." Aurelius breezily suggested, "If you can best my girl, perhaps I'll give you the contest you crave."

"Are you gonna play hide-and-hunt?" asked Arni. "Can me and Quinny join?"

Both six-year-olds did their best to plead with their eyes.

"Nay," said Aurelius. "At least, not today. Traipsing through these wilds was your Uncle Far's one wish, and so we must persevere. Besides, your Uncle Larkin should be waiting on the shore by now."

"Which way?" asked Quintrell.

Carric, who was seven and smug, asked, "Don't you have ears? Listen!"

The whole group left off talking, and Farley's heart skipped at the faint sound of distant waves. The ocean. It was taking half of forever to walk toward Vanora through the featureless woods that were apparently some kind of Pred hunting grounds. Now, the Starlit Mountain loomed, and her magic shimmered softly in Farley's periphery, so different than Morven's, yet familiar enough to ground Farley.

This was the place to which a young Freydolf Rakefang had run in order to seize a better future for himself. It stood to reason that it was also a good place for Farley to make his new beginning.

Lifting three-year-old Medric from his shoulders, Aurelius spoke to Quintrell. "Follow Carric and take this stripling along. See if you lads can steal up on Larkin."

"Yes, Papa!" Aurelius's fifth son beamed, lifting his arms to accept Medric, whose ankles jingled with bells.

But the littler boy's hand went to his dagger. "Nay! Not you! I can do it!" Lip out-thrust, he dodged Quin and trotted after his brother.

Thus rejected, Quin looked to Arni, who shrugged and caught his hand, running with him into the trailless woods ahead.

Ulric silently extracted himself from their group, going after them.

"Tree-cat territory," supplied Aurelius. "And there's always the odd bear."

With a startled glance, Torio asked, "This is your people's

idea of a playground?"

"They have to learn somehow."

Snorting, Torio lengthened his stride to catch up with Ulric. The children would have a rear guard. And better. Farley, who had Dessa's arm through his, gave her hand a grateful pat when he caught the telltale burst of magic that meant she'd sent Char and Nyx after the boys.

Something else bothered him, though. "Why don't Carric and Medric trust Quinny? He wouldn't hurt a sparkfly."

"Oh, aye. Neatly pinpointed." Aurelius fluttered his fingers vaguely. "No Pred, even one as small as Medric, cedes leadership to someone they consider ... weak."

Carden, who'd been conversing with Ulric most of the way, fell in step with Aurelius and mildly pointed out, "Quin isn't weak."

"Ulric understands, but his boys ...? They haven't met Frey." With a faint grimace, he added, "They probably never will."

As far as Farley could tell, Ulrica's namesake was a decent guy, if a bit stiff. He'd been nothing but polite, despite having to play host to a group of outspoken, overly familiar Flox from the countryside.

"Quintrell's strengths don't match my people's standards." Aurelius frowned. "I wanted him to know his brothers, though. I thought I could give him that much."

Hadwin said, "He has me."

Aurelius's glance was fond. "Aye, by the fangs. And I shan't complain. My two Harrow sons *should* back each other up."

"Don't your other sons want to take your name?" Carden inquired.

"I doubt Ulric or Mauritius would set aside the prestige that comes with being a Rakefang. They've seized the reins of a founding family's holdings. *And* made elite matches." His smile twisted. "Can you imagine what their wives would say if they suddenly adopted the name of a dockside nobody? Nay, I raised my sons to have better sense."

"You're *not* nobody," Carden gently interjected.

"Nay, but my pedigree isn't up to my people's standards, either. Though none can deny that the heirs to Rakefang have eyes of Harrow gold. Even down to wee Candra."

That was Ulric's youngest, a baby girl that Ulrica had barely set down since their arrival.

"What about Larkin?" Farley asked. "Is he vying for a name change like Hadwin did?"

"Not sure. I've barely seen the lad since he went off with Flaygore. One of my brothers. The tolerable one. According to Flaygore, Larkin took to the sea like one born to it. He may never have returned to shore if not for my insistence. And incentive." As they crested the bluff above a white sand beach, a grand ship with red sails came into view, anchored a little way from shore. "Yon ship is mine until he wrests it from me by completing his rite."

"What're you making him do?" Farley asked. "Aside from giving us a lift."

Aurelius snorted. "Only *now* you think to ask?"

"Well ... I've been busy with my own plans."

But the man ran lightly ahead, skidding down the bluff's steep slope in order to capture his fourth son. The embrace seemed to startle Larkin, but Aurelius's son didn't fend him off, and Farley guessed he was glad, even if he didn't show it.

Although Aurelius usually referred to Larkin as a *lad*, his son had grown enough to vie for his rite to adulthood. The guy had to be close to Freydolf's height, with the same rangy physique and hair color. Quin was wrapped around one of his legs, even though Larkin's pants were wet past his knees.

Then Aurelius framed his son's face with both hands and spoke earnestly to him, which caused Larkin's expression to soften. Pred never liked admitting they had a soft side, so Farley looked off over the water. Today, the sea was a peaceful blue-green with barely a ripple.

Until his first glimpse, Farley never would have imagined you could put so much water in one place. Or that—even without magic—it took on a life of its own. Colors and moods and movement. The sea rolled and roared in a restless way that he kind of understood. Not in the same way he understood magic, but he was sure of one thing. Farley wanted to board a ship and ride those waves to new places.

His attention drifted to Larkin's inheritance. The *Moontide* was newest ship in the Harrow fleet, and Larkin Rakefang was her captain.

The thing was a testament to Aurelius's paternal pride. And to the depth of his pockets. How long had he been preparing this grand gesture? Farley wasn't sure how much time it took to build a boat, but it was pretty obvious that this scheme was the long-range variety.

Quintrell collided with Farley's hip and wrapped both arms around his waist. Arni was on his way, too, walking backward up the slope. His guard was up, and his hand was on the hilt of the knife at his side.

"What's up Quinny?" Farley asked.

"Larkin's angry."

"About what?"

Wide golden eyes blinked up at him. "I don't think my brother likes Flox very much."

"Oh. Well, he's Pred."

"*I'm* Pred."

"Good point." Farley smoothed his hand over silky auburn hair. "But Larkin didn't grow up with Flox like you did. He doesn't know any better."

Arni caught up and took a position between Quintrell and Larkin. What was going on down there?

Quin asked, "Will you teach him to like Flox?"

"Sure. No problem. I mean, deep down, he's a Harrow, too, isn't he?" But when Farley looked toward Aurelius and his son, his heart sank. Aurelius was being extra flowery, and even at this distance, Farley could hear the sweetness in his tone. Not good.

Larkin wisely averted his gaze and spat an affirmative like it was a curse.

Hardly the most opportune time for Farley to offer an introduction, but he wasn't about to go nubless just because a Pred snarled. Nudging Quin and Arni toward Carden, Farley slipped down the sandy slope and kept his hands loose at his sides.

Thankfully, Torio was good at this sort of thing. He was all poise and courtesy as he introduced Larkin to Dessa. "She is your uncle's masterpiece. Few know that a thirteenth mountain was found, and your parents are adamant that we continue to be circumspect. Can we count on your discretion, Captain?"

Larkin politely offered his hand, but he said, "She's a statue."

"Yes and no. Dessa is a mountain. Or more accurately, the heart of one. It is rather a long story, but such things help to pass the time for fellow travelers. I look forward to regaling you."

Aurelius spotted Farley's approach and warned him off with one of the hand signals they used during hunts, then backed in his direction.

Farley quietly asked, "Is there some kind of problem? Quinny was upset."

"Perhaps I set the bar too high." Aurelius pursed his lips. "This is very likely shock. He'll adjust to the idea."

"What idea?"

"Aggie, for one. You for another. And to a lesser degree, Quin's attachment to young Arni."

"They're best friends. Practically from birth."

"Aye." Aurelius drummed his fingers against his thigh.

"Have I really changed that much?"

Farley didn't see the problem, but then ... he wouldn't. He'd been looking up to Aurelius since he was newly nubbed. "Doesn't Larkin know about Tupp and Frey? About your being lord governor? About Hadwin becoming a Harrow? About what his grandpa did to me?"

"Nay. It would seem he was completely unaware of the close connection our families enjoy. My letters must have gone astray, as they sometimes do when the recipient is at sea." Aurelius sighed. "All will be well. We've reached an understanding."

"Looked pretty reluctant to me."

"This is hardly the time for understatement."

Farley searched Aurelius's face. "What do you want me to do?"

With a chuck under his chin and a thin smile, he raised the bar for Farley as well. "Make me proud."

When Larkin pulled Hadwin aside for a hushed—and heated—conversation, Farley got on with his own plans for the remainder of the day. "Are we close?"

"It's not far." Aurelius gestured along the shoreline. "Frey's hideaway was snugged up right against Vanora herself."

"A hiding place?" demanded Carric.

"Unca Doff's special cave," Quinny boasted.

"Who's *that*?"

Blushing, Quin amended, "Freydolf Meadowsweet. He's your uncle, too."

Carric looked to his father for confirmation.

"Aye, the Gray Mountain's Keeper is your grandmarm's

brother. In a way, your Uncle Frey has gained even more prestige than that enjoyed by hilltop families."

"But he said *Meadowsweet*," the boy grumbled. "That's not us."

"Have you never heard tell of bond-brothers?" Ulric asked archly.

Such stories must have been good, because Carric's expression shifted to one of grudging interest. "He swore an oath, with blood and everything?"

Aurelius promised, "Everything was in order. I witnessed the ceremony myself. Making Meadowsweet a name that's known the whole world over."

"That's *us*," bragged Arni. "We're Meadowsweets."

"And I'll be the most famous Meadowsweet of all," vowed Farley. "But first ... where's this sea cave of Frey's? Or have you forgotten?"

"Perish the thought."

Farley fell in step with Aurelius, who led the way toward a monumental jumble of scrap rock that stretched from Vanora's sheer face, right out into the sea. He craned his neck, looking up toward the Pinnacles, which was home to Vanora's Keeper and to the many apprentices and journeymen who were in his care. "Do they actually pitch out their rubble here?"

"They do. Or did once, half an age ago. Still, it's best to keep your guard up."

"What a mess."

"Morven's barrens are certainly more orderly." Aurelius indicated the heights. "These days, they keep useful remnants in storerooms. This jumble is older than most of the capital."

Farley eyed the heap critically. "It might not be the best stuff, but it's not worthless. Aren't they afraid of poachers?"

"This part of Open Territory is famous for ghosts. Nobody comes here. Which should mean that Frey's boyhood trove has been similarly safe from thievery, if not from the elements." Aurelius crouched before a rocky outcropping and pulled a handful of sand away from its base. "The entrance is buried."

Farley dropped to his knees and began pulling. Quinny was quick to help, and that interested Arni, who brought over a couple of big clamshells to use for shovels. Medric tried to outdo them by stabbing at the sand with his little dagger. Carden brought him a shell of his own, which was both safer and somewhat more productive, although it also seemed to mean that Medric could now order Carden around like a servant. Farley wouldn't have put up with it, but his older brother seemed amused.

Aurelius wasn't.

Ulric wisely stepped in.

Carden received an apology.

Medric was allowed a hunter's topknot.

Peace restored, they made steady progress. Farley smiled to himself as two sorts of hands pulled together. Fair Flox with blunt nails. Clawed Pred, all bronzy brown. This was the sort of cooperation that had built his home. Funny how shocking it was to everyone else. He glanced around, curious about Larkin's reaction, but he and Hadwin were still off by themselves. Farley thought they might have been arguing, but ... honestly, it was hard to tell with Pred. But weapons stayed in sheaths, so it was probably all right.

"He'll come around," Aurelius murmured.

Farley cheerfully pointed out, "You did."

"Slanderous brat," he returned fondly.

"Should we look for another way? There's other boats."

"Nay." Aurelius sat back on his heels and gazed toward his sons. "I'll rest easier knowing you and Kite have Larkin to smooth the way. He's a well-traveled guide. A fluent translator. Truth be told, the papers I've promised him will effectively make him my successor."

"And I'm the blot on an otherwise appealing contract?"

"I can't think why he's being so cagey. The lad's always liked languages and culture. He has the makings of an excellent agent."

"He called me a bleater."

"Admittedly rude, but not inaccurate. Also ... beside the point." Aurelius slowly shook his head. "Perhaps Ulrica can suss out what's anchored in his harbor. Tomorrow. Over breakfast."

"What about dinner?" Farley's stomach growled.

"What's your pleasure?"

It was casually offered, but a Pred only hunted for their own. Farley tucked his chin, not that he'd ever been able to hide much from this man. "Since you're offering and all ... I could do with a rabbit."

Aurelius smoothly returned, "Aye. You shall have one."

As soon as the gap was wide enough, Aurelius suggested Quintrell wriggle through. "You push, we'll pull."

"Yes, Papa!"

Heedless of the tunic his father had no doubt ordered especially for the occasion, Quin drew his dagger and slid into the widened entrance. He became stuck partway through, but Arni pushed at the soles of his boots. Moments later, Quin's voice carried from inside. "I'm in!"

"Need a light?" Arni called.

"Nay, there are little holes to let it in." And a moment later, he exclaimed, "This is so good! It's full of treasure!"

Farley shot a look at Aurelius, who rolled his eyes. "Oh, aye. It's a veritable trove, and we've a treasure box to fill."

"What kind of treasure is it?" asked Arni.

"Gold and jewels?" guessed Carric, who was finally shifting sand like it mattered.

"Dawnstone and freshstone!" Quinny answered from within. "And songstone and dapple!"

Carric's pace faltered. "Just rocks?"

"So many statues!"

Aurelius signaled to Hadwin, who'd been given the unenviable job of traversing Open Territory with a trunk strapped to his back. After rejecting several finer, more ornamental chests from the stash in the Rakefang's attic, Aurelius had opted to take a sturdy trunk from Harrow Shipping's dockside warehouse.

Farley had to wonder if Aurelius expected Hadwin to haul the rock-filled trunk back out again. Based on his grim expression, Aurelius had left him in suspense on that point. But Farley doubted Hadwin's penance would be pushed that far. Not with Larkin's longboat beached a short distance up the shore.

Quintrell reached through the opening, passing Arni a bit of blue, which turned out to be a freshstone cradle guardian. The little feline's front paws must have snapped off, and part of its head had split away, yet Freydolf had mended the little statue with local stone. The join would have been invisible, if not for the contrasting colors, and the result was a blue tree-cat with a particolored face and white boots.

Frey had lavished this little one with care and with magic. Farley could see it shimmering hopefully. Having glimpsed the sun, it knew ... it wanted.

"I remember that one," Aurelius murmured, uncapping his canteen. "It wants fresh water. Cup your hands, Arni. There's a lad."

He dribbled a little into Arni's palms, snorting when the feline shivered to life and leapt for him. Teensy, tiny claws snagged in Aurelius's tunic as it tried to climb.

Farley laughed. "He remembers you."

"Not with any great affection. Trying to spoil another set of clothes, you little terror?" Aurelius scooped up the tree-cat and thrust it upon Medric, as if glad to be shed of it. But his eyes held a mercenary gleam as he watched his grandson sheathe his blade and sit in the sand to play.

Noting Carric's envious gaze, Farley asked, "Do *you* have a cradle guardian?"

"Who doesn't?" The boy haughtily bragged, "I get a new one every year. During my birth festival."

"Because your grandfather sends them," drawled Aurelius. "You're welcome."

"Did Frey make them?" Farley asked, even though the answer was obvious.

"Every last one," assured Aurelius. "Not many can say their bath toys and cradle guardians are a Keeper's handiwork."

"We're all spoiled," Farley cheerfully assured. "Everyone Frey loves has a statue or three as proof."

Carric's cheeks turned pink. Farley had forgotten that Pred didn't speak of love with the same ease as Flox. Aurelius never seemed to mind, though. Maybe because Flox ways were rubbing off on the Harrows. Just like Pred ways had become normal for the Meadowsweets.

Arni grinned at Carric. "My first one was a tiger. His name's Stripe."

With a superior air, the older boy revealed, "Mine's a wolf."

"What kinda stone?" Arni quizzed.

"Starstone."

"Hey, mine, too!"

This seemed to further disgruntle the Pred boy. "And titian jade. And dawnstone. And sunstone."

"Those are real good." Arni went back to pulling aside the sand Quin pushed out of the cave. "My favorite right now is a songstone dragon."

Carric's eyes widened, and he turned to his grandfather. "*I* want a dragon."

"Best try to keep up, then." Aurelius angled his head toward the task at hand. "Or I might forget to mention it to Frey."

The boy dug in with fresh vigor.

Not long after, Farley overheard Arni whisper, "Don't worry. *I'll* tell Uncle Doff for you."

Carric pouted, but he didn't refuse the favor.

When it was his turn, Farley crawled into the grotto. Aurelius passed him a lantern and followed on hands and knees.

"It's smaller than I remember."

"Because of the sand?"

Aurelius hummed. "I suppose I was only sixteen when Frey got himself banished. Not yet in my prime."

"Should I say something about your *always* being magnificent?"

"I'm not fishing for compliments, brat." Aurelius settled back against a smooth patch in the stone wall. "Though you wouldn't be wrong."

Farley sat with his back to the Pred—mostly because it would annoy Aurelius that his guard was down—and took his time just ... *looking*. He'd heard the story of Frey's sea cave at least a dozen times. Sometimes from the man himself, sometimes from Ulrica, since his sister had tracked it down later. If he was right about her hints and boasts, Aurelius had been here more than that one time Frey brought him. This hideaway had become Ulrica's escape, a safe place to meet with her hunting partner ... and future husband.

Little sparks of color caught Farley's eye, and he dragged his fingers through white sand flecked with chips of color. Once upon a time, when Frey was younger than Farley was now, there'd been no servants to sweep up after him.

He eyed the setup again. Rusty tools. Candle wax. Tinder box. Frey must have always sat where Aurelius was now, with that smooth patch for a backrest, facing the shelves he'd carved into raw stone. Long and narrow, they were exactly the right size for cradle guardians.

Chipped and broken.

Mended and propped.

Farley noted a dawnstone wolf with a starstone tail and a whimsical set of white horns mounted upon a brownstone mouse. Some little guardians must have been handed down over generations, for fur and scales had worn smooth in spots. All showed signs of Frey's gentle meddling, for in addition to the mending, there were lingering signs of his magic. How many hours had he spent comforting these castoffs and misfits, assuring them that they were loved and lovely? Unless Farley was mistaken, Frey had already been binding one sort of stone to another, giving them a part of himself that nobody else had ever wanted.

"I hope the trunk we brought is big enough," Farley said softly. "They miss him. Bet he misses them, too."

"Aye." Aurelius casually asked, "Did Tupper put you up to this?"

"I doubt it would've occurred to him." Farley plucked a songstone falcon from the collection, running his finger lightly over chipped wingtips. "He'll be glad I thought of it, though."

"Him and Frey both."

Farley looked his fill, then glanced over his shoulder. Aurelius lounged there, watching him. Like he was waiting for something.

"I wish you were coming with us," Farley quietly admitted.

The man's gaze subtly softened. "If I did, would you really be leaving home?"

For several moment, Farley couldn't even breathe.

Aurelius had a pleased light in his eyes. "Well, then, brat. Are you going to bid me a *proper* goodbye?"

Farley cleared his throat. "Guess so. Since you asked."

And there on the verge of a vast ocean, in a grotto laced with familiar magic and lovingly-mended guardians, where no one could see him acting so nubless, Farley crawled into Aurelius's arms and held on tight.

"I've done all I can," the man eventually murmured. "Use it to best advantage."

"You'll see," Farley promised. "I'm going to be magnificent."

"I found a ghost!" called Farley, who'd followed teasing hints of Frey's magic in among a series of old pilings. According to Torio, there must have been a pier here, at some distant point in the past. Its remains were almost like a colonnade, though its thick stone columns listed, drunken and derelict.

Torio turned from the ancient column they'd been admiring. Frey had clearly borrowed the thing as a practice block, lacing its surface with delicate sprays of flowers, curling peacock feathers, and the seashells he'd eventually taken for his signature.

Tipping back his feathered hat, Torio echoed, "Ghost?"

"A statue." Farley pointed. "According to Hadwin, this part of the forest is meant to be haunted, but it's only because there are guardian statues."

"They posted a guard *here*?" Torio asked skeptically.

"Pretty sure they only dumped him here." Farley beckoned. "He's damaged, but not fatally. And I think Frey marked him."

"One of Freydolf's statues?"

"Nope. This statue's gotta be ancient, but ... I think Frey felt sorry for him. See? Here." Farley rested his fingertips against the chest of a life-sized statue of a man who stood gazing out to sea, one hand outstretched. Or ... it would have been, had the hand not been snapped off at the wrist.

Carved from starstone, he showed signs of salt rime and weathering. Still, his nobility shone through, perhaps because of the circlet at his brow. Flowing cloth draped the figure, making Farley curious how it would move if he stirred. Because something about his posture brought dance to mind.

"He's Keet," Farley murmured.

Torio inclined his head, but then he flicked his fingers toward the figure's feet. "Notice the pedestal?"

Farley swept a bare foot over smooth stone. "Kinda big. Oh, I get it. He's meant to have a partner."

"Paired statues are common on Vanora."

"Is he reaching for his partner?"

Torio hummed as he ran his fingers lightly over white stone. "Statues return to the pose in which they were originally carved. Ah, here is his name. No. Two names. Pollim and Eullia. They would translate from Cantl as *verse* and *refrain*. Common enough. Keet are all about music."

Hardly surprising, as their people lived on the slopes of the Songstone Mountain.

Farley murmured, "I wonder which one he is ...?"

"I see you found Frey's favorite sob story." Aurelius strolled up, already bare-chested as he twisted his auburn hair into a knot, ready to hunt. "Poor old relic. Somehow or other, he and his partner were parted. Wouldn't surprise me if she was acquired by a Pred conqueror."

"But this is the Pred capital," pointed out Farley.

"Aye, it is *now*. But in days of old and yore, our people— like all people—had their beginnings on First Continent. Frey theorized that the two starstone lovers were cruelly parted. Pollim may have tried to stop the one who stole Eullia. Or perhaps their original positions linked their hands. Either way, the damage and the deed were done." With a little twirl at the mark Farley had found over the statue's heart, Aurelius added, "He might have become one of the terrors you'll be hunting down, if not for Frey's meddling."

Torio whistled softly. "He *changed* this statue. I think he strengthened his ... ah! Yes, here it is. Farley, can you see it?"

Farley wasn't sure what Torio was talking about. "See what? Where?"

"Frey did what he could to make the wait easier. Or so he said. No idea what he was going on about, actually. Maybe you can wheedle an answer out of him yourselves." Casting a look toward the deepening sky to the east, Aurelius said, "Pollim will be waking soon. And you'll be wanting that rabbit."

By the time Farley dragged his attention from the puzzle the Keet statue represented, Aurelius had slipped away.

Squinting into the sunset glow, Torio asked, "Am I imagining it?"

"Tell me where to look," grumbled Farley. "What am I looking for?"

"Magic."

Farley snorted, since that wasn't much help. They could both see magic, supposedly a rare affinity. Really useful, too, when it came to stone trade.

He considered Pollim more closely. There was the original magic of the stone itself, which was clean and strong and steady. And there was another sort of magic, which was linked to the original sculptor and their master mark. That magic held lingering threads of a hopeful sort of happiness. This was a good statue, but the break threw off the balance, and Farley didn't like how it felt.

Separation.

Suffering.

Sorrow.

Then something glinted briefly. "Hold up." Circling Pollim, he tilted his head. And found it. "You're right. It's barely a thread, stretched taut, and leading ...."

Both of them raised their arms at the same time, pointing out across the sea.

"What's that way?" asked Farley.

"Far Continent."

"Our destination! What're the chances ...?"

"Slim at best. It's a whole continent."

"And it's where I'm going." Really. Truly. Finally.

The light shifted, and stars gained enough strength to stir all of Vanora's children. The Keet dancer's clothing caught the sea breeze and fluttered lightly against Farley's skin. The feathers upon his head ruffled, and Pollim's mouth formed a startled little 'o' at finding a partner in easy reach. He angled his head and offered both his hand and an uncertain smile.

"You might have to teach me the steps, but sure, Mister. I like dancing as well as the next Flox." It was always nice to see a statue's delight in doing what it had been made to do. "My name's Farley, by the way. Farley Meadowsweet. I can't promise anything. I mean, I might not be able to find your partner, but if you wanted ... if it'd help any ... I think I could get you back to Frey."

"Surely you jest!"

Aurelius had barely placed a limp rabbit across Farley's palm when he began his haggle. "He's as scrapped as the rest of Frey's collection. Nobody will miss him if you bring him to Morven."

"You're serious?" Then Aurelius's tone shifted from incredulity to something vastly more petulant. "You're serious."

Farley gazed toward the bonfire Ulric had kindled, where Aggie was taking a turn dancing with Pollim. "Frey would be happy. Tupp would be happy. And if I can find his partner, even he'll be happy."

"She could be rubble," groused Aurelius.

"No, she's out there somewhere. You can ask Torio. They're still connected."

Aurelius turned to Torio. "The size and weight of the pedestal alone ...! It'll be deucedly awkward."

"Oxen?" suggested the Grif.

"Through Open Territory?"

Farley thought the drama was just for show now. "Barge to the docks, where Harrow Shipping is more than equipped to hoist him onto an ox cart. Load his pedestal on a clear night, and he can ride next to you on the driver's seat."

"But not yet. Not right away," cautioned Torio. "What if that much further is too far? If their bond snaps ... I do not like to think of it."

Aurelius drummed his fingers against the side of his leg and sighed. "Oh, all right. If you somehow manage to find his lady fair, send word. I'll bundle him up myself, and Frey can see them reunited."

"You're fond of him," guessed Farley. "Of Pollim."

"Aye, I suppose I am. He's part of my history with Frey. A good memory." Aurelius quietly admitted, "I'd like him to have a happier ending than this."

"Deal." Farley eyed Larkin's longboat and the lights aboard the *Moontide*. "Unless ...! Hey, do you think we could bring him with us? Instead of the other way around?"

"That's a thought." Aurelius looked to where Larkin sat with Hadwin, sharing the contents of a flask while they oversaw the turning of skewered meat.

Farley saw that Quinny was there, too, fiddling with the pouches at his belt. He was rarely without them. They held salt and spice and herbs from home. If he could get away with it, Farley would let the boy prepare his rabbit for him. Given the enthusiasm with which Hadwin was tearing into his own dinner, he'd done the same.

Aurelius asked, "What do you think, Kite?"

Torio began to nod. "It would vastly improve our chances of reuniting the pair."

"Aye. I'll hand down the order. If Larkin balks—and I expect he will at every turn—you'll likely have to stow Pollim in your own cabin."

Farley perked up. "I get a cabin?"

"Naturally. It's large-ish, though far from lavish. In fact, it doubles as a storeroom. One you can fill as you please." Waving at the Keet dancer, Aurelius said, "Far be it from me to criticize a man for squeezing in some last-minute packing. He can be part of your baggage."

Dinner and dancing stretched long into the night. The former because Hadwin and Aggie had clearly tried to outdo one another in the hunt, so there was an excess of game. The latter because Pollim kept inviting everyone to dance with him, even little Medric, who finally fell asleep to the statue's swaying.

Farley would have had trouble sleeping anyhow, so he danced all night.

Dawn was still a while off when Larkin rowed out to the *Moontide* to fetch some of his crew to move Pollim's pedestal into Farley's stow. Torio spoke softly to the statue, and Farley thought Dessa might have helped, because the Keet dancer walked a little way into the water and pointed to the ship.

Afraid he'd walk into the deep and be lost, Farley splashed to his side and hooked their arms together. "Come on back. You won't have to wait long. We sail with the tide, whatever that means. And there was something about favorable winds. But we're leaving today. And every day after this one, we'll be a little bit closer."

The Keet gently embraced Farley and petted his hair.

"I can see why Frey liked you so much." Patting Pollim's back, Farley muttered, "You're both a couple of softies."

"And you're not?"

He turned to Carden, who'd somehow been able to sleep. His eldest brother was sensible that way. Early to bed, early to rise, and always there for his family.

"Nope. I'm the daring one." Farley guided Pollim out of the lapping shallows and gave him a push toward Aurelius, who was fussing with the pedestal.

"If you say so." And the big brother who'd been the only father Farley had known—up until Aurelius anyhow—dragged him into another hug. "I suppose it's pointless to ask you to be careful."

"Yeah, of course. I'm going to have adventures, and

those are never safe."

"It's what you've always wanted."

Carden had to look up at him. Usually, Farley liked that proof that he'd grown up, but right now, he wished it was easier to hide his face, to hide his sudden dread over casting off this final tie to his kin. So he breezily said, "Goodbye, boring life. No more milking cows and making cheese."

"Were you really bored?"

"Not the whole time. But I was waiting the whole time, and that was hard."

"Harder than adventuring?"

"For me, yeah." Farley poked accusingly at Carden's shoulder. "Hey, you've been to as many new places as I have. So far."

"Travel is interesting, but I don't fancy a journeyman's life."

"Half the reason Morven likes you is because you're the settling sort."

"And Dessa favors men with a streak of wanderlust?"

Farley glanced toward the spot where Torio slept with his head cushioned on Dessa's lap. "I'm not sure if she loves Torio because he loves to travel ... or if she loves travel because she loves Torio. Either way, it means I'll be going."

"Come home sometimes?" Carden whispered.

"With heaps of stories and souvenirs," he promised.

"Then there's really only one last thing to say." Carefully tapping horns with him, Carden spoke their mother's words almost like they were a benediction. "Be brave, and do your best."

1

Misbegotten

Two Years Later ...

Farley didn't want to be backhanded for breathing wrong, so he focused on the soundless drag of air in and out of his lungs. Not easy while climbing a rain-slicked slope so steep, it was nearly vertical. The fading storm may have masked small noises until now, but fitful gusts and odd droplets made for scanty cover.

At times like this, Farley was wretchedly aware of the difference between those born for the hunt and those trained to keep up. Larkin moved like molasses—rippling, folding, and frustratingly slow. Utterly silent. The show-off.

If their prey had been a buck or bunny, Farley might have hung back until the Pred pounced. But tonight was different. Magic frizzed across his field of vision. From under the brim of his hat, he squinted at its quavering tendrils. Farley knew the look and feel of every kind of magical stone. A little closer, and he'd have this one sorted. Of course, that could also mean that whatever they were tracking would be close enough to know they were coming.

Farley touched Larkin's heel.

The Pred kicked free and flipped the blade in his hand, ready to slash down. But when Farley made the signal for ambush, Larkin melted back to his side. In the dim glow of their shuttered lantern, eyes of Harrow gold looked like honey in the sun, but nowhere near as warm or sweet.

Farley gritted his teeth behind his smile. After two years, he was used to this Rakefang's disdain. He put up with it. He could even sort of understand it. But he didn't have to like it.

Larkin's words puffed against Farley's ear, barely audible. "These woods are empty."

"There's power here. More than usual. Be careful."

"I move with care because I am Pred, *not* because you bleat caution."

"Only a dullard would call these woods empty. Right now, my eyes are better than your ears." Farley glibly quoted the man's father. "If the nearest is dull, reach for a better blade."

Annoyance flickered across Larkin's face, but Aurelius Harrow hadn't raised fools. "Lead on, Meadowsweet."

Taking a slightly different heading, their careful chase continued.

Thinning clouds broke, spilling enough moonlight over the landscape for Farley to get his bearings. He grimaced, though. They'd purposefully chosen an overcast evening in case they were dealing with moonstone or starstone. Sure, there were other varieties that stirred after sunset, but Torio had recommended narrowing the field.

Farley sought signs of movement among the trees below. The others had taken the longer approach, where the slope was more gradual. Larkin angled his weapon, indicating the trail where shadows slipped from tree to tree.

Not that Farley needed the help. When he focused just right, Dessa's magic blazed bright as a star. Her petulance grazed his mind. *"Wait for me. I don't like this one."*

Danger was half the reason Farley loved these side jobs. He wasn't going to let Dessa and her lionesses have all the fun, but Aurelius Harrow hadn't *fostered* fools, either.

"I'll be careful," he promised softly. "Can you tell what we're facing?"

Larkin eased closer, as if trying to eavesdrop. "Well?"

Farley shrugged. Dessa's thoughts took odd turns, especially where facts and feelings were concerned. Unsurprising, given the differences between flesh and stone.

"I won't let him touch you." Possessiveness edged her vow.

"Thank you, Dessa sweet." Farley's ears tingled, and he bit his lip. He hadn't meant to let slip Frey's pet name in Larkin's hearing, but she needed soothing. Clearing his throat, he tried again. "What kind of stone?"

"Cracked and crazed."

"Weakened?"

She brought out one of the newer words in her vocabulary. *"Warped."*

"Well, yeah. Guess it'd have to be."

Farley kept right on climbing. Ever since they'd taken on the first of these jobs for Freydolf, chasing down rumors of a moonstone Misbegotten in Drom, he'd seen terrible things. At least this time, they weren't hunting down a murderer. Only a killer.

"Did she give a straight answer this time?" asked Larkin.

"Same as usual. Go for a clean break."

When artisans worked with stone from one of the twelve magical mountains—*thirteen*, if you counted Dessa—it was possible to wake the resulting sculpture. Master-marked statues became stone guardians. They took on a life of their own, ruled by their mountain's magic and guided by their maker's hopes. But every so often, something went wrong. Any statue whose original purpose became twisted was considered a Misbegotten.

Farley reached a ledge and struggled onto it, only to find Larkin waiting for him with pointed patience. Signaling for light, Farley caught his breath while the Pred lifted a slat on their shuttered lantern. Its warmer glow lent color to a moon-silvered landscape, showing stone that looked wet with blood.

Rock in this part of Far Continent was red, even two days' journey from Yulla, the Red Mountain. To the untrained eye, it looked the same, which was why so many hacks and charlatans were able to pass off dull stuff for the magical stone that woke to flames. Only someone with affinity could tell the difference.

Larkin signaled, demanding a direction.

Farley pointed to where magical currents drifted from a jagged crevice. He made the sign for *slowly*, but his warning went to waste. Larkin shuttered his lantern and prowled through the opening without a backward glance.

The sudden absence of light wasn't half as disorienting as the sudden suffusion of magic. Sparks and sparkles dazzled Farley, who slowly worked his way forward and reached out, searching for the wall. His hand met something solid, but it wasn't earth or stone.

Larkin rounded on him, a sneer in his undertone. "Do you need someone to hold your hand, bleater?"

"That'd be a big help, thanks."

"I cannot track that thing if you cling like a milk-faced weanling."

Farley was glad the dark hid his expression. If Larkin knew he was grinning, the tongue-lashing would probably end. But insults were so much better than the stony silences that had marked their passage from the Pred capital to Far Continent. These eruptions of verbal viciousness meant Larkin was his mother's son, and that gave Farley hope. The stubborn brute might be warming to him.

"I can track it easy," said Farley. "But the trail's so bright, it's all I can see."

"Blinded?"

"Totally."

"It wasn't this bad last time."

"It's different every time." Magic was shifty like that.

Larkin stepped so close, Farley could feel the heat of him. "Use your other senses."

Doing that also meant letting down his guard. Something Farley did as often as possible, if only because it irked this guy. Closing his eyes, he lifted his face, effectively baring his throat. "I want the salvage."

"I thought you weren't interested in dull rock."

"This time's different." When they broke a statue, the stone's magic might be lost, but stone didn't need magic to be pretty. "I'm gonna keep the whole lot. Titian jade is your mom's favorite."

He could almost hear Larkin gritting his teeth, but he only asked, "Which direction?"

Farley pointed.

Larkin grunted. "I'll carry you."

"No chance. I can walk."

"If you die, my future is forfeit, and if you step in that direction, you'll fall."

Skeptical, Farley edged a toe forward. There was a drop, and possibly … water. Squinting against the glare, he asked, "Is there a pool?"

"And signs of death." Larkin turned his back and crouched. "Skeletal remains."

"The missing livestock?"

"Among other things. Get on."

"I'm too heavy."

"Don't insult my strength."

So Farley pushed his cloak back, wrapped his arms around the other man's shoulders, and thought heavy thoughts.

Larkin failed to notice. Not a total surprise, since the Pred had twice Farley's bulk, and all of it muscle. Larkin merely went up on his toes, bounced a few times to test his balance, and sprang from the edge he'd warned Farley about.

It wasn't a long drop, but it was unexpected. Farley borrowed a bit of Torio's native tongue and swore into Larkin's ear.

The Pred's huff sounded amused.

"What?"

"Your pronunciation is still abysmal."

"So I've got an accent." It hadn't taken long to catch on to the fact that Larkin was fluent in all the main trade languages and every regional dialect they'd run across thus far. When Torio had asked, it came out that Larkin spoke even more languages than his mother, having picked up a couple of obscure tribal languages in order to distinguish himself.

In a recent letter, Aurelius had suggested that Farley might learn from his son. Which was a good idea—in theory—if firming his grasp of Prose and Skrit hadn't felt like reckless endangerment. Larkin never gave pointers. Only criticism.

To Farley's surprise, they were in the open again. He was used to caves that went on for days, like the labyrinths that wove through Morven. This one hadn't amounted to much. More of a gate. Or perhaps a back door.

Larkin all but dropped him beside a tumble of stones that may have been a building at one point. The two of them stood at the top of a long, gentle slope, and on the opposite hilltop, stark against the starry sky, were the moonlit ruins of a grand house. With a little imagination, Farley could almost see how it must have been, a prosperous estate like those in the Pred capital, where houses like small fortresses loomed over their holdings. So different from the Flox, who gathered their homes close and rode out to farm the surrounding land.

"There," Farley breathed, pointing. Ever since he'd started on this path, it had always bothered him that Misbegotten magic was so flashy. Like the sculptors responsible for waking their creations hadn't known how to make the magic behave.

"I see it." A few heavy heartbeats later, and Larkin added, "It sees us."

"Titian jade, right?" He liked to point out how often he was right. Which was *always* when it came to stone.

"Be ready."

"Yep." Farley's boot knocked against something that scraped hollowly against underlying stone. Crouching to investigate—and to make himself a smaller target—his fingers brushed across something cool, smooth, and curved. Locating a socket, he glanced down to identify the skull. Horse. Farley pivoted slowly, surveying their surroundings.

What had probably been a pasture at one time was now a bonefield. Farley touched a set of curling horns that gave him the creeps, even though it was from an ordinary ram. A bare ribcage jutted nearby, and Farley guessed it must be from one of the big, docile oxen that pulled most carts on this continent.

"Sure are a lot of them," Farley remarked. "Strange nobody looked into it until now."

Larkin said, "Losing one or two animals in a season is unremarkable."

Farley paused to think. "How long's it been since that house was lived in?"

"It was on the map."

"The notes on your map were in Yamer," he grumbled.

The Pred spared him a glance. "That guildhall was built six centuries ago, more or less."

"Okay, that'd add up." Farley slowly rose. Larkin's posture was relaxed, but that didn't really mean anything. Pred were ridiculously confident. "Does it look dangerous?"

"Nay." In a flat tone, he added, "They were Grif."

"The statue's Grif?"

"The artisans who commissioned a guardian statue to tend to their flocks were Grif."

"Was that on the map, too?" Farley hated having to pester for every little detail. Torio was way more generous when they talked.

"Nay." Angling his knife toward the Misbegotten, he said, "The statue is a Pika slave."

"Oh. I get it. I guess that's ... historically accurate." Farley blinked, trying to clear his vision. It didn't always work when a nearby statue was agitated.

Nestor, who'd been quietly looped around Farley's neck, tensed. Then the little snake butted his head against Farley's jaw. "Uhh ... I don't think it's happy we're here."

"They never are." And more snidely, "If you plan to *use* that weapon, loose it."

The big, two-handed ax had been a parting gift from Ulrica, who'd bullied her brother into explaining its use in situations like this one, when a break was necessary to stop a statue.

Dessa's voice rang through Farley's mind. *"Char! Nyx! Go to him!"*

At the same time, Larkin warned, "Here it comes."

Farley already knew that, since the statue had pulled itself together in order to attack. The excess of magic retreated, allowing him to see a slender figure gliding silently toward them. Moonlight gleamed against polished jade. The guardian stone bent long enough to pick up a pale bone, which he waved over his head.

"Is that supposed to drive us off?" Larkin scoffed.

"Statues do what they were made to do. He's probably trying to protect his flock."

"Pitiful."

It really was, but it was also dangerous. A local shepherd

had filed a complaint with the Keeper of the Redstone Mountain. Two of his children had been badly frightened when a statue had come out of the trees and picked up one of their lambs. His daughter had tried to rescue it by driving the thief away with a stick, only to be dragged by the ankle to the edge of a bluff and tossed over.

Like all of Aurelius Harrow's contacts around the world, Yulla's Keeper had received a letter extoling the skills and bravery of Torio and Farley, who could be trusted to discreetly deal with any number of odd jobs involving magical stone.

"Move!" snarled Larkin, who sidestepped the statue's headlong assault, kicking its legs out from under it and driving it to the ground with an almost casual push to the back of its head. Slowing it down. Giving Farley an opening.

The stone guardian scrambled to his feet and swayed there. Like all the other Pika statues Farley had seen, he had a slight build, delicate features, and long ears reminiscent of a rabbit's. This one was dressed in a smock that left his legs and feet bare, and there was a heavy collar around his neck.

Writhing clear of Larkin, the statue was close enough to strike, and Farley had the ax in his hands, but ... it was only looking up at him. Like it was trying to decide how to deal with a man with curling horns. Well, *horn*, in Farley's case.

Then it stepped right past his lax guard and grabbed his wrist, pulling him toward a blockish formation near the hut that resolved itself into a line of troughs. Water caught starlight, and Farley spotted a lamb huddled against the trough's side. Worried for it, Farley's steps lengthened. Which was probably really, *really* stupid. Because the next thing he knew, the statue had him on his knees and by the horn, and he was pushing Farley's head down.

Piecemeal impressions rasped into his mind.

Dessa had used the right word for this one—*warped*.

Farley's hands found the trough's edge and he pushed up, gasping for air and shaking wet curls from his eyes. He was wondering if Larkin was planning to step in anytime soon when two black shadows leapt over the trough, swarming his attacker and driving the statue to the ground.

Nyx and Char were two of Dessa's guardian statues, and they'd always been protective of him. While they harassed the titian statue, Larkin loomed large.

"Why did you hesitate?"

"Didn't you see him? He was kid."

"It's a rock."

"And he's sad," he muttered lamely.

"It's ... a ... rock," Larkin repeated. "Give me your ax."

Farley immediately gave in and held it out.

"Call off your cats. They're in the way."

"Char. Nyx." Farley held out his hands to them. "Good work."

The lionesses looked between him and Larkin and wisely slunk to Farley's side. When the ax fell, Farley kept his gaze firmly fixed on Char's nose. She licked his. A new trick. Not to be outdone, Nyx licked his ear. Then Dessa was there, skirts billowing as she knelt before him.

Cool hands cupped his face, and she asked, *"Not hurt?"*

"I'm fine, Dessa. Just a little tired."

"I didn't like this one."

"I can see why. Now." He leaned into her touch and promised, "You're not alone, Dessa sweet."

Then Torio was there, standing over them, gazing out over bone-strewn acres. "What a chilling scene."

"Yeah," Farley agreed. "The little guy made a lot of mischief."

"Sympathizing, are we?" Torio's tone was light as he crouched before him. "Did it speak to you?"

"Not in so many words, but ... images. He was made to fill the trough from that spring back there and lead the animals to drink. It was nice here, way back when. He kept them safe from predators."

Larkin stalked over and thrust a fistful of grass under the lamb's nose. It bleated weakly and nipped at the blades.

"The little guy was trying his best, only the grass got choked out." Farley waved at the abundance of bones. "The animals he'd bring would slowly starve, and he knew that wasn't right. So he started killing them to keep them from suffering."

"A shame," Torio said.

"Can we bring him?" Farley asked. "What's left of him?"

"You still want it?" Larkin sounded exasperated. "It tried to kill you."

"I'm not so sure. I mean, he knew I was thirsty."

Torio passed Farley his canteen and remarked, "The pedestal is inside the cave mouth. We should bring it, too."

"Who's going to carry it?" asked Larkin in a tone that clearly communicated, *Not I.*

Dessa acted, pulling the Pika child into her arms and glaring a challenge. *"This stone was strong and beautiful. Once."*

Farley knew Torio wasn't really his master any longer, but he still looked to the Grif for answers. "He tried to learn a new way, to adapt." The next bit just sort of slipped out. "I'm glad Tupp wasn't here to see this."

"The young master would have been furious."

Fury hardly seemed to fit Farley's placid next-older brother, who was content to sweep chippings and oversee baths back home. But only if you'd never seen Tupp take the side of a stone.

Torio grimly said, "Even if he never meant to, this statue became quite the predator. And he might have learned to harm more than livestock. That girl. Now you."

"It mistook him for a ram," said Larkin.

Farley simply shook his head. It had been another adaptation. The statue had hoped for better company, but his outlook was so skewed, it would definitely have ended badly.

"At least we can return this lamb to that girl." Torio stood and shook out his feathered cape. "After that, I decree a respite. We'll sail south, toward Itzel."

"The Dawnstone Mountain?" Farley liked the sound of that. Pink stone was soothing.

Torio said, "Perhaps some time among actual Pika will ease the weight of this one's demise."

Larkin snorted again. "It's a rock."

"It is. And dull rock, at that. Thanks to you."

The Pred's eyes narrowed. "Are you blaming me?"

"No, my good captain. I am thanking you. As is Dessa."

Larkin spared her a glance, then muttered, "If we're bound for Itzel, Pika customs are … well. At least warn him."

Was that a note of concern? After such a poor showing, Farley had expected nothing but disdain.

"A lecture *is* in order," Torio agreed. "As well as a refresher in Liric, since we are due in Fwan territory before long."

"Leave me out." Larkin dropped the lamb into Farley's lap and grumbled, "I'll get the pedestal. Let's get back to the *Moontide* before the rain returns."

The Pred stalked off, and Torio offered Farley a hand up. As taloned fingers closed around his wrist, Farley asked, "What's his problem?"

"Let's call it … family resemblance. He is as vicious as his mother and as fair-minded as his father." Torio's lips quirked into a sardonic smile. "A charming combination."

"You think Larkin is charming?"

"Surely you can see it, given your years under Ulrica's loving heel." Torio's tone was as amused as the gaze that followed the Pred's swift retreat. "You had him worried."

2

Catchpenny Wares

Farley left the ship early, eager to have a look around. Up until now, his exploration of Far Continent had been limited to the environs of the Redstone Mountain. Grif culture seemed to place a high priority on artisan crafts, so Torio had dragged him from one guildhall to the next, showing off his homeland's many specialties.

He'd half expected Torio to take him to see his kin, but the man insisted he didn't have anyone left in Grif territory. "Wanderlust is a family trait. My only remaining family are traveling performers."

"Will we meet them?"

"Who can say?" Torio had answered vaguely.

"Don't you want to?" Farley pressed.

"I can hardly send a letter to my sister in care of First Continent. It's vast. Crossing this continent can be done in a matter of weeks, but that one? Months would be required, as well as careful planning and, ideally, a caravan."

"I want to see every part."

"Certainly. *Eventually*. It's worth all the time and even the risks."

"As long as we don't skip anything, I don't care about the

order." He reminded, "We're going everywhere."

"Even home?"

Farley tossed back, "Certainly. *Eventually.*"

Farley had learned a whole lot more about tides and favorable winds since boarding the *Moontide*. This first tour had them chasing good weather. Winter in the tropics sounded too good to be true. But that was weeks and weeks away, and Farley was more interested in enjoying today. This port was on the outskirts of Grif holdings, but they'd soon be in Pika territory. His experience with their race was limited to a handful of statues back in Morven's galleries ... and references that were either insults or insinuations. Firsthand experience was sure to set matters straight.

Shops crowded the extra-wide road that led from the port into the city, and he looked his fill until his belly complained about skipping breakfast.

A familiar scent caught his interest, drawing him into one of the side alleys. Sure enough, a cart heaped with fragrant melons stood outside a shop. The seller was a burly fellow with a gray complexion, and both he and his dapple mare wore fresh flowers. A few of Larkin's crew were also Oxus, so when the man glanced his way, Farley formed a polite greeting with both hands.

The fellow cheerfully returned the gesture, then called into the shop.

To Farley's delight, a gangly, slope-shouldered man emerged. His tunic was kilted up above knobby knees, and his skin was a deep, dark brown. Who else but a Drom would buy a glut of melons? The fruit was prized by their people.

Both men turned to Farley, who swept off his hat. "Good morning, homelander. That's a fine harvest. Could you spare one? I'm looking for breakfast."

The Drom hurried forward and bowed low. "Welcome, and welcome again! These ears have not heard such natural

Verit in many a season. How is it that a Flox has wandered so far from the green pastures of New Continent?"

"I'm traveling with friends." He proudly added, "We're connected to the Gray Mountain."

The shopkeeper was properly impressed. "You are as welcome as rains. And you have a taste for melons, young sir? These are dear, but perhaps in exchange for a story or two for me and my good friend ...?"

This time, Farley was properly impressed. Drom hospitality was famous, but it wasn't given in haste. "Thanks, and thanks again!"

"Fine manners." The shopkeeper beamed as he beckoned Farley inside.

"I went to Drom with my business partner. He'd lived there for a while, so he made sure I wouldn't offend anyone with my clumsy enthusiasm." Bowing low, Farley gravely added, "Please, be patient, since I too easily forget myself."

They strolled past rolled carpets and lanterns strung on chains, clustering against the ceiling. Shelves were lined with specialties he'd seen everywhere in the Drom capital—perfumed oil, pungent spices, and colored glass. Farley noticed that shades of pink were predominant. A sure sign they were nearing the Dawnstone Mountain, which was famous for its rosy hue.

The Drom, who introduced himself as Zaalenis Hashbaz, served cubes of melon alongside a salty cheese and cold strips of grilled meat. He apologized over and again for his lack of preparation and the meagerness of every serving. All part of being a good host.

Farley did his part by complimenting everything, both with words and by humming over every mouthful. Best of all were the mugs of spiced ale, which he suspected was the very stuff Aurelius raved about whenever he was feeling nostalgic. Apparently, he'd never found an equal to old Master Platt's reserve. But this ...!

"Do you make it yourself?" Farley asked.

"My brother and I dabble a little," Hashbaz admitted humbly.

"Any chance you'd part with some?" Farley made the Drom hand sign that meant he wanted to dicker.

Hashbaz beamed. "You bring back good memories." And then he said something in an aside to the Oxus merchant, who'd introduced himself as Corvullin.

"What did you say?" Farley barely knew any of the First Continent languages. Just a little Brohg, which was meant to help him get along in Clow territory. They'd get there eventually.

In warm tones, Corvullin spoke in Terse so Farley would understand. "My good friend says I should listen well, for no one haggles like a Flox. I am prepared to learn."

Farley grinned and followed through with his plan. If this went well, he could secure a cask for Aurelius. But why settle for good when you could barter for better?

He haggled Hashbaz to a fair price for one keg, then asked, "Heard any rumors lately? Ghosts? Monsters? Strange things lurking only by day or by night?"

The man drummed his fingers on the table. "Are you asking to trade tales?"

"Only if they're good enough." Farley leaned forward. "My friends and I take on the sort of jobs that involve rogue statues."

"Tell me more of this business, and I'll part with a second cask."

Perfect. Farley cheerfully countered, "If my tale is good—which it is—I'll allow you to ship four casks a year to Morven."

"Am I paying tribute to your Keeper, now?"

"More like our lord governor, who has connections you might find valuable. And the sense to part with coin when he finds something superlative." Farley touched the fingertips of both hands to his forehead, then his lips, and bowed his head in a Drom expression of gratitude. "May your efforts bear fruit that is heavy and sweet."

Hashbaz burst into rusty laughter. Topping off Farley's mug, he urged, "Tell on, and we shall see what we shall see."

When Farley finally meandered back out into the market, he was pleasantly hazy, flush with triumph, and in possession of a telling tale. He touched the flower behind his ear, a gift from Corvullin, and hoped that Prahkreet was on Torio's itinerary.

Hands tucked into his sleeves, lest he be accused of shoplifting—*and* to keep one of his small daggers at his fingertips—Farley easily found his way into the stone-seller's quarter. Magic beckoned. Stone whispered. A lot of the stuff was cheap, the sort of catchpenny wares that appealed to dullards. In one stall, heaps of beads stood in dusty baskets. He wouldn't have given them a second glace, but for a forlorn burst of magic from somewhere within the pile. Farley checked his stride and backed up.

"Good day to you, marm. Mind if I take a look?" Farley waved his hands over the basket. "I want something special, something *particular*. May I move them around?"

The wizened Grif gummed a smile and handed him a bag. She also watched him with a hawk's eye, lest he palm any beads.

Farley poked through the upper layer, searching for the lone bit of brightness, sure it would be songstone. He knew what it was like, being an uncommon stone trapped among so many dull rocks. Farley was probably the only

Flox anywhere who hadn't been content to stay in Morven's foothills. Sure, he'd had it easy. He could have milked cows and made cheeses until the end of his days, living comfortably with friends and family, with nothing more exciting to look forward to than the annual festivals.

But how could you stay put once you found out about faraway lands and foreign cultures? When Torio Kite the wanderer became his master, Farley had made up his mind to be a wanderer as well. Why stay when you could go? Why blend in when you could stand out? So he dug through the shabby basket, determined to find that one stone that sparkled with aspirations.

Tupp would have understood.

Frey would have called him a good picker.

Mercifully, Farley didn't have to upend the whole basket. Holding a green bead between thumb and forefinger, he offered the old woman a slim coin, not even bothering to barter. The trinket was too sweet-natured to be stingy about, and he was feeling generous.

The trade was good, and as Farley strolled toward the next stall, he offered it to Nestor, who took it into his mouth. The little snake liked being entrusted with things. He might be small, but he was a proper Heartstone guardian. The first ever to stir.

"You're late!"

Farley hadn't realized he had an appointment. Swerving toward Larkin, he cheerily asked, "Am I?"

"Where have you been?" the Pred demanded.

"Here and there. If you can't track me down, Dessa always knows."

Larkin glowered at the slight to his skills. "We have business to conduct."

Farley brightened to see Torio leaning against the entrance to a courtyard filled with large blocks of dressed stone. Even from here, he could see the wax seals that served to certify stone as authentic. Hurrying to the Grif's side, Farley asked, "What's a stone market doing here? We're a long way from either Itzel or Yulla."

Torio inclined his head. "This city is midway between the Dawnstone and Redstone mountains, but convenient to half a dozen middling guildhalls. They also cater to stone merchants and journeymen who travel through this port."

"Is there *really* going to be anything worth looking at?" Farley whispered. The whole place had a lackluster feel to it.

"Aurelius wants Larkin groomed for the business. This is more for his benefit than your brother's."

Farley wasn't sure if he meant Freydolf, who was a Meadowsweet on account of Tupp, or if he meant Carden, who'd asked Farley to keep an eye out for practice blocks. Either way, he was skeptical they'd find anything. But Larkin was a dullard, so it was all the same to him.

Farley said, "I guess we should back him up. Since Aurelius asked."

Torio said, "I don't expect to find anything, either. But we must go through the motions for the young captain's sake."

"Will he listen to us?"

"He has little choice. And he does not like it. Or you."

"He's coming around. Sort of." Farley tried not to be offended. "I wouldn't mislead him. Not about stone."

"I know that. You know that." Angling his beaky nose toward Larkin, who was introducing himself to the merchant, Torio quietly added, "*He* must learn that, and so we must teach him."

"He's smart. He'll figure it out."

Then Larkin called for Torio, and there was more of the longwinded gallantry that paved the way for a possible sale. Having already navigated his own deal earlier, Farley wandered through the courtyard, then into an inner room where blocks of all sizes were arranged by color. The merchant who ran the place had to be a dullard, because most of the stones he'd brought in were sad specimens, probably taken a long way from their mountain's heart. Some were probably even taken from their foothills, good enough for furniture or fountains, but Farley couldn't imagine parting with coin for any of it.

Or was he just spoiled?

Morven had been under his very feet, and he was acquainted with spectacular masterworks, some of whom he counted as friends. Only dazzlers like Dessa turned his head anymore.

Maybe modest stones like these were good enough for an apprentice's practice block. Was this the sort of stuff he was meant to bring back for Carden? Farley *could* see the sense, but he rebelled against it. His oldest brother had to have progressed in three years. He deserved finer stones than these.

Determined that such a travesty never happen, Farley stole back to Torio's side. Larkin needed backup, even if he didn't acknowledge that he and Farley were practically brothers.

With small headshakes and subtle signals borrowed from Pred hunts, they helped Larkin see past the flowery words of the simpering salesman.

When a long slab of freshstone caught Larkin's eye, Farley muttered, "If you want a new threshold for your parlor, it's handsome enough."

He was overheard by a youngish-looking man who seemed to work in the shop, a big fellow whose muscles were likely needed whenever there was stone to be shifted. Catching Farley's eye, he winked.

Larkin's questions grew more pointed, and his mood soured.

The Grif merchant's smile faltered as his hopes of a sale dimmed.

Talk turned to trade routes and the trustworthiness of stone peddlers.

Easing to Farley's side, the big guy remarked, "You've more affinity than most."

"Some of those blocks may as well be made into beads," Farley countered. "I've seen loads better."

"Oh, there's better than these. But don't disparage a stone's potential simply because their ambitions don't match your own."

Farley gaped at him. It was the sort of thing Tupper would say.

"Your hands," he said. "They're too soft for you to be a sculptor."

Over the last couple years, Farley's calluses had rearranged themselves some. He'd always hated drudging, but he'd pitched in plenty. However, churning butter hadn't hardened his hands much, and he didn't spend much of his free time swinging his ax. Neither was he expected to do much aboard ship. Farley wasn't exactly a layabout, but he had more books than blisters.

He stiffly said, "Not everyone with affinity serves stone."

"I meant no slight. I'm only trying to sort you out." He offered a big hand. "I'm Artor. Your accent ...? Where are you from?"

Farley tipped back his hat to look up at him, then took it off. "We sailed from New Continent. Farley Meadowsweet. I call Morven, the Moonlit Mountain, home."

Artor's eyes widened. "You're Flox!"

"Sure am. Say, are you Ursa?"

Nodding, he tentatively revealed, "In days of old, my forefather was one of Morven's Keepers."

"Then what are you doing on this continent?" Farley ventured, "Are you a journeyman?"

"The child of a child of one. My grandsire was part of a crew." Artor shrugged. "I came into my affinity late. I can't boast a mountain's call, and there's no one to recommend me to a guildhall. Journeymen come and go through this port, and some are willing to show me things. But they're barely here long enough to teach me more than trifles."

"My brother started late. Carden was a father three times over before they found out he had any affinity. Now, he's apprenticed to Morven's Keeper."

Artor looked envious, but he flashed a wry smile. "Good for him."

"So what do you do? Other than shift unambitious blocks."

"Would you like to see?" He gestured toward a door. "I've been working in there."

Farley didn't expect much. There was no great magic emanating from the direction Artor led him. The door led into a hall, which in turn led to a series of small rooms. "You live here?"

"Yes. I get room and board, and Ketik didn't care if I changed the floor."

The *floor*. Artor's tiny room had been fit with a mosaic.

"I don't have many statues. Still trying to figure out …."

But Farley wasn't listening. Artor's statues were nothing special, but they didn't try to be anything they weren't. The lines were simple—all graceful curves and high polish—and none of them were marked. But they radiated happiness, as if they were pleased to have been chosen and proud of their transformation.

"The floor," Farley whispered.

Artor stopped his rambling apologies and looked down. "I work with dull stone a lot."

"I'd hardly call your mosaic *dull*." Residual magic shimmered throughout the intricate pattern, glowing with affection and lending the room a peaceful ambiance. "Did you do this on purpose?"

"Do what?"

Farley gaped at him.

"Ketik was pleased. He said I could do his receiving room next, if I want."

"What terms?" Farley asked sharply.

Artor slowly shook his head. "You mean pay? Well ... he gave me a place. I'm grateful he thinks enough of my work to–"

"*I'll* give you a place."

"Pardon?"

"I'll give you a better place than this." Farley folded his arms over his chest. "Morven would like you. Frey might even make you an apprentice."

Artor's bewilderment multiplied. "Frey?"

"Freydolf Meadowsweet is Morven's Keeper. And my brother. Frey would take you, no question. Though we're not headed there directly. Torio promised me a look at First Continent before that, and even a quick look will take time." This was probably the most interesting haggle Farley had ever attempted. "Do you mind being a journeyman for a while first?"

"Me, a journeyman?" He sounded hopeful, but Artor still hesitated. "That Pred ...?"

"Larkin. He's captain of our ship."

"I'm not very good around Pred."

Did this guy not know that Morven's Keeper was Pred? Not that Frey counted, exactly. Still, there were Aurelius and Ulrica to consider. "I don't blame you, but I bartered hard for my place in his family. I'm kin to Larkin, even if he doesn't like it. It's a long story, but if you come along, there'll be lots of time to tell it."

Just then, Torio called from the shop's direction.

"Here! You need to see this!"

Torio strolled their way a moment later, feathers aflutter and a bemused smile on his face. "Why have you cornered this good Ursa?"

"This is Artor. I'm bringing him to Frey."

Torio spared the man a quizzical look, then indicated the room. "May I see?"

"Yes, of course. Be welcome."

The Grif stepped into the room, lightly touched a few of the statues, and peered at the contents of a work bench. Pivoting, he offered his hand to Artor. "I agree with Mister Meadowsweet's assessment. Do you have a contract fee we will need to cover for your current master?"

Artor quickly shook his head. "Nothing like that. Nothing formal."

Farley said, "I'll bet this merchant's downplayed Artor's skills, making it seem like he's doing him a favor."

"Business has its perils." With a smirk, Torio pointed out, "Artor has no contract to protect him, but that also means his employer has no means to hold him back. I'll have a word with Larkin about what we'll be carrying away today."

"Just like that?" Artor ventured. It wasn't a protest, really.

Torio said, "Your handiwork speaks for you. Did you wish to speak for yourself?"

"Should I?"

"Work out a verbal agreement with Farley. When I can get word to Harrow, there will be a proper contract. We won't sail for a few days. Time enough to stow your things aboard the *Moontide*."

"Who's stowing what on my ship?" growled Larkin, who'd stolen up behind them.

Farley stepped between him and Artor. "This guy should be apprenticed to someone better than a two-bit rubble salesman."

Artor made a soft noise of protest.

"I'm right!" Farley insisted. "And so I'm bringing him to Frey."

Larkin's expression hardened, but he looked to Torio.

The Grif said, "I'll support this young artisan's decision, should he choose to journey with us. And I will mourn his loss, should he choose to remain here."

"Well?" demanded Larkin, eyeing the Ursa.

Artor drew a quavering breath but steadied himself on the exhale. "I want to go to Morven."

Larkin grunted and turned to Farley. "Where are you going to put him?"

Farley didn't even hesitate. "He'll bunk with me."

"Your name?"

"Artor Oldtree."

That earned a raised brow. "Contract?"

"None."

A smile slowly crept onto Larkin's face. "I'll inform your former employer that you've heard a mountain's call."

Though he moved to follow, Torio paused long enough to ask, "Are you attempting to outstrip your brother?"

Farley frowned. "You mean Artor would be competition for Carden?"

"I am referring to Tupper." To Artor, he added, "While his brother is unsurpassed as a picker of stones, Farley may yet distinguish himself by finding artisans suited to Morven's heights. You will be welcome, Artor Oldtree."

"Thank you."

Backing away, Torio pointed to Farley. "Bring a cart from the ship." And pointing at Artor, "Don't leave a single loose stone behind. They love you."

Once Torio strode away, Farley asked, "Want help packing?"

"There isn't much." Artor sank to a seat on his pallet. "How can he tell? That they love me, I mean."

Farley's lips twitched, and he shook his head. "Let's just say Torio's in a position to know."

3

Deucedly Affectionate

Artor insisted that he could manage alone, and Farley admitted, "I'll need to make room in my cabin."

"Room?" came Dessa's worried whisper. "*Make room?*"

With a promise to return with a cart before evening, Farley hurried toward their ship. "I'll tell you all about it as soon as I get there. Are you staying out of sight?"

"*Yes, I'm keeping my promise.*"

"Thank you, Dessa sweet."

She only sighed.

Even though they'd explained things, she didn't like any circumstance that parted her from Torio ... and to a lesser degree, from Farley. She refused to believe that they needed to keep her safe. What could be safer than having her with them?

Torio refused to take her into public places. Dessa complied, but she didn't like it. And Farley felt bad for her. At times like this, she grew increasingly quiet.

He found her sitting on the floor in Torio's cabin, the lionesses sprawled around her while she petted their ears.

Nyx moved aside, making room for him.

"You look like a girl with a lapful of kittens," he teased, dropping to a seat.

No answer.

Dessa had draped herself in the travel cloak he'd adapted for her. Farley had all but unraveled Torio's feather cape to learn the knack to making one, then used that knowledge to add a generous ruff to Dessa's. The black feathers, with their green and purple sheen, gave her an air of elegance, and she liked matching her Keeper. Whenever they did leave the ship together, the hooded cloak with its flutter of feathers helped to hide Dessa's features.

Easing back the deep hood, Farley gently rearranged a loose curl. "You changed your hair again."

"Farley." She slipped her arm through his and immediately calmed, which was nice, since it meant the fireworks ebbed away.

Dessa counted as Freydolf's masterpiece, and she was a tribute to his skill. None of the other mountains' Keepers had given Torio a chance, let alone tried to figure out how to wake the new magical stone he'd carried across all four continents. Frey had found the way, but this was new territory. Nobody really knew the consequences of giving shape to a mountain's heart.

Farley had been the first to notice that Dessa could make little alterations to her appearance: the fullness of her skirt, the trim on her cuffs, the addition of a necklace or bracelet. Maybe it was because he'd already discovered that Nestor could change his shape. When the little snake was alert to danger, he could flare his scales outward, like a cobra's hood. He could also flatten himself in order to press through narrow cracks.

With a little nudge, Dessa repeated, *"Farley."*

"I like it." He tweaked a curl. "Very Floxish."

She smiled then, a hopeful, wistful sort of smile. *"Farley wants to go home?"*

"Well, yeah. Eventually. Did you think I was homesick?"

"Missing Morven? Missing Freydolf?"

"They were on my mind, but I have my hands full with my own mountain and my own keeper." Farley firmly said, "It's like I've told you, Dessa sweet. You and me and Torio—we're at home together."

She took his hand and pressed it to her cheek, leaning into his touch.

Farley wasn't stingy with his affection. In a way, Dessa felt like family. She'd called him, and he'd answered, and so he was bound by her magic. He knew the ties were there because he could see them, and he'd already figured out what it meant. That part hadn't been hard, since Morven had formed similar bonds with Frey, Tupp, Carden, and even his young nephew Hewey.

He'd gone so far as to confide in Aurelius, who'd helped him sort out his priorities. And maybe his feelings.

Mountains chose Keepers, but they also looked to their future. A mountain's call carried far, and those who answered became journeymen, apprentices, and successors. Torio was Dessa's Keeper, and she needed him in ways that made the Grif uncomfortable. Unlike the other twelve Keepers, his mountain wasn't a vast topographical feature. She was a lady, and she gave every impression of being in love.

Not for the first time, Farley wondered if Torio ever kissed her.

Dessa might be stone, but she sure felt like a girl. If Farley closed his eyes, it was easy to forget that she was a gleaming masterpiece. She rested her head on his shoulder, and he wrapped an arm around her, pulling himself closer. "He'll be back soon," he soothed. "He'll always come back."

"Like you?"

"Me, too," he agreed easily.

Torio might be skittish about being the object of a statue's affection, but Farley didn't see the problem. He'd kissed a few. His first big crush had been on a member of the Triads. Tupper had butted in—of course—taking him aside and offering to answer any questions, which had been really embarrassing. But Tupp, who was good at listening to stone, had also listened to him. Without laughing or teasing, he'd considered the matter from both sides with a grave sort of sympathy. To Tupp, the statues were people, and their feelings mattered. He'd gently let Farley know that the girl in question didn't want to break his heart.

What Tupp didn't get was that Farley's heart had always been safe. But his brother wouldn't have understood. Because Tupp was happy to settle down and stay put, and Farley had always known he couldn't.

So he doted on Dessa, trying to show Torio that it was simple.

And his former master looked on with the oddest mix of exasperation and envy, as if Torio couldn't decide if he was relieved that Dessa took so well to Farley ... or if he was jealous of the attention he paid her.

"I made a friend today. Artor has a way with stone that reminds me a little of Freydolf. So I invited him to sail with us." He rested a cheek against soft curls. "Are you ready to make a new friend?"

"You won't make me hide from him?"

"Nope. I'll introduce you straight away."

"Will he be afraid?"

"That would be silly."

"People are silly, sometimes."

"Mmm. Yeah, they are. But Artor's stones love him, and that means he loves stone."

"Will he love me?"

"He might. Would you like that?"

Dessa sighed softly. *"Where's Torio?"*

"He and Larkin are resupplying the ship before we move down the coast toward the Dawnstone Mountain." Farley patted her head. "Want to lend a hand? Artor will be moving in with me, so I need to make room for his stuff in my cabin."

"I'll help." She pressed her lips to his cheek and murmured, *"Love you, Farley."*

When Farley returned to the stone seller's shop with a cart, he found Artor on his hands and knees, loosening and lifting the stones of his mosaic floor. He asked, "You didn't set them permanently?"

Artor started. "Hey, again. Wow. I didn't hear you arrive. Am I late?"

"Nope. Can I help, or is there an order to it?"

"Not really." He shook his head, then softly asked, "Is this all right? I wasn't sure I should be bringing my floor, but then I couldn't bear to leave it."

"Torio said to bring your stones. I'd say these count." Farley pulled the dagger from his boot and began flipping up the tightly-fitted stones and adding them to a crate that would probably be too heavy for him to budge once it was full. "Hang on. I'll bring the cart inside. Better to load this onto it now."

Artor agreed, and they resituated. Farley started pitching mosaic tiles into his hat. While they worked, they started swapping little details. Normal stuff like favorite foods and first jobs and cradle guardians.

"I'll introduce you to Tap once we're aboard ship. He's a

freshstone stallion."

"I also have one to show, but I'll have to bring him out later, once the stars are bright." With a sidelong look, Artor ventured, "Who's that with you?"

Farley eyed him curiously. "You can sense a stone's magic?"

"Not really. At least, not right away." He pointed in the vicinity of his own throat. "Your uhh ... your little buddy keeps peeking at me ...?"

So much for subtlety. Farley tickled the nose of the guardian who was supposed to be staying out of sight. "Guess we can get into it a little. Can you keep a secret?"

Artor's brows drew together, but he said, "Yes."

Unwinding the snake from where he'd draped himself, Farley turned him loose on the tile. "This is Nestor. Frey made him for me."

"Morven's Keeper did?" Artor reached out, offering his fingertips to the little snake.

Farley waited for the inevitable question.

"This opacity. Is it possible ...?" Artor's voice dropped to a whisper. "He *isn't* smoky crystal, is he?"

"Nope."

"But ... none of the magical mountains yield black stone."

"That's what people say."

Artor smiled faintly as Nestor slipped between his fingers, then rubbed his head against one big knuckle. "He's wonderful."

"We try to keep it quiet, since there are mixed opinions and mercenary types at every turn. Joining up with us means you're in on the sorta-secret of the thirteenth magical mountain." Farley went back to collecting mosaic stones. "You'll get the whole story once we're safe aboard the *Moontide*."

Accepting that with a nod, Artor changed the subject. "Will there be room for all this?"

"It'll be fine. You'll see. My cabin isn't fancy, since it's basically a storeroom, but I'm nowhere near close to filling it. And besides that, I'm used to sharing. Big family."

Which brought questions about Farley's kin. It took a while to rattle through all his siblings and their families, but Artor seemed interested, and it helped pass the time.

"So your brother's babies have a brownstone nanny?" Artor asked with a laugh.

"I'd say Haimish is Yona's, through and through, but he lends her a hand when *she's* lending a hand, so it works out. But the family keeps growing, and everyone wants their statues to be Frey's handiwork. His stuff's what Aurelius calls 'deucedly affectionate.' So I'm looking for just the right blocks. Redstone would be good, since Frey thought he could manage a fire-eater, but Tupp asked for more brownstone. Not sure where I'd find any on this continent, but ... yeah. I'm keeping an eye out."

He suddenly felt bad for only talking about himself. "What about you? Do you have brothers and sisters?"

"Brothers, after a fashion. My parents died when I was still too young to be on my own, so I was taken in by our neighbors." He looked at Farley, as if wanting to gauge his reaction. "I was raised by Pika."

"Yeah? Were they good to you?"

"Always."

Something in Artor's smile made him wonder. "Am I missing something?"

"I think so. You ... don't know much about Pika, do you?"

"I know they're small in stature, kinda like Flox. And that they're often compared to rabbits because of their ears. And that a lot of them are herbalists and healers. Aurelius *insists* on Pika-made medicines." He thought back and shook his head. "People like to hint that there's more, but they're always really vague about it. Even Torio."

"Oh, there's more."

"And you're an expert. Maybe you can give me some pointers?"

Artor said, "If we're headed deeper into Pika territory, I'll have to."

"There it is right there! The knowing look. That hint of insinuation. You're holding something back."

Artor laughed. "The first thing you need to know about Pika culture is that they don't hold back. They're generous, especially with their affections. Basic etiquette involves a lot of touching, and most of the courtesies involve kissing."

Farley tried to picture Larkin in a situation like that and snorted. "I'll hang back and let Torio handle things."

"They won't let you." Artor's smile was definitely still in the knowing category. "You're Flox, and that makes you a true novelty on this continent."

"So they're going to want to meet me?"

"Mmm. Think of it as collecting. For instance, once a collector discovers that there are twelve mountains, they'll want a stone from each of them."

Farley was well aware of this tendency. It was one of the reasons Torio was so protective of Dessa. For a certain subset of the world's population, she represented a tempting acquisition.

"Many Pika collect experiences. They'd boast about simply meeting a man like you. Or better, that they'd crossed palms with such a man. Or touched his hair. Or shared a meal ... or a dance ... or a kiss ... or more." Artor's tone was frank, and his gaze was direct. "The Pika will vie for your attention, and they'll try to outdo one another."

"Are you speaking from experience?"

"Yes."

"But you said they were good to you."

"Always," he repeated. "I never minded. But you might, so I'm erring on the side of caution."

Farley grimaced. "I want to make a name for myself, but I'm not looking for that kind of attention."

Artor scooped up Farley's hat, emptied its collection of

tiles into the crate, and returned it to Farley's head. "Keep your hat on," he advised. "And stick close to that Pred brother of yours. He'll make an effective deterrent."

"That doesn't sound like much fun."

Offering his hand, Artor said, "There are forty-six ways to say *yes* to a Pika, but there are a few ways to say *no* in a manner that doesn't leave room for counteroffers. I can teach you."

"Forty-six words that mean *yes*? Doesn't that get confusing?"

Artor blinked, then broke into a low, rolling laugh. "Who said anything about *words*?"

The cart creaked up the gangway. Larkin loomed ominously on deck, but he only nodded to Artor. Farley was surprised at him. The Harrows might have been very Pred, but as merchants, they usually made more of an effort toward diplomacy.

Once they were out of earshot, Farley whispered, "Kind of stingy with the welcome and introductions. That was Larkin, by the way."

"Oh, he came by the shop earlier and spoke to the boss on my behalf. There were papers for me to read and to sign." Artor softly added, "He *hired* me. I'll have both a place and an income."

"Larkin made you join the crew?"

"Nothing like that. I've been retained as a journeyman, and my main duty is to assist you and Torio." His chuckle was a little forced. "It makes more sense in hindsight, but Captain Rakefang was very clear that I'm contractually bound to keep Torio Kite's secrets. If I betray that trust, he said he'll carve out my heart."

"And you still signed?"

"Well, I was hoping the language was mostly figurative."

"Nope. He'd totally do it."

Artor sighed gustily. "Have I made a terrible mistake?"

"Not a chance. We're a stroke of luck, and you'll forever bless the day we met."

Farley swung open the hatch they needed to get the stone-laden cart below. Right away, homey barn smells surrounded them—straw and oats and a hint of the oil he used on the harnesses. "We bring the carriages aboard this way. Here's the stable. Those four black horses? They're mine. I'll introduce you later."

In a way, this area had become more crowded than Farley's cabin, mostly because he kept finding things that he wanted to bring back home. Torio teased that a Flox was still a Flox at heart, meaning that deep down, Farley was still a farmer. Which was nonsense. Even so, Farley did spend his otherwise empty days at sea rearranging this collection.

Under every window, he'd lashed buckets. They held seedlings and saplings, mostly of fruit trees and fruiting shrubs that could be added to Morven's small grove. There was a lemon tree and another kind of citrusy fruit that had thick green peels. On an island they'd visited, he'd spotted a variety of apple tree that had skin as dark as Dessa's cheeks, with fragrant, red-veined flesh. There was a nut tree, too. And he'd been babying along a couple of twigs that—if they survived—would bear red pears.

But he was especially pleased by his makeshift chicken house.

Larkin had refused the first time Farley requested space for them. He'd snapped and snarled all the way up until the day Farley's pockets started peeping. One look at the fuzz balls, and the captain wavered. So Farley had coaxed again, reminding him that their ship's cook would be happy for a ready supply of eggs.

It was a hassle, but over the intervening months, Farley had built up a decent flock, and from time to time, he provided a roasted chicken or pheasant for Larkin's supper. He couldn't wait to see Tupp's face when he saw these birds. Chickens with blue feathers. Pheasants with gold. He'd be dazzled by them ... and by Farley.

"This one's mine. *Ours* now. There's a trick to the lock." Farley beckoned Artor closer.

Farley wore a heavy key around his neck, but it was mostly for show. If anyone ever lifted it from him, all they'd get for their trouble was a decoy. The actual key that fit his door's padlock was a dainty piece of workmanship, courtesy of Aurelius Harrow. It was an antique of Oxus origin.

Half a dozen cogs decorated the lock's face, and three different keyholes spun in and out of view when you turned them. It'd taken Farley days to unravel the lock's puzzle, and even now, he felt silly for taking that long. None of the doodads on the front did anything except stymie the uninitiated. But if you flipped up the padlock to admire the wreath of flowers that had been worked all along the edge, you might notice a slot hidden in the heart of a flower.

Showing Artor the right spot, Farley inserted the teensy key, and the well-oiled lock came open with a faint *snick*. Heart light, he swung the door wide. "Welcome home, Artor Oldtree."

That's when the lionesses pounced.

4

Winsome Ways

A series of thuds next door, followed by Farley's sharp reprimand, had Torio shaking his head. "Do you think Farley is trying to test the fellow's mettle? If Artor was not made of stern enough stuff, Larkin would have frightened him off long before now."

She offered no opinion.

Torio cocked an ear. The wall against which he leaned was thick enough that while he could hear the excited lilt of Farley's voice and the deeper timbre of Artor's replies, he couldn't make out their words. "All seems well."

Still nothing from Dessa, who stood utterly still in the corner, her face averted.

He held out a hand. "Will you come and meet the new boy?"

"I did not call him."

"That honor is mine to claim. And Farley's. But you don't have to call him to befriend him."

"I have no friends in this place."

"There's Harrow's son. He knows you're here, as do the members of his crew."

"They shy away."

"They're in awe. As am I. What have you done to your

hair?" He crooked the fingers of his still-outstretched hand. "Let me see."

Her fingers settled lightly on his palm, and he urged her even closer. As usual, once invited, she came easily into his arms.

"*Is it good? Is it ... pretty?*"

"Quite charming." And because she didn't seem to understand, Torio added, "As was your previous style *and* the one before. You know, you don't have to change yourself to suit some imagined fancy of mine."

"*You don't care?*"

Torio couldn't understand Dessa's fretting. "I am irrevocably yours, woman. What more is there?"

"*There's more!*"

"Is there? I cannot be more than I am."

Dessa looked away.

He knew he'd fallen short again, but what was he supposed to do? He was hers for every day that remained to him, and by the same token, she was his lifelong responsibility. Without exception, that was the way of things between a Keeper and their mountain. And yet ... Dessa wasn't satisfied by his duty to her.

Torio hung his head and offered a pleading murmur. "*Dessa.*"

A shimmer of magic, much subtler than her usual emotional outbursts, stirred between them. He recognized it—how could he not—for it appeared whenever he spoke her name. She fit her arms around him, face upturned.

Dessa wasn't exactly complicated.

Neither was she terribly subtle.

But Torio didn't think there was anything simple about their bond. In some ways, his mountain was ancient, as old as the world itself. Yet he'd been the one to wrest Dessa out of peril, and he'd spent years searching for help. Tupper had heard her voice, and Freydolf had given her form. And by his very blood, Torio had played a part in bringing to life the Heartstone Mountain.

Harrow had likened the day of Dessa's waking to a wedding. But hadn't it also been the birth of something entirely new? Her simplicity, her limited understanding, her hopeful innocence—they made her seem so very young. And that put Torio in a quandary. He could be Dessa's Keeper, for that had been his role from the beginning. But could he—*should* he—answer her persistent yearning for more?

He didn't have an answer.

Not yet. Not today.

Tucking her arm through his, he said, "Farley is waiting for you."

"*Farley.*" His name was as soft as a sigh. "He *loves me.*"

"And he's eager to show you off." They strolled to Farley's open door, which offered a promising view. Char had somehow managed to pin Farley to the floor with a casual paw, holding him in place while the young man roughed up her fur. Artor sat beside him, leaning against the wall while Nyx sprawled between his legs, her head over his heart while he scratched behind her ears. The young Ursa's expression held wonder and delight.

A fierce gladness took Torio by surprise.

He wanted this for Dessa—acceptance, admiration. She was a beautiful mountain, smaller than all the rest, necessarily rare, strikingly potent, and ... sensitive. From the start, she'd inspired fear. Over and over, they'd been driven out. He wasn't sure how much she'd understood back then, but some of it must have filtered through.

She'd been called ugly and accursed.

He'd been called a charlatan and worse.

Torio rapped lightly. "Is young master Oldtree ready to meet our Dessa?"

Farley's face lit up, and he gave Char a shove. "Dessa! No need to be shy about Artor. See how much your lionesses like him?"

"I know. I always know."

Artor whispered something to Nyx, who let him up. Gaining his feet, he came to greet Dessa, offering his hands in the fashion of Pika. She looked between them, uncertain how to respond. Torio inclined his head toward the young man. "A simple greeting. Place your hands in his to give him permission to proceed."

Farley was at Torio's elbow a second later, demanding, "A greeting? Show me how!"

So Dessa tentatively offered her hands to Artor, who carefully enfolded them, then bent to kiss her cheeks, one side and then the next.

Dessa looked startled, then flustered.

But Farley barreled right past the gesture. "Was that a Pika thing?" Then to Dessa, "Artor was raised by Pika. Useful, huh? He can teach us all about their culture."

Torio gave the Ursa a sharp look.

But Artor's gaze was fixed on Dessa's face. "I understand that this is a rare honor. Hello, Dessa. I'm pleased to be traveling with you, and I hope you'll count me as a friend."

"How nice." Dessa looked to Torio, adding, *"He has a gentle touch. Morven will want him."*

Implying that she didn't.

Torio had to own that he was relieved.

His mountain's lips quirked. *"I know what I need."*

Implying that she craved some other quality, one that he and Farley shared.

"We can hear her, since she called us," Farley boasted. "Torio is Keeper, and I'm ... well, I can hear her, too."

With a courteous nod to Torio, Artor asked, "What should I call her stone?"

"Heartstone," supplied Farley. "Dessa is the Heartstone Mountain."

"May I ask your impression of her quality?" Torio posed.

Artor, who still held Dessa's hands, gave them a squeeze before stepping back. "Give me a while? My affinity is a little different. I respond more strongly to a stone after I've spent time with it."

"And yet ... the lady is curious."

The Ursa's gaze swung immediately to Dessa, and with a small shrug, he said, "I feel as if I'm in the presence of magic itself. You stir the soul, lady."

"He compliments me?"

"He has made an attempt," Torio murmured. "Anyone's words would fall short."

Dessa searched his face. *"You compliment me?"*

Torio ruefully said, "If you cannot tell, then I, too, have fallen short."

Quite early the next morning, Torio made his excuses to Dessa and trailed after Larkin, bound for the shop of a Drom merchant that Farley had befriended the previous day. If only the lad's winsome ways worked half so well on their young captain.

Torio did admire Farley's refusal to quake before Larkin Rakefang, who looked disturbingly like his grandsire, a man whose casual cruelty had left Farley with a snub horn and a healthy dose of circumspection. Not that he applied it to Larkin.

With less caution than he was capable of showing, Farley jogged along the pier, catching up. "Dessa is helping Artor unpack," he reported.

Farley wasn't quite as long in the leg as Torio, but he walked with an extra spring in his step so that Torio no longer had to check his stride. The lad—now a man of twenty-two—had been foisted on him when he was barely showing nubs. Even then, it'd been clear as skies that Farley would be better suited to *this* life than his former.

As was his custom, Farley slipped ahead and turned to walk backward in front of Torio. "Hashbaz is a good guy. Say, are we going to visit Prahkreet once we move on to First Continent?"

"You have an interest in the Oxus homeland?"

"The merchant who was there yesterday made it sound amazing. Is it worth going to see?"

"It is. Although I wonder if our captain would be willing to follow us so far inland."

"We can't stick to port cities *all* the time." Farley grabbed his arm and pointed to something in one of the stalls. "Say, what's that for?"

This is how it always went, and Torio supposed that he enjoyed it. Farley was seeing this part of the world with new eyes, and his enthusiasm over every discovery was ... refreshing. Travel had palled during Torio's search for answers about the black stone he'd found, but showing Farley around was reminding him why he'd chosen this life.

The only way to forestall Farley's nonstop gush of questions was to slip into lecture mode. Early on, he'd confined himself to Verit, but with increasing frequency, Torio had lapsed into his own language, which was the primary trade language on this continent. Farley's fluency in Terse had improved by leaps and bounds.

Today, Torio sprinkled in common Liric phrases, which would come in handy once they moved further into Pika and Fwan territory.

Their piecemeal conversation didn't faze Larkin at all. "Are you coming? Or are you going to natter further about Fwan idioms?"

Ignoring the young captain's censure, Farley asked, "Do you know any others?"

Larkin frowned, then offered, "Turn away from odds and spares. Peace and plenty come in pairs."

"No kidding?" Farley looked to Torio for confirmation. "That's a thing?"

"The saying springs from Fwan superstition. According to their traditions, odd numbers are bad luck. All the best things come in twos."

Larkin added, "If you want to enter Fwan territory, we'll only be allowed to do so if we have an even-numbered party."

"Good thing we have Artor, then!"

The Pred's jaw tightened, and he pointedly looked past Farley to Torio. "You still intend to traverse First Continent?"

"We do."

"I have … new information. Would it be possible to visit the Freshstone Mountain first? There is something I need to take care of in the Basq capital."

"New information?" Torio echoed, honestly surprised. "From where?"

Larkin's expression took a turn toward the surly. "I have my connections."

Farley's eyebrows slowly lifted, but he held his peace.

Torio acquiesced with a nod. "I've only had the pleasure of visiting Meridian twice before. So long as our arrival doesn't overlap with one of the Basq sacred tidal festivals, suit yourself."

To Torio's surprise, Larkin's gaze dropped, and he sketched a hasty bow. Clearing his throat, he gruffly repeated, "Are you coming? This was a matter of some urgency, was it not?"

"Not sure," Farley admitted. "But I've got a feeling it'll turn out to be a job. The rainy-day kind."

Dessa's voice inserted itself into Torio's mind. *"Will we hunt?"*

He let his steps lag and murmured, "Too soon to tell."

"I can hunt."

"I know no other mountain so capable of defending herself."

"I'll defend you."

"While that reverses the usual arrangement between mountain and Keeper, I appreciate the sentiment."

There was a lull, but it was the brooding sort. Torio waited to see what else his mountain had to say.

Finally, Dessa said, *"I hope there will be a hunt."*

Torio wasn't sure how he felt about the brutal efficiency with which Dessa had dismantled her first Misbegotten. While he was grateful that she'd leapt to Farley's defense, it had been unsettling to learn that she could shift her forearms into scythe-like blades ... and that she could wield them with enough strength to split stone.

In that moment, he'd wished he was back in the balcony of Freydolf's workshop, sharing a bottle of wine and a game of Pinnacles with Aurelius. Because Torio dearly wanted to ask where he'd found the courage to let a huntress like Ulrica under his guard.

"Torio?"

His name. She didn't often use it, and so he still wasn't used to it. Somehow, his mountain's call was more potent when it was personal. "I'm here, Dessa."

"Will there be a hunt?"

"Are you so eager to stalk prey?"

Another, longer lull. Dessa shyly said, *"If there's a hunt, you take me with you."*

Torio stopped in his tracks and hung his head. How had he missed something so obvious? "Even if there is no Misbegotten behind this Drom's tale, I'll take you for a stroll this evening. It should be fine if we're careful."

Happiness blazed across their connection with a fierceness that could be frightening.

Yes, Dessa was powerful. There was no telling what her limits were ... assuming she had any. But her stone wasn't warped or cracked or crazed. She was as far from a Misbegotten as a statue could be, because Dessa had been shaped by a master sculptor of superlative kindness.

"I apologize."

"Why?"

"For keeping you closed up aboard ship in my clumsy attempt to defend you." He started walking again, lest he lose sight of Larkin and Farley. "I asked Freydolf to give you form so we could walk together."

"I can walk."

"And so we shall. Wait for me?"

"I have been waiting. I was always waiting."

Torio ruefully replied, "I'm doing my best, Dessa."

"You are trying," she agreed.

His shoulders relaxed, but something about her tone made him suspicious that his best efforts were still falling short. Lest he further try her patience, Torio conceded the matter in silence, allowing her the last word.

"Welcome and welcome again!" exclaimed Hashbaz, whose gaze flicked uncertainly in Larkin's direction. "I didn't expect you back so soon, friend Farley. Was there something more this humble merchant can supply?"

Farley was either missing the subtext or—more likely—ignoring it. Torio was about to step in and reassure the shopkeeper when Larkin filled the awkward silence.

"Fine day, homelander. This is a handsome rug." He indicated one of the many woven ones displayed upon the walls. "If we were not so far from their territory, I would swear the artisan was Tisk."

Hashbaz drew himself up to his full height, and Torio could see him rethinking his stance on this particular Pred.

"You have a discerning eye, sir. There is a family of Tisk who settled among the Fwan. Theirs is a small guildhall, and I am one of the few merchants they trust to sell their wares."

Larkin rubbed his chin. "How was such a connection made?"

"How is any connection made? A friend of a friend." And when the weight of Larkin's gaze became too much, Hashbaz confessed, "My brother is a buck of some standing, and he endeared himself to their household while escorting a bevy of Pika does to see the flowers."

Torio saw the boast.

Fortunately, so did Larkin. "May his good fortune add to the glories of the Cloisters."

Hashbaz relaxed noticeably. "It has and may again. But look closer at the delicacy of the workmanship! This is a traditional motif, representing the pollen harvest. Early summer finds Hesper's fields and terraces awash in titian poppies."

"There is a smaller harvest in autumn," Larkin countered. "Less well known, yet highly prized."

"There'll be flowers? Can we go see?" interrupted Farley.

"Possibly." And their captain's gaze shifted to the Drom. "Especially if the tale you told has any merit."

"About the monster in the mountain pass," Farley

helpfully clarified. "Can you tell us more about it?"

"Which road?" demanded Larkin. "Is it in Pika territory? Or near a Fwan settlement?"

Hashbaz slowly said, "The tale I told is true, but there is little else to tell."

"Tell it anyhow."

Farley jumped in. "I'll bet we can help."

"Papaver Pass is remote, and warnings have been posted along the road. My brother assures that blue skies favor travelers and curiosity seekers alike. The way has only proved dangerous during storm season."

"Any mountain path can become treacherous in rain," scoffed Larkin.

"Who can deny it, homelander? Poor footing can cause someone to slip down," agreed Hashbaz. "But rather than falling to their deaths, these poor fools climb to theirs. The bodies are always found *above* the road."

5

Southbound

"**S**o Larkin is more like a bodyguard?" Artor asked.

"That's probably how he sees it. He'll be in big trouble with his parents if something were to happen to me." Farley leaned back against the ship's rail, enjoying the ruffle of wind through his hair.

Even with three of them to do the work, clearing and freshening the ship's stable had taken all morning. Torio sprawled in a scrap of shade a short distance away, dozing with his head propped on Dessa's thigh. Magic looped between them in contented swirls.

Turning to face the water, Farley leaned out. "We could be kin, but he doesn't want that. Not from a bleater like me."

Artor frowned deeply. "Where I come from, that's a rude word."

"Same where I come from. I think he says it here because he can. Back home, there'd be consequences."

"Did you stumble across a bad omen the day you met?"

One of the first things Farley had learned about Ursa culture was that they found meanings in strange places. "What counts as a bad omen among Ursa?"

"A fish bone in the stew. Red clouds in a purple sky. The

ringing of bells after dark. Dreaming about turnips."

That last one stumped Farley. "Why would anyone dream about turnips?"

"I have no idea, but if they did, it's a portent."

"Is it okay if I ask ...?" Then with a shrug, he just went ahead and did. "When did you lose your parents?"

"I was almost eleven."

"And by then, you learned all of these sayings and sightings and stuff?"

"Yes. The good signs and bad signs have been part of my life since cradle days. They're woven into every memory, and those became precious."

"Do you believe them?"

"Is it hard to tell?"

"Well, you kind of sound like you're half-joking whenever you reel off a new one."

"I suppose I can laugh about my heritage because I can see another side now. My Pika brothers found the more mystical aspects of my upbringing charming, and they indulged me for my parents' sake." Artor quietly added, "I think deep down, I *do* believe them. Every one."

"Even the thing about turnips?"

"Oh, that one especially."

Farley asked, "Are they all bad omens?"

"There are twice as many good ones!"

"Like what?"

"Three eggs in a nest. A dove on the windowsill. Being knocked on the head by a falling pinecone."

They *were* charming traditions, and Farley was looking forward to learning more. "Well, I don't know if anything portentous happened the day I met Larkin, but I definitely started the dance on my wrong foot. And probably snapped a twig while I was at it. Which is committing simultaneous sacrilege in both Flox and Pred cultures."

Artor laughed. "I'll take your word for it. He does seem

to hold a grudge. I wonder why?"

"I *know* why. His dad loves me like a son."

"Making you ... a rival for his affection?"

"Don't see how. Aurelius has loads of affection." Rolling his hand, he tried to figure out how to explain Aurelius to someone. "We rely on him, and we respect him. He's ... he's *important*. To all of us."

"Does Larkin not approve of you because you're Flox?" ventured Artor. "Pred are said to be ... elitist."

"I don't think so. Larkin's not like that. You know, he chose his whole crew, and none of them are Pred. And slurs of endearment aside, he's never treated me like I'm not a person. He mostly treats me like I'm annoying."

"Are you?"

"Maybe." And because it was privately funny, he cheerfully added, "Probably."

"So what will you do about him?"

"Keep wearing him down. He'll eventually have to admit I'm amazing. It's only a matter of time."

Artor chuckled. "That doesn't sound like much of a plan."

"I don't need a more complicated one. Not for him."

After two years, Farley figured he knew enough to *survive* Larkin, but that didn't mean he *knew* Larkin. Oh, he'd sorted out lots of everyday things. Larkin was really very boring. He did the same stuff over and over, like the ship would sink if he didn't keep a schedule. And when he wasn't being the captain, he mostly stuck to reading or writing letters.

For a Harrow, he dressed plainly, and he never drank any kind of liquor. He pitched in right alongside the crew whenever it was needed, and none of them showed any sign of fear around him.

Not much else stood out. Just random stuff.

Given enough time, even the most careful people let their guard slip. Or at the very least, they slipped into old habits. Farley knew for sure that Larkin was happier at sea than on land. In a way, he seemed as tied to the *Moontide* as Torio was to Dessa. But Farley couldn't tell if it was because of the ship or because of the sea … or if the two were so closely entwined that they were one and the same.

But a shipbound Pred was still a Pred, and that gave Farley an in. He made a point of always knowing where Larkin was. He didn't need to turn. Simply kept his gaze firmly locked on the water as he softly asked, "Does he look busy right now?"

Artor glanced around, then answered, "Not especially."

"Perfect. Ever seen a Pred in action?"

"No. Never. Mmm. Would I want to?"

"From a safe distance, sure. I suggest the rigging." Farley started to back away. "Larkin may hate me, but he loves to hunt me."

Pivoting, he ran lightly across the deck and took the stairs to Larkin's post two at a time. Without fanfare, Farley drew the dagger at his waist and threw it hard. The blade stuck into the decking at Larkin's feet.

"What are you trying to do?" Larkin growled.

"I heard about this game from your mom. Sounded fun." Farley bounced on the balls of his feet. "Want to play?"

Larkin glared.

Farley innocently asked, "Not up for a little exercise?"

Without a word, Larkin gathered up his hair and twisted it into a knot.

Entertaining a Pred was as simple as becoming prey. Larkin had the advantage here. This was his ship, and he knew every creak and crack of her. But Farley liked challenging him. He held his ground while Larkin dragged off his shirt and set it aside.

"Shouldn't you be running?"

"Shouldn't you signal your crew?" countered Farley.

Larkin whistled sharply. His glittering gaze never left Farley's face when he bellowed, "Clear the decks. This won't take long."

With grunts and a few chuckles, most of the crew went aloft, evacuating their captain's hunting grounds. This wasn't their first game.

Farley had made enough mistakes during previous bouts to be wiser each time they played. A ship this size had its share of dead ends, but it was also a Pred ship. The design incorporated double entrances, subtle footholds, hidden throughways, and rails that doubled as runways. Because no Pred liked to be cornered.

The ins and outs made possible a prolonged game of chase.

Technically, it was a friendly contest, but Pred weren't the friendliest of opponents. Back home, these games had always been swift, unpredictable, and ruthless enough to be unsettling, yet Farley had never once believed that his life was in peril. But against Larkin, Farley went in with a thready heartbeat and a vague sense that he might not see tomorrow.

Well, Larkin wouldn't *actually* get rid of him, but he probably wasn't opposed to a little bloodletting. That was all part of the fun when it came to Pred games.

Larkin dominated. Always. Hardly a surprise. Farley never expected to win. His goal was to stump his pursuer and steal precious minutes, to prolong the game, to beat his previous record.

He treaded lightly on dangerous boards.

He ducked into one hidey hold, then stole to the next.

He ran along the upper deck's rail, tossing a wave to the audience up in the ropes.

Spreading his arms wide in silent plea, he hoped for some hint as to where Larkin was lurking. It wasn't cheating so much as ... utilizing valuable resources. And the crew liked to meddle. One of the Oxus lifted his chin toward one of the doors that led below. A Selk held up thumb and forefinger. A good sign. Farley had only missed Larkin by moments, and so far, the best way to stay out of his grasp was to shadow his steps. A risky business, given how quickly Larkin could turn the tables. But Farley did it anyhow.

For a while, he met with success, minutes passed without any sign that Larkin had located him.

Nobody was signaling from above, but all eyes were riveted. Definitely a bad sign.

Farley tried for retreat, only to have his feet swept out from under him. A hand in his hair controlled his descent—and cushioned his fall—before the dagger he'd thrown flashed before his eyes.

Going limp, Farley offered a rueful smile. "All right. I yield."

"Mother told you about this game, did she?" asked Larkin, a mocking light in his eyes.

"Yeah. She did."

"Who did she play it with, I wonder."

Farley answered, "Your dad."

"Do you know why?" Larkin asked silkily.

He ventured, "Because it's how Pred have fun?"

"This," he said, snapping Farley's blade back into the sheath at his waist, "is a courting game."

"I am *really* sure nobody mentioned that part." He thought back over the particulars and grinned. "Though it makes the story extra funny, you've gotta admit."

"I wouldn't know," Larkin said stiffly. "I've never heard that story."

Farley grabbed his collar, holding danger close. "Ask your dad to tell you."

He sneered. "Why should I?"

"Because!" This was a prime opportunity. "We can compare notes and try to figure out which one of them is exaggerating!"

Larkin blinked. "You are an intolerable nuisance."

"That was your dad's first impression of me, too. Like ... almost the first words out of his mouth. But he said it with a smile, and he kept a close eye on me after that. That was nice. I liked it. And he thought it was funny that I thought it was nice. I didn't know any better back then, about Pred, I mean."

"You learned." Larkin's gaze flicked to Farley's broken horn.

Angling his head so Larkin could see, Farley shared, "It didn't hurt, exactly, but it was awful."

"My grandsire was always cruel."

"I noticed. But you've never been cruel to me. Thanks for that."

Larkin snorted and his hand tightened. "You will never best me."

That was so obvious, it was almost a dumb thing to say. Farley patiently pointed out, "I'm not trying to win."

That seemed to stump Larkin for several moments. "What are you after?"

"This." Farley wanted him to just get it already. "Pretty much this."

"My claws at your throat?"

The tone was so much like Aurelius's taunting affection, Farley couldn't hold back his smile. "Happened a whole lot for a long time. By now, it feels like home."

Larkin's scowl had a distracted quality, and he let Farley up, waving a hand. "You may consider your suit rejected."

"Consider me relieved." Farley waved at Artor and called, "Fun, huh? Wanna go a round with us sometime?"

With an incredulous expression, Artor raised his voice. "Thank you, *no*. And if there's anything I can do for the captain to keep me on his good side, he'll find me willing."

Larkin ignored the offer, hoisting himself up a nearby ladder in order to retrieve his shirt.

But Farley wasn't opposed to shouting, "Like what?"

"It would have to be stonecraft." Artor paused in his descent. "Would a mosaic floor be appreciated?"

To Farley's surprise, Larkin turned to gaze at the journeyman. Finally, he said, "I've heard of such things.

Aye, that would be appreciated. If ...."

Artor simply beckoned for more.

Clearing his throat, Larkin asked, "Could you use freshstone and starstone?"

"Certainly." Reaching the deck, Artor came to stand beside Farley, but his gaze stayed on Larkin. "I've always found blue cooperative with white. Shall I draw up a few things so I can get a sense for what kinds of patterns you favor?"

"Aye. Do that."

Farley couldn't put his finger on why it was important, but he was quite sure Larkin had done something startlingly new. Well, maybe a few things.

They'd practically had a conversation, for one. And Larkin had been in a good enough mood to almost, sorta hide a joke under his usual grumbling. But even more than that, he'd *wanted* something. And let it show.

Starstone he could understand, since Larkin had grown up along the shore where Vanora was situated. The whole Pred capital had been built with white stone from the vicinity of the Starlit Mountain, so it had to feel like home. But what about freshstone? If the guy liked blue, he'd never let on. As far as he could tell, most of Larkin's clothes were green.

But that pause. That tone. That request.

Yes, Farley was sure they were important.

And finding out why sounded like fun.

Torio brought his problem to Larkin.

"Somewhere quiet," the younger man mused aloud. "Aye, I know a place. We used to picnic on a certain island when I was small. It's not far, and it's not inhabited. Your lady could stroll to her heart's content."

"No one goes there?"

Larkin smiled faintly. "It's an old conquest, belonging to my great aunt, who has named my father as her heir. He already considers the place his own. He's been managing it for years. There's little more than a dock, a cottage, and a half-wild fortune in titian poppies."

"And nobody meddles with them?"

"That would be foolish."

Torio pointed out, "Anyone could steal ashore once the red-sailed ships were away."

"There used to be a caretaker. Someone Aunt Lissie stranded there. But in recent years, Father took other measures. Guardian statues now defend its shores."

"Dare I ask why your aunt stranded someone there?"

Larkin hesitated. "I think it had to do with a shipment of silk slippers. I don't recall if they'd approved inferior beads for their embellishment or if the slippers had been dyed the wrong shade of yellow. Aunt Lissie has always been creative in her censure."

"By any chance, was your father close to this aunt?"

"Oh, he's her favorite. And she's his. They're both fiends for fashion."

"Dessa is already looking forward to it." Torio bowed. "Thank you for indulging us."

"Can she hear everything you say?" Larkin asked curiously.

"Sometimes, she seems to divine my very thoughts. But yes, we are ... attuned. As is Farley." Torio touched the black rings in his ears. "And not entirely because she has me pierced."

Larkin opened his mouth, hesitated, then shook his head.

"Something on your mind?"

"It's not my business."

"There are few I can speak with about Dessa. And you can hardly be more meddlesome than your mother. Did you know she allied herself to my mountain while Dessa was little more than a block?" Torio fluttered the fingers of one hand. "Ask what you will. I'll answer if I can."

He lowered his head. It was almost a nod. To Torio's mystification, Larkin also lowered his gaze.

"Do your people know you've formed a life-bond with someone ... unlike yourself?"

"Ah." Torio let his own gaze drop. "I should probably quibble terms, but put simply, *no*. My only remaining family is currently on First Continent, and I haven't told my sister about Dessa. Perhaps more to the point, I have no idea what Quilleria will make of my ... turn of fortunes. But what does that matter? What's done is done."

Larkin gazed out over the water. "Did you mean for it to happen?"

"How to say it." Torio knew his mind on the matter, even if he didn't speak it. But Harrow's boy had him curious. These weren't idle questions. "I never sought this future. There was no plan. I was reckless and unprepared, and there were so many consequences—some daunting, some dearer than I could have guessed. But what I never meant for myself ... was still meant to be."

"Aye." And with a little more confidence, Larkin repeated, "Aye. What's done is done."

Torio studied the younger man's profile, then admitted, "I fully expect Quilleria to tease. But I know she'll take Dessa's part, and once they begin to conspire against me, I will grumble. Yet I'll be glad, because it will mean that another person cherishes my mountain."

"Though not as much as you ...?" countered Larkin.

"Such is my right, as Keeper," Torio agreed easily. And

because one of the dearer consequences of his journey was friendship with Aurelius Harrow, he casually asked, "Do you ever play Pinnacles?"

"My grandsire decreed it an unseemly dockside game." Larkin's expression was difficult to read.

"Because he could not best your father?"

Larkin snorted his way to a smile.

"So you had to learn it on the sly."

"Aye." Larkin gazed over the water. "Out here, Father was freer and fiercer and *ours*."

Torio could imagine it and smiled. "I wonder. Did your inimitable father teach you well enough that you could best me?"

"Are you claiming superiority?"

"At Pinnacles? Possibly." Torio honestly missed his bouts with Aurelius. "Care to find out?"

Larkin slowly said, "Perhaps. To pass the time."

Torio accepted that with a nod, content that he'd left Harrow's boy an opening.

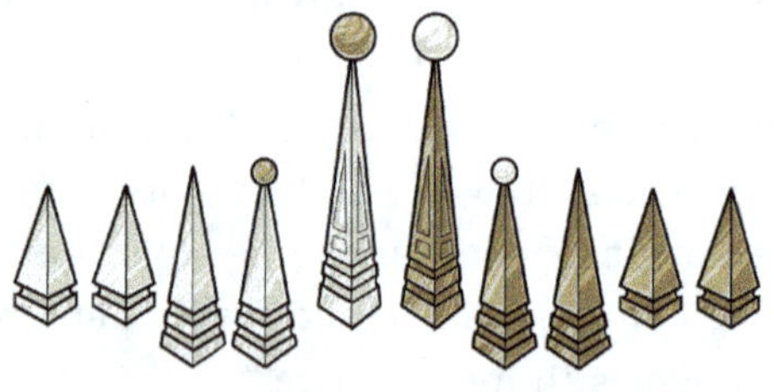

Every time they sailed into a port, Farley expected everything and nothing. *Everything* because they'd be in a new place, so it just *had* to be amazing. But also nothing, because he didn't really know *what* to expect. Even if he tried to guess, he'd be wrong. Because as the people and places changed, the rules changed. Finding his footing in unfamiliar settings was fascinating.

"The cobbles!" Farley elbowed Torio, who was scanning shop signs. "Did you notice?"

"Hmm?" The Grif glanced down. "Ah. Local stone. Quite lovely."

"*Lovely?*"

"Not as lovely as you, Dessa sweet," Farley assured. "You're too precious for ordinary things like cobbles and thresholds."

"*Precious,*" she echoed. "*Because heartstone is rare.*"

"We've been over this," Farley gently chided. "You're scarcer than gemstones and dense with magic, but that's not why we care about you. Can't you feel it?"

She calmed, even without Torio chipping in. Farley wondered if that was progress. She was in a good mood today, but so was Torio. They were always subtly swaying each other. Taking a page from Flox courting tradition, he pretended not to notice.

"What's this city called again?" he asked.

"It's an old name in the Tauke dialect the translates as Morning Sky," said Torio, who paused to study the labels on bottles in one of the shop windows. "You know you're in Pika territory when the shops stock petalberry cordial."

"The pink stuff?" Farley had picked up a fair amount of Liric, but speaking a language was different from being able to read it. "Is it good?"

"Quite lovely. The Pika are as famous for petalberry products as the Fwan are for pollen."

"Maybe I should buy some? For Aurelius, I mean."

"I doubt they'd part with a bottle. The cordials are jealously guarded."

"They won't sell to foreigners?"

Torio quirked a smile. "Given the chance, they would serve you cup after cup. Should you be offered any, I recommend stopping after one."

"How come?"

"Petalberry cordial is heady stuff." With a sidelong

look, he asked, "How much did Artor tell you about Pika hospitality?"

Farley glanced ahead, to where Artor ambled along at Larkin's side. In addition to finding Hashbaz's brother, their plans had expanded to include the procurement of blue and white chippings from one of Morning Sky's stone merchants. Larkin really did want a mosaic floor in his quarters.

"Artor was more straightforward that you've been. Although I'm not sure I believe him." Farley shook his head. "I can't really picture any of it."

"Keep your eyes open and your wits about you, and you won't need your imagination."

Up to this point, Farley had been focusing on the stonework and statuary they passed. Not only were the cobbles pink, the same local stone faced most of the buildings. Hues blended through shades of rose and rust, with titian jade accents hinting at the relative proximity of the Sunset Mountain. At Torio's urging, Farley turned his attention to the people.

Pika were now predominant, and they seemed generally upbeat and friendly. Farley tried not to stare, in large part because he'd been coached not to make eye contact, but Pika had tall, furred ears that could only be called rabbity. And clothing in this part of the world was adapted to make room for short, puffed tails.

Unlike Flox, who were universally fair, or even Pred, whose coloring stayed in a tight range of bronzes and browns, Pika coloration varied widely. Their hair—and their fur—could be black or white or anything in between. Their build was generally lithe, and so far, all the Pika they'd passed were a little shy of Farley's own height.

It took longer than it should have for him to notice something odd. "Where are the women?"

"Pika women are always cloistered in an inner city."

"Why?"

Torio explained, "Only one in ten children born to the Pika are female."

"Doesn't that mean they'll dwindle?"

"Not at all. Their population increases at a brisk pace."

Farley puzzled over that for a while and finally asked, "Are they like Flox? Big families?"

Torio shook his head. "They are a beautiful race, with qualities much desired by other cultures. And oftentimes they were conquered and kept."

"As slaves."

"That's the simple truth. Throughout the eras, Pika were carried off to every continent, and in every place, children were conceived. And in every case, the child was born Pika."

He was putting it delicately, but the meaning was clear enough. Still, Farley had to ask, "Even if the mother was Flox or Clow or Tisk?"

"Always. This has allowed for their steady increase, and it's led to the variety we see today."

Farley peered around with greater interest. Were the Pika with gray fur descended from Oxus? Did the red-gold ones have Clow ancestry? What about the spotted ones?

"It's said that Pika females chase after fads, seeking partners who'll give them the most beautiful children. You'd be very popular if the ladies of this land were to learn of your golden curls."

"I'm not going to settle down with a Pika wife."

Torio blandly countered, "Your assumptions are quite Floxish."

"That's not how it works?"

"No."

"How else *would* it work?"

"Ah, well. You're a clever boy. Sort it out. One warning, though. Make friends all you like, but take care how you respond to offers of brotherhood. Pika have their own definitions for the words we loosely translate as friend, kin, and brother."

"Yeah, yeah." Artor had covered some of that earlier. "Though this doesn't seem like the kind of place where I should have to keep my guard up."

"Be your usual self and enforce your boundaries. They'll be charmed, and you should survive with your virtue—such as it is—intact. If you want more details, bring your questions to Artor."

"Because you're too embarrassed to explain?"

"Yes." And firmly changing the subject, Torio said, "Pick up the pace. We're falling behind."

"Heart of a lion," Farley teased.

Torio favored him with an aloof gaze. "I'm only thinking of Dessa."

"I also want to know how it works," she chimed in.

Farley grinned sheepishly.

His former mentor smiled blandly and dropped a hand on his shoulder.

As they walked on, he left it there, which was unusual. Farley shot him a look from under his hat brim.

Torio met his gaze and gave a squeeze. "A friendly warning to others. Since you're already drawing attention. No, don't look. It will only encourage them to try."

"Try what?" he ventured, risking a peek despite the warning.

His former master snorted.

"Try what?" echoed Dessa.

"I'm not sure, Dessa sweet. But I'll let you know if I figure it out."

Torio sighed. "What am I going to do with the two of you?"

"You're a Keeper," pointed out Farley. "Try to keep up."

Torio lengthened his stride. "The young captain and Artor went into that shop. I believe it's the place we're meant to inquire after Hashbaz's brother."

As they came even with double doors set with pink and

green glass, Farley studied the sign, which featured billing doves perched on a fruiting branch. "Are those meant to be petalberries?" he asked.

"That seems likely." Torio opened the door and beckoned him through. "The name on the sign is a play on words."

"Doesn't translate?"

"The closest thing in Verit would be ... Bill & Coo."

The interior was hushed and cool and smelled like drying herbs and tea flowers and a sticky-sweet scent that he couldn't quite place ... and wanted to taste. Out of habit, he removed his hat and scanned a large room that was divided into two sections. Half seemed to be dedicated to the preparation of herbs, like an apothecary. The rest was taken up by low tables surrounded by cushioned seating. A few customers reclined on these tufted lounges.

Farley averted his eyes, his attention next drawn to a large cage where doves cooed softly. He'd never seen the like and wondered if the birds served a purpose. That's when Artor snapped his fingers. The Ursa's eyes were wide, and he gestured urgently for Farley to return his hat to his head.

Oh.

Whoops.

It was way too late, but he jammed it into place with a muttered apology. To Artor, who'd warned him. Or maybe to the shopkeeper, since by Flox custom, wearing a hat indoors was bad manners.

Suddenly, another person insinuated himself under the wide brim. He was so close, so fast, Farley's training failed him. Not that he wanted to skewer this Pika, who was probably really harmless. Or maybe just curious.

The Pika's skin was dark, and his hair was black. Large brown eyes seemed to be laughing at Farley, but then his arms wrapped around Farley's neck, and a warm cheek pressed to his as he spoke right into Farley's ear. "You made three mistakes, and I fear I must chastise you for all of them.”

The voice was mellow and amused.

“I did something wrong?”

“Not *wrong*. Perhaps … unwise?” The Pika drew back to search Farley’s gaze before resettling with his opposite cheek pressed to Farley’s. His low laugh was husky. “Are you not going to push me away, lovely locks?”

“Oh. You happened so fast, I forgot.”

“What a nice thing to say.” He proceeded to nuzzle Farley’s ear.

“Hey, you speak Verit!”

“I wonder what else we have in common.” The Pika somehow managed to lean back and press close all at the same time. “We are up to six mistakes, Farley. Where is my push?”

Recalling Artor’s lesson, Farley set his hands against the Pika’s shoulders and gently pushed.

“Be firm.”

He pushed harder, and this time, the Pika stepped back. Long ears swayed into view, and Farley tipped back his hat to see better. Small, squat rings pierced their outer edges. Several had tiny bells attached, which twinkled softly, and two were set with dawnstone beads.

The Pika let his ears dip and rise, and Farley watched in frank fascination.

“Do you want to touch?”

“I’m not supposed to.” Farley knew that much.

“I would let you.” His smile was winsome.

He wouldn’t mind, huh? Farley was sure that there was a taboo surrounding Pika ears. And tails, for that matter. He glanced toward his companions for some clue as to what to do.

Larkin was looking on with a beleaguered expression.

Torio had a hand over his eyes, and he was doing a

terrible job of hiding his laughter.

Artor seemed to be trying to coach him, but the gestures weren't making sense.

"Yeah, umm ... no. Thanks, but ... better not. We just met, and all."

The Pika shook his head and took a more serious tone. "That will not do, you know. You cannot push with words that pull. You are too curious, too courteous. It makes me want to keep trying."

Farley thought back over what he'd said, but then the Pika was snug against him again. He ventured, "One push isn't enough?"

"Rarely."

So he took the man by the shoulders again and set him at arm's length. "Hello, by the way. I'm Farley."

"I know. My brother asked me to look after you, and it is clear as Bezel's heart that you need me."

Farley caught on, then. "You're Hashbaz's brother."

"Half-brother. We share a mother." Dark lashes fluttered. "My given name is Zaalenis Jubalzayn, but I would be delighted if you were to call me Jubilee."

6

Bill & Coo

Farley spooned a generous serving of petalberry confit onto his bread and took a bite. Compared to other blind tastings of foreign fare, this one wasn't much of a risk. Pika wouldn't guard something so stubbornly if it wasn't exceptional. He'd had a few unpleasant surprises this way, but that only made the first taste of something new more exciting.

Petalberry was hard to describe as a flavor. It didn't compare to anything he'd eaten before, but there was a tang to it and—at least in this marmalade-like preparation—a lingering sweetness. "If I can't buy the cordial, can I get this? Melina would be wild for it."

"Your sweetheart?" inquired Jubilee.

"Sister," Farley countered, keeping his attention on the food Torio had ordered for all of them. There were rounds of soft bread, the glistening pink confit, and tiny cups of a hot, bitter drink generously laced with spice.

The Pika leaned against him. "Are *you* wild for it?"

"I might be." He was doing his best to follow Artor's advice and overlook these little bids for attention. Apparently, it would be as rude for Jubilee to neglect him as it would have been for Farley to keep his hat on indoors back home. "I'm surprised Aurelius never brought back any of this stuff."

"One reason petalberries rarely leave these shores is that they don't keep well." Jubilee rested his cheek against Farley's shoulder. "They're best eaten as soon as they're plucked. During their brief peak, all other activities are suspended for the harvest. We only have days to create the jellies, candies, and cordials that preserve their flavor until the next ecstatic frenzy."

"Which makes them too dear to be sold to just anyone," added Artor, who'd taken the seat across the table from Farley. He was keeping a close eye on Jubilee, but he didn't seem worried. "Private sales *can* be arranged, should someone vouch for you."

"I would vouch for you," Jubilee immediately offered.

"Really?" Farley turned to look at him, and their noses bumped. "Hey, too close. I might accidentally knock you with my horn."

Jubilee studied the horn for a moment, then cozied back up with his head resting on Farley's shoulder. He repeated, "I would vouch for you."

"That's incredibly generous," said Artor. "Thank you."

Larkin, who'd been ominously silent this whole time, said, "I will manage the exchange."

"And I'll come along," Artor hastily offered. "To ... lift things."

And undoubtedly to smooth things over. Farley thought Larkin looked grateful. He and Artor were definitely getting along, which was a nice surprise, but Farley had to wonder if he'd ever *not* be at the bottom of the pecking order.

He sighed, then asked, "Do all Pika stick this close?"

Jubilee warmly assured, "Usually."

"Always," countered Artor, whose smile was almost wistful. "He's treating you like family."

Farley relaxed a little.

Immediately, the Pika slipped an arm around his waist.

He must have looked worried because Artor chuckled. "Still familial. Probably because Hashbaz extended hospitality and asked him to look after you."

Farley risked another glance. "I think he's actually teasing me."

Torio, who was also entirely unperturbed, said, "He's protecting you. If not for Jubilee, all the others in this shop would be clamoring for your attention."

"Uh-huh." Farley wasn't believing it for a second. "You sure it's not because the rest of them are afraid of our Pred?"

Larkin's gaze flashed dangerously.

Artor shook his head, chuckling. "Torio's right. Jubilee got to you first, and you haven't sent him away. The others are keeping their distance out of respect for his good fortune. And, I think, a prestige that has little to do with us."

Farley glanced around the shop. "Are you the owner, Jubilee? Or do you work here?"

"Work here? I *play* here." He gestured toward a stool on which a lap harp rested. "I am a musician. A bard, if you will. I travel a fair amount, and I hear things. My brother's letter said that you liked one of my stories well enough to come see me. Very flattering."

"Will you play for us?" asked Farley, who'd only seen pictures of harps in storybooks.

Jubilee's ears trembled enough to send his little bells into tiny peals. "You break rules so carelessly and remake them just as carelessly. Ah, lovely locks, you could rule over me so easily, yet I can see you will not try."

Farley wasn't a stranger to cultural differences, but the Pika way of life was as different as could be from a Pred's. On the upside, nothing about Jubilee felt dangerous. But that didn't necessarily mean Farley was comfortable. He could almost hear Ulrica criticizing him for letting the Pika under his guard. But he kind of wondered what Tupper would have done in the same situation.

Probably taken it in stride. And calmly looked Farley in the eye before bluntly asking, *"Did you listen?"*

Fine. He'd listened. So what had the Pika said?

That Farley had made mistakes.

That curiosity could be misinterpreted.

That firm refusal wasn't rude.

That Farley needed Jubilee.

All of which put Farley on more familiar footing. Because Jubilee had something Farley needed, and maybe this whole time, the Pika had been trying to draw him into a trade. "Could you teach me?"

Jubilee didn't flirt or flutter this time. He asked, "What do you want to learn?"

Terms? How could he set any when he wasn't even sure what he was lacking? "Show me my mistakes so I can learn from them. Be a friend to me so I'll know how to befriend other Pika. And keep protecting me, since you seem concerned." He shot a look at Artor and asked, "Or did *you* want to ...?"

"*I* will!" interrupted Jubilee. "Lessons will proceed in Verit, your own language. Will that not be best for lending nuance to your understanding?"

"There's no need. We're not staying in Morning Sky," interjected Larkin. "Tell us what we need to know, and we'll be on our way. *We* are enough to keep him safe."

"Is that your wish, gentleman Flox? To be guided and guarded and kept from me by this Pred?"

Farley said, "Larkin's right, though. We're leaving."

"*We* are," Jubilee agreed. "Since I will accompany Farley wherever he goes in our lands."

Torio frowned. "Very generous of you, but ours can be a dangerous business."

Jubilee arched his brows. "Are you saying you and your Pred cannot guarantee *my* safety?"

Farley was kind of impressed that he'd sorted out the two most experienced fighters. He was only a little miffed at being overlooked. Then again, Farley *did* have a lot to learn.

"I can open paths for you. A bard is always welcome." Ears rising, he casually added, "I can even gain entrance for you into a Fwan holding not far from your destination. They will undoubtedly be grateful if you can make the mountain pass safe for travelers."

"Grateful farmers," grumbled Larkin.

"Grateful *stonecrafters*," countered Jubilee. "Stonecrafters with close ties to Hesper's Keeper."

Farley perked up. "Would they have blocks of titian jade?"

Jubilee's eyes took on a shine. "I look forward to finding out."

Torio murmured, "That *would* be a welcome turn of events, since we've not been approved for a visit to the Sunset Mountain."

Larkin relented with a sigh. "I suppose he *would* even our numbers."

Farley glanced around the circle, making a quick tally, and he noticed the color seeping into Torio's cheeks. So Larkin had included Dessa in the party? Nice. "Is it far, this mountain pass?"

"A few days on foot, but it will be a pleasant walk at this time of year."

"Oh, we're not walking." Farley cheerfully boasted, "I have a carriage."

Farley turned his stallions loose in the corral Larkin had reserved for them while Torio oversaw the unloading of their carriage. Perched on the top rung of the fence, Farley went to remove his hat, remembered himself, and resigned himself to leaving it in place.

Jubilee, who seemed to think it was his duty to keep Farley within arm's reach at all times, leaned against a fencepost, propping his chin on folded arms. "You learn quickly."

"I'm not likely to make the same mistake twice." Farley scanned the vicinity. "As far as I can tell, not a single soul on this continent knows the meaning of 'common as curls.'"

"Uncovering your exceptional hair *was* your first mistake."

"You said I made more than one."

"Look at me," urged Jubilee.

Farley did, waiting for the Pika to say more.

Jubilee's smile turned saucy. "This. Prolonged eye contact is an invitation."

"An invitation to what?"

"Shall I show you?"

"Let's go with *no*. Definitely *no*." Farley gestured between them. "I'm thinking—as a bard and all—you're good with words. Try those first."

"And if words fail?"

"Like you said, I learn quickly. Say it plainly, and I'll catch on."

Jubilee folded his hands together. "Flox are modest folk."

"We are," Farley agreed easily. "Can't you teach me any customs that take that into consideration?"

"Certainly. I can teach you our songs and our dances. I could tempt your palate with sweets and savories that can only be found within our borders. I could even bring you up into Itzel's heights to show you the morning sky from atop the Dawnstone Mountain."

"Sure. That all sounds good."

"And in so doing, I would be neglecting the simplest of common courtesies."

"That's not *your* fault, though. I'm the one being rude."

Jubilee kept his gaze on the horses when he asked, "If you only accept the more mundane commonalities we share and do not explore our differences, have you truly traveled beyond your borders?"

Oh, yes, the bard was good with words.

Farley gently cuffed his shoulder. "I'm not agreeing to anything yet, but I do see your point. I stepped away from several Flox traditions when I moved onto Morven. Stuff that was normal for Pred felt strange and even daring, but now it's normal."

"Can you give me an example?"

"Easy. Did you know that Pred bathe in groups? The ladies have their room, and all of us guys are together in another. It took forever for my older brothers to give in and join. But it's all good, because there's songs and stories and lessons and goofing off. It's a family thing." Farley cleared his throat. He hadn't realized how much he missed it. "It's the best, but we wouldn't have known that if we weren't willing to change."

Jubilee smiled hopefully. "I could arrange for space at a bathhouse."

"That was *not* the point. But thanks. I think."

"Pika families are different. 'Close as kin' means something different here."

"How do you know so much about Flox?"

"Travel."

He left it at that, and Farley didn't think he should pry. Instead, he tried to meet Jubilee partway. "Can't we be friends without all the extra closeness?"

"Have you found me discourteous thus far?"

Farley had to admit that while Jubilee was all kinds

of coy, he was doing most of his fluttering from a polite distance. "Nope. I think you're being considerate, but you're also kind of a handful."

"I could keep both your hands full."

He shook his head in disbelief. "I can't decide if you're exhausting or funny."

"You aren't the first to be in such a quandary. My race excels at keeping others off-balance." Jubilee sought his gaze. "Do you find you want me closer?"

"Nooo. Weren't we just admiring how considerate you're being?"

The Pika's ears, which poked through holes alongside his hat's crown, quivered. "How sensitive is your nose?"

Farley rubbed at his uncertainly. "Am I meant to be smelling something?"

"Me." With a serene smile, Jubilee explained, "Many people find our scent alluring."

"Oh. Huh. I didn't notice. No offense."

He waved away the apology. "To answer your earlier question, *yes*. I believe we can cobble together something resembling friendship, even if I'm never allowed to run my fingers through the gold of your curls."

Farley couldn't help laughing. "How big of a mistake would it be to let you?"

"Ah, you tempt me to lie."

"Honesty will get you farther."

Jubilee beamed. "I live to please!"

"Okay. Good. First question, because I'm having trouble here. If I can't look a Pika in the eye, where am I meant to be looking?"

He saw Jubilee's smile widen and realized he was still making eye contact. Seriously. What else was he supposed to do?

The Pika beckoned for him to join him on the ground, so Farley swung a leg over and squared off.

"A lesson," Jubilee said, reaching up to frame Farley's face with his hands. "To look at me like so, directly in the eyes, is to invite more." Gently, he turned Farley's head a little to the side. "Like so."

He was still looking Jubilee in the eyes, but from a slight angle. It wasn't a huge change, and it didn't feel all that different. If anything, *he* felt coy now, like one of the girls who ringed the festival square, hoping to be chosen as a dance partner. "Hey, that's all it takes? This is okay?"

"Entirely correct," Jubilee assured, his hands falling away.

"What else?"

"Your dashing Ursa guided you through assorted refusals?"

"Yeah, but will I need them? I mean, you're here."

Jubilee's smile tilted slyly. "I cannot be overlooked. You may yet need to rebuff me."

"Couldn't we skip that part?"

Very slowly, the Pika reached up and turned Farley's face ever so slightly to the side. "Perhaps once you stop encouraging me to try."

"I guess that's fair. But what else?" Farley beckoned with both hands. "Aren't there any Pika courtesies that *don't* involve kissing?"

"A clasp for greeting, a kiss for peace, a meal for welcome, and a dawn for sharing—these are the basics of Pika hospitality."

"Seems normal enough to me. Except the dawn one. Is that literal, or does it have to do with the Dawnstone Mountain?"

"If you were to accompany me into Itzel's heights, we could share the dawn in fine style."

"Could you really take me into her galleries?" Farley admitted, "I want to go, but Torio wasn't sure we'd get a chance. Last time he was here, he ... well, he didn't leave on the best of terms. So he told me not to get my hopes up."

"It *might* be done," Jubilee said cautiously. "I would be pleased to try."

Farley offered his hand. "A clasp for greeting?"

Jubilee did take his hand, but only to pull them flush. "This sort of clasp, lovely locks."

"I should have figured," he grumbled.

"Yes, you should have. Where is my push?"

"Getting there," promised Farley. But then he wrapped his arms around Jubilee. "Pred are terrible at hugs, and Torio's awkward about affection. So this is nice. For the record, this is a family thing for Flox."

Jubilee relaxed into him and whispered, "Yes, I remember."

Farley added up all the hints. "You've known other Flox besides me?"

"A long while back. When I was a little boy." Jubilee revealed, "I was born on New Continent. We're homelanders, you and I."

Farley's carriage was a somber affair—understated, elegant, and imposing. The rig and the four black stallions that pulled it were probably the first real spoil of war ever claimed by a Flox. He'd gone over the whole thing at least a hundred times while waiting for Dessa to be ready to travel, learning its ins and outs. Sliding panels. False bottoms. Pressure points. Hidden catches. Little by little, he'd uncovered its secrets.

The letters and ledgers had gone straight to Aurelius, and Farley had asked for Ulrica's help in sifting through the small arsenal he'd teased into the open, piece by deadly piece. The valuables he'd traded back to Ulric, the new head of the great and noble house of Rakefang.

Even the stallions had helped line his pockets, because once Ewert spread the word, stud fees came rolling in. But best of all, thanks to the carriage, Dessa could travel in style. And secretly.

"Ride up top with me," Farley invited.

"This belongs to your Pred captain?"

"Nope. It's mine."

"It's strange to me that someone so young would own something so grand yet choose the driver's seat for himself."

Farley simply shrugged. He knew many Pred kept servants—even slaves—to take care of things they were too lofty to do for themselves. But he was proud of his rig and of his four brave boys. They'd been good company while at sea, helping to fill the long hours when there was nothing better to do than study the wind and waves and stars. He'd curried them to a high gloss and polished their hooves, shoveled their leavings and doled out their feed. They looked to him now, and he sat tall in the driver's seat.

With a bemused smile, Jubilee passed up an instrument case before making use of hand- and foot-holds that were intended for men with longer limbs.

"Is this a harp?" Farley asked.

"Yes, though a smaller one than I use at the Bill & Coo. This one is more convenient for travel."

"Will you play as we go?"

Jubilee looked pleased to be asked, but he warned, "It would draw attention."

Farley promised, "We'll be there and gone, so it won't matter. These four are *fast*. Want to meet them?"

"I'm not opposed to becoming better acquainted."

"Names for now. We'll get you under their noses when we stop to rest them." Farley whistled sharp, released the brake, and gave the reins a flick. As they picked up speed, he stowed his hat.

"That will *definitely* draw attention."

"There and gone," Farley assured easily. "Now, about their names. Don't laugh. They were named by a Pred family, so it's not their fault."

"Consider my curiosity piqued!"

"Didn't you ever notice how Pred names are? Well, family names anyhow. First names are fancy, but family names are supposed to sound fierce, to strike fear in the hearts of lesser races."

"Like bounders?" Jubilee inquired knowingly.

"And bleaters," Farley acknowledged with a quick smile. "They're fine stallions and fond of flattery."

"Tell on while I tune."

"The lead pair were Wreckage and Havoc," he said, nodding to each in turn.

"Distinctive." Jubilee stowed his case and propped a leg, leaning the harp against his shoulder. He plucked a few notes and fiddled with a knob. "Memorable."

"Can't argue with that. The second pair were Conquest and Blade."

"Were. You don't call them by these names?"

"Nope. I have nicknames for all of them, and they're smart enough to answer to them."

"And what Floxish endearments did you bestow?"

"Don't laugh," Farley warned anew.

But Jubilee did, even before he heard a single nickname. And he did it with his harp, letting it laugh for him. Who knew an instrument could be so cheeky?

Farley told him anyhow, mostly because he was pleased by his adaptations. "Wreckage is Rexus now, because he's so regal. And Havoc is Hillock, since he's so hard to budge when he's feeling lazy. Then there's Conquest, who really should have been named Coquet, he's so eager for attention. And Blade will forever be Blaze, for obvious reasons."

"Clever."

"If you say so," said Farley breezily. "I'm going to let them run."

Jubilee soon had to clamp a hand over his hat. It was a fancy thing, all creamy suede and wine silk, which may have been why he—wisely—took it off and stowed it next to Farley's under the seat.

The stallions cooperated when Farley eased them back to a sensible speed, and their ears pricked when Jubilee struck the first notes of a travelers' song. They shook their manes and picked up their feet. Farley wasn't sure if they were dancing to Jubilee's tune or if the bard was letting the team set the beat.

Sun on his shoulders. Wind in his hair. Head nodding. Heart light. Farley doubted there was a finer way to travel.

7

Waiting on the Weather

Torio leaned against a sun-warmed boulder atop a grassy slope overlooking the long curve of the lake where Jubilee had suggested they water the horses. Although there was a village nearby, Larkin wanted to stay here, and Farley had been all for camping in the woods. They could hunt and fish, and the quietude meant that Dessa was able to roam.

"Is the warped one near?"

"Not that I can sense." Torio's gaze drifted toward the low mountain range that was their destination. "We're still too far away. Where are you?"

"Near."

He knew that. What he really wanted to know was what she'd found that was making her so happy. But Torio stayed where he was, searching the sky. The day was fine, and the afternoon would be hot. A good day for lazing.

Still, they needed a change in the weather.

This was familiar territory, scanning the skies for rising clouds. He'd done the same, week-in and week-out, before being rewarded by the thunderstorm that had made it possible for Freydolf to wake Dessa. Thankfully, this was the right season for rain. He doubted they'd have to wait for long.

"Are they right?"

Torio turned his head to consider Dessa, who'd been picking flowers. Her arms encompassed a bouquet of yellow blooms. He asked, "Can a flower be wrong?"

She sat beside him. *"Are the stems long enough to weave?"*

"Is that what you were after? Let me have a look."

These weren't the titian poppies for which the entire area was famous. They were ordinary wildflowers, but they were a cheery color … and they'd made his mountain happy. "Fortunately for you, Miss Aggie taught me this skill at the same time she was showing Miss Dulcie and Miss Yona."

Dessa closely watched his hands, then chose a few flowers in order to follow his lead. She was clumsy and so cautious, as if she didn't want to bruise a single stem, even though she'd been quick enough to snap them.

His crown was finished first, and he settled it over her hair. "For my lady."

"Am I beautiful?"

"You are," he assured. "And not because of a humble man's lopsided garland."

His playful gallantry backfired on him, for it put the loveliest smile on her face. And Torio was keenly aware that he'd spend the rest of his life trying to draw it out again.

He tipped his head back, turning his face into the sun. A sidelong peek confirmed that Dessa had mimicked him, eyes closed, her face tipped. It was nice, this casual togetherness.

"Where is Farley?"

"Hmm. Probably swimming by now. That was his intention."

"Is that safe?"

"The lake poses no great peril."

Dessa tutted at him, which was amusing. *"Is he safe with Jubilee?"*

"Ah. I see your point. Our boy won't come to any lasting harm if he's cornered and kissed. Besides, he's not alone. Artor and Larkin are keeping an eye on them."

She leaned against him and ventured, *"Kisses are harmless?"*

Belatedly, Torio realized that he was alone. With Dessa. Even the lionesses, who'd followed their carriage on foot, were off ranging the woods.

Before his scattered thoughts could figure out a graceful way out, Dessa's hand found his. The black stone had soaked up enough sun that she felt almost feverish.

"Show me?"

"See here, Dessa ...!" he protested weakly. But his traitorous imagination was wondering how warm her lips would be under his. And this was an idyllic setting for a first kiss.

"Isn't it my right?"

Maybe? He was fairly sure they'd been headed in this direction from the very beginning. Freydolf had warned him in little ways. So had Aurelius. Because all of the statues created by Morven's Keeper were deucedly affectionate.

"Torio?" Her voice was barely a whisper.

For her sake, he rallied. "Can a kiss be wrong?"

"I don't know. I don't know how. Do you?"

"Well, yes. I suppose I do."

"How?" And with a small frown. *"Who?"*

She didn't know. Nobody in his current circle of friends did. It was so much easier to let them believe he was a bachelor. That way, he never had to talk about a past best left buried. But Dessa deserved to know. "I suppose I owe you a story. It's old and sad and ... mine."

"You're sad." She looked worried. *"I made you sad?"*

"No, lady. This isn't your fault." He fixed his eyes on

the cloudless sky while he framed his confession. "In days of old and yore, when I was a much younger man, I took a bride. I had a wife, Dessa."

"*You love her.*" She sounded so confused.

"Very much," he agreed softly. "And in the usual way of things, there came a child. I had a son, Dessa."

"*You are so sad.*" Her confusion had turned to alarm.

"Less than before, but always a little. Because I lost them."

"*Is that why you travel? Is that where we're going? To find them again?*"

What a thing to assume. Torio used plainer words. "A fever crept in and stole them from me. They died. Do you understand about death?"

"*Tupper told me. He told me Graven's story so I would understand.*"

"Very conscientious of the young master." He sighed and said, "I don't like to think of you being sad."

Dessa's mood shifted. "*You love her. She is lost, but you do love her.*"

"Did you stop loving Ulrica or Dulcie or Chelle, even though you can no longer see them every day?"

"*No.*"

"Is Freydolf still precious to you, even though he's far out of reach?"

"*Yes.*"

"Do you love Farley, rascal though he be?"

"*Yes.*"

"And does loving him mean you think less of me?"

"*No.*"

Torio searched her face for signs of understanding. "Can you imagine what it would mean to a man who has known so much sadness and loss to have a lady who will never leave him?"

Slowly, he could feel the bloom of happiness, brighter than any bouquet.

"I make you happy?"

"Did you not know?" He lowered his voice. "I thought you could tell."

"I know. I do know. But you never ...."

Not for lack of wanting. But she had to know that as well. "Having traveled far and wide, I'm in a position to know that most Keepers do not kiss their mountains. Not even Freydolf."

"I am your lady."

"You are."

"Your ... your second lady."

"Very true."

"You kissed that lady? Your first lady?"

Torio might have enjoyed forcing Harrow to quibble him into a corner before admitting defeat, but he wouldn't do that to Dessa. She needed to be cherished, and she was trying to tell him how.

"Enough," he begged. "Enough, Dessa. I'll show you. Please, let me show you. It's so much easier than words."

She went still and silent. Expectant.

Yes, Dessa was a mountain, but his mountain wanted to be his lady. And she craved the kind of belonging that led to kisses. He was going about it all wrong, at least by Grif standards, but they *were* bound. As good as wed.

The hand he lifted to her cheek was trembling. She was so good at making him tremble. Just a little, he promised himself. Just enough to reassure her.

But Dessa startled him. She was good at that, too.

Her lips parted under his, and the kiss deepened.

Magic twirled across his senses, so close he could taste it. He knew she was pleased, even triumphant. But she didn't understand *why,* and that was important to him. So even though magic sparked and fizzed against his affinity in exciting ways, he drew back and firmly tucked her under his chin.

"Dessa?" he ventured.

"*I am here.*"

"I must confess, I'm confused."

"*No. You love me.*"

"That ... wasn't what I meant." He knew the answer, but he asked anyway. "How did Freydolf manage to give you a mouth?"

He could almost feel her smile, though it was hidden against his shoulder. Her laughter chimed brightly in his mind, and pinions and pinfeathers, if it didn't make him want to kiss her again.

Farley turned sharply toward the grassy hilltop where Torio had slipped away with Dessa.

"Something amiss?" asked Artor.

"Nope. Dessa's happy."

"How can you tell?"

"I can always tell." Farley tapped his fingers distractedly over his heart. "Probably part of hearing a mountain's call. At least, that's the going theory."

"Do you know why?" Artor amended, "Why she's happy, I mean."

"I could guess." Really, Farley didn't need to. "I mean, it's gotta be Torio. But more importantly, can you un-scare those kids? They were here first."

"They're not children."

It was Farley's turn to ask, "How can you tell?"

"Long practice. It's all in the length of the foot and the fullness of the tail." He bobbled a hand. "The number of earrings can also be a hint, but one far less reliable."

To Farley, the pair of Pika who'd taken one look at Larkin and scarpered had looked like teens—thin, startled, and understandably wary. But he didn't think they were gone-gone. Not with their blankets and canopy still a bright spot on the shore and their kettle steaming on a tripod over a small fire.

Artor turned to Larkin and asked, "Do you mind sitting in plain sight. Right there? And if Jubilee would stay with you, to show your peaceable intentions."

Farley thought Larkin might skulk off to hunt, but he did as he was told. Though when he caught Farley looking, he did curl a lip.

Jubilee cozied right up to the Pred and began to strum his lap harp.

For his part, Farley got ready for a swim. He'd wanted to since they'd rounded a bend and spied the lake, but he'd had to care for his team first. Even with Artor's help, it seemed to take forever. He chucked his boots, set his hat with more care, and shimmied out of his breeches.

"So bold!" called Jubilee, who was watching him from under his lashes.

Pulling his tunic over his head, Farley said, "I'm keeping the undershorts. What's the big deal? Isn't this how Pika swim?"

"Swim?" he echoed vaguely. "This is a popular place to bathe."

"Isn't it the same?"

Larkin snorted. "Their ears. They don't like getting water in their ears."

Jubilee's flattened to either side, and with a shudder of distaste, he said, "We do not."

Farley checked to see if Artor was having any luck. He'd coaxed the two Pika into conversation. His voice was deep and slow as he asked, "Can we bring aught but peace to a place of peace? We are travelers with simple needs—water for our horses, a shady place to rest—and this man wishes to swim. Outlandish, is he not?"

"Hey," protested Farley. "This isn't strange where I come from."

Artor beckoned as he continued in soothing tones. "You can see he's unarmed. Can we not trade names and share this bit of shore in the manner of neighbors?"

Farley spied one pair of ears, then a second. The Pikas' eyes were wide, but they were listening as Artor introduced himself as a member of their community.

"... and that good man is our ship's captain. A Pred, true, but a merchant. He comes to trade, not to take. And this man is Flox, a kindly people, by and large, though this one has an adventurous heart."

With a wave, he called, "I'm Farley."

"I'd wager that none of your brothers ever met a Flox," Jubilee called out. "Ursa are rare in this territory, too. Will you be the first to meet palms with them?"

Gasps.

Whispers.

And finally, "Jubilee the Traveler?"

He flashed a smile and kept right on plucking notes from his harp.

Farley asked, "Are you famous or something?"

"I am little more than your guide and guard." Jubilee nodded toward the other two Pika. "Mind your lessons."

And suddenly, Farley was caught between one guy with titian hair and his friend, whose coloring was all mottled grays. The double embrace turned awkward when one of them dropped to his knees and began petting Farley's leg.

"He's *bald*," gasped the titian one.

"Not everywhere," countered the gray, who gently tugged one of Farley's golden curls.

Two at a time was a little much. He'd have to do this in stages. Neatly catching the gray's wrist, Farley guided it away from his hair, but he also slipped an arm around his back. With his face slightly averted, he cheerfully repeated, "I'm Farley Meadowsweet. What's your name?"

Gray eyes widened, and pale cheeks turned pink. "Forgive me. I should have asked first, but you're so lovely and strange." His gaze flicked longingly to Farley's hair.

"No harm done. What should I call you?"

"I'm Greysallow."

"Nice ta meetcha, Greysallow." And because he really didn't mind, Farley tipped his head. "Go ahead. It's only hair."

"Even your horns curl!" exclaimed Greysallow.

Artor chuckled and gave Farley an approving nod. So far, so good.

Turning his attention to the other one, he asked, "Hey, you. What's so strange about my legs?"

Crouching next to him, Artor said, "Ursa also have sparse hair on their hind limbs."

The titian-haired Pika blinked soft brown eyes and wrinkled his freckled nose. But then his ears strayed to a new angle, and he asked, "Are you going to take off your breeches, too?"

"Would you like me to?" countered Artor.

Lashes fluttered, and he tugged at his ears, which Farley noticed were bare of rings. "I haven't finished my readying. Neither of us has."

Artor's expression softened. "*Nobody* here is on offer. Perhaps Farley will give us swimming lessons."

"Sure. Happy to." Farley was interested to note that Artor had his face slightly turned, as did this blushing Pika who scooted over to kiss the Ursa. It was one of the more reserved greetings, shyly given. So not every Pika was as forward as Jubilee.

"Should I ...?" ventured Greysallow.

"My friends tell me it's only polite, but I'm new to this stuff."

"Sounds lonesome." And with his gaze full of concern, Greysallow went up on tiptoe to deliver a soft kiss. He promised, "For as long as we're together, you'll have good and gentle company."

Farley was feeling increasingly foolish to have worried over Pika customs. He cut an accusing look in Jubilee's direction. The bard's lips were twitching.

Then the second Pika flung his arms around Farley's neck. "Your name is pretty, and your hair is pretty, and I want to be neighborly, too. Will you let me keep you company?"

He quickly checked Artor, who nodded amiably.

"I'm glad you like my name. What's yours?"

"Hespero!"

"Like the Sunset Mountain?"

Grabbing a handful of his vividly orange hair, he said, "*Lots* of titian tufts are named for Hesper. It's so *ordinary*."

Farley could only shake his head. "Tufts?"

"Bitty brothers, newly named." Wriggling closer, Hespero dropped a perfunctory kiss on the corner of Farley's lips then urgently whispered, "How come your horns are uneven?"

"That's a really good story, but is it okay if I get wet first? I've been wanting a swim all morning."

And ... that was it. No propositioning. No need to push. Farley shot another look at Jubilee, who was attempting to draw Larkin into conversation. It seemed increasingly possible that his first friend among the Pika wasn't exactly typical. He'd have to ask Artor's opinion later.

Greysallow and Hespero were easy to impress. They exclaimed over his shallow dive and his arm strokes. They were equally impressed when his hair hung in wet ringlets almost to his shoulders. He was really overdue for a trim. Questions came at him thick and fast, but he gave as good as he got. They only had to pause from time to time to get translation help from Artor, which was when Greysallow and Hespero realized that Farley had needed to learn their language.

He talked in Verit.

They wheedled for stories.

He brought out Tap.

They shared their picnic.

Sitting together in the shallows, the Pikas' heads practically on his shoulders while they dreamed up more questions, Farley thought to ask, "When will you get earrings like Jubilee's? Are they a rite of passage thing? They are for Pred."

Hespero gaped at him. "You don't know?"

"I wouldn't be asking if I did know."

The titian-haired Pika gently poked at one of the blue droplets Farley wore. "But you have two."

Farley smiled crookedly. "I think your earrings must mean something different."

Greysallow stole a peek in the bard's direction. "He's a father. A ring for each child."

"Wait, what?" Farley craned his neck, counting. Then he ducked back, whispering, "That's a lot of tufts."

"He's a popular consort." Greysallow wistfully explained, "Black fur has been in vogue for a while. Unlike gray. Gray is boring."

Hespero heaved a sigh. "We'll be lucky to get any rings."

"Well, you're my first gray and my first titian, so you're amazing to me."

Leaning into him and fluttering his lashes, Hespero asked, "Am I beautiful? Have I enchanted you?"

Farley delivered a teasing fingertap to his nose. "*I'm* not the one you need to impress."

Hespero accepted the mild rebuff by dimpling, and Greysallow lowered his voice conspiratorially. "There are other ways to gain a lady's favor."

Both looked in Jubilee's direction.

"Like music?" Farley guessed.

Greysallow bashfully admitted, "I'm good. Getting better."

Hespero gave one of Farley's earrings another careful poke. "So you're *not* a father?"

"Nope. I wanted to travel more than anything, so I didn't take a wife."

"Wife?" ventured Greysallow.

"A Floxish tradition. He means a lady," said Artor.

"Just … take one?" Hespero snorted. "You make it sound easy."

"Well, sure. It's not *hard*. I'd have had to pick a girl and court her, but I didn't bother. All the girls I knew wanted to settle down, not go adventuring."

Jubilee spoke up then, proving that he'd probably been eavesdropping for a while. "Tell them, lovely locks. Tell them how many girls there are in a Flox village."

"Oh, yeah. That'd be different from here, wouldn't it." Farley almost felt bad, so his words came out like an apology. "Where I come from, there's the same number of boys as girls. So when we marry, we pair off."

They gaped.

For quite a while.

Then tittered a little, like it must be a joke.

"It's true," said Farley. "I swear it is."

Finally, Hespero leaned past Farley to ask his friend, "Maybe *we* should travel?"

Greysallow fidgeted. "But we'd have to *leave*."

"Might be worth it." Hespero pointed out, "Farley says we're *amazing*."

"For now, maybe we could be a little adventurous." Greysallow cautiously asked, "Farley, do you want to spend tonight with us?"

"Well," he answered slowly. "We planned to camp here. You, too?"

"There's a place not far from here." Greysallow pointed across the water. "An island. If we had a party of four, we could reserve one of the east-facing alcoves."

That sounded a lot like sharing the dawn, and Farley

wasn't sure what to do. "Oh, well ... there's only three of us."

Hespero angled his head to the side, practically pointing with his ears. "You could invite Jubilee the Traveler. Then we would be four. And if he was to bring a lantern ...!"

"Yes, that!" urged Greysallow. "Ask for that."

Farley said, "I'll just see if he's interested. Sound okay?"

They nodded eagerly.

"No promises," he warned. "We might be ... busy."

Again nods.

So he sloshed to his feet and tramped across the bank toward the tree where Jubilee looked on with an indulgent smile.

"How much did you hear?"

"Enough."

"What do you think?"

"That wet cloth does little to contribute to Floxish modesty."

Farley glanced down, sighed, and crouched with his arms wrapped around his knees. "Consider yourself pushed. Now, what should I tell my friends? Is the alcove and the lantern going to be a problem for someone like me?"

"Not at all," said Jubilee, without a hint of teasing. "If their offer pleases you, you should accept. For both of us."

"Can you tell me what's supposed to happen? I need to know if there's some kind of tradition or taboo involved." His curiosity warred with frustration. "Tell me where the door is hung and how the hut is thatched."

"This tradition is harmless enough. Drinking long into the night. Sleeping in close quarters. Waking early to watch for the sun." Jubilee beamed at him. "If the dawn sky is pink, it means you will have good fortune in your next venture."

"Nice. Say, though. They seem really interested in *you* being there. How come?"

"When young bucks invite an adult to accompany them, they hope to learn from him. There are many intricacies involved in Pika etiquette, and all of it is handed down by word of mouth. And as you were so kind to point out, a bard has a way with words."

"Does that mean ...? Are you going to kiss them?"

Jubilee beckoned him closer.

With a sigh, Farley closed the distance between them.

"They will want to talk. From what I overheard, it will likely be about consorts, travel, and possible apprenticeships. If they know *me*, they're probably also aspiring musicians or songwriters. I expect to share songs and stories." Running his fingertips across the stubble beginning to grow along Farley's jaw, Jubilee quietly added, "I will keep my promise. You will be safe."

Farley admitted, "It does sound fun."

"Tell your friends that I will supply both a lantern and a bottle of petalberry cordial. And if they have instruments, they should bring them."

"Okay, sure. Anything else?"

Jubilee dragged his finger along the other side of Farley's face. "I look forward to seeing if the sky will blush in your honor."

With Jubilee's name—and coin—to guarantee their success, Greysallow and Hespero hurried off to secure passage on the ferry to the island, which Farley couldn't see from this part of the shore. "Have you been there before?"

Jubilee hummed. "I have seen many places. This one more than once. It is lovely in summertime."

The next couple hours were busy. Larkin hunted, and Farley fished. Artor went into the village with Jubilee, who needed to procure the promised cordial. By the time Torio returned, savory smells were coming from the direction of the cookfire, where a bare-chested Larkin presided.

At the news of Farley's intended side trip, Torio simply turned to Larkin. "What do you think, Captain?"

"Harmless."

Torio accepted that with a nod. "Unless you want Dessa to send the lionesses after you, I suggest introducing her to Jubilee."

"You don't mind?"

With a bland look, he said, "Use your Floxish wiles to haggle some discretion out of him."

"Or I could ask nicely."

"Or that." Torio's smile was tentative.

Farley held his gaze, affecting innocence.

Torio lowered his gaze. "Should we … talk?"

"I probably know as much as I need to." He strolled into the woods a little way, and Torio followed. "At least, that's how it works in Flox villages. And Ulrica almost flayed Tupp for not saying anything. So I'm the one who should be asking if we need to talk."

To Farley's surprise, Torio looked sad. "Sometime soon. Perhaps aboard ship. When you don't have a gadabout bard on your arm."

He went to the man's side. "I don't understand."

"I don't think Dessa does either. Not truly."

"*He loves me.*"

Torio flushed, and Farley cheerfully said, "Yes, Dessa sweet. *That* has never been in question."

The Grif now looked exasperated, which was better, but not best. And Farley wasn't much for patience. "*What?*" he whispered, holding out his hand. "Spell it out if you have to."

Long fingers tapped lightly against his palm, but the man didn't trace any letters there. Instead, he clasped Farley's hand and sighed. "I never mentioned ... and I felt Dessa should understand. You, too. I don't talk about it because ... it seems so long ago. Another lifetime."

Farley crowded even closer and forced Torio to look him in the eyes. "Dessa's terrible at secrets, so I'll find out either way."

Torio looked miserable. "It's not that I'm ashamed. Never that. It was always easier not to talk about it."

"If you're haggling for discretion, it's yours," Farley quietly promised. And then he did his best to listen. *Really* listen.

His former mentor spilled his secret in a handful of words that wrenched Farley's heart. He couldn't think of a thing to say, so he cautiously pulled Torio into his arms and hoped it was the right thing to do.

Torio bowed his forehead until it touched Farley's shoulder. "I was your age when it happened. Barely wed for two years."

Farley tutted. He'd lost someone, too, but it had been the other way around. He'd been just a nubbin when his father died.

"My boy would have been sixteen this year."

Throwing back his head, Farley blinked hard.

"Do not cry," Torio warned.

"I'm not. I kinda want to, though. I mean he was so *little*." Farley's voice cracked, and he swore softly. "Okay, yeah, I'm crying. But can you blame me? It's like finding out I had a little brother, but I missed out on teasing him."

Torio groaned and straightened, but he didn't pull away. He crushed Farley closer, tucking him under his chin, all shaky breaths as he tried to swallow back his grief.

"Why is he crying?"

"Because he's sad, Dessa sweet." His voice only wavered

a little.

"Why are you crying?"

Farley kept it simple. "Because I care about Torio."

"Torio is mine."

"He is."

"And you are mine."

"No doubt."

After a long pause, Dessa asked, *"It's not good enough?"*

Farley hesitated.

Then she ventured, *"Maybe you should kiss him, too?"*

He laughed, because what else could he do? Even Torio snorted. But that's when the thing Torio had said earlier finally clicked, about Dessa not truly understanding. Yes, Dessa was a living, thinking heart of a magical mountain. She'd found a man and a boy to answer her call. But Dessa was stone, and her Keeper was flesh and blood and bone.

In a way, it was simply another cultural difference. Something they could work through. But there were things Dessa hadn't grappled with, like loss and grief and regret. And unlike Farley, she probably couldn't imagine what Torio had suffered. Not now. Not yet. Maybe not until she lost *them*.

"Did you kiss him?" checked Dessa, who sounded worried. *"Did it help?"*

"I'm hugging him hard," Farley promised. "And he's hugging me back. Will that do?"

"Will it?" And more fretfully, *"Am I not enough?"*

"Skies above, woman," Torio grumbled. "You and this brat are more than enough. Better than I deserve. But stop asking him to kiss me. His is no more Pika than I."

"He'll be fine," Farley promised. "When he talked, you listened, didn't you? Remember how it felt when we first listened to you?"

"Oh," Dessa breathed. And her mood took on fresh sparkle. *"Oh, I do."*

Farley relaxed against Torio, figuring he should make the most of a rare show of affection. This was only the second time the man had pulled Farley close.

"How do you do that?" muttered Torio.

"What did I do?"

"I wish I knew." He stood there, stayed there, and finally he said, "Dessa *needs* you."

"I coulda told you that."

Torio's hold tightened. "Don't go far, and don't go for long."

Farley had never really tested to see how far he could go. Dessa's hold on him was a good thing, but he knew better than to stray. Once a mountain claimed someone, they needed to stick close. He and Torio couldn't leave without putting a strain on a bond that was linked to their very lives. "You think that island's too far?"

"No." Torio released him with traces of reluctance. "Just ... don't lose your way back."

"Because *Dessa* needs me," Farley teased.

Torio simply flicked his snub horn with a curving talon. But it was enough for Farley.

It was pretty nice knowing that where you wanted to be was also exactly where you were needed.

Jubilee adored Dessa on sight, vowing to carry the secret of her existence close to his heart until such a time as he could sing of her beauty far and wide. A decent outcome, even if the bard had fluttered and fussed enough to make Torio step in.

Farley leaned over the gondola's side, mostly so he could trail his fingers in the water, but also so he could put some distance between him and Jubilee.

"A push would suffice," reminded the Pika.

"Pushing just means more touching," countered Farley.

"Very good. You're quick to grasp the essentials."

With a nod toward Greysallow and Hespero, who were chatting with the oarsman standing at the prow, Farley said, "Those guys have been easy enough to get along with. *You're* the only one who's begging to be pushed."

"I'm keeping all the rest at bay."

"So you say." But Farley relented enough to sit straighter, and when their shoulders bumped, it felt friendly. He peered off toward their island destination, which mostly looked like a giant rock jutting above the lake's surface. Boats bobbed alongside several docks, and he could make out people moving up and down ladders. "Are those caves?"

"Day-Peep is a dawnstone monolith riddled with private alcoves. The very walls are said to lend peace to the troubled and respite to the weary."

If so, Farley doubted it was because of the stone. While the island glowed with the characteristic pink of dawnstone, they were a long ride from Itzel. He wasn't picking up much in the way of magic. Just a scattering, like there were stone guardians posted here and there. Maybe he could poke around and find them.

"Do you have any affinity?" asked Farley.

"Oh, some. A trifling amount, really. Mother was part of a journeyman crew, and stonework is a family tradition." Jubilee said, "I know enough to appreciate fine craftsmanship when I see it. And a masterwork when she is introduced."

"Hush," grumbled Farley, with a glance toward the oarsman at the stern. He'd already figured out that Pika had long ears—in the sense that their hearing was excellent—

and a love for news and gossip. Any rumors started here would probably reach Morven before they did.

Jubilee obliged, folding his hands around a box tied shut with fancy braided cords.

"Is that the lantern?" Farley asked curiously. "What's it for?"

The oarsman behind them chuckled, and when Farley looked up at him, he winked.

"Hush," Jubilee answered in an amiable undertone. "Save your questions until we are there."

Sunset was painting Day-Peep's walls red, and they were near enough for Farley to catch the flutter of pink banners and a faint snatch of music. In some of the alcove entrances, lights were already showing, flames behind tinted glass— copper and coral, ruby and rose. Farley guessed the different colors had to mean something, but he stowed his questions and tried to memorize every detail.

Quiet seemed to be expected. The guys who came to meet the ferry worked without words, and Greysallow and Hespero left off talking. Farley arched his brows at Jubilee, who only patted his knee and took the lead.

The dock was strung with lights that were too tiny to be practical, but Farley decided they were as dainty as festival cakes, lending a celebratory note to the end of the day.

They passed a thin strip of beach—all pink sand and white shells. Farley had to wonder why there were shells in this lake. They certainly didn't have any in the rivers and creeks back home.

Jubilee exchanged murmured greetings with a Pika whose hair and fur were white with black spots, and then they entered a tunnel flanked by a pair of starstone guardians.

Smooth stone underfoot. Soft light overhead.

A staircase took its time spiraling upward, and they passed several doors. Farley wondered why they weren't scaling ladders like the people he'd spotted earlier. Their guide unlocked a narrow wooden door, then presented

Jubilee with the key ... and a kiss. Then the bard sought Farley's gaze and held out his hand. "Come along, it's a small tradition. Show him how it's done, my young friends."

Greysallow beamed at Farley, then offered his hand to Hespero, who took hold, allowing his friend to pull him through the door.

Farley mimicked Hespero, letting Jubilee draw him into a low-ceilinged room hung with tapestries. The first thing Jubilee did was unbundle the lantern, which had been stowed in one of the embroidered bags he'd allowed Greysallow to carry. Candlelight gave a warm glow to pink glass. Jubilee hung it from a hook near the curved opening in the far wall, which offered a view of the eastern sky.

If Hespero's exclamations were anything to go by, their alcove was especially fine. Cushions heaped the corners, and a series of small tables held covered dishes. Farley lifted a few lids, then stepped out onto the ledge, which dropped away without so much as a railing. He sat with his legs dangling over the edge, peering around. Many other alcoves dotted the wall, but theirs was nearest the top of the monolith. So Jubilee really *was* wealthy, famous, or both.

After some consideration, Farley decided that it didn't matter. Not really. If Jubilee had wanted more respect, he would have insisted on it. So this was fine. No need to change.

"Oh, no!" Hespero exclaimed. "Oh, be careful!"

"That's dangerous," agreed Greysallow, who took Farley's arm to pull him back.

"Not for a seasoned adventurer." Farley laughed and let them pull him inside, where Jubilee had been making other small preparations.

"I don't like heights," confessed Hespero.

"I've never minded them when there's good stone underfoot." Farley tapped his toe against the polished floor. "Now, scaling the ship's rigging took some getting used to, but that was more about the roll of the ocean than the height."

They had a dozen questions about sailing and sailors.

All the while Farley talked, Jubilee slipped the braided cords from the box he'd carried in. As it happened, the case held the promised bottle of petalberry cordial, as well as a set of four tiny cups. The bard arranged them upon one of the tables but didn't pour. "A meal first, for you shall need your strength. Then music, lest the cordial go to your head and keep my songs from finding their way into your hearts."

The food was good. Farley wasn't sure why Hespero and Greysallow insisted on feeding him his first taste of anything, but they mostly seemed excited to share. So he went with it. They chatted about favorite foods and festival fare. All too soon, they'd cleared every last tray.

Fingerbowls with fragrant water to wash up.

Braziers to chase away the dark and warm the alcove.

Hespero pulled cushions into a new arrangement, and Greysallow produced a lute. His ears dipped toward it as he tuned, and Farley couldn't decide if he was feeling shy ... or angling them to listen. Maybe both.

Jubilee uncovered his harp, then arched his brows at Hespero.

The titian-haired Pika scuttled to his pack and returned with something Farley had never seen before. The polished wood box had a hole like a lute, but instead of a neck and strings, the thing had been fitted with a row of bent metal tabs.

"That's your instrument?" Farley asked.

With a small nod, Hespero ran his fingertips over the metal bits, and as he did, notes rang out, clear as a cascade of small bells.

Farley crowded closer. "Do that again!"

Smiling bemusedly, he obeyed, and this time, he played a song, light and sprightly and perfect for dancing.

"That's amazing. Can I try?"

Laughing softly, Hespero pushed it closer to Farley. "Haven't you ever seen a music box before?"

"No. Never." He tried to mimic the flicking motion the Pika had used. Coaxing music from it wasn't any trouble at all, and he grinned. "It's easy, but ... also hard. How long did it take you to learn?"

Hespero bumped shoulders with him. "Am I amazing again?"

"I'm certainly impressed."

"Would a Flox lady be impressed?" he asked shyly.

Farley hummed. "Thinking of becoming Hespero the Traveler?"

"If there was a way. And if Greysallow came with me."

Jubilee drew a laughing cascade from his harp. "I know a song about a journeyman bard. Would you like to hear it?"

Each Pika took a turn. Greysallow would not sing, but he played well enough to Farley's way of thinking. And Hespero had a sweet singing voice, which only gained strength when Jubilee and then Greysallow added their accompaniment to his ballad.

Then Jubilee suggested, "The cordial?"

With much ceremony, the pink glass bottle was passed around and admired. Jubilee unstoppered it and poured a tiny glass for each of them. The liquid was predictably pink, but Farley was intrigued by how thick it was. Slow as syrup, the stuff caught the lanternlight and glowed its way into each cup.

He accepted his and waited for the others.

Greysallow held out a hand, protesting, "It's his first sip!"

Jubilee cautioned, "What's traditional for Pika need not apply to our Flox friend."

"But ... it's petalberry cordial." Hespero sounded so disappointed, like Farley was missing out on something special.

"So it is." Jubilee shifted around the table to sit beside Farley. "If I may?"

He took Farley's cup, then held it carefully to Farley's lips. This wasn't much different from the others slipping him morsels over dinner, so he cooperated. The cordial had the same sweet tang as the petalberry confit he'd eaten earlier, but also a subtle sting. It might take a few glasses, but he thought it could make him tipsy.

The other young men raised their own cups and tipped them back.

Licking his lips, Farley accepted his cup from Jubilee, asking, "Do I want to know what's traditional for Pika?"

Jubilee offered a knowing smile and a small shake of his head.

He held another sip in his mouth, trying to decide how he felt about drinking something that was thick enough to coat his tongue and throat. He was still curious, though. "Thanks for sparing me …?"

The bard quietly warned, "Three glasses from now, you'll be asking me to demonstrate."

Farley licked his lip as he contemplated the tiny cup. "It's that strong?"

Jubilee only shrugged.

Hespero swooped in to top off his glass.

Greysallow asked for the tale of his snub horn.

And Farley soon lost track of how much cordial he'd swallowed. Keeping tabs was trickier when his friends kept refilling his glass before he could finish.

Music happened. Jubilee knew so many songs, one for any occasion. And Greysallow had a lute lesson, and Hespero sang whenever Jubilee asked, which was often. Then they were teaching him a Pika dance, which had simple steps but a lot of arm positions. Farley offered to show them a Flox dance, and Jubilee really must have been a homelander, because he knew the tune and played it well.

"Which town did you stay in?" Farley dropped to a seat beside Jubilee and leaned against him. "I'm from Hayward."

"Oh, you know how it is. Journeymen rarely stay in one place for long."

"There aren't *that* many towns. I've been to all the ones around Morven." Farley slouched lower, resting his head on Jubilee's shoulder. That gave him a good view of the Pika's ears and earrings. "Is it a secret?"

"We aren't famous for secrets. Pika are simple and merry and eager to please."

"S'perfect," Farley murmured. "Always keep it a secret that you've got a secret."

"I fear you are drunk, lovely locks."

He hummed and smiled and asked, "Where's my push."

Jubilee did push him. First to his feet, then onto a bed, where he landed with his head on a pillow. After that, they covered him in blankets, turned down the lantern, and ... someone pet his hair until Jubilee's soft music sent him into sleep.

Farley knew it was a dream when he heard his name and glanced over his shoulder to see a young Grif hurrying to catch up. He turned to walk backward, happy to wait. The lad's smile was the same as Torio's, as were his blue eyes. But his hair was fine and black, with a silky shine that reminded Farley of Dessa's stone.

The boy reached out, and Farley caught his hand, pulling him to his side. He slipped an arm around his waist to show that they were friends, maybe even brothers.

Off to one side, Torio looked on. He didn't comment, but he watched them with a funny little half smile. Like when things were better than good. Like when he was really glad.

Farley hugged the young Grif tightly. Hugged him because Torio wanted to but couldn't. And there was an appreciative hum.

The dream slipped away.

Farley opened his eyes. The lantern still cast a soft glow over the alcove. By its light, he could tell that the black hair under his nose was Jubilee's. "Mmm... mornin'?" he murmured.

Jubilee patted his shoulder. "You are an early riser."

"Usually, yeah. Somewhere wayyy off in that direction, it's time to milk the cow."

Lifting his head and cocking an ear, Jubilee asked, "Any ill effects from the cordial?"

He rolled onto his back, scratching at morning stubble. "Not really, no. Thirsty, I guess."

Jubilee hummed in a pleased way. "Petalberries are truly a treasure. But I fear the sky will not blush in our favor. I am sorry."

Farley peered in the direction of the east-facing arch. The sky was lightening, but dawn was still a while off. Just then, a faint roll of thunder sounded, and an answering gust of wind carried the scent of rain.

"It is not a total loss," Jubilee quietly promised. "Burrowing together while listening to the rain can be entirely pleasant."

"Don't give up so easily."

"Optimism will not redirect the storm."

"No, but I'm going to check the horizon, which is also wayyy off in that direction. Rain here doesn't always mean rain there."

The Pika conceded with a sigh.

Farley threw back the blanket, catching a glimpse of black-furred legs under Jubilee's nightshirt. He crossed first to the water pitcher and drank two cups. When he turned back, Jubilee perched on the edge of the other bed with its heaped pillows and blankets. He must have found Greysallow, given the color of the ears that perked up. Jubilee shook his shoulder, and the younger man emerged enough to loop his arms around Jubilee's neck and pull him down. The bard laughed and murmured something. Farley suspected kisses.

Circling to the other side of the bed, he found Hespero's shoulder and gave it a poke.

He was already awake and smiled sleepily. His hands lifted, then quickly dropped to clutch the edge of his blanket.

Farley angled his head toward the other two. "Is that how you say good morning in these parts ...?"

Hespero gave a small nod.

"Teach me?"

He let the other young man pull him down into a hug that included a nuzzle to one cheek. "First light, first kiss," he mumbled, as easy as *good morning*.

It kind of made sense, given the nature of dawnstone, so Farley returned the greeting. "First light, first kiss. Want me to bring some water?"

Hespero nodded and pushed to a seat, ears flopped to his shoulders as he peered around. "Did I miss sunrise?"

Another soft growl of thunder answered, and Farley thought it might have been closer.

"Oh." Hespero sounded disappointed, but he rallied a little. "I'm glad we're not in our tent."

Greysallow sat up and pulled his friend close for their own morning greeting. "Fortune favored us both. Thank you, Jubilee. And you, Farley."

Jubilee suggested, "Let us have a look at the sky, then burrow until breakfast."

Hespero kept a blanket bundled around his shoulders as he shuffled from the bed. Farley handed him a cup of water, earning another sleepy smile. Greysallow checked the cooled teapot from last night and poured himself the dregs, which he swallowed with a slight grimace. "I volunteer to go down to the kitchen, if need be. Must have tea. Preferably hot."

"Later," countered Jubilee, who drew the younger man toward the arch.

Greysallow looked awestruck and followed gladly enough. By the time Farley and Hespero joined them, the pair were huddled together as they peered into the murky morning sky. Backtracking for another blanket, Farley threw it around them, then joined Hespero under his. It wasn't raining yet, but the damp air held a definite chill.

In the distance, a narrow band of lightening sky hadn't yet been overtaken by clouds.

"Come on, now," coaxed Farley. "Don't disappoint Itzel's get. Can't you feel them trembling?"

"Are they?" Jubilee looked his way.

"Sure they are. They live for this moment."

"Dawn's first kiss?" suggested Jubilee.

"Sounds about right," Farley answered, then addressed the distant horizon. "So don't dawdle."

Hespero pushed up under his arm. "Dawn never hurries, and yet she's never late."

"Here comes the rain," warned Greysallow.

Droplets spattered around them, but in the distance, the sky turned peach, then pale gold. For a moment, there was a peep of the sun's bright rim, before gray curtains of rain closed around them, hissing into the lake below.

They ducked back inside, shedding blankets and shaking rain from their hair and ears. Hespero and Greysallow slipped away to bring tea and breakfast, and Farley hunted down his socks. "No blushing daybreak for me," he remarked. "I don't think it's unlucky, though. We needed the rain."

Jubilee drifted toward their bed and sat amidst the cushions. "Unlucky? Indeed, no. Not when the sky took on the same shine as your fetching curls ... albeit briefly."

"Guess that's one way to look at it." With a shrug, Farley added, "Sure. If that's good fortune, I'll take it."

"Because you will hunt today?"

"That's the plan. Whatever's in that pass will be on the move until sunset." Farley hesitated. "You'll need to stay back. It'll be safer for you."

"If you think you will abandon me here ...!"

"Nope. In the carriage should be fine. Can you handle a weapon?"

Jubilee's ears dipped. "No."

"That's all right. I'll leave one of the lionesses with you and Artor." Farley paused again. "Are you ... nervous?"

"There is something I did not mention. About the story ... and my part in it."

"Your part?" Farley echoed, crossing to the bed.

Jubilee smiled weakly. "I have firsthand experience, you see. With the monster you will hunt."

"Do you know what stone?"

He shook his head. "I did not see it. I felt it."

"Your affinity."

Jubilee curled in on himself. "I was little more than a tuft, new to the continent and homesick. Mother brought me along to cheer me up, but ... none of the crew knew the rumors. Barely twelve words of Terse amongst us, and our guide offered no warning."

"Was it raining?"

"No. The skies were an endless blue, but we walked through a few puddles during our climb."

Farley reached for Jubilee's hand. "What happened?"

"My uncle pushed me up into the branches of a big pine and begged me to keep climbing." He sighed softly. "So I did."

"And ...?"

"It did not find me."

Farley felt sick. "The others?"

He shook his head. "After, when they found us, they sent for Hashbaz."

"He *knew*," Farley realized. "He always knew the rumor was true. And he sent us to you ... to put things to rest?"

Jubilee tugged Farley's hand up and brushed his lips across his knuckles. "Every coin in my coffers is yours if you can vanquish that monster. Please, Farley. Beggar me."

8

Persistent Drizzle

Farley all but pushed Jubilee inside the carriage. "Don't be stupid. Stay put, and stay dry. Leave this to me and Torio."

"And me."

"Yes, Dessa sweet. You most of all. Say, could you ask one of the lionesses to mind Jubilee and Artor?" He nodded at her reply and looked to Artor. "Nyx will be close."

Artor wrapped an arm around Jubilee. "I'm sorry we can't be more help."

"It's fine. We'll go do this and be right back. Nothing to worry about." Farley closed the door and backed up ... straight into Larkin.

The Pred glowered.

Farley gave his arm a pat. "Yeah, I need you, too. More than I'm gonna admit, but only because I don't want to embarrass you. So ... which approach should we take?"

Gaze fixed on Farley, Larkin crouched right there in the road and pressed his fist into the mud.

Startled, Farley responded, dropping down to set his own knuckles on the ground. He had no problem letting

Larkin take the lead in any hunt. But calling Farley into line like a partner? That was new. "Why are you taking this time so seriously?"

Larkin lifted his chin. "Your wee snake is already hooded."

Farley reached for Nestor, who was wrapped around his snub horn. The little guardian butted his fingers, and yeah ... he'd adopted his more threatening aspect.

Next, Larkin angled his head toward Torio. "Your master went quiet even before we reached the terraces."

Torio was with the horses, his gaze on the treed slope, his hand on Nyx's broad head. He'd volunteered to stay back and stand guard—just in case.

"Yeah, that's kind of a bad sign. No offense or anything, but ... are we enough?"

"I would have preferred to seek stone while it remained still."

Farley slowly nodded. "Should we? It's not too late to pull back. Try again tomorrow."

"I also wish to return to the *Moontide* without further delay." Larkin's shoulders lifted. "We have been enough before. Does that change here?"

Honestly, Farley didn't know. Pulling the brim of his hat lower against the persistent drizzle, Farley asked, "Where are you, Dessa?"

"We're climbing. There's something among the trees."

"She and Char are already above the terraces," Farley reported. The slopes below Papaver Pass had been terraced long ago. Though they were choked with weeds now, here and there an ancient fruit tree suggested that this had been an orchard. Maybe a whole farm. "You found something? What sort of something?"

"Like a quarry. Like a bridge."

"How is a bridge like a quarry?" he muttered. And because there was only one person he could ask, Farley returned to the carriage. "Jubilee, is there a bridge through the pass?"

The Pika's initial puzzlement vanished. "An old aqueduct. *Very* old. It's probably nothing more than ruins."

Farley turned and found Larkin looming behind him. No need to relay information. Instead, he asked Jubilee, "Anything *else* up there?"

"In days long gone, there were fortresses in every pass. Defenses against conquerors." Jubilee flashed a wry smile at Larkin. "Pred, mostly."

"An abandoned fortress with Misbegotten defenders," Larkin muttered. "And you only mention it *now*?"

"I truly don't know what you'll find." Jubilee reached for Farley's hand, even though it was dirty. "I could only post signs and spread stories to warn away the unwary."

"Is there a quarry up there?"

The Pika again pleaded ignorance.

Larkin said, "If they built ductwork and fortifications from local stone, they would have quarried it nearby."

Farley extricated his hand from Jubilee's and closed him in again. "Do you want to take the road?"

"Nay. Too many switchbacks, too many surprises." Larkin pointed. "Straight up, through the trees."

"Okay, sure. You should go first."

"Is there no magic that you can track?"

"Maybe when we're closer. This *is* supposed to be a safe distance."

Nodding toward their destination, Larkin asked, "What has she found?"

"Dessa? Can you sense another statue?"

"I don't understand." Uncertainty seeped through her tone.

"Is there a Misbegotten here?"

"Something is wrong with them. They are wrong."

"Warped?" Farley checked.

She hesitated again. *"Shattered ...?"*

"It's already been broken?" Farley glanced at Larkin. A

serious break usually put an end to the magic that brought stone to life.

"*Not shattered,*" she muttered. "*Splintered ...?*"

"All right. So long as we know it's here. Once I'm closer, I'll be able to tell."

She immediately demanded, "*I will find where they are.*"

"That would be a big help. Thank you, Dessa."

"Well?" asked Larkin.

"I guess this one's different from the others we've hunted. She's uneasy."

"She's always uneasy when you're being reckless."

Farley rested an upraised hand under his heart. "I'll have you know she loves me *because* I'm reckless."

Larkin only snorted and started up the slope.

Tossing Torio a jaunty wave, Farley followed, though not in a close, companionable way. There were rules when hunting with Pred, some of which he'd learned from Aurelius. But truth be told, Farley owed most of his training to Aggie. His little sister was silent as stone when on a hunt, and since he was often her hunting partner, she'd decided he needed to keep up.

Rain pattered lightly, fine as mist and clinging to everything. Under the circumstances, freshstone made sense. Plenty of daytime guardians were shaped from the stuff. Stick them in a fountain, and they were on duty from sunup to sundown. And there was an aqueduct? Simple. Except that this didn't feel like blue stone.

The attack on Jubilee's family had happened on a day it had rained. But if this Misbegotten attacked every time it rained, wouldn't people have sent for help sooner? So not necessarily *every* rainy day. What other factors might be in play?

A sheltered position that the rain didn't always reach, making the amount of rain or the direction of the wind a factor. Or maybe Farley's gut was correct. This didn't feel like freshstone, so one of the other daytime stones. Sunstone and dawnstone needed a glimpse of the sun. Brownstone and dazzle needed it to be daytime, but they required scent and snow respectively. Dapple had to have mist or fog or fine rain, and that *could* be the condition that kept this Misbegotten inactive for long stretches. Redstone could stir by day *or* by night, but it wanted fire. Not a fit here.

On the edge of the forest, Larkin glanced back. Farley was privately pleased, since that meant he'd been silent. He made a quick hand signal to ask if he should change course.

Larkin crisply answered in kind—*stay with me*. Which probably meant he thought Farley needed babysitting.

The Pred glided into the trees, naked to the waist, hair knotted, blade in hand. Farley knew his hat limited his senses, but he preferred his layers. Sure, raindrops on his hat brim might mask sounds, but what did that matter when your prey was silent? Better to keep the rain out of his eyes. They were his best asset. But there was no sign yet of magic on the move.

Up under the trees, the rain tapered to odd drops from where the water had collected among the leaves. Farley tipped his hat back and peered around. If there was a Misbegotten stirring, it had to be higher up. "Anything, Dessa?"

"Empty road. Hills beyond. Village below."

Larkin had stopped and turned. He looked annoyed that Farley had spoken.

But how else was Farley supposed to get information? He spread his hands in mute appeal and replied to Dessa is low Terse. "No sign of trouble? Guess that's good. Did you find a building? Or someplace a building used to be?"

"Well?" hissed Larkin, who'd backtracked.

"Nothing on the road or beyond the pass," Farley reported. "Jubilee did mention that the bodies were found *above* the road. I'm guessing the old fortress held the high ground."

"And nothing is here?"

Farley was about to confirm that when something stirred. He raised a finger, held his breath. Larkin remained still.

Warily, Farley gestured for Larkin's hand.

Brows lowered, the Pred thrust it forward.

Onto his palm, Farley spelled, **W – A – T – C – H – I – N – G**.

They remained otherwise motionless, each scanning a different section of the wood. Finally, Larkin bared his teeth and signaled for Farley to follow.

Twice, they crossed the road, which was a rutted mess, well-mired by the rain. Only when the pass itself came into view did Farley spot stonework between the trees. Larkin circled toward a rain-washed ruddy wall, then put it at his back and beckoned for Farley to join him.

At a sign, Farley unstrapped his ax, though it was a hassle to carry around.

Arched brows invited an update.

"Dessa?" he whispered.

"Some walls stand. Some have fallen. There are caves and a well." More petulantly, she added, *"They fear me. They flee before me. I'll return to your side to keep you safe."*

He simply hummed. It wasn't as if he could stop her. Very little could.

Larkin jabbed his shoulder, a scowl ready.

Farley made a face. "I still can't tell what kind of stone it is."

"Does it matter?" he softly grumbled. "Any rock we break becomes rubble."

Farley still felt like he was missing something. "Why doesn't it attack? Why *does* it attack? What was it made to do, and how has its purpose twisted?"

"It murders travelers," Larkin reminded.

"It defends the pass," corrected Farley. "I want to find

its pedestal. Maybe that'll help."

Larkin swept an arm. "Where? Does a pedestal have any magic, or is it only the statue?"

"A little," Farley replied, tensing when a nearby tree released a shower of drops. "There's always a little."

"Can you track it?"

"Sure." Farley grudgingly added, "Once I'm close enough."

"And we're not?" he asked silkily.

He shook his head.

Larkin frowned. "Which direction did she take?"

Farley pointed.

"And no pedestal?"

"No." Dessa would have mentioned finding it.

With a curt nod, Larkin muttered, "Stay close."

He cut across in a different direction than Dessa had taken, zigzagging like he was searching for prey. Farley soon had stone under his feet, a badly overgrown trail that had once been fit with pavers. They were skirting the ruins of what must have been the old aqueduct. Not many sections still stood, but they paused in the shelter of a partial arch. Russet rubble led uphill toward the fortress, but Farley's attention snapped to one side. He started toward the tantalizing hint of magic, only to have Larkin grab his arm.

A brisk hand signal reminded him who was leader in no uncertain terms.

A second ordered Farley to ready his weapon.

Larkin stole toward an overgrown gap in the rockface that became more pronounced once they were closer. Farley followed him into a hushed area with squared-off walls where stonecutters had harvested blocks for the aqueduct. It wasn't magical stuff, nor was it the soft pink of dawnstone. Farley probably would have liked the rust color better if the rain-wet stone hadn't looked so much like blood. Still, he pocketed a couple of rocks to show Artor later. The color might appeal to him for future mosaics.

"Well?" Larkin loomed close, gaze darting.

"Pedestal. Probably." With a helpless gesture toward thick vines, he added, "We're dealing with brownstone."

The Pred simply motioned for him to proceed.

Farley waded in. Thanks to the rain-wet foliage, his pants were soon soaked through, and his boots were developing a squelch that would definitely make Larkin peevish. But it didn't take long for questing fingers to find a brownstone disk half lost in the surrounding vines.

Satisfaction quickly turned to puzzlement. Pushing further into the mess, which was hip-deep and difficult to navigate, he brought his axe into play, cutting vines that were showy with flowers. The scent was subtle ... but sweet enough to stir brownstone.

"Thought so." He found a second and clambered up onto it. If the statue's base hadn't been elevated, it may have been overrun. From his new vantage, he spied a third. Then a fourth. "Larkin! You better have a look," he called softly.

The Pred pivoted enough to consider Farley's face, then backed toward him. "What did you find?"

Farley was worried. "I've seen something like this in the Cavern. Four pedestals. One for each leg."

"That would be a very large guardian. Hardly subtle." He crouched to study the first pedestal Farley had found, using his blade to clear away vines. "Rainflowers."

"Lemme guess. The flowers only open when it's raining?"

"Aye."

That had limited this Misbegotten's chances to stir. Only on rainy days when these vines were in flower. But Farley felt like they were still missing something. The statue was on the move. So why hadn't it attacked?

Larkin's eyes narrowed. "There's an inscription. It's a memorial of some kind, to honor a band of Grif who defended the pass during a Pred incursion. Their names are here. You're wrong, Meadowsweet. This monster isn't a behemoth."

"Good." Indicating the four pedestals, he added, "I wasn't looking forward to trying to cleave anything on this scale."

"Guard up." Holding his gaze, Larkin said, "There are four of them."

When Nyx's hackles rose, Torio left off petting the lioness in order to draw the heavy blade Harrow had commissioned for him. Gleaming black and etched with a pattern of feathers, the weapon served a single purpose: to split stone.

Torio may have been lax in his training during the years he was hauling a formless chunk of power around in a swaying wagon, but Harrow had challenged him to more than bouts of Pinnacles. Running, climbing, sparring ... and countless games of hide-and-hunt that left Torio's heart in his throat and his muscles taut with a renewal of strength.

While neither of them had ever put it into so many words, Torio knew that Aurelius Harrow enjoyed their friendly rivalry. But it had also been preparation. For the journey, yes. The Pred was no stranger to travel and understood a traveler's needs. But also because—in much the same way that Aurelius had secured the *Moontide* for Larkin—he'd wanted the best possible foundation for Farley's future.

Leaves quaked and grass blades bowed, gently beaten by the rain. But the dipping and dripping foliage made pitiful camouflage against a man who could see magic itself.

Rapping on the side of the carriage, Torio warned, "Something's here."

A window panel slid open enough to see out, and Jubilee whispered, "What do you see?"

Torio raised a finger to hush the bard, then pointed toward one of the overgrown terraces. "We are being watched."

"By what?"

"A guardian." Almost at once, he had to indicate another direction. "How unusual. There's another, and yet ... it's the same. Dessa, what did you and Farley find?"

"They come together. They fly apart. One and not one. Like ... like the Triads ...?"

"A good analogy," he murmured. "This grouping ... are there three then?"

"Four."

"Is Farley aware?"

"Farley knows."

Jubilee pushed the window open a little further. "Will it attack?" he whispered. "I thought you said we'd be safe here."

"We haven't been attacked," Torio quietly pointed out. "What sets them off?"

"The rain?"

"We're dealing with brownstone. It's stirring, and yet it stays back." Torio hated to admit it, but he said, "This isn't the behavior of a Misbegotten."

Artor crowded close behind Jubilee and squinted through the drizzle. "Can you see the statue? Its form might give a hint to its original purpose."

Moments later, the nearer statue rose and stepped into the open, giving them a clear view of rain-slicked brownstone.

Torio grimly remarked, "Well. That's certainly very traditional."

A stone griffin leapt from its terrace down to the next, then sat back on its haunches. The statue was easily as large as Nyx, equipped with a beak, talons, and wings that would be able to bludgeon with every beat.

Jubilee whispered, "You're Grif. Is it not attacking because you're Grif?"

"Possibly. If that was the wish of its maker." Torio risked a glance at the Pika. "What of the other victims?"

Right away, he shook his head. "They have been all sorts of people from all sorts of places."

Torio scanned the sign that marked the uphill road, a bold thing with pleas for caution written in all the major trade languages. "You were thorough. Terse. Verit. Prose. Skrit. Cantl. Liric."

A sudden flare in magic pulled his attention back to the stone griffin, which was moving closer, head cocked to one side. It wasn't an attack, but it was now fixed on him. Ominous, but again … not the behavior of a Misbegotten. Warped statues were more driven by some twisted, lingering purpose. This one seemed reasonable.

"Tell me again," Torio said, not taking his eyes from the statue even though the second one had moved into the open. "Why was your traveling party attacked?"

"Because we were traveling through the pass. To an artisan hold beyond." Jubilee's gaze was similarly fixed on the stone guardian. "It had rained earlier. It was a pleasant day. We were in no hurry, talking and laughing and … totally unprepared."

"A harmless company, yet these statues interpreted your arrival as an attack."

"Foreigners?" he ventured. "My mother and her kinsmen are … were Drom. We were newly arrived from New Continent."

Torio's gaze jumped to the statue, then back. "You were speaking *Verit*."

Jubilee nodded.

Artor nervously asked, "Should you have *said* that in Verit?"

Their watcher was on the move again, and its head now cocked to the other side.

Readying his weapon, Torio moved toward it, speaking

broadly in his native tongue. "Greetings, homelander. It is always a pleasure to see one of the noble creatures for which my people are named. Tell me, good griffin, do you also have the heart of a lion? Come now, let us reason together."

Farley caught movement at the top of the quarry wall. No, not movement. Magic. It limned a brownstone griffin who crouched there, wings slowly spreading. It looked ready to swoop in, but stone was stone. It couldn't actually fly, and the wall was high enough that Farley doubted the statue would risk the leap.

"There's one," he warned, jumping from the pedestal and backing away.

"Out!" Larkin quickly outpaced him toward the quarry entrance, snarling, "We're outnumbered. Where's Dessa?"

Farley couldn't see her, but he always knew what direction she was in. "That way!"

"They have found Torio. They have found Farley." Dessa sounded distraught.

Farley's heart sank. Of course she would choose Torio. But then magic flared as a second griffin burst from the trees. Not good. "Dessa, is Torio under attack?"

"He will not tell me!"

High-stepping through scrubby undergrowth that slapped wetly against his legs, Farley did his best not to distress her. "Oh, you know. He's probably fine, then. Did he have anything useful to say?"

There was a brief pause, during which Farley risked a glance over his shoulder. The first griffin had worked his way down from the high ground, joining the second.

"Do not speak Verit, or you will be marked as invaders."

"Dessa sweet," Farley groaned. "You and I are speaking in Verit now."

"Did they hear?"

"Yeah. They heard."

"I am coming."

An instant later, Farley could tell. So could the griffins, who broke stride. That gave him and Larkin time to reach a more defensible position, up against a standing section of the old aqueduct.

Larkin demanded, "What *about* Verit?"

"They attack foreigners. Our language gives us away."

Dark eyes glittered with annoyance. "So where are the other two?

"Torio may be under attack."

Char streaked onto the scene, bowling over one of the griffins. They tumbled together, but the brownstone statue fought its way free and galloped away, the lioness close on its heels. The other griffin veered off in another direction, probably to avoid Dessa, who strode into view. It bothered Farley that they were headed downhill.

"Safe." Dessa stopped before him, her glossy surface rain-wet. A cold hand briefly grazed his face, and she calmed visibly. *"Farley is safe."*

"Doing my best!" He managed a smile, then looked to Larkin. "Well, leader?"

The Pred scowled. "It's much easier to destroy the ones that are warped and reckless."

Farley nodded. "They're working together."

"So are we," Larkin snapped. "It's only stone, Farley. We are superior."

Rolling his eyes toward Dessa, he said, "Should I be pleased to finally out-rank something, or should I take you to task for insulting a lady?"

Larkin sucked in a breath, exhaled on a growl, and muttered, "Present company excluded."

"Yeah, yeah. I usually am. But that's a whole different problem. This one's got a new twist. I don't think these statues are Misbegotten."

"Nay. They're faithfully serving their intended purpose."

"Kind of a shame to break them. They're all ... historic."

"They're also murderers."

"Aaand they're back." Farley nodded toward a different approach, where two stone griffins trotted out of the underbrush. "Hold up. Where did Char go?"

"To Torio." Dessa's forearms slowly shifted into sharp-edged scythes.

Larkin grunted, probably in surprise, but he looked impressed. Leave it to a Pred to appreciate a well-armed woman. Larkin said, "Fend them off while Meadowsweet and I return to the carriage and defend its retreat."

Dessa's answering smile was surprisingly sweet, considering the fierceness of her answer. *"I am here. I am enough."*

Torio circled away from the carriage, moving uphill in the direction the others had gone, talking all the while. "Your form is a favorite of mine, for my people are your namesakes. Your maker must have been truly stalwart to have wrought such delicate magic. Your bonds are strong, and although you are four, your purpose is one."

He beckoned for Jubilee to close the carriage shutters and be still.

With a showman's flourish, he kept up his nonsensical patter. "It's not many years past that I met another brownstone griffin. That guardian was the workmanship of a notable acquaintance of mine. Indeed, I'm proud to say he counts me as a friend."

Torio always had a gift for the continual patter required to drum up an audience for a show. Grand words to pull in a crowd and stir their interest. Ah, Quilleria would have been proud.

Leaning heavily into the rolling patterns particular to entertainers, he kept up his one-sided conversation. "That fine man's statues are only fierce when the need arises. You are much the same, are you not? I can see that you believe a threat is present and that your fierceness is needed. Dear friends, it has been centuries since the Pred bothered to trek this far inland."

Both griffins slowed, and their attention flicked past him, perhaps already dismissing him.

And to Torio's great dismay, one of them turned back, skulking toward the carriage.

"No, no! Keep with me. You've given that man enough grief. Follow me toward the young captain and my audacious comrade, and along the way, you can show me the land you live to defend."

Their ties to it were deep, which meant their options were few for resolving this mess.

Moving the statues to a different location, even to one of the Twelve, would devastate them. Yet times had changed. Travelers and traders were everywhere, especially upon the magical mountains. These four would have to be bundled up and locked away in some Keeper's storerooms, much as the truly Misbegotten.

"You'll have to trust this pass to the future and retire.

Not that you'll thank those who must secure your new berth. Itzel's latest Keeper is Keet, and Hesper's is Selk. You'd consider either of them prey."

Despite his momentous news, the guardian statue didn't look back.

Torio raised his voice, switching to Liric. "How many languages have you learned to mistrust? Are my Verit-speaking friends the only quarry you seek? Or do the Fwan to the north have reason to tremble?"

The griffin paused, and its head turned.

"How is your Skrit?" Torio inquired, switching to another of the trade languages.

Hackles rose, and the statues' heads swung to consider him again.

Dessa's voice was suddenly clamoring for his attention. *"Do you need me? Nyx is unhappy. What is happening?"*

"All is as well as can be expected," he replied evenly, leaping onto the first set of terraces and striding to climb onto the next. "How is Farley faring?"

"They have found Torio. They have found Farley."

Her distress over having her attention summarily divided cut him. "Go to the boy."

"I want you."

He couldn't think how to answer that. And then he didn't have to.

She switched tones, snippily asking, *"Do you have a message for Farley?"*

So he passed along his warning, and her priorities shifted. As did his.

One of the griffins lunged forward, and Nyx sprang to his defense. With a muffled thud, they collided in midair and slammed to muddy ground, scrabbling against each other. Torio took advantage, scrambling up another tier, only to turn back with barely enough time to raise his blade.

The second guardian's beak closed over it, and it clacked

over the obstruction, clawed feet drawing back to swing at his belly. Torio swiftly planted a boot against the statue's chest and shoved it to the terrace below. No small feat, considering its weight. And not much help, as it quickly found its feet and coiled to leap.

Torio readied his blade, eyeing the statue for weak points. The thing was beautifully rendered from fine stone, but it had been left to the elements for centuries. Weathering had weakened some of the joins. If he angled his blade just so, he might rob it of a wing. The break probably wouldn't end the life it had been magically granted. Not when its existence was linked to three others. But ... well. One thing at a time.

He firmed his stance.

His opponent hesitated.

Torio glanced over his shoulder, hissed in relief, and ducked, even though Char's leap would probably have cleared him. She crashed into his attacker with enough force, a wing was wrenched awkwardly to one side. The lioness seized it in her jaws and twisted, dragging the struggling griffin backward. Then with a wrench, she snapped stone, and the guardian contorted, its body forced into its resting form before it teetered to the ground. Magic retreated, slipping away toward the other three members of the set, leaving dull stone in its wake.

Even though he was enormously grateful, Torio shook his head to see it. "A shame."

Char used her back paw to flick mud at her toppled foe and joined Nyx in harassing the other griffin. So Torio cut across the terrace and topped the next, aiming for the spot where he knew Dessa—and therefore Farley—would be. Only when he reached the woods' edge did he glance back to see if the lionesses were done toying with their prey.

He really should have checked sooner.

All three of them crashed into him.

Farley wasn't prepared for Dessa's scream.

He dropped to the ground, covering his head, heedless of consequences. Everything was anger. Everything was fear.

Larkin flipped him onto his back in the mud and snarled something Farley couldn't hear.

When the Pred hauled back as if to slap him, Farley managed enough air to grate out, "Torio. Something happened to Torio."

Real concern flashed in golden eyes, which probably should have been heartening, but then Larkin hauled him up and tossed him over his shoulder. With every step, Farley gasped for air. He'd been in this position before, and it wasn't bringing back fond memories. But when he tried to push away, Larkin slapped the back of his thighs, snarling, "You're dead weight. Act like it."

Farley went limp. Though after a few more punishing leaps, he did brace an arm against the Pred's back to keep his belly safe from any further bruising. Dessa's wail had cut off, so Farley was gathering his scattered wits. He could now tell that Larkin was skidding downhill at dangerous speeds, that he was following after Dessa, and that the two stone griffins were close on their heels.

Slapping the Pred's shoulder, he warned, "They're catching up!"

Larkin hooked an arm around a sapling, using it to swing them to a stop, and he shoved Farley off.

From his ungainly heap in the underbrush, he watched Larkin ready the ax Farley hadn't realized he'd dropped. He peevishly pointed out, "That's mine, you know."

"I prefer Torio's blade," Larkin retorted haughtily. "This thing is too small for me."

With a double-handed swing, he clipped the tips of feathers from a griffin wing. The bits of stone dropped to the ground, but it wasn't a bad enough break to affect the guardian. Still, both statues backed off, their claws flexing in the soft earth as they circled in opposite directions, preparing to pounce.

Farley staggered to his feet, drawing the blade at his hip. It wouldn't do much against statues on this scale, but he had to back up Larkin somehow. "Retreat is the plan, yeah? Outpace these guys and come back on another day to get them under wraps."

Larkin snorted. "They hurt your mountain's Keeper."

"I'm ... not sure. But yeah, I think so."

"Do you really think she'll forgive it?"

"Dessa," Farley called. "They're guardians. They're only trying to protect their home."

"So am I."

Somewhere behind them, stone cracked with ominous finality. And then the two lionesses bounded to their defense, tangling with the remaining griffins, keeping them from escape. Dessa strode to one and beheaded it. Only ... she didn't stop there. Her blows didn't cease until the forest floor was littered with brown rubble.

"Torio," Farley muttered. "I gotta get to Torio."

Larkin must have agreed. At least this time he didn't toss Farley over his shoulder. An arm around Farley's back steadied him to the mess at the base of the slope. Stone chunks were barely recognizable as statuary, and the earth was scraped bare in spots. Torio slumped at the base of a tree, pale and wheezing for air.

"Hey," Farley managed, dropping to his knees beside him. "Hey, Torio. Torio?"

The man blinked and stirred, immediately wincing.

"Better hold still." Farley wracked his brain for what to do. Carden had given him a lesson or two on basic home remedies, and he'd sorta paid attention. But mostly only to the part about teas to get rid of the ache back when his horns were making their first turn.

Larkin grimly said, "Stay put. I'll bring help."

He was barely gone when Torio levered onto an elbow. "Help me up."

"You're hurt."

"I need to calm her."

Farley nodded shakily. "Yeah, you do. But I don't think you're gonna make it up this slope."

Torio sucked in a hitching breath, then fought for a bigger one. "Dessa! Come here, woman! You're worrying Farley!"

Silent rage ended in a rush that rattled Farley's heart.

A moment later, Dessa dropped to her knees beside them. *"You're alive? You're alive!"*

"Yes, yes. I live." Torio reached for her hand and closed his eyes. "A little worse for wear, perhaps, but I'll mend. What about you and the lionesses? You promised Freydolf that you wouldn't take risks, yet you're brawling with brownstone. No cracks, I trust?"

Farley watched numbly as Torio stole Dessa's fury and her fears.

If only his were as easy to dismiss. Hanging his head, he admitted, "That was scary."

Dessa's face turned his way. *"I scared you?"*

She truly had. The echo of her scream still had him queasy, but she might not even have realized what she'd done. It had been so ... primal. He scraped up a smile. "Nope. Torio getting hurt scared me."

Her head tipped to one side. *"Torio is hurt?"*

"Yes. Torio is being brave for us, but he's in pain."

Her gaze swung back to her Keeper, and she asked, *"Are*

you *cracked?*"

"You know, I believe I am," Torio said lightly. He turned his head, gazing past them. "Help is on the way, though."

Farley pivoted.

Larkin strode beside Artor, Jubilee jogging to keep up. Farley must have looked confused because the Pred flatly explained, "Most Pika are better versed in medicine than healers in other parts of the world."

"But you're a bard."

Jubilee shot him an impatient look, which kind of threw Farley off. So he stowed his questions and watched as the man fussed over Torio, asking questions in a low, soothing voice.

Suddenly, Artor was kneeling at Farley's side. "Let's have a look," he ordered.

"I'm fine. Torio's the one who …."

But the Ursa briskly cut across his protest. "You did your part, Farley. Let me do mine."

"You're a healer?"

Artor said, "The Pika who took me in were apothecaries. I learned alongside all the tufts in our covey."

"That's really useful." Farley winced when Artor found a particularly tender bruise. "Flox don't really have healers. Mostly home remedies."

Just then, Larkin bent over Torio and growled, "Does Dessa understand what I'm about to do?"

"No, not really."

"I would prefer not to lose my life."

Torio squeezed Dessa's hand and said, "Even if it seems like he's hurting me, it's to help me heal. Stay calm."

Larkin waited a beat, then asked, "Ready?"

Farley certainly wasn't. Not for Torio's strangled cry or for him to fall back, pale and unmoving.

Artor was the one who lunged forward, his hand closing around Dessa's wrist before she could retaliate. "Don't, lady. He's fine. He'll be fine."

Rousing enough to intercede, Farley crawled between her and Larkin, though his gaze never left Torio's waxen face. "He'll be fine," he echoed, needing to believe it.

"Dislocated shoulder." Jubilee's voice was low and urgent. "Bring the carriage nearer, please. It's better if we move him while he's unconscious."

Larkin stood and hauled Farley to his feet, spinning him so his back was to Torio. "Did Father neglect healing lore?" he asked haughtily. "A hunter must be able to render aid to their partner."

"Nobody's ever been seriously hurt."

"We'll see you better equipped. For today, trust us."

The shove toward the carriage was only the sort to get him moving. That's right. They needed the carriage. He forced his legs to move.

Artor caught up and placed a steadying hand under his arm.

As shaky as his legs were, he needed it.

"Can you teach me?" His mind was racing. "Frey made sure I knew how to mend stone, to bind and support a bad crack in case something were to happen to Dessa or the lionesses. But … Torio?"

"Certainly. We could trade lessons, if you like."

That surprised Farley. "Yeah, sure. Take your pick. Herding cows? Making butter? Bartering with eggs?"

Artor proposed, "I was thinking more along the lines of handling weapons and tracking rogue statues. Vastly better than hiding in carriages."

"You'd be willing to help? It's dangerous."

"I'd hardly sit back." Resolve lent his gaze a touch of steel. "Let me be more useful."

9

Gaining Entrance

Farley was right beside Torio when the man's eyes opened. He leaned forward, grip tightening on taloned fingers.

With a faint sigh, Torio creakily asked, "Do I look *that* bad?"

"We should probably go back to Morven soon, pick up those other two lionesses Frey wrote about."

"I thought you didn't want to curtail our tour of First Continent."

"Changed my mind. And besides, there's Artor to consider. We promised to bring him to Frey."

"I don't need further convincing. We can visit the interior another time. Limit ourselves to Nerida and Shiri."

"Shouldn't we skip the whole thing? Sail home now?"

"The captain had business in the Basq capital, and the Songstone Mountain is in a homeward direction, more or less." His grip on Farley's hand was reassuringly steady. "We can certainly adjust our plans, but there's no need to scuttle all of them."

"Maybe we should hold off with the hunts ...?"

"I'll heal while we travel. By the time we find another job, I could be back in fighting form." His smile tilted wryly.

"All of this consideration isn't like you."

Farley knew it. But Dessa's scream still rang in his ears, as did the thing she'd said ... about protecting her home. Back in Hayward, home had been a good place. Farley had known everyone, and he'd known everything anyone needed to know to make the most of every day. Even on Morven, where the community was smaller, Farley had gotten used to a sense of timelessness and stability. But here, far from everything familiar, there was only Torio.

"I thought you were better in a fight."

"This." He waved limply at his torso. "Was more fiasco than fight. How can any man defend himself against a fluke?"

"Dessa wanted to be here."

"Where is here?"

"That Fwan holding Jubilee was talking about before. It took a while, but he talked our way in. Well, most of us." After some debate, they'd left her and the lionesses in Larkin's care outside the gates. Or perhaps it was the other way around. She'd only agreed—under protest—because it was the only way to make certain that Torio could get the care he needed.

"I've disappointed you."

Farley frowned at the floor. "If something were to happen to you, everything would be ruined."

"Yes and no." Torio's gaze held no criticism. "It *is* true that everything would change. But it takes more than the death of someone dear to ruin a man."

He glanced up, feeling awkward. "Dessa destroyed those griffins. They weren't Misbegotten, but that didn't matter. Not to her. Because she was protecting her home."

"Ah." Torio's gaze swung to the ceiling. "Then I think we're as safe as two men can be, despite the risks that come with travel."

"Guess so."

"A Fwan holding, you say? Have you been able to explore?"

"Jubilee warned me not to wander around by myself."

"He's right. Very unlucky. But you should get him to take you around. This is as far as we'll go on this continent ... at least for this visit." He withdrew his hand from Farley's hold. "This is a rare opportunity, not to be missed. Don't you live for such things?"

"You ... wouldn't mind?"

"Weren't you going to see if they had a block of jade to tempt Frey?"

"Yeah. You're right." Farley wasn't an idiot. He could tell Torio was stealing his fears and shifting his focus. But he shot to his feet and said, "Guess I'll do that. You need anything?"

"If you can convince Dessa to hold her tongue for more than a few moments, I might be able to get some rest."

Farley huffed a short laugh, then raised his voice. "He's looking better already, Dessa. But he'll get stronger faster if we let him sleep."

Torio drew as deep a breath as his ribs allowed and released it on a sigh, then mouthed, "Thank you."

Touching his hands to his lips, Farley spread his arms wide in Floxish custom, returning gratitude for gratitude.

Jubilee took one look at Farley and seized him by the arm, steering him toward a set of double doors at the end of a wide hall with low ceilings. The room turned out to be a necessary, and everything was arranged in pairs. Two basins. Two tubs. Two cisterns, one of which was faintly steaming.

"Though their homes a generally rustic and earthy, being snug underground, the Fwan are a fastidious people. You are looking entirely too downtrodden for me to show you off about the holding. Buckets are there. Fill a tub."

Farley asked, "Which one."

"Strictly speaking, we should fill them both, but I won't mention the breech in etiquette if you don't." Jubilee rummaged in a cupboard, then shook out a simple white tunic with lacings at the collar, then a pair of loose brown pants with a double row of buttons down their front. "Fwan are born in pairs, and they believe in pairs. They spend their entire lives with a counterpart within reach."

"My brother has twins. A boy and a girl. They're mostly inseparable."

"We're in a place where that is both expected and enforced." Jubilee located a second set of clothing. "For the duration of our stay, we'll be a pair. When I take you around, stay close. Fwan are suspicious—even frightened— of singles and odd numbers."

"I don't mind." Farley eased out of his mud-smeared tunic. He hated to set it anywhere, since the room was really clean.

Jubilee took it off his hands. "I'll wash your things while you wash yourself. Provided you'll allow me to stay. Strictly speaking, I need to."

"Yeah, of course. I'd be grateful."

Jubilee accepted that with a no-nonsense nod. And he kept his back turned while Farley lowered himself into the bath.

"Did the healers say anything extra about Torio?"

"He cracked a rib or two, and his bruises will turn spectacular colors. But nothing dire." Jubilee tipped a bucket of water into the deep sink holding Farley's clothes. "Given time to mend, he'll make a full recovery."

"We're headed to First Continent next, and it's supposed

to be warmer there."

"It is." Jubilee's ears angled toward the sound of his voice, though his back remained turned. "A lazy sail under sunny skies would do him good."

"I wish you were coming with us." It just sort of slipped out, but why not?

Jubilee didn't acknowledge the remark.

Maybe he needed time to think about it?

Farley sniffed at strange bottles and found something that was probably for washing hair. Only after he'd dunked a couple of times in an effort to get the lather out did he ask Jubilee for a bucket of fresh water for a final rinse.

"Allow me?"

Farley bowed his head and let the Pika douse him. "Something wrong?" he asked softly. "You're not usually this quiet."

Jubilee's ears lifted, and he gave an odd little headshake before launching into a rambling explanation of Fwan beliefs that filled the space between them with interesting tidbits and useful insights.

All the while, Farley couldn't get rid of the idea that the other man was hiding behind his own words.

Farley tried not to stare at the two Fwan tasked with showing them around. He'd seen his share of Fwan statues, even some sketches of Frey's, but firsthand was fascinating.

In a very general sense, Fwan seemed to have a similar build to Flox and Pika. Their skin was really tan, and they had white freckles that stood out against it like spots on a baby deer. And at the inner corner of large, thick-lashed eyes, a black stripe ran straight down on either side of their noses. Farley was especially intrigued by Fwan antlers, which grew straight up instead of curling like Flox horns. On older Fwan—like their guides—the antlers developed a prong. They were pale ivory and velvety, and he was curious if they felt as fuzzy as they looked.

As best as Farley could tell, these two were performing some kind of inventory. Jubilee spoke to them in low, respectful tones.

Since they were conversing in Liric, Farley couldn't follow. He quietly asked, "Is there a problem?"

Jubilee beamed at him. "Our hosts are taking their time reassuring themselves. It helps that we are dressed alike, but they seem to wish your ears were longer or that I would sprout horns."

"Not much chance of that," he muttered in Verit.

"Wishful thinking, indeed."

Farley spread his hands and smiled at their hosts, keeping his tone light. "So it's not just numbers that matter? Matching is important, too?"

"Only for sticklers. We are a pair, and that *will* suffice."

The Pika took Farley's hand and switched back to Liric. Whatever he said did the trick. Although the Fwan eyed his unsymmetrical horns with traces of suspicion, his tone changed, and his partner held the door open for them. At least ... Farley was pretty sure they were male.

Their tour began with a stroll along raised paths of packed dirt. While there were no houses Farley could see, woven fences defined boundaries. They weren't arranged in neat squares like back home. Instead, gently curving meadows nested together, interlaced and overlapping like feathers on a bird's wing. The spaces in between were planted with different things—some with grasses, others with flowers. A few held fruit trees that had been carefully pruned so that they didn't overstep their boundaries.

Beyond this warren of meadows, more low buildings showed.

"The center of their holding," Jubilee translated.

Farley glanced back the way they'd come. "Looks like they stashed us as far away as they could."

"Best to focus on the fact that they *did* extend hospitality. They have expressed their gratitude several times for your bravery in dispatching the mountain's monster."

"You told them I did it?"

"You and Torio, yes." Jubilee smiled innocently.

The Fwan took turns talking in lyrical tones. Their mannerisms were graceful, and their expressions were pleasant. And yet ... Farley was growing increasingly distracted. Finally, he leaned into Jubilee to whisper, "Are Fwan like Pika?"

"In what sense?"

"Are there more men than women?"

Jubilee shook his head. "They are enviably balanced."

Farley peered around, then finally admitted, "I can't tell them apart. Like ... at all."

"You will be fine if you treat them with equal courtesy."

"I'd have done that anyhow. I was only wondering."

Jubilee seemed amused. "Just as well you lapsed into Verit."

"Is it rude to wonder?"

"You are fearless in your ignorance and unabashed in your interest. A charming combination. But let us err on the side of caution where Fwan feelings are concerned." The Pika suddenly laughed. "Is it their antlers, I wonder? Unlike your people, both the men and women grow them."

"Oh! Well, yeah. I guess I was thinking along those lines. But they're all sort of ... umm. Flox girls have more curves ...?"

Jubilee's eyes sparkled.

Farley was feeling defensive. "They all dress the same, too."

"Yes."

"And their hair is the same."

"Yes."

"Well, how do *you* tell them apart?"

"I do not need to. Pika do not discriminate."

Farley snorted. "Yeah, yeah. I know you'll kiss anyone. So what about our guides? Are they a couple?"

Jubilee casually looked them up and down. "Both male. Twins, of course. Siblings remain close until they form marriage bonds, usually with another pair, then they can safely form new households." Switching to Liric again, he asked something.

Their guides seemed startled, then glanced Farley's way.

Both had questions, and Jubilee slipped into confiding tones.

Twin brothers traded a look. One shrugged. The other smiled.

Jubilee said, "They were planning to lead you to the stone you covet, but ... would you like to meet their family? We would be welcome in their home."

"Really?" Farley quickly qualified, "I want a look at their stone, but yeah. If they don't mind, I'd love to see a Fwan home."

As Jubilee translated—at considerable length, so he was definitely embellishing—their expressions softened. Gesturing to a side path, they resumed at a quicker pace, heads together as they conferred.

"What did you tell them?"

"That you are missing your many nieces and nephews back home, and that they are probably missing their adventurous uncle with equal wistfulness."

Farley frowned. "How'd you know *that*?"

Jubilee gave his hand a squeeze. "You are a sentimental drunk. Very talkative."

"I don't remember."

"Hespero especially was coaxing for stories. You all but

promised to help find them brides."

Farley weakly asked, "I did?"

Jubilee hummed an affirmative. "At which point, Greysallow applied to me for lessons in Verit. And for guidance across the vast and lonely sea to the place you spoke of with so much fondness."

"They want to go to Morven?"

"With all the audacious passion of young bucks in love."

"And ... you'd bring them?"

"I can be audacious. And sentimental." Jubilee searched his face, then answered, "Perhaps."

Farley wanted to coax for a more certain promise, if not actual passage on the *Moontide*, but their guides called out. One beckoned to hurry them along. The other whistled sharply, and children erupted into view, seemingly from nowhere.

Jubilee nodded toward a long, low mound covered with wildflowers. "We are here."

"An underground home? Hey, that's great!" Startled into looking back, he asked, "Have we been passing houses all along?"

"A few, yes. But this is a diverse community. There are Pika and Grif and even a pair of Tisk. These Fwan are outliers, rather progressive on the whole." Jubilee gestured between Farley and the distant east. "Like many other similar communities, they are bound together by their craft. These good people are all stoneworkers, which practically makes them kin to the likes of you and me."

Another adult Fwan appeared, quickly followed by another. The only reason Farley could tell them apart was because one of them was pregnant.

Introductions were offered, and Jubilee explained, "These men share a household since their wives are sisters. It suited them to remain together, since it meant none of them had to be parted from their twin."

Farley answered distractedly. He was a little busy.

Counting heads, two-by-two, he confirmed that there were ten children, and every one of them wanted a closer look at his curling hair and curling horns. "Hey, why me? Why not you?"

"Little Fwan are taught to be wary of strange Pika." His smile didn't waver. "I will win them over by and by. I am always in high demand when it comes to bedtime stories."

Glancing at the sun, Farley asked, "Will we be here that long?"

"Such is Fwan hospitality."

By the time Farley was presented to the ladies of the house, he had a child on each hip ... and attitudes toward him and Jubilee had warmed considerably. "I don't get it. They seemed so suspicious earlier. Now they're all smiles."

"You were battered and bloodied and besmattered— hardly the best of first impressions. And I believe they feared you were going to demand a fine stone as a sort of bounty. But you are as mercenary as a buttercup, and ... well, look at you."

Farley had dropped to one knee in order to listen to a lisping explanation in a language he couldn't even understand. "What's she saying about her doll?"

"The doll's name is Ninny. And that child is boy."

"Gotcha. Nice to meet you, Ninny. You must be happy that your young master loves you so ... much." He squinted at the house. "Hey, now. Hey, Jubilee. There's stone here."

"They are crafters, lovely locks. To one degree or another, they share your affinity."

One of the adults clapped their hands, calling out, and the children ran toward the mound. Jubilee offered a hand up and they followed. Only after they'd partially rounded the mound did a wide front door come into view, as did a garden and a shed. Based on the contented curl of magic in the air, the latter had to be a workshop. The stones weren't large or especially potent, but they were happy. And that said a lot about these people.

The front door was wide and low, and two stones had been set into the lintel—pink and orange.

While Farley watched, the oldest of the children reached up, each placing a hand on one of the stones before bowing through. The next two had to jump to accomplish the feat, and even though they were short enough to stroll under, they also bowed before entering.

Farley glanced at Jubilee, who asked their guides.

The twin brothers moved in front of the door, and they each placed a hand over the blocks of dawnstone and titian jade. They took turns relaying their explanation, and their demonstration was a more polished rendition of their children's actions. Giving the stones a caress, they smiled at each other, then bowed through the door.

Jubilee said, "Apparently, it's a Tisk tradition, adopted by all the sculptors who live here. Most choose a stone for which they have special affinity or affection. They say the morning and evening stones lend strength to the timbers that hold up their hopes for a happy home—day in and day out."

Farley touched stone worn smooth by the peaceful press of so many hands. "It's a nice tradition."

Resting his hand against the companion stone, Jubilee said, "It is."

They ducked through together, stepping down into a large central room. Even though the home was essentially buried, there was no lack of light. Farley counted twelve skylights, which marched along the ceiling in predictable pairs.

Everything came in pairs. Two hearths. Two pumps set over two sinks. Two doors set in the far wall. And opposite them was something that had Farley's curiosity going crazy. The entire wall, from floor to ceiling, was crowded with a series of interlocked round baskets. Pointing, he asked, "What are those for?"

Jubilee repeated the question, and the children shouted answers, then stampeded the structure. Clambering up, they disappeared two-by-two through round openings, then leaned out, beaming with pride.

"Beds?" Farley ventured.

"In Fwan cities, larger versions of these are a pair's whole home. Such warrens are complex to navigate and crowded."

Farley thought they looked like oversized fish traps. Or maybe a little like the nesting baskets Tupp had added to their coop back home. It never would have occurred to him that people might put them to similar use. "Can I take a closer look? The kids back home would absolutely love it if we made these for them."

Jubilee conferred and patiently relayed, "They're not simple to make, but you and I will have one for our bed tonight, so you'll get your look."

"Oh, I can figure this out, easy. Me and my whole family, we're basket-makers."

When this was relayed, it caused a stir of excitement with the ladies of the house, who apparently wanted him to prove it. Reeds were brought, and he didn't mind showing off a little. Quick and careful, he began a basic pattern.

Jubilee relayed, "They know that one. Another, please."

"You're looking for something new? How about this?" Farley's fingers flashed through another pattern, this one a little more complicated than the last ... though not one of his mother's best.

The pregnant lady came to sit by his side, and she waved for him to stop.

"Know that one, too? Okay. I've got just the thing." And much slower, since he needed to manage more strands, he began a woven band that was the basis for the baskets Flox girls used to carry this and that. Right away, the lady leaned closer, intent. "Found a good one, yeah? Get your own reeds. I'll go slow."

Jubilee spoke to the men, who seemed surprised, then grateful.

This was one of those patterns that required his full attention, so he was tuning out Jubilee. It was easy enough, since the man was speaking in Liric again. But eventually, he noticed that there was a rhythm to the Pika's speech ... and that his voice was changing at intervals. Jubilee was telling a story. The children were quiet, and their fathers had also been drawn in.

It was so familiar.

Almost like home.

Farley hadn't wanted to be stuck there, had been eager to get away since he'd come into his nubs. Maybe even before that. But he didn't hate where he'd come from. Maybe he even missed it a little. And today, he guessed he had another reason to be glad for that little thatched hut in Hayward.

He might not understand Liric, but he understood basket-weaving. And families. And home.

And sometimes, that's all a guy needed in order to find welcome ... or to show himself grateful.

The following morning, Farley woke to a familiar gouging in the ribs. He cracked an eye and snorted softly. He and Jubilee had company. Over the course of the night, three different sets of twins had stolen into their basket bedroom. Thanks to the bowl-shaped bed, they'd slid down and burrowed close.

Easing away from one set of nubs, he found another. He adjusted again, only to find Jubilee's eyes on him. The Pika lifted his ears, sending tiny peals through the bells he wore, which inspired soft giggles in the nubless little ones he cuddled close.

"Mmm ... mornin'," Farley murmured. "This gonna get us in trouble?"

Jubilee smiled. "Only with Artor and Torio, if they are the sort to worry."

Farley blinked. "Dessa sweet? Has Torio asked after me?"

"Three times."

Grimacing, he asked, "What did you tell him?"

"That you feel happy." She ventured, *"Why are you happy?"*

"I met some good people. We're guests in their home."

"We? Who is with you?"

"I'm with Jubilee."

"Why not with Torio?"

"He's resting, remember?"

"I know." It was almost a sigh.

Farley usually thought of stone as patient. Not Dessa. "Yeah. Healing takes time. I'll check on him once I can get away."

"From Jubilee?" Dessa sounded intrigued. *"Did he kiss you?"*

Farley chuckled. "We're all on our best behavior."

After a few moments, her voice came again. *"He makes you happy?"*

"Guess so," he said vaguely. "Are you letting Torio rest?"

More sulkily, she answered, *"I'm on my best behavior."*

Farley laughed again, then stretched. Heads popped up as sleep-tousled, stripe-faced children lisped morning greetings in Liric. He echoed them, then tried again when Jubilee corrected his pronunciation. This further endeared him to them, so much so that he feared that they wouldn't let him up and out, but then parents were calling, and the little ones guiltily scurried away.

He closed his eyes until he felt fingers in his hair.

"Yeah?" Farley tipped his head to meet Jubilee's gaze.

"Perhaps." Jubilee's ears quivered. "Perhaps if I were welcome."

It only took a moment to understand. "Yeah, of course. Everyone on Morven would love the company, and there's plenty of room. You should go. Hey, maybe Larkin could even give you a letter. That kind of thing helps, especially when you have to travel through Pred territory."

"Very generous," Jubilee murmured. "But ... would *you* welcome my presence."

"Sure I would. It'd be great." He was imagining Tupp's reaction to all the kissy greetings. "Of course, I might not *be* there. We plan to explore the whole world, you know."

"But if I let you go now, that place, that mountain ... it is the surest way to find you again?"

"Yeah, it is." Farley ventured, "You gonna travel with us after you get Greysallow and Hespero settled?"

Jubilee nodded slowly. "Perhaps."

"I'm glad." And because it looked like the Pika needed it, Farley sidled closer and hauled him into a hug. "Guess I'll just have to miss you in the meantime."

Long ears trembled, and he muttered something about young bucks.

Farley held on, sniffing surreptitiously. He wasn't sure what the deal was with a Pika's scent. Maybe Flox were immune? Maybe Jubilee had been teasing again. But he seemed serious about going to Morven, and that really did make Farley happy. It was nice knowing that Jubilee hadn't wanted to part ways, either.

Breakfast was surprisingly sedate, considering how many people were at the table. The children applied themselves to roasted vegetables and a clear soup with no complaints and a minimum of slurping. Last night's dinner had been lively enough, but the mood had definitely shifted. Nobody spoke, and Farley was reluctant to break the silence to ask why.

He arched his brows at Jubilee, who'd been seated directly across from him.

The Pika winked and tapped a finger to his lips.

Farley nodded gratefully and held his peace.

Once every plate and bowl had been cleared, the adults brought out a second course ... to cheers from the youngsters. Amidst the sudden babble of voices, the Pika admitted, "I'm as mystified as yourself, lovely locks."

He conferred with their hosts, and one man gave an explanation that inspired the occasional interjection from his twin, followed by more questions from Jubilee. While Farley waited for a translation, the ladies continued down the table, setting shallow bowls at intervals. Like he and Jubilee, everyone sat across from their counterpart, and now they each had a shared dish between them.

The children babbled, pointing and reaching into their bowls.

"Seems like this is the favorite part of breakfast," Farley remarked, peering into his bowl. "I can see why. Smells good!"

Dough balls and nuts and bits of fruit appeared to have been coated in sugar and spice and baked together, then drizzled with honey. Each set of twins pulled off warm, bite-sized chunks and popped them into their mouths, all smiles.

"A family tradition," Jubilee reported. "Based on local tradition from the men's hometown. The first meal of the day serves as a reminder. They have a saying, of course. Fwan do like their sayings."

Farley reached into their bowl and tweaked a bit of the sticky bread. It was light and sweet and rich with an unfamiliar spice.

"You didn't mention that before. I want to hear some of these sayings."

Jubilee licked his fingers and cheerfully relayed, "Life is sober. Life is sweet."

For a little while, Farley focused on eating, lest the Pika get more than his fair share of the treat. A pot of strong, dark tea appeared, and it was good. "Would it be rude to ask after the spices and the tea? My sisters are bakers, and I'd like it if I could bring them something new."

Jubilee made inquiries, then reported, "I'm assured this is nothing special. And that their little mercantile stocks tins of both. I assume you'll want to visit it?"

"Yeah, I do. And I also want to know if they'd mind if I showed them my guardian." He nodded toward one of the littler children, who'd brought a cradle guardian to the table. The starstone puppy no longer stirred, but it was well-made from good stone. Farley had been catching hints of stone magic since last night, but this was his first glimpse of a statue in the household.

Jubilee asked.

By the looks of things, the child received a mild scolding.

"If it helps, go ahead and tell them that I can see magic. That's how my affinity works." Tapping his chest, he added, "Let them know I brought my cradle guardian to the table, too. Because he's the best."

This time, Jubilee seemed to be interceding on the child's behalf. Words flew, and Farley found himself the object of intense scrutiny. Then both brothers pointed unerringly. Right to the place where Nestor had been hiding under his shirt, loosely coiled around Farley's arm, right above his elbow.

Farley grinned. "They knew something was up, but they were too polite to ask?"

Jubilee arched his brows. "It would seem that we're in the home of the leaders of this artisan hold. These good men are both sculptors."

Indicating the starstone pet, Farley asked, "Who made

the pup? It's really good."

When Jubilee relayed the question, the men indicated the pregnant woman, who seemed flustered by the attention. Then direction was given, and the children were sent scurrying. They returned, each clutching at least one small statue. The older twins boasted two each—one for day and one for night.

More questions. More answers.

The Fwan were clearly impressed that Farley called Morven home, and they wanted to know about the Statuary, about Freydolf, and ... about the availability of moonstone for trade. Farley's hopes for a haggle rose considerably.

Soon the daytime members of the menagerie ranged freely along the table, and Farley coaxed Nestor into the open. The black snake coiled around Farley's teacup, then unscrolled to bump noses with a freshstone lamb.

Exclamations led to translations. Farley asked that Torio be allowed to make explanations.

Breakfast was finished in haste, and Jubilee relayed their gratitude for the hospitality.

Before leaving, honorary Uncle Far explained the Flox tradition of tapping horns, then delivered gentle ones to each of the children in turn. One for each antler, of course. Because even numbers were important.

Then with Nestor safely coiled around his snub horn, Farley followed the twin sculptors back along the paths toward the fringes of their holding, where they'd unknowingly left a man of considerable importance with the barest scraps of hospitality. Or so Farley had assumed.

To his relief, it looked as if Artor had been seeing to Torio's comfort. Trays of food and a pot of tea crowded the scanty surfaces.

Even so, Farley asked, "Need anything?"

"We're comfortable enough," Artor assured. "You?"

"These guys have big families, just like Flox. Been goofing off with theirs since yesterday, but I think we might be back to business. Do you speak Liric?"

"Only the basic courtesies, but Torio is fluent."

Clearly, since the Grif was now holding audience with as much dignity as his injuries would allow.

"I wish Larkin was here," Farley sighed.

Jubilee cozied up to Artor and delivered a kiss, then revealed, "You shall have that wish and more. Once reinforcements arrive, we're bound for the gates."

"Reinforcements?" Farley whispered. "Are they worried our Pred will attack?"

"I exaggerate," Jubilee soothed. "They're assembling a welcoming committee. Ah, see? Here they come."

Footsteps sounded in the hallway, and with a quick rap, a breathless group of men and women filed in. They looked rumpled and flustered, as if some had been dragged from bed and the rest pulled from their work. One guy was still clutching a riffler, and Farley identified three kinds of rock dust on their work aprons.

Two Grif were part of the group, and conversation immediately jumped to Terse, so Farley could follow. A pair of Pika leaned into each other, a gray and a dark brown. Most intriguing were the two who must have been Tisk. Their eyes were angled, their ears were pointed, and their hair was green. *Green.*

The man and woman were eyeing him with similar interest, so Farley offered his hand.

Unfortunately, they addressed him in Liric. Farley looked to Jubilee for help, and he stepped smoothly into his continuing role as translator. But he seemed to hesitate over something the Tisk were saying. He quizzed them closely, then looked to Farley. "They're curious how a cloudstrider found his way to Far Continent."

"A ... what? I don't understand." He waved to the pair

and said, "I'm Farley, and I'm Flox. I don't know about any ... what'd they say? Cloudstriders?"

Jubilee bobbled his hands, his expression bewildered. "A creature from Tisk lore ...? I don't know many tales from First Continent, so I couldn't say for certain, but to them, you're a legend come to life."

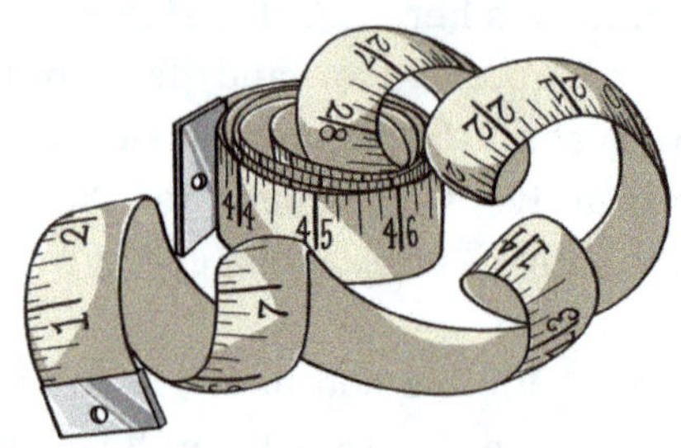

Farley wasn't feeling very legendary as he squirmed through a narrow gap between two blocks of redstone in order to get at the dawnstone column that was exuding hopefulness from the row behind. "This one's the best yet," he called over his shoulder. "Master quality. Frey would be in love."

A measuring tape hit him on the back of the head and dropped to the floor.

"You'll have to measure for me. I can't get through."

"Yeah, yeah. I can manage that much."

"Be exact," warned Larkin.

"Fifty-seven. And a smidge."

"Smidge," scoffed the Pred, who'd been welcomed through the gates with tentative courtesies. "Well? Is that length, width, or height?"

"Umm ... that's how big around it is. It's a column. Aaand it's taller than your tape measure."

With a hissed expletive, Larkin slapped his ledger onto the top of one of the large redstone blocks Farley had already assessed, then climbed atop its neighbor. From this vantage, Larkin glared between him and the offending block. "Ah. I see," he said snippily, crouching to make a notation.

"How many more blocks *are* there?" Farley asked. He might have been whining. A little.

Larkin sighed.

Ever since Torio confirmed the nature of their stone affinity and explained the grading system that Freydolf and Aurelius had worked out, Farley had been stuck doing inventory. And while an artisan holding didn't hold a candle to the vastness of the Statuary, this storage shed was cram-packed. Farley wasn't exactly chained to a workbench or chipping daisies into cobbles, but he was tired of the monotony and minutia.

These were the same sorts of blocks that Aurelius was always bringing home for Frey. Of course, the Keeper's personal agent didn't scrounge through sheds like this. He went straight to other Keepers to get the highest quality rocks. These blocks were mostly middling. Nice enough. They'd stir if master-marked. Some were even better, perhaps because of the good relationship these holders had with the Keepers on this continent.

Aurelius planned to publish the new grading system, try to normalize it. Ambitious, but it seemed like the man was willing to tackle monumental tasks if it could benefit his brother-in-law ... and his sons.

"Do you want that one?" Larkin asked.

Farley hadn't realized he'd been petting the pink column. Dawnstone liked touch, and this one had been rather lonesome, hemmed in as it was. "I wasn't kidding. Frey would love it. And this block would probably make a good daytime guardian. Maybe another nanny, since the family's probably grown again."

"If you say so."

"Try. It's worth offering for and carrying back."

Larkin grunted and made another mark. "Next?"

Farley sighed and rapped yet another block of redstone.

"It's good. These are all good. With the right sculptor, they could even be great."

"Which means?"

"Middle of the second tier."

"Measurements?"

Farley obliged, but he asked, "Wanna get outside after this, do some hunting. Or maybe fish? I saw a lake."

"Three more rows. Six to a row." The Pred squinted thoughtfully and added, "There's titian jade in the far corner."

"I know. It's the only thing keeping me going." Farley cautiously asked, "If it's good enough, will you help me haggle for it?"

"Aye, but I *won't* shift the nine rows of stone between it and the door."

"The shed walls are plank. I say we make a back door."

Interest sparked in Larkin's eyes, but he answered casually. "Aye. It could be done."

Farley returned to his task. It was a pain to have to do the measuring part, too, but it'd be worth it if Larkin would manage the exchange. Part of it was his fluency in whatever language was needed. Part of it was the intimidation factor. And Farley had another motive, as well, because he wasn't done bartering for Larkin's better opinion.

Finally, they reached the back. "That the one?"

"Hoping so." Farley had been saving best for last. Feeling a little silly, but completely justified, he rested his fingertips against glossy orange. "Hello. Have you been waiting long? I know what that's like."

The magic was sleepy, but it stirred. A little slow. But steady and stubborn. And Farley smiled.

"Quality?" asked Larkin.

"Ohhh, it's not as lofty as the dawnstone, but it's real good. I'll surrender whatever coin it takes." He sought Larkin's gaze and added, "I want it for Tupp."

"And the dawnstone?" he checked.

"That's for Frey. He'll know what it needs."

"Aye. Measure your rock." Larkin dropped to the floor, unsheathed a blade, and carefully worked it between boards.

Farley did his part, calling out dimensions like he'd been doing all afternoon, though Larkin didn't stop his investigation of the wall to write them down. His blade rasped, and he crouched and tested more boards. The shed must have been really old, for sunlight lit the seams.

"This faces west," he realized.

"Aye."

"And the sun's near to setting."

"Aye."

"Hey." Farley dared to suggest, "Can you hurry?"

Larkin shot him a look, then glanced at the titian jade. With a thoughtful frown, the man stood, raised a boot, and casually drove it through the wall. He must have weakened the joins. Or maybe the weathered wood was just that brittle, because three wide boards snapped off, falling to the grass beyond. Sunlight angled through, ruddy and right, and the titian jade's magic swelled.

Perfect.

"You look pleased."

Farley's smile widened. "Pleased as a Pred who's about to carry off some wealthy so-and-so's front step. Only … I'll pay for it properly. But I feel triumphant. It's like finding treasure."

Larkin snorted. "Magical stone *is* treasure."

"Ever want one? A guardian statue?"

He hesitated but shook his head. "What for? An anchor?"

Farley shot him an incredulous look. "I can't believe you said that while surrounded by a whole community of sculptors."

Larkin wrenched free another board, widening the shed's new back door. "I don't see any outraged sculptors. There's only you and me for the moment."

"While it's the two of us," Farley ventured. "Have you ever heard of a cloudstrider?"

"Naturally."

"So they're real?"

"Nay. They're fiction."

"Those Tisk. They called me one. Said something about my being a legend." He shook his head. "I don't think Jubilee was teasing about it."

Larkin knelt to apply his blade to a crosspiece, then squinted up at him. "I heard stories of them whenever we visited the Songstone Mountain. As the name suggests, they're creatures who've tamed the very clouds and live among them. But I don't see how you could be one. If I'm recalling the lore correctly, they're not ordinary men. In drawings, they have four arms."

"Oh, hey! There's a statue of one on Morven. Four arms. Riding on a cloud. Songstone."

"Odds are the sculptor was Keet."

Just then, a shout rose, and a pair of Fwan were hurrying their way.

"Better start apologizing," muttered Farley.

"Why?" Larkin stood to his full height. "They're only asking if we're injured."

"They're not angry about their wall?"

The Pred offered a casual greeting, speaking smoothly in Liric. Then he smirked down at Farley. "Only that we're late for dinner."

Farley didn't trust that smirk. He'd seen it too many times. And ... he'd missed it. So all he said was, "You are *such* a Harrow."

Larkin doubled down by looking smug.

10

Deepening Waters

Even though Farley offered to drop off Jubilee in the little city where Greysallow and Hespero lived, the bard insisted on keeping his promise. He'd stay by Farley's side for the duration of his stay on Far Continent.

The drive back to the coast was crowded, for two large blocks of magical stone weighed down Farley's carriage, as did two cases of petalberry cordial. And another of Fwan spice tins. With scant room inside the carriage, Larkin sat on the roof—head high, gaze fixed, nose lifted to catch the first scent of the sea.

Stowing everything aboard the *Moontide* took some doing. The crew helped bring everything aboard, but Artor was the one Farley entrusted with lashing down his purchases in their room, while he saw to the securing of his carriage and the settling of the horses.

"How do Pika say goodbye?" he wondered aloud.

Jubilee didn't pause in his strumming. "That all depends on the circumstances."

"How do you say goodbye when you don't want to?"

"Mmm ... probably at some length, and usually until dawn."

"That's when we're supposed to sail."

"So all I have is tonight?"

"Yeah. I guess. I mean … it's not a fancy alcove or anything, but I could ask if you can stay the night. Larkin probably wouldn't care if you wanted a look at the morning sky from here."

"Do you plan to tie me down in your cabin like so much magical stone and carry me off as a souvenir of your travels?"

Farley wondered at his tone. "Do you want me to?"

"What I want …." The bard pressed his palm to his strings, silencing them. "What I want is to spend the night with you on my arm. Come, see the town with me. I will return you before the sky blushes over our behavior."

"What's there to see at night?"

"I will show you." Jubilee's ears strained forward, as if eager for Farley's answer. "Refuse me, and you will always wonder what you missed. And there is much you would. A night market. Music in the streets. Assorted food carts. Comfortable seats in cozy shops that offer sips and tastes of food found nowhere else in the world."

"Well, when you put it like that … sure. Show me around some."

Jubilee inclined his head and promised, "You will not regret it."

Goodbyes weren't Farley's favorite thing. He mostly ran off, hoping to avoid all the tears and hugs and last-minute advice. When it was time to go, he just wanted to be gone. If Tupp hadn't sent Graven after him the day they left

Morven for good, Farley wouldn't have had to make so many promises he hadn't been sure he wanted to keep. To be good. To stay safe. To come back.

Jubilee's version of goodbye was so much easier to swallow.

Farley bought a cloth bag that glittered with mirrors and beads once his arms were so full it was awkward. Then he lightened his purse further trying to fill it. All sorts of people milled through the night market, and the wares seemed more exotic than the daytime stuff. Maybe it was the lanternlight. Maybe it was the company. It could also have been that flashy green drink that had fizzed enough that Farley sneezed.

They dawdled in stalls, then sat at tiny tables.

Jubilee liked to stop and listen wherever buskers played.

Farley couldn't pass up a traveling merchant who sold fire-eaters in all shapes and sizes.

At a flower cart run by an Oxus couple, Farley let them guide his choices and presented Jubilee with a lavish bouquet.

The bard murmured over the extravagance, but he didn't seem especially pleased.

Farley said, "They called them journey flowers. I thought they'd be appropriate. Like a good omen."

Jubilee guided him to another cart, ordered drinks, then claimed a table for two. The bouquet was so big, it hid much of the bard's face. "I'm not free to follow. I'm spoken for."

"Okay. I don't know what that means here. Back home, it'd mean you share a promise with a girl. One to marry."

"It's a little like that." Jubilee's smile seemed forced. "I'm fortunate to have found favor, but that favor binds me. I won't be free to choose my own path again until my rings number ten."

"Your earrings?" Farley did a quick tally. "So you're missing three? Couldn't you go get them pierced? I'll bet Larkin's equipped."

"You tempt me, lovely locks. But I'm a man of my word."

Farley hesitated over asking, but he really wanted to understand. "Does that mean you're gonna have three more kids, then ... leave them?"

Jubilee's face clouded. "It's different here. Ladies keep their daughters close and bequeath their sons to the coveys they favor. My role has never been parental. Bartering for Greysallow and Hespero will be similar, though. If their brothers permit it, I would become the head of a new covey."

"You're hiring them?"

"I'd be acquiring them." Jubilee sighed. "It's more than employment. We would become brothers ... a household. And I would look to our home and its future."

"Meaning you could colonize." Farley sipped at the drink that arrived. It was sunset colored, not too sweet, and it burned a little going down. "Didja know Morven's technically a Pred colony. Mostly Flox, but Aurelius gets to be lord governor."

"You were conquered?"

"Nah. We're protected. And we're family, thanksh to Tupp."

"The brother you're trying to outdo?"

Farley hesitated. "When'd I ever say that? I'm loads better than Tupp. He's a good guy, but ... y'know ... kinda shlow. Lucky, though. Magic loves him."

"Dessa loves you."

"That's diff'rint. Lika sisser."

Jubilee plucked the glass from his hand. "If you're drunk, you won't be able to enjoy the other places I wanted to take you."

"Mmm. Water? Where's one of them lil couches when you need one?"

"I know just the thing." Jubilee downed his own drink, then offered his shoulder. "The walk will do you good."

"You're kinda good at goodbyes," Farley declared. "Hardly hurts at all."

"What a nice thing to say." Jubilee softly promised, "You can rely upon my greater experience."

Farley stumbled up the stairs and shuffled along the deck on unsteady feet. Dawn wasn't far off, but for some reason, Jubilee hadn't wanted to stay long enough to share it with him. He'd simply supported Farley up the gangway, placing him in the hands of the *Moontide*'s night guard. Maybe it was better that the *goodbye* part of Jubilee's goodbye was so hazy. And it was definitely for the best that the Pika had curtailed the evening. Otherwise, Farley might not have noticed.

One foot in front of the other, he sauntered sloppily across the deck, colliding with the door to the captain's cabin. It wasn't locked, so he let himself in and dropped to a seat on the edge of Larkin's bed.

Claws found his throat, and the tip of a blade touched his ribs.

"Jush me, Cap'n Rakefang, sir." He shook his head, trying to clear it.

"You're a fool several times over," growled Larkin.

"Yeah, I get that a lot."

"Why are there flowers in your hair?"

"For luck. They're ... rosha- ... rucksha- ... uhh." He gave up on the word. "Journey flowers."

"Roxolani," Larkin supplied.

"Thassit. What you said. For luck."

"You're drunk."

"I think so, too." Farley held up four fingers. "The lass three drinks were extra nice."

Larkin sat up and began checking him over. "Did that Pika toy with you?" he growled.

"Nope. He manfully reesh– reeshtrained himself." Farley reeled his hands vaguely. "I think maybe he likes Floss ... Flosh? My kinda folks. So's nothin' persh'null. N'less it is. But thass not the point."

Angling Farley's face toward the windows, Larkin sniffed and scowled. "You're not making any sense."

"Wordsh are hard right now." So Farley thrust up one fist in a Pred hand sign.

Larkin snorted. "You want to hunt?"

"Yep." Easing from the bed, Farley tried to crouch, but he landed on his backside. Still, he planted his fist on the floor. "We gotta hunt."

"Are you serious?"

"Coursh I am. Magic matters."

Heaving a sigh, Larkin struck a match and lit a lamp. To Farley's relief, he lowered himself to one knee and pressed his own fist to the floor. Pred were serious, too. For them, what mattered was the hunt.

Farley squinted against the light, then blinked up at Larkin. "You look so much like Frey."

"So I've been told. Repeatedly." He reached, then pressed a cup of water in Farley's hand. "Hardly surprising. We both resemble my grandsire."

Wrinkling his nose, Farley said, "Yer nothin' like him. Truss me."

"Thank you." He made Farley take a drink.

"Frey's nice. A good brother. He's big."

"Aye, compared to a bleater like you."

"He scratches my head sometimes. Tupp, too." Farley feared Jubilee was right. He was a sentimental drunk. "I mean ... Tupp doesn't scratch me. Frey scratches Tupp."

Larkin eyed him warily.

Farley hiccuped delicately.

"I'm nothing like Uncle Frey."

"Nobody is." He took another gulp of water and scratched at the base of his own horn. "Are you ever gonna admit we're practically brothers?"

"Nay."

"Liar."

Larkin dropped a heavy hand on top of Farley's head. It wasn't truly affectionate, but neither was there any meanness to the move. It was almost like the Pred was curious about Floxish curls. Farley closed his eyes and tucked his chin and waited.

"You're such a child," Larkin muttered.

Farley smiled and said, "Shut up."

There came a tentative scratch at the base of his snub horn. "Is there any reason I shouldn't be tossing you out of my cabin?"

"Oh! S'right!" The haze cleared a little, and he lunged forward, taking hold of Larkin's nightshirt with both hands. "It's Pollim! He's half-frantic, tryin' t' get my attenshun."

Larkin frowned. "Who?"

"The starstone Keet yer dad made ya bring 'board for me. His partner's closh ... *close*. So you an' me ... we're gonna hunt her down!"

While the crew readied to sail, Farley worked his way back down to his cabin and found the lionesses pacing outside.

Artor opened to his knock, saying, "Torio also noticed, and we pulled Pollim to the window. There was barely enough starlight, but he's stirring. Help us calm him down!"

"We understand, friend. Truly. Here's Farley now. He's been interceding on your behalf." Torio had Pollim by the shoulders, and his voice was pitched to soothe. "Farley, *tell* him. Otherwise, I fear he'll throw himself overboard and be lost."

Getting between his mentor and the distraught statue, Farley slapped his hands to Pollim's cheeks. The Keet's gaze sought his, wide and worried.

"Larkin'll hunt, and he's Pred. That means shuccessh." He wished he wasn't slurring so much. "It means good thingsh."

Pollim's countenance crumpled like he'd be crying if he could.

"Hey, now. Shoosh. Keep it together. Your partner'sh not cracked or broken. I can feel it. You're still bound together. N'it's good, strong magic. Betcha Eullia feels it, too. Knows yer closh ... slose ... *close*." And even though Farley knew the answer, could *see* the way a strained thread of magic had thickened to rope, he asked, "Which way should we go?"

The handless arm swung unerringly, pointing the way. Past the harbor. Out to sea.

"Thought sho. Good thing we have a ship, huh?" He patted and promised, "We'll sail at sunrise. Me'n Torio'll guide Larkin, and we'll find the placsh. While you're resting, we'll be hunting."

Torio wrapped an arm around the Keet's shoulders and said, "We won't leave without her. I swear it."

"We'll wake you again as soon's there's stars," Farley promised.

Pollim trembled, touched Farley's cheek, lapsed into his resting posture, and stilled.

"Dawn," said Artor.

Farley hung his head. "Okay. I better go make sure Larkin knowsh which way ta go."

Torio grabbed the back of his shirt. "*I'll* provide the bearing."

"*You* should be n'bed." Farley gently poked the man in the wrapped ribs. "Reshting."

"Fine advice from the man who was out all night." He addressed Artor. "Lace him into his hammock if necessary."

"But ... I wanna be the one ...!"

"I won't rob you of your prize or the pleasure of securing it." Torio gently straightened Farley's floral crown. "You're barely standing. Get some sleep."

"Guessho. Guessh I better." Farley practically fell onto his hammock, which creaked and swayed. His eyes closed while Artor stole his boots and covered him with a blanket.

A cool hand touched the side of Farley's face, then swept the hair from his brow. *"Wake up, Farley. Torio says you need to drink something."*

He rolled onto his back and swiped drool from his chin. "That so?"

"Do you hurt?"

"Been worse." Summoning up a grateful smile for Artor, who stood a little back, a steaming cup in his hand, he admitted, "I'm thirsty."

Artor unobtrusively helped him sit up. "What drinks did you sample?"

"Ohhh, all kinds of things in tiny little glasses." He took a sip, then a longer swallow of the tea. Clearing his throat, he admitted, "I don't remember the names, but they were good. Different. Interesting. So was the food."

"Sounds like Jubilee kept it light. Though according to Larkin, you were tipsy enough to forget caution."

"I don't drink much. Never got a taste for wine, so it's just the odd mug of ale."

Artor gestured for him to take more tea. Farley downed the last of it, and the Ursa next passed him a canteen.

"Farley?"

"Yeah?" He quirked a smile and asked, "Did I worry you? Sorry."

"You were happy." Her brow puckered slightly. *"You were happy to leave him?"*

"Nope. But I was happy for the time we spent together." This was probably going to be important later. "I already had good memories of Jubilee, but he wanted to add to them. We explored the city together."

"Because you couldn't explore with Torio?"

"Partly, yeah. But also because Jubilee and me, we're friends, too." He leaned his aching head into her palm. "You can share memories with all the different people you care about. Like Artor, here. You and he have been becoming friends."

"He can't hear my voice."

"Hearing isn't everything. Or did you forget Chelle?" Farley smiled crookedly at her expression, then brought Artor into the conversation. "My brother's wife is deaf. Doesn't bother Tupp any."

"I cannot write messages."

As far as he and Torio could tell, reading and writing were beyond a statue's abilities. Even the librarian statues in Morven's archives didn't read the books they tended. They simply knew the books in their keeping. Somehow.

"Did you have something you wanted to say to Artor?"
She shook her head.

Artor ventured, "If you have deaf kin, why not teach Dessa to speak with her hands?"

"Spelling into her hand doesn't work. Chelle can read, but Dessa can't."

The Ursa frowned, and when he spoke again, there were gestures to accompany his words. No, they *matched* his words. "I have deaf kin, too. Brothers in my covey who cannot speak, but they still have a lot to say. Like this. Would Dessa like to learn to speak with her hands?"

Farley was sitting near the wheel, idly gnawing on a late lunch when Larkin refolded his map with an expression that was hard to read. "You're sure it's here? *This* island?"

The crew had sighted land earlier, and Larkin had been oddly reticent ever since.

Farley said, "If you don't believe me, ask Torio. This is the place."

"I can't decide if Father will be outraged or embarrassed."

"Why would Aurelius care?"

"It's *his* island."

Farley missed a beat. "Aurelius owns a whole island?"

"Nay," Larkin blandly replied. "He owns *three* and maintains property on two others."

"He sometimes mentions estates." With a frown, Farley asked, "Property way out here? What's he want islands for?"

"Traditionally, for conquest. More practically, for escape." With a wave at their destination, he said, "This one happens to be both inheritance and investment."

"There's something valuable here? I mean ... besides Pollim's partner?"

"Once we're closer, you'll see for yourself."

Sure enough, when they rounded the island, bound for a cove along its southern shore, a wide sweep of land came into view. "Titian poppies!" Farley exclaimed, finding his feet. This entire side of the island was in vivid bloom, gaudy orange and gold.

"The second bloom is less showy than the first, but it's no less valuable."

"Hey! I see statues!" Farley leaned out over the railing, straining for a better look. "Are they Frey's? They feel like Frey's!"

"Aye, they would be, since Father commissioned them himself."

He couldn't get a good look at them, which was frustrating. "They're not very big."

"Smaller is better," Larkin said dismissively. "They only have to be as tall as a flower in order to harvest the pollen. More importantly, is this where the hunt takes us?"

Early on, Farley wasn't sure if the bond between Pollim and Eullia was going to take them onto this shore or pull them straight past it. But now, he and Torio were convinced that starstone Keet's partner was hidden somewhere here. *Where* was another question. The island was little more than a low rise with wide meadows that sloped to the shore. There were no trees. Only a small, white building.

"Who lives in the house?"

"It's more of a hut. You should feel right at home."

Farley wasn't going to be offended. Not when Larkin had been unusually talkative all day. Was he in a good mood because of the hunt? Or was it just that they were back aboard his ship? "Yep. Looks real cozy. Want me to check the thatching?"

Larkin offered a token sneer.

For a while, he was busy barking orders. The *Moontide* slipped up to the dock with hardly a bump, and the crew soon had her moored. He set a few boundaries, then gave the crew leave until nightfall. Returning to Farley's side, Larkin admitted, "I'd already planned to stop over. Torio wanted someplace private to stroll with his lady."

Too excited to eat anything else, Farley tossed the last bits of his bread at a sea bird. "I want a look around. Should I wait for you?"

"No need." Larkin gathered up his hair and began knotting it. "Let's hunt."

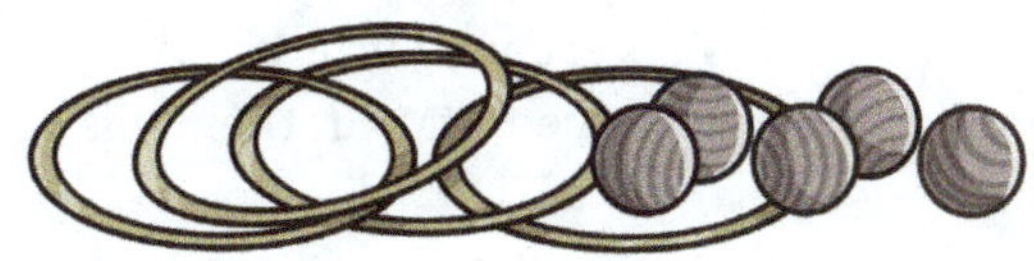

Torio wasn't planning to rob Farley of his fun, but he wasn't about to be completely left out. He was strolling down the gangway when heavy steps creaked the boards.

Artor asked, "I'd like to help. And ... I'm curious. Did you really follow a thread of magic all the way from New Continent?"

So Torio spun out the tale of Pollim and Eullia, such as it was.

"And you can *see* the magic that binds them?" Artor pointed along the path they were following. "What does it look like?"

"I cannot speak for others with similar affinities, but there is light and movement and especially connections. To a statue's maker, to the one they were made to protect, to a place. Or in this case, to a partner." Torio skidded down a sloped bank to the sandy shore and lowered himself onto a seat upon a stone.

Artor quietly asked, "Are you in pain?"

"I can manage. Just not at any great speed. Go on ahead. If you follow the shore, you'll catch up to them."

"This isn't the direction they took."

"Nooo. The lad chose a more headlong bearing, but this path is kinder to the crops."

"I don't think there's any hurry. Not if we're dealing

with starstone." Artor stayed close and smiled when Char and Nyx drifted to his side. He tugged affectionately at their ears and asked, "Did you always know what it was? Magic, I mean."

"Not at all. I didn't have any contact with the Twelve, and I was never tested for affinity. If there were stoneworkers in my lineage, they must have been on my mother's side, and I never knew them. We were wanderers. Performers." With a low laugh, Torio confessed, "My father was a traveling magician."

"Ah, I always liked those kinds of shows. Did you have an act?"

"When I was small, I took part in the acrobatics and balancing acts. When my aptitude for languages became apparent, my father put me upon the stage." He doffed an imaginary hat and spread his arms wide. "Come one, come all! Let the Grand Master of Miracles amaze and amuse you!"

Artor asked, "Was it fun?"

"It was travel, and I loved that part. But also the acrobatics and the buffoonery and the audience's smiles." Torio levered to his feet and leaned gratefully on Artor's arm. "My sister took over once my father's wanderlust was sated. Somewhere out there, the show goes on."

They proceeded at an easy pace. Eventually, Artor asked, "Where's Dessa?"

"She sent the lionesses to me, but she followed after Farley."

"There's no danger, is there?"

"None." Torio was sure of that. "At least, not from the statue they're seeking. I cannot guarantee Larkin won't lose patience."

Even as slow as they were going, it didn't take long to round a bend that let onto a smaller cove. This one faced southeast, and Farley and Larkin stood on the grassy slope above the water.

"How long are you gonna do this?" Farley complained.

"Hold still."

"But she's right over there!" Farley argued, pointing at the water.

"Hold still, or I'll pin your feet to the ground with my daggers!"

"Since when do you nitpick?"

Torio suggested, "Call over one of the harvesters? They're better equipped than you are for the task, Captain."

Larkin left off plucking at cloth with the tips of his claws. He scanned the meadow he and Farley had tramped through and called, "Can we get some assistance over here?"

Artor whispered, "Who's he talking to?"

"There are six statues in this field. Pollen harvesters. Climb up if you want a closer look."

Just then, a sunstone creature emerged from among the flowers. A creation of pure whimsy, quite unlike any of the other statues Torio had seen Freydolf produce. She was a tiny person, barely reaching Farley's knee, and she had pointed ears, a crown of stone poppies, and tapering fingertips on all four of her hands. Slotted into her abdomen was a glass vial, half-filled with golden pollen.

Larkin addressed her. "He was careless. Can you rescue the pollen on his clothing?"

She smiled and bobbed her head, then began to rapidly pluck at Farley's pants.

Although she worked quickly, Farley's patience ran out. He kicked off his boots. "Here. Have at 'em." Unbuttoning and unbelting, he let his pants drop to his ankles and stepped out of them. He peeled out of his tunic, too, and skidded down the slope to the shore. "I'm going in."

"Wait! Farley, this isn't a lake," warned Torio. "Anything could be lurking."

"Dessa went first."

Torio was well aware. "She's less palatable to hungry sea monsters."

Farley snorted. "I haven't seen a single sea monster. I'm starting to think they're nonsense tales."

But he held his ground when Torio raised a finger and asked, "Dessa, what have you found?"

"Water. Weeds. Darkness."

He tried not to worry about how far she'd gone already. "How deep are you?"

"Deep. No starlight could reach."

"Is it safe for Farley to follow?"

"Too deep, too cold." She added, *"Let me help, Farley."*

"All right, Dessa sweet." He crouched in the shallows and flicked his fingers in the water. "But keep talking. I want to know what you see!"

"So do I," interjected Artor.

Farley grinned his way and held up an arm, pointing with his whole hand. "She's walking in a straight line. Eullia must have gotten free and started walking home."

"Only to be stopped by the sunrise," said Torio. "And at a depth that starlight couldn't reach."

"How long do you think she's been stranded down there?" asked Farley. And before anyone could answer, "Hey, Larkin. Was the one who stole Eullia a Harrow?"

The Pred frowned thoughtfully. "Nay. I believe Aunt Lissie wrested control of this island from others."

"Pollim is quite old," pointed out Torio. "His attire, the weathering, and even the fact that his partner was carried off, point toward a century when conquest was more typical."

Farley ventured, "What happens to a statue that's underwater for hundreds of years?"

Larkin snorted. "Your lady might find a reef with a starstone heart."

"Should I bring tools?" asked Artor.

"If it comes to that." Torio asked, "How are you faring, Dessa?"

"Close, now. Very close. Poor, sad thing."

"Yes, I imagine she would be sad," he murmured.

And then she spoke, but the words weren't for him. *"Here you are. Were you lonely? I understand."*

Farley shot to his feet and took a few steps into the water. "Can you carry her?" And to Artor, he reported. "She's carrying her back."

Minutes dragged by, though Torio thought Dessa was moving faster now, surer of her way back than she had been of the way forward.

Farley kept up a running commentary, impatient as ever. "Is she a good match for Pollim? Well, yeah ... I knew she was starstone. I can tell that much. But what does she look like?"

Artor turned to Torio. "Do stone guardians see as we do?"

"Yes and no. I've always been under the impression that they see *more* than we do. At least ... that's the way of things with master-marked statues."

"And this pair is master-marked?"

Torio was a little surprised that he'd retained anything from the books Freydolf heaped on him. "Yes, they *are* a Keeper's work. I recognized Master Reesee's signature. He was one of Vanora's early Keepers ... and prolific. Paired statues were his specialty, and even today, the Pinnacles is famous for them."

Artor looked impressed.

Uncomfortable with the attention, Torio pointed to Farley. "There seems to be a turn of events."

Farley was knee-deep now, hands on his hips, head tipped. "I mean, I assumed a Keet would be with another Keet. No, it doesn't *have* to be that way. It just mostly works out that way. I dunno why. Well, look at us! You didn't call another rock, didja? And we're amazing together."

Torio had caught enough of their exchange to be curious what Dessa's scattered descriptions meant.

The water stirred.

Farley waded further, as if to help, but he halted when black and white stone broke into open air. Dessa was cradling a still statue. There were a few barnacles, and seaweed had snagged on the statue's limbs. All six of them.

Pollim's partner definitely wasn't Keet.

"Oh! So *that's* what you meant!" Turning to seek his gaze, Farley blurted, "Hey, Torio. Turns out Pollim's partner is a *he*."

"Do you want to try your hand?" Artor offered.

"Not a chance." Farley stayed right where he was, leaning against the mizzen mast, watching Artor clean up the rescued statue. "I don't have the training. And besides, Eullia has taken a liking to you. You're good at gaining trust."

"Am I?' The Ursa searched the statue's face. "How can you tell?"

Farley twirled a finger. "His magic began reaching for you after you knocked off the first few shells, and now it's looping around you in a friendly way. He's grateful, and he wants you to keep going."

A smile bloomed on Artor's face. "I've never had a conversation with a statue before, even secondhand."

"Well, this isn't like it is with Dessa. I'm mostly guessing, but I'm also really good at guessing." Not as good as Tupp, though. "I can't actually hear stone. I see the magic. That's it."

"And that's amazing." Artor ran his polishing cloth over the section he'd just cleared, then murmured, "Now then, what next?"

"That clump by his knee."

Artor circled the statue, then knelt to consider the new problem. "Did he tell you, somehow?"

"In a way. He coiled his magic there in a tight, spinning ball, like he was trying to draw your attention to it. He really doesn't like barnacles."

"I can imagine they'd be uncomfortable." Artor was using the same kinds of small tools that Freydolf used for fine work. With both care and confidence, he returned to his self-appointed task. Then he quietly addressed himself to Eullia. "I can't get it all done before sunset, friend. But we've many days ahead of us. You'll be feeling more like yourself soon."

Looping magic brushed and clung to Artor's fingers. It was sorta cute, and it kinda reminded him of how magical stone responded to Carden, his oldest brother and Frey's only apprentice. "Betcha there'll be two of you, now," he said softly.

Artor glanced his way, then past him. "Oh, yes. Two of them."

Larkin and a couple of his crewmen maneuvered Pollim out onto the deck. At first, Farley thought he was grumping at them, but once they were a little closer, he realized that the captain was explaining the intrinsic value of magical stone ... and the pricelessness of master-marked guardians.

Had the crew been so in awe of Dessa because she was the first living statue they'd ever seen? Farley doubted many statues went to sea. And finished pieces were generally shipped in boxes. As members of Larkin's crew, these folks would be handling a lot of magical stone in the future. Farley guessed he'd better mention it to Torio. During this crossing, the Grif could lecture while he loafed.

They'd set sail almost as soon as Eullia was aboard. Far Continent had vanished behind them. Now, they sometimes slipped past other islands, but Farley didn't think any of those could hold a candle to Aurelius's.

The sky was clear, and out here, the stars would be brilliant, perfect for waking starstone. Farley studied Eullia, who was only familiar because he'd met the Statuary's lone songstone guardian. A lean figure in puffy pants that gathered at the ankles above shoes with pointed toes, he had long, straight hair, through which pointed ears peeped. But most notable were Eullia's four arms, which were gracefully arrayed, one pair curving up, the other pair reaching forward. And in one clawed hand, he gripped Pollim's missing one.

Farley asked, "Did Torio say anything to *you* about what kind of creature he is?"

"Only that the Furl are popular figures in Keet tales."

Furl. He turned the unfamiliar name over in his mind.

A whistle piped three times, high overhead, and Larkin snapped to attention. Someone shouted and pointed, and Farley barely caught movement out of the corner of his eye. His first impression was that he'd seen the sail of another ship, but it was gone. Running to the rail, he leaned over. "What was that?" he exclaimed.

"Tail fin," Larkin said through clenched teeth. He strode further along the deck, to where a length of knotted rope coiled, and kicked it overboard.

Ripples spread outward from where the fin had vanished, but Farley couldn't see what made it. "Is it one of those whales that Frey was always on about?"

"Nay." With a grim smile. "It's one of those sea monsters you don't believe in."

"No kidding?" Farley trotted to the opposite rail, peering downward. "Will it come back?"

"Oh, aye. It's hunting."

A scaly muzzle suddenly erupted into the air, followed by a long, lean body covered in scales. They caught the sun and swirled with rainbow colors. Farley gaped at the sheer size of the thing as its upward momentum slowed and it arched sideways in a lazy flop, hitting the water with a thunderous slap that tossed water in every direction.

Farley wiped droplets from his face, then blurted, "Didja see that?"

"Quite clearly."

"It was big."

"Aye. Easily twice the length of the ship."

The resulting ripples were bigger than they looked. They hit the *Moontide*'s side, and she jounced fretfully. Larkin barked orders, and the crew started doing things with the sails.

Farley asked, "Are we in danger?"

"Nay. He feeds below the surface. We are above it."

"What if he tips us over?"

Larkin muttered, "Don't give the old brute any ideas."

Farley couldn't tell if the Pred was kidding. "He's not people."

"Nay," he sighed. "You can stop your bleating. He's not interested in us, but he's feeling frisky. Enjoy the show."

As if on cue, the whiskered muzzle appeared once again, shooting high into the air. This time, Farley noticed that the thing had legs tucked against its sides. "You know, if you scaled him down, he could be Dart."

Larkin spared him a baffled look.

"I had that box in stow Tupp sent along. A delivery for that fountain dragon, one of Frey's old commissions ...? Anyhow, he looked a whole lot like that."

Torio arrived then and propped a hip on the rail. "A frolicking steelfin. I didn't expect to see any until we were further south."

Farley was indignant. "You *knew* about those?"

"That such things exist in the world? Certainly."

"Why didn't you *tell* me?"

"And spoil the surprise?"

He considered that and lapsed into an easy grin. "Got

any more like it?"

Torio said, "Some equally stunning. Others quite a bit smaller. A few you might like even better."

As the steelfin once more lunged up out of the depths, Farley stared hard, trying to memorize every sparkling prism of the moment.

The crew got the ship moving, and they left the frisky sea monster behind. Artor went back to chipping at barnacles, and the crew scattered to other tasks. All except Larkin, who moved to that same spot where he'd kicked the rope overboard earlier. It struck Farley as odd, so he kept watching.

Larkin must have felt eyes on him, because he glanced back. With a fierce look that spoke warnings, the Pred stalked off to do ... whatever it was captains did.

Farley waited until he was thoroughly busy before stealing over to the rail to see what Larkin had been looking at. The rope was still there, dangling over the edge. Knots ran down its entire length, and with every roll of the sea, the wide loop at the end skimmed the water's surface.

Strange.

Torio tipped back the last of his wine while watching the sunset. His deck chair, an extravagance foisted upon him by Harrow right before departure, was always a good place to loiter. Today, it afforded a fine view of three men attempting to solve a puzzle.

Farley, Artor, and Larkin were trying to place Pollim and Eullia upon their pedestal. To no avail.

"Stop thinking like a Flox," Torio cheerfully called. "They're not dancing at a festival."

Hands on hips, Farley countered, "You know how they fit together?"

"Only because I've heard the ballad on which this pair is based."

Larkin brushed his finger across his mouth, then gripped the back of his neck. "Aye. He's right." And then, "Aye. It's no use. They were pulled apart while they were stirring."

Torio tipped back his hat to study the deepening sky. "Not much longer now."

"How *do* they fit?" Farley marched over and stole Torio's empty goblet. "Show me."

Slouching deeper into his cushions, he said, "No need. Larkin has sorted it out."

Before Farley could turn to the captain, arms surrounded him from behind, emulating the posture of Eullia's lower set of arms. Larkin said, "It isn't a dance. It's capture."

"Agreed." Torio fluttered his fingers between the two of them. "Natural enemies who become friends, then allies, then heroes. Or so the story goes."

"Tell it!" demanded Farley, looking to Torio, then leaning into Larkin in order to catch his gaze. "One of you better start talking."

Larkin snorted and stepped back.

"Later," Torio promised. "No doubt they'll reenact their story all through the night. Although I'm holding out hope they're capable of more than their rote."

"Should be," said Farley. "Pollim is really personable. And a good dancer."

"True. But he was on his own, then. Reunion may change him."

"Doubt it." Farley shot him a challenging look. "It's not like they ever really lost hold. Frey made sure of that."

Torio conceded with a nod and stood, lest he miss the moment.

They spread out, each wanting a view as the sun touched

the horizon and slowly sank. Most of the crew drifted closer, forming a loose circle around the two starstone statues. Things quieted to background noises—water parting, ropes creaking, sails rustling.

Dessa slipped to Torio's side just as the bright rim of the sun winked out. *"Can you see them?"*

"You know I can."

"How do they look?"

He flopped a hand back and forth. "Magic isn't an exact language. I have little confidence that I'll find the right words to explain what's underway."

Seeking. Testing. Blending.

And yet, it was also like Farley had said. Neither statue had ever been completely lost to the other while their bond remained intact. But distance must have been like a pain for two who'd always been meant to be one.

Darkness deepened.

The starlight strengthened.

Pollim's head turned.

Eullia lowered his arms to cradle Pollim's missing hand to his chest. He hung his head, and his Keet partner stepped forward. He reached up, and his head tipped to one side as he tried to catch his partner's eye. Alabaster fingers brushed a pale cheek as if to wipe away a tear. Then the Furl tried to give back the hand he held.

Pollim smiled and looked to Artor.

The journeyman simply nodded.

Eullia sought Dessa and pressed a set of hands to his heart before opening them in a show of gratitude that was startlingly Floxish. She waved to them with both hands. No, not quite. She was waving them together.

Farley chuckled and did the same. "Don't be bashful. You're among friends."

Without further urging, Eullia captured Pollim, pulling him into an embrace that was doubly snug, and Pollim hid his face and twined his arms around Eullia. And they stayed that way, locked together. Torio doubted anything could part them but sunrise.

When nothing further happened, the crew began to murmur.

Larkin mildly called, "There, now. It's safe to light the lamps. *All* the lamps. I'll bring out a cask of ale."

Dessa plucked at Torio's sleeve. *"How do they look?"* she asked again.

With a sigh, he pulled Dessa into an embrace. "They look like this."

She wrapped her arms around him. A moment later, a second pair of arms slipped beneath his cloak, encouraging him closer.

"I hadn't realized Furl anatomy was in your repertoire."

"Only to understand."

"And what do you understand?"

Dessa finally said, *"They are like me and my lionesses, cut from the same block."*

"Hmm?" Torio hadn't noticed that particular detail, but it didn't surprise him. He asked, "Can you sense the lionesses that are waiting back at Morven?"

"No." And more thoughtfully, *"Maybe once they are bound to me?"*

"After that, they will not want to range, even if they could."

"And you?"

"Hmm?"

"Would you range if you could?"

Torio rested his cheek against her hair and gazed at the starstone pair. "What does it matter? I can't and I shan't. We are as bound as they are, but in our own way."

"You cannot go. You belong to me."

"As if I could forget." And because it clearly needed to be said, he whispered, "Have *you* forgotten? I couldn't go until we could go together."

Dessa softly added, *"And I belong to you."*

"Irrevocably."

After a few moments, her voice came again, almost shy. *"They seem happy. To me."*

"They wouldn't be together now if you hadn't gone into those dark waters alone. None of us could have found him … or reached him."

"They were alone, and now they're not."

Torio brushed his lips against her brow. "I'm proud of you."

Dessa's response left him rather dazzled, but then Farley was there to slap his back and lure Dessa away with the promise of dancing. And sure enough, instruments began tuning, and Artor was there, pressing a mug of ale into his hand.

Torio sank to a seat in the chair Aurelius Harrow had provided for his comfort, and Nyx came to rest her chin upon his knee. He stroked the fur that Freydolf Meadowsweet's skill had rendered thick and soft, and he let himself count these many blessings. His mountain's words rang true, even when he applied them to himself. *I was alone, and now I'm not.*

11

Man Overboard

Within a few days, Farley noticed a definite change in the air. Warmer. Softer. By the end of the week, the air thickened toward sultry, so he shed layers along with the rest of the crew. The sun seared his fair skin, and Artor scolded and smeared him with salves. Night air grew heavy, and Farley's cabin was too stuffy for sleep.

Rolling out of his hammock, he stole toward the deck, thinking to watch Pollim and Eullia act out their tale. Torio still hadn't kept his promise to tell it, but Farley had worked most of it out. It wasn't too hard. The starstone statues were so expressive, their story didn't necessarily need words. But Farley still wanted to hear it.

Up on deck, he scanned the starry sky.

The only lanterns lit were the ones at stem and stern, a safety precaution against nighttime collisions. Someone would be in the crow's nest, and another guard should be strolling the decks, keeping an eye out. Farley wasn't sure who might be on duty since the sailors were always trading turns. He got on with some crewmen better than others, and he dared to hope one of the Oxus was on patrol. They were easygoing and usually happy to swap tales.

Stealing across warm deck boards, Farley paused in a deeper patch of dark alongside one of the longboats. Wait. He backed up a step, looking up and down the length of the ship. One of the longboats was missing?

A hand touched his shoulder, and Farley turned in surprise.

Pollim had found him, and he offered a gesture of welcome.

"There's a boat missing," Farley said in low tones. "Did something happen?"

The starstone Keet smiled and nodded. Taking his arm, Pollim ushered him toward the stern. Eullia met them there, stepping closer and cautiously reaching for Farley.

"It's okay, go ahead." This wasn't the first time the Furl had betrayed his fascination. "I don't mind."

Clawed fingers slipped into his hair, teasing out unruly curls before moving along to follow the curve of his horn, the whole one, before giving Farley's cheek a small pat.

"Do you know what a cloudstrider is?"

A sharp nod. Another caress. Eullia stepped back, apparently satisfied.

"Guess I'll ask Larkin for more details next time he's in a good mood."

Pollim gestured stiffly toward the stern. Artor had restored his missing hand, bracing the join with a cuff and bandages until Frey could take a look. Farley was hoping the master sculptor could connect the stone so Pollim would regain the use of his hand.

Eullia came around behind Farley, gently nudging him forward, reinforcing their message.

"He's here?" Farley asked.

Larkin *did* take a turn on the guard rotation.

Farley gestured for the starstone statues to stay back, then with more stealth than he might have otherwise used, he dropped to his belly and crept to the rail.

Black sky. Black water. Stars blazing above and reflected below. At first, he couldn't see anything much, but that's only because he wasn't looking in the right direction. The sound of a hushed voice guided his gaze to where one of the longboats glided in the *Moontide*'s wake. They were towing it? Farley frowned in confusion. What was Larkin doing? Fishing?

But then someone laughed. Someone other than Larkin.

Moving over by a few rails to improve his view, Farley called upon his Pred training to calm his hammering heart. Slow, deep breaths. He focused his straining senses so they could bring him the information he'd need to overwhelm his prey.

Larkin's posture was relaxed as he spoke to a woman who seemed to be in the water.

She laughed softly and answered, then pushed up on the longboat's edge, bringing her face closer to his. With the dark and the distance, it wasn't like Farley could see details, but ... yeah, they were kissing.

When Larkin pulled back and stood, Farley gawked as the man stripped, then dove, knifing into the inky sea. The woman also left the boat behind, slipping underwater in apparent pursuit. Scaled coils briefly gleamed in the starlight, and a fishtail lightly tapped the water. They surfaced to the side, arms around each other. And ... yep, definitely more kissing.

Farley rolled onto his back and stared up at the sky, giving the couple some privacy.

As surprises went, this was a big one.

He wondered if Aurelius knew that his son was courting a mermaid.

After that, Farley kept a sharp eye on Larkin. He kept a safe distance, too. Some of it was embarrassment, but there was also a longstanding Flox custom in play. Traditionally, the folks in his hometown pretended not to notice when a boy and girl paired off. They weren't acknowledged as a couple until their families announced a wedding day.

But Farley was curious.

Probably stupidly so.

There was a statue of a mermaid in the courtyard of Aurelius's house back on Morven. The freshstone guardian was good friends with Ulrica, who'd claimed her as a sister way back when Quinny was born. Farley had always assumed Nerine was the product of some past sculptor's fancy, but ... apparently, mermaids were as real as steelfins.

He could ask Torio. That would be simplest. But what if his questions somehow got back to Larkin? That might lead to painful consequences. And besides, Farley really, really wanted to figure this out on his own. Larkin's lady friend was the most interesting thing going on right now. At least, it was better than watching Artor set tiles or language lessons with Torio.

Farley hung over the railing, peering into the deep blue water as they cut through it with a churning of foam. Sometimes, he was sure he caught movement under the surface. Could be fish. Then again, it could be anything.

Something splashed, but by the time he looked, there were only ripples, quickly lost in the ship's wake. Was she there? He moved further toward the stern, eyes alert ... but also blind. Because he ran smack into Larkin, whose scowl was back in full force.

"I thought I saw ... a dolphin maybe?"

"Aye. It's possible."

"And something like seaweed. Kinda." He wiggled his hands. "Rippling. Green."

Larkin's jaw clenched. "It doesn't grow in these depths,

but sometimes snarls of it are cut adrift."

"So ... seaweed?"

"Aye." Larkin repeated. "It's possible."

The whole mood aboard the *Moontide* shifted when clouds piled up on the horizon and swells gained enough height to be exciting. Clambering into the nets near the bow, Farley whooped as they climbed and plunged in a wild ride that left him soaked to the skin.

He might have stayed longer, but Larkin barked orders and sent him below to dry off and make certain that everything was lashed down, including Pollim and Eullia, who'd been stowed at the first sign of a storm. Farley knew his stuff was fine, but he'd planned to double-check the horses and chickens anyhow. And Artor.

"You okay with all this?" Farley used a hand to indicate the motion.

"I haven't decided yet." Artor looked a little green. "Will it get worse?"

"Not sure what to expect. This is already rougher water than we saw on our first crossing. If the stories are true, things'll get pretty wild." Tempering his excitement, he offered, "Want me to bring a basin from the galley, just in case?"

Hugging Char and Nyx, who bookended him snugly, Artor wryly said, "Better that than your hat."

Farley laughed and went to see what he could find.

Minutes later, he was back on deck, squinting into rain that seemed to be falling sideways. Unless it was the ship that was sideways? He clung to the open doorframe, then felt bad for letting in the weather. Shutting it behind him, he settled for gripping its sturdy handle.

The other crewmen were too busy to notice, but Larkin quickly spotted him. "I told you to go below!" he growled.

"I did. And now I'm back. You can't expect me to hide. It's my first real storm!" Over the Pred's shoulder, he saw a wall of greenish water rising higher than they stood. "Whoa."

Larkin flattened him against the door as the wave hit, drenching them.

"Does that happen often?" Farley asked, trying to be cheeky.

"You are twelve times a fool if you think you can outwit these waves!"

"Thirteen times!" he countered.

"Get. Below."

Farley wheedled. "Just a little longer? I'll be careful."

Rain slicked the deck, and another wall of water appeared ahead. This time, the *Moontide* rose to meet it, skimming the wall with a speed that left Farley's stomach behind. The ocean tossed them up, and for a breathless moment they teetered in a still place. Farley thrilled over the sensation. Then, the nose dipped, and they plunged into a valley of water that opened below them.

That was slightly less fun. Actually, it was terrifying.

Farley hadn't realized he was yelling until Larkin snarled and drove his claws into the wood of the door.

He roared into Farley's ear. "Grab my belt."

Fumbling, he found enough room between the many blades sheathed at Larkin's waist to get a grip.

Golden eyes bored into his. "If you let go, I'll kill you."

Oddly reassuring.

"If you really want to ride this out, I'll lash you to one of the masts."

Farley brightened. "Yeah?"

Larkin shook his head. "You really *are* thirteen times a fool."

Then they were climbing again, but this time, Farley felt more secure. Larkin's confidence made it possible to believe that the *Moontide* could ride safely through any storm. When she plunged, he whooped, and Larkin rolled his eyes.

"Do you know where we are?" Farley asked.

"Afloat."

"Is that all?"

"It's enough." Larkin scanned the sky and sea, then checked the positions of the few members of the crew that remained on deck.

"Is everyone safe?"

"Aye. Now get below before your guardians decide you're not."

Farley sucked in a breath as the ship crested another huge wave. Then he laughed. "I'm *fine* Dessa. I'm with Larkin."

"Aye, and you're keeping me from my rightful place."

"A little longer?"

Larkin frowned. "You're not afraid?"

"Not with you here."

That caused the Pred's eyebrows to rise. "If you trust me so much, you should listen. Your place in all this is below."

Lightning flashed, and Larkin cursed.

"What?"

Ignoring him, Larkin hollered something to the man at the wheel. Shouts rang out all around, barely audible over the roar of waves.

"Everything okay?" Farley checked.

Larkin fixed him with a look of pure annoyance. "You are cold. You are wet. This can only impair your chances of ...."

Lightning sliced, and something cracked. One of the masts snapped and fell, dragging red sailcloth and tangling ropes down to the deck. Larkin twisted to see, and Farley's cold, wet fingers lost hold of him. The ship shuddered, and instead of rising cleanly over the next swell, she wobbled. Another greenish wall of water came at them sideways, and when it crashed across the deck, Farley lost his footing, sliding on his hands and knees across the boards.

"Idiot!" Larkin was on him in a moment.

"I'm fine, Dessa!" He put as much cheerfulness as he could into his tone, despite how rattled he was. "Larkin's with me."

The deck rolled. The broken mast swung their way.

Larkin drove a blade into the deckboards and held on.

Farley only had a moment to register that this might be really bad, and then another wave pounded around them, making it impossible to breathe. Dessa's voice was screaming at him as he went tumbling again. Something cracked against his knee, then pain hit his elbow. He was dizzy from rolling and from lack of air when the pitch of the ship momentarily left him and Larkin high and dry.

Shaking his hair out of his face, Larkin only had time to growl out three words. "Don't. Let. Go."

And then they were falling.

Water swallowed them, spun them, buried them. Farley's thoughts were nearly drowned out by Dessa's scream, but he couldn't draw breath to lie again.

Torio would be so disappointed.

Aurelius wouldn't be surprised.

Ulrica was going to kill something.

Mother would cry.

Tupper might name a kid after him, but that wouldn't fix this. There was only *one* Farley, and he was it. Plus, it'd be no fun at all if he wasn't around to impress the kid and teach him all the stunts he used to pull.

Something bumped him from behind.

Then Larkin turned traitor and let him go.

Farley flailed weakly, and bubbles escaped.

Scales coiled around his waist, pulling him in a direction that might not be up, and he pushed weakly against his captor. Water rushed, and then he broke the surface and choked down a breath. But it felt like the rain was trying to drown him, and a wave slopped over him. Afloat might be fine for the *Moontide*, but not for him. His hands fumbled, searching for something to hold onto.

More silken scales.

Then hands met his, guiding his arms around someone's shoulders. He clung, focusing on coughing, sneezing, and breathing. He hurt. Everywhere.

Eventually, he registered a voice. Someone was calling him by name. Larkin.

He lifted his head, calling, "Here! I'm here!"

Strong arms locked around him from behind. Larkin had found him again.

Lightning flashed, and in that brief moment, Farley was looking into the face of a beautiful woman with eyes as green as storm-tossed waves. She looked worried, even wary. This had to be Larkin's mermaid.

"Which way?" Giving him a squeeze, Larkin growled, "Which way is the ship?"

Farley pointed.

"How do you know?" asked the lady in accented Verit.

"Dessa." He probably shouldn't be holding somebody else's girl, but he couldn't imagine letting go. "Dessa's screaming for me, and ... it hurts."

"Are you cut?" Larkin asked.

"Not sure. But being this far from Dessa. It hurts."

Larkin gruffly pointed out, "You're not her Keeper."

"But I will be." He pointed again. "She called me, too. She's calling me now."

The Pred muttered something to the mermaid, whose coils rippled with movement. Then Larkin asked, "Can you calm Dessa from here?"

"She knows I'm alive. But she's not happy. At all."

Larkin wiped the residue of the next wave from his face. "The sea's too frantic for us to reboard, but we can get closer. Will that help?"

"Should do." And when another flicker of lightning offered another peek, Farley ventured, "Thanks, miss. You saved my life." And with a forced laugh, "We sure are lucky, huh, Larkin?"

"Hardly." Larkin's voice went all silky. "But you *knew* that, didn't you?"

"Well, yeah. But it's not like I'd tell. Flox don't meddle with courting couples." He turned a little toward Larkin. "Does your dad know? Or ... your mom?"

"Nay, and I'll thank you not to mention it."

"Okay. So are you gonna introduce me?"

Larkin grumbled, "He's the one. I told you he was an unholy terror."

She laughed, and then her cool cheek pressed to Farley's. "Livia." She spoke right into his ear. "You may call me Livia."

"Nice ta meetcha. I'm Farley. So ... you're a mermaid?"

She gently mussed his hair. "Some do say so."

Waves still carried them up and down, but Livia navigated steadily in the direction of home. As the pain of separation eased, Farley found it easier to think beyond his next breath. "We're still really far away," he said. He was cold, and he knew enough to be a little worried.

Larkin asked, "How long can you hold your breath?"

Farley hesitated. "Will that be faster?"

"Much."

"Guess we better."

"Aye, it's for the best. Livia?" Larkin's tone was so different when he was talking to someone he cared about.

"We're ready."

Farley didn't have to do anything. Not even hold on. Trapped between Livia and Larkin, he could feel the sway of strong muscles and the building speed. Underwater, there was no storm, no interfering waves, but there was also no air. He grabbed Larkin's wrist, and he must have signaled Livia, because she surfaced.

He sagged into Larkin, who made him let go of Livia. The rearranging was awkward, and he wasn't sure he wanted the Pred to be able to read his face, but Larkin said, "She can swim faster this way."

"How are you hanging on?"

"There are harnesses for me. I'm secure." He searched Farley's face. "Livia and I have been swimming together since I was fifteen."

Farley boldly asked, "You sharing a promise?"

Larkin looked decidedly vulnerable when he said, "It's more than that."

"Will you tell me?"

"Why should I?"

"Because I'm family," he reasoned. "She's practically my sister."

Dark brows slowly lifted. "You'd claim kinship with Livia?"

"Why wouldn't I? She's gonna be your wife, isn't she?"

"We're irrevocably bonded. I'm her husband." Again, that uncertainty crept into Larkin's expression. Ducking closer, he confessed, "We have twin daughters."

Farley thumped his shoulder. "I'm already an uncle? That's the best kind of news! Also, they're gonna love me."

Larkin pushed him down and gruffly ordered, "Hold your breath." And then, "We're ready, Livia."

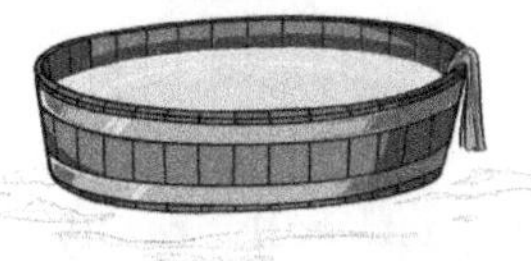

Farley had a hard time closing his hands around the bottom rung of the rope ladder that the crew dropped over the side.

"Do you need to be carried?" goaded Larkin.

"Please."

"Truly?"

Larkin made him turn around and hold onto him again. Farley clung like a toddler while the Pred scaled the ladder without any sign of difficulty. Near the top, Larkin quietly asked, "Are you still alive?"

Farley nodded.

"Then I've kept my promise."

Oh, of course. Just fulfilling his promise. Farley simply nodded again. Then his leg bumped a rail, and Larkin released him. Knees giving out, Farley sank to the deck, shivering, salt-slicked, and sodden.

An instant later, two lionesses accosted him. Nyx caught his tunic in her teeth and pulled him away from the rail, and Char pressed up behind him. When the first lioness released him, it was into the second's support. Their tails lashed him there. Char nosed his ear, and he flung an arm around Nyx's neck.

"I know, I know. I'm sorry. Please, don't fret." His teeth were chattering, and his voice was mostly gone, but they listened intently. "You did g-good to stay with Dessa on the ship. Don't ever j-jump after me, no matter what. This ocean would s-swallow you up, and then wh-where would Dessa be, huh?"

Dessa bent over him, and he summoned up a weary smile. "Hey. Made it back. Sorry 'bout that."

"*You are mine.*"

"Totally am."

"*You fell.*"

"I did."

"*Are you cracked?*"

"Nope. No cracks. Just really, really tired."

Then Torio was there, kneeling before him, pale and furious.

Farley quailed before the man's displeasure. "I ... mighta made a mistake."

Swearing volubly, Torio declared him a fool in every trade language and a few dialects that nobody but Larkin had heard of, then hauled him into a fierce embrace. Ignoring the wet, he covered Farley with his cloak, which was a Grif thing. Without a word, he was promising loyalty, protection, and affection.

Farley wanted to tease him for being too shy to say it. But he hung his head and offered a creaky, "Sorry."

"I would have been sorrier." And with definite snap, "Pinions and pinfeathers, man! You're going to get me killed!"

"You?" Farley thought that unjust. He was the one who'd nearly drowned.

Totally serious, Torio said, "She was ready to pitch me in after you."

"Oh, that'd be b-bad. Don't ever do that, Dessa." And even though it wasn't really any more convincing this time, he added, "I was f-fine. I was with Larkin."

"I made so many promises," Torio groused. "To your mother. To your brothers. To both Harrows."

"Then you better k-keep me from c-catching cold," Farley suggested.

With another oath, the Grif hauled him bodily to his feet, hollering for hot water and extra blankets. Torio tried to support him toward the stairs, but Farley shook his head. "Dessa," snapped Torio. "He's a bit overgrown for me to be lugging around. Bring him to Artor."

She scooped him up and flowed across the boards, the gathered crew parting before her.

"Sorry, Dessa," he whispered.

"Farley is alive. Farley is here."

She spoke with lofty pride, as if the rest didn't matter.

Farley doubted he could dismiss the past few hours half so easily. Not when what had almost happened was finally beginning to sink in. Tremors had begun by the time Dessa transferred him into Artor's waiting arms.

The Ursa got straight down to business, stripping wet clothes and flinging them into the corner. He scolded Farley the whole while he toweled feeling back into frigid limbs.

Submitting without complaint, Farley responded at appropriate intervals.

"Yes, Artor."

"Never again, Artor."

"You're right, Artor."

"I promise, Artor."

The door slammed open, and Torio directed the placement of a washtub in one corner. Buckets of water followed, with conscripted crew members offering brief words of relief and encouragement. Once the door closed behind them, Torio wearily announced, "The girls are warming themselves beside the galley stove, so resign yourself to a bed of stones tonight."

"S'fine," Farley assured as Artor lowered him into water that steamed lightly and stung his toes.

For a while, he just sat there, soaking in the warmth.

Artor draped his own big blanket around both Farley's shoulders and the bath itself, then hurried off to brew some kind of tea. It'd probably taste awful, but Farley would welcome the added heat.

He was still grimacing over his second cupful when Larkin glided in, bringing a kettle of hot water and bottles of Pred remedies. One of the bottles held an oil, which Larkin added to the water before urging Artor to rub more into Farley's extremities. The pungent stuff wrinkled his nose, but it had a warming effect, so he didn't complain.

Larkin requisitioned one of the crates from Farley's stow and used it for a stool. Sitting opposite, he slid his feet into the washtub, forcing Farley to make room. Then Larkin emptied the kettle into the bath and grimaced as the renewed heat hit toes that must still have been cold.

The captain's hair was lank against his face, and he smelled faintly of mulled wine. However, Farley got the impression that this was the first chance Larkin had taken to sit.

"Better give him some of that tea," Farley suggested.

Artor was quick to comply, passing him the same cup Farley had used, and Torio dared to begin toweling the Pred's hair for him. When Larkin submitted to it all without a fuss, Farley guessed he wasn't the only one in shock.

A big brown hand reached for him, and everyone went very quiet and very still.

Was he ...? Yeah, he was.

Larkin determinedly kneaded at the base of Farley's horn.

Eventually, the captain spoke. "If you ignore my orders again, I'll ship you home in a barrel addressed to my mother. And should you survive the journey, she can brutalize what's left of your hide."

"Yessir," Farley offered meekly enough.

Surprise registered on the man's face. "So this works?"

Farley's face heated. "Did Aurelius somehow put you up to this?"

"Nay, you told me yourself. You were drunk and pining for Frey."

"Remind me not to drink. Seems like I only embarrass myself." He lowered his gaze to the hairy legs and clawed feet warming in his bath. Did this count as group bathing? For Pred, this almost, kinda meant ... family.

"Thanks for not letting go," Farley mumbled.

"Aye."

"And ... I'm sorry I didn't listen."

"Aye."

"Hey, are you gonna do like Hadwin did?"

"What did my older brother do?"

Farley could have rattled off a whole list of things, but he kept it simple. "Are you gonna change your name to Harrow?"

Larkin's expression slowly softened, and he looked so much like Frey in that moment. Farley swallowed against the lump in his throat. He didn't wish himself home, and he wouldn't take back anything. Not really. Not even near-drowning, if it meant that Larkin saw him as more than a duty. Pred ferocity was a fine thing when they were bent on protecting someone they considered their own.

"The matter was raised," Larkin said carefully.

Even though it was foolhardy to let someone see how much you wanted something, Farley had his hopes up. "It'd be good for business."

"Aye, there's that." Larkin's brows lifted. "Though I suspect Father's offer had sentiment at the heart."

"Gonna carve it out?" Farley prodded. "Feast upon it with ready fangs?"

"You sound like Mother."

"You're worried about her, ain'tcha?" He prodded Larkin's knee. "On account of Livia."

"Hmm."

Farley turned to Torio. "He went and married a mermaid."

The Grif didn't look especially shocked, so maybe mermaids weren't such a big deal. Torio said, "An interesting combination. A sea captain and a sea wife."

Larkin's eyes flashed warnings.

Patting his knee, Farley said, "I don't think your folks will mind. Especially not Ulrica."

"That woman is a meddler in matters of the heart," said Torio. "She lives for love stories that pit a poor, unsuspecting pair against insurmountable odds."

"Torio's one of her victims," Farley proudly reported. "On account of him being destined for a lady trapped in stone."

Larkin looked from face to face. "You think they'd accept Livia?"

Farley chuckled. "You'll have Ulrica by the fangs the second you tell her she's got granddaughters."

"*Daughters*?" Torio exclaimed, sounding startled this time.

"Aye. Twin girls." With a rebellious glint in his eyes, Larkin declared, "They're the first Basq ever to have eyes of Harrow gold."

12

Dangerous Business

Farley overslept. He wasn't sure how long, but his stomach snarled at him until he dragged himself out from between the two lionesses. Making it to his feet hurt more than it should have. He was still clinging to his hammock, checking out his new bruises, when Artor arrived with a tray of pots and shears and gauze.

"You're in pain!" he exclaimed as Char and Nyx butted affectionately at his thighs on their way out.

"Sorta, I guess. I got knocked around some, but I don't think it's serious. Nothing broken or anything."

"Better let me look."

Farley didn't protest since he kind of wanted the second opinion. His whole body ached in ways it never had before. He hissed and flinched under Artor's gentle prodding.

Finally, his friend agreed, "None of this is dangerous, but take it easy for a little while. No games of hide-and-hunt with Pred until you lose the limp."

Farley hadn't even realized he was favoring one leg. Other things were commanding more of his attention. "Anything on that tray edible?"

"The tea ...?"

"Doesn't count."

Artor chuckled. "No, it doesn't, but you'll be grateful for your dose. Also, I overheard Larkin telling the cook to save back a portion for you at lunchtime, so once I have you sorted, check in at the galley."

Then he applied some kind of warm salve to abused skin, wrapping whole sections of his body in gauze before helping Farley into clean clothes.

He smelled like an herb garden, but the stuff had limbered his sore muscles. "Better already," remarked Farley.

"*Tell me* if you're in pain. There are other things I can do to ease it." Artor pushed a second cup of tea on him.

Farley had downed the dose when Torio poked his head inside, looking tense. "Awake, I see."

"Did *you* bring me anything to eat?"

The man immediately relaxed. "No, but I know where a meal can be had. The captain is asking for you ... well, for all of us."

"Why?"

"Probably to tell us the same things he just finished telling his crew." Torio pointed up. "While the *Moontide* isn't floundering, repairs will still drive us into port, and the nearest is Turncove."

Farley shook his head. "Never heard of it."

"Neither have I," admitted Artor. "Should we have?"

"Oh, it's famous enough. Or infamous. The Mard aren't likely to take on a Pred, though, so it should be fine."

The Grif sounded doubtful.

"Who are the Mard?" Farley asked. He couldn't recall the name from any books.

Torio quietly answered, "Seafaring clans, for the most part. Shrewd in their business dealings."

Something about the man's expression worried Farley. "Anything else I should know?"

"Nothing worth mentioning." But reaching for Farley's

hand, Torio spelled it out upon his palm, so Dessa wouldn't overhear. P - I - R - A - T - E - S.

Farley trailed after Torio and Artor. His limp was slowing him down some, but so was his curiosity. The port city was unlike anything he'd ever seen. The underpinnings were crooked, weathered, and rusty, like all the building materials had been salvaged from—or savaged by—the sea. Yet over the top of all the dilapidation were splashes of brilliant color.

Vivid hues stained every building, and painted sailcloth stretched over walkways. Curtains of shells and beads spanned the doorways of most shops, and old buckets and barrels had been commandeered as makeshift gardens that put Farley in mind of his shipboard one. Nothing about the place was orderly or tidy, and he couldn't really decide if he hated it ... or loved it.

Lagging behind to identify a spindly fruit tree in a washtub, Farley was startled when the shop owner leaned out a nearby window to ask him something.

"Sorry, I don't speak ... whatever you're speaking."

Mard were a strange bunch. For reasons that seemed to boil down to cultural differences, the men wore masks on the upper halves of their faces. They were garish, sometimes even ghoulish. Larkin suspected the goal was intimidation. Torio leaned toward trickery since the Mard could swap their identity with a quick change.

The man smoothly switched to Liric, in which Farley was barely conversant. But he'd been warned—and threatened—not to listen to or linger with any of the locals, who were apparently specialists in illegal trade.

"No, thank you. And have a nice day," he offered, tapping the brim of his hat and moving along.

He walked on, waving to Artor, who'd paused at a shop entrance, waiting for him. He pointed inside, then ducked past a burlap flap. Torio must already be in there. Artor had wanted to stock up on a few things—medicinal stuff—and Torio had decided it was essential. Farley was glad for the necessity. He doubted Larkin would have let him off the ship otherwise.

What were the Mard going to do? Kidnap him?

Chimes pinged over the entrance to an alley lined with more scavenged planters. Farley turned in, amused to find vegetables thriving in everything from butter churns to old boots. Ahead, he caught the sound of flapping wings and contented clucking. With a vague idea of finding out if there was another variety of chicken available, Farley kept walking.

The alley opened into a kind of pavilion. The roof was high at the center, steeply sloped, and hung with dozens of cages. Songbirds and poultry populated most of them, though he spied some showier birds that had to have come from First Continent. Monkeys peered at him from behind the bars of one cage. A bored looking tree-cat glared at him from another. But in the very center of the pavilion stood a much larger cage. He worked his way around the clutter to get a closer look, because a flash of pink plumage had him curious.

But ... no.

Oh, no.

Not plumage at all. He'd mistaken silken finery for feathers. In the central cage, huddled in some kind of flowered robe, a girl slumped against her prison wall, head nodding as if she were about to doze off.

Stealing closer, Farley crouched beside her and softly asked, "Miss? Say, miss, are you in some kind of trouble?"

With a whimper, she jerked away, tumbling away from the bars with a flash of furred legs. She had the usual delicate features, and her hair and fur were the color of milky tea. Farley didn't have to be a healer to see exhaustion in the smudges under wary eyes.

"Sorry, miss. My fault." He politely turned his face away, giving the girl time to rearrange her clothing and compose herself. "Didn't mean to surprise you like that."

"You speak Terse," she mumbled.

"Sure do. Though I'm told I have a funny accent. What's a Pika doing here?"

Her eyes, which were the strangest shade of pink, widened considerably. "You know my people?"

"Well, yeah. I came from Far Continent. Well, it's not just me. I'm traveling with friends." Farley kept his voice low, not wanting to draw the attention of the kind of shopkeeper who stocked pretty girls. "I befriended a few Pika. Learned heaps of stuff. You're my first Pika girl, though."

Long ears slowly lifted. "You are not Grif."

"Nope." Farley swept off his hat. "The name's Farley, and I'm Flox. My people come from New Continent."

"Farley." She crawled across musty straw to get closer. "I'm Tsing."

"Nice ta meetcha," he softly returned, tapping one of the cage bars. "So how come you're in here, Tsing?"

"Our ship," she began, her gaze darting nervously toward a different entrance than the one Farley had used. "We were overtaken, and the Mard boarded. Those terrors ... they never leave a male alive, so my brothers made me s-swear to live. And then they died."

Farley's heart clenched. "I've got to get you out of here!"

"Buy me!"

He frowned. "You can't buy *people*."

She reached through the bars, grabbing him by the front of his shirt. "Buy me quickly!" she begged. "Before I'm discovered!"

Discovered? Farley took a longer look, but all he saw was a bedraggled girl, the sour-smelling straw, and flies buzzing around the untouched food on a rusted plate. "Help me out, Tsing. What am I missing."

Her desperation ebbed into despair, and the girl's voice dropped. "I already told you, Farley the Flox. Mard never leave males alive. They're sure to notice their oversight eventually."

Oh.

Farley only needed a moment to rearrange the facts, then he swore under his breath. "I *really* gotta get you out of here."

Tsing pulled at an ear. "Do you have enough coin to buy my life?"

"Probably. Who do I talk to?"

When Farley tried to stand, Tsing's hold tightened. "Please! Please? Promise me you won't walk away and never look back."

"I wouldn't do that."

He didn't let go.

"Hey, I won't abandon you. I'll swear it any way you want. How do Pika promise stuff?"

"How do Pika do anything?"

Farley snorted. "Fine. You know what? I can swear it three ways."

Grabbing Tsing's hand, he pulled until it pressed over his heart in the Pred fashion. "I'll be back."

Linking their wrists in Grif fashion, he swore, "I'll buy you."

Then Farley carefully pulled Tsing right up to the bars,

kissing the quavering young man and promising, "When I leave this island, I'll bring you with me. Satisfied?"

He stifled a whimper and nodded.

"Buck up, will you? I gotta find my friends. They'll help."

This time, when Farley pulled back, Tsing let him go. With a hasty wave, Farley backtracked to the street at the end of the alley. Unsheathing his blade, he chose a dented watering can and rapped out a smart sequence of beats. They carried quite well and earned him a few strange looks. But he kept his head down and repeated the pattern.

After the third time, an answering *rat-a-tat* beat came from the direction of the docks. Shortly after that, people in the street stopped, turned, and scattered. Farley could only be grateful. This barter might require a touch of conquest, and that was Pred territory.

Larkin strode Farley's way with teeth bared and blades drawn. Looming large, he growled, "Why are you alone?"

"I've been doing some shopping."

"You agreed to stay with Torio and Artor."

"I did. Mostly." Farley flapped a hand at the shop into which they'd gone. "They're right over there, and I'm with you, so it's all good. More importantly, I want you to handle a haggle for me."

Larkin's eyes narrowed. "I'm busy with–"

"Not too busy for this." Farley grabbed Larkin's hand and dragged it closer, pressing it over his hammering heart. "Truly. This haggle's too important. And I don't know the language. Or how much is fair. But I've never wanted anything more than I want this to go well."

"That's what you said about that block of titian jade."

"This is way more valuable." Farley backed into the alley, beckoning for Larkin to follow. "Make this happen, even if it costs me my last copper."

The man glanced at the sign, and his mouth thinned. "What have you done?"

"Met someone lovely. Made a vow."

Larkin's brows shot up, and then they were before the cage.

Farley hurried forward. "I'm back, Tsing."

He struggled to his feet, only to shrink back, using Farley for a shield.

"It's only Larkin. Him and me are on friendly terms. He'll handle the haggle for us ... so we can be together."

"What ...?" Larkin's eyes were wide and wider. "*Farley* ...?"

With an innocent smile, he asked, "So how much does—oh, say, a *girl*—usually cost?"

In a strangled tone, the Pred asked, "For how long?"

"For good. Tsing will come with us. I already vowed it three ways." Farley guessed he'd teased enough. "Better us than anyone else in this port."

"Granted."

"Tsing's in trouble. I want to help, but I need yours."

Larkin grimaced. "Aye. I'll broker the purchase of this doe, but you will be the one on the binding block."

"The what now?"

"There are laws on every continent against the buying and selling of individuals. But the Mard bend the rules to suit themselves. If you want her, you'll pay their price and take her as your wife in a public ceremony. All of Turncove will celebrate long into the night."

"Just to cover up the fact that they're selling girls?"

"Aye." Larkin quietly added, "I didn't think you were the sort to make a pledge so frivolously."

"Tsing's life is on the line."

"And so you'll claim the rest of it ...?" challenged the Pred. "You'll see this through?"

Farley kind of wanted to point out that he could pretend as easily as the Mard. The wedding was for show. But he thought it was kind of sweet that Larkin was taking it so seriously. So Farley placed his hand under his heart and bowed in the Pred fashion. "Thank you for brokering the price. I'll wait here for the good news."

Larkin surprised him then, addressing Tsing. "You could do worse, miss."

When he'd gone, Tsing softly asked, "Why did you do that?"

"Because he's the son of a first-rate merchant. Scary-good when it comes to barter."

"Not that. He thinks I'm a doe."

"Oh! Well, yeah. He'll probably be annoyed later. Or relieved. Does it matter?"

"Why would you antagonize a Pred?"

"He doesn't like to let on, but we're practically brothers. So it's my solemn duty to make trouble for him whenever possible." Farley sat and offered his hand through the bars. "We'll set him straight after, let him know you're a brother, not a sister."

Those soft pink eyes flashed with surprise. "Brotherhood is a sacred gift."

Whoops. Farley quickly explained, "I'm offering the Floxish kind of brotherhood. I hope you don't mind? We'd be close as kin, but ... well ... where I come from, brothers are for backup, not for kissing."

Tsing's ears slowly sank. "I don't understand."

"I had a hard time understanding Pika customs, too. Guess we'll both just have to do our best."

Clinging to Farley's hand, Tsing brushed a kiss across his knuckles.

"It'll be okay. You'll see." And because talking was the only thing he could do right now, Farley asked, "Do you have any affinity? For stone, I mean."

"I'm not versed in stone lore."

So he rattled off a little about magical mountains, master sculptors, and living statues, and Tsing crowded as close as the bars allowed. When his ears angled away, Farley fell silent. The door banged open, and a husky Mard in a garish, fanged mask ambled through, dragging the end of a cane across cages as he passed. The animals shrieked and chattered in fear and confusion, and Tsing's grip tightened enough on Farley's forearm, there'd probably be new bruises.

Farley snorted and softly said, "Look at Larkin."

The Pred wandered in, hands behind his back, expression supremely bored. Right behind him came Torio and Artor. The Grif took in the sight of him and Tsing, huddled together on either side of the bars, and his confusion resolved into a cold fury. Artor frowned and gestured meaningfully at Tsing, who nodded several times. Another gesture, and he darted a quick kiss to Farley's cheek. The Ursa's gaze softened, but he pushed closer to the Mard, using his greater bulk to intimidate.

And then Dessa was reaching for him. *"Farley?"*

"Hmm?"

"Is what Torio said true? You chose a bride?" She sounded genuinely confused. *"I thought you loved Jubilee."*

Farley softly begged, "Not *now*, Dessa."

"If you are not in love, are you in danger?"

As if those were the only two possibilities. He looked pleadingly at Torio, who turned away to—very quietly—speak on his behalf. Which was probably only going to confuse matters more, since it sounded like the Grif had believed whatever Larkin related about him and Tsing. Farley chuckled.

Tsing looked incredulous.

Farley smiled at him.

"Torio says you are well ... and that I must wait. I don't like waiting."

"Everything's fine," he promised Tsing and Dessa both. "Trust me."

Because Larkin's purse dangled from the Mard's ragged claws. Which meant the deal was made.

"What manner of man hath horns?" the slaver asked

in stilted Verit. He was probably making an effort out of deference for his Pred customer.

Larkin ignored the question and growled, "Uphold your pledge. The girl is his to take."

The Mard's mask didn't completely hide his leer as he fitted a key into the cage's lock. "Our first binding this moon! All of Turncove will raise a cup and wish themselves in your place!"

With a clank and a creak, the door swung open.

Tsing didn't move, so Farley gently freed himself, limped past the Mard, and entered the cage. He helped the Pika to his feet, staying between him and his former captor. Back still turned—an insult in most cultures—Farley flatly asked, "What now?"

"Lead her to the block," the Mard replied. "Hear that? Wedding bells are already tolling."

A raucous clatter had begun in the distance, quickly spreading. *Bells* was overly generous for the racket. It sounded like the people of Turncove were bashing cook-pots together.

Tsing got up under his arm—one part huddle, one part support. Long ears pressed flat against matted hair, but determination flashed in his eyes. That was good.

Farley spared him a smile. "I guess they're throwing us a party."

"Their joy cannot compare to mine."

The Mard bellowed a laugh. "She *likes* the lad? Now, that's a twist! Don't keep her waiting."

Larkin sighed. "You're the one we're waiting on. Where's the binding block."

"Where else? Center square!"

He led them out, a skip in his step, calling for his neighbors to spread the good news. He wavered between several languages, and Farley pieced some of it together. Something about a pink-eyed doe taking a fancy. And a strange buck, which had to mean him. People cheered him on as they passed by, urging him to manfully mount the bidding block. Or … well, something along those lines. Judging by Torio's flush, not all their suggestions were polite.

They proceeded in a tight knot, and Farley let the noise fade into the background as he turned his attention to Tsing. "This is going well."

"Is it safe to hope?" he muttered back.

"Sure. You outwitted them all, and you're keeping your promise to live. That's worth celebrating with a ceremony. Hey, got any ideas about a vow?"

Tsing shook his head.

"What about names. Do you want to take mine? That's how it works for Pred bond-brothers."

"My name is all I have left of my brothers."

Farley said, "Then keep it. We'll just hafta consider you an honorary Meadowsweet. Kin in every way that matters, yeah?"

"You're too kind."

"Not sure this counts as kindness. Nobody with any decency would've left you in that cage." With a quick glance at the masked crowd, he quietly added, "Or put you in one. Really, you're lucky I was snooping around."

The binding block, which had probably once been a bidding block, was small enough that Farley and Tsing had to cling together, lest one jostle the other off.

Larkin asked, "Is there someone who officiates?"

"Nothing like that." The Mard said, "He can claim her any way he likes."

Frowning mightily, Larkin gestured for Farley to get on with it.

So he invented a pledge on the spot, pitching his voice so that only Tsing would hear. "You were alone, but now you're not. They think you're a girl, but we know better.

Your family gave you this chance, and you've made the most of it. I'm Farley Meadowsweet, son of Hayward, fostered by Aurelius, friend of Morven, and bound to Dessa and her get by stone magic. These wretches want me to claim you, and I'll do it. For your sake, not for theirs. Welcome to the family, Tsing. As far as I'm concerned, we're brothers."

The Pika flung his arms around Farley's neck and hugged him tight.

On every side, the Mard cheered.

Farley checked on his friends and couldn't help grinning. Larkin was definitely annoyed. Torio was looking dazed. But Artor's solemn gaze held approval. Farley wasn't sure if the Ursa simply appreciated his sacrifice ... or if his greater experience meant he saw through their pretense. He leaned toward the latter and offered a small nod.

Artor returned the nod, adding another hand gesture that Farley didn't know. He really wanted to learn more of this silent language.

Hugging his bride, Farley asked, "Is that it?"

Shouts rang out, rough voices making lewd suggestions.

Tsing's seller, who seemed to have some kind of authority over the proceedings, called, "A kiss to satisfy the romantics!"

Farley cocked a brow at Tsing, who didn't even hesitate.

It was one of the kisses he'd learned from Jubilee. The grateful kind.

"Get down here!" snarled Larkin, who drew two of his blades.

Artor held up his hands to Tsing, swinging him down, then beckoned for Farley to follow suit. The minute his boots hit the ground, Tsing went right back to clinging.

Farley raised his voice to be heard. "*Now* what?"

Torio dropped his own cloak around them both. "If you must behave impetuously, at least do it properly. Take your new lady under your wing."

"You really expect me to be proper?" Black feathers rustled as he fit his arm around Tsing's shoulders and leaned. "How about we get out of here?"

"Eager for the nest?" Torio's tone was light, but his gaze was wary.

"You could say that. Tsing's in danger."

The Grif's expression shifted into something closer to suspicion. "You're laughing at me. What have you done?"

"Weren't you paying any attention? I picked a bride. Tsing and I will be very happy."

Torio frowned. "You shouldn't take the wedding of souls lightly."

"Not you, too." Farley let slip a chuckle. "Worried Tsing will break my heart?"

"Not if you can smile like that."

Artor's big hands landed on both Farley's shoulder and Torio's. "Farley's bride is worth twenty times what Larkin parted with. Shall we get the young lovers aboard before someone else recognizes this one's rarity?"

Larkin grumbled, "No one will fault the groom if he is hasty."

So they ran. Or tried to. Farley limped along until Artor hefted him. Torio offered to carry Tsing, but the Pika muttered, "I can keep up. Just run."

Whether it was Tsing's huskier tone or his rebellious glare, Farley thought maybe the Grif caught on.

Torio shot a beleaguered look at Farley and repeated, "What have you done?"

Farley grinned at Tsing, and to his immense pleasure, his new bond-brother smiled back.

Torio brought up the rear and stayed at the top of the gangplank until Larkin was able to gather enough of his crew to post a guard. Suddenly, every shipwright and rigger was a potential threat to Farley's future happiness. Except … now that he thought back over all that was said and done, the wedding had been more about rescue than romance. Had his own circumstances colored his perceptions? He really wanted a private word with the brat. Ideally without Dessa playing go-between.

"How long until we complete repairs?" Torio asked Larkin.

"At least two more days."

"I'll encourage Farley to keep to his cabin."

Larkin grunted. "Wouldn't that doe be encouragement enough?"

Torio lowered his voice. "Farley has never wanted to settle down. Nor would he take advantage of anyone's—especially a lady's—misfortune."

The Pred inclined his head.

"I'll have a word with both of them. Sort out what needs to be done."

"Assure them both that the crew is aware … and armed. She's safe."

Torio excused himself and went below, striding along the hall to where Farley's door stood open. Artor was there, but Farley was missing.

His confusion must have shown, because Artor said, "He went to the galley. Tsing hasn't had any kind of meal in days."

"I see. Yes, of course." And sweeping a bow, he said, "I am called Torio."

Tsing dipped a small nod, gaze straying to the door.

Farley sauntered through with a heaped tray. "Hope you like spicy food. The fish soup is definitely a Harrow family recipe, and it'll test your mettle. But I found bread and butter, and I'll open a jar of petalberry confit … since this is a celebration."

As the savory smell of chowder filled the room, Tsing's stomach growled.

Artor nudged the Pika toward the room's small table, which was bolted to the floor. Farley unburdened himself and lifted a chair from its hook on the wall. Grabbing a second, he sat beside his bride, pressing a spoon into her hand before buttering a thick slice of bread.

The look she gave him held nothing more than weary gratitude.

Farley waited until she'd taken her second spoonful of the chowder before seeking Torio's gaze and lifting his brows expectantly.

Torio had no idea where to begin.

Over and again, this young man surprised him. How did Farley navigate cultural differences with such ease? He wasn't the least bit flustered at the way Tsing leaned into him. Had those scanty hours with the two Pika boys from the lakeside camp been enough to inure him to their people's lack of boundaries? Farley was rightly interpreting Tsing's closeness as a familial bid for comfort.

And when those bids were repeated three times in quick succession, Torio took a longer look at Tsing. "Do you mind if I ask your age?"

Pink eyes lifted briefly, then returned to her meal. In silence.

"Hey, yeah! How old are you?" asked Farley, undaunted. "It's hard to tell with Pika. Are you my big brother? Or my little brother?"

The Pika softly replied, "That depends on *your* years."

"*Brother*?" Torio echoed, feeling like the last let in on a joke, for Artor's gaze held bland amusement. But facts aligned quickly enough for him to exclaim, "You did well to hide it. Pinions and pinfeathers, lad, you're lucky to be alive."

With a wan smile, Tsing leaned more firmly into Farley.

"So? How old?" demanded the Flox. "I'm past twenty."

"I'm not."

"That's perfect. I always wanted a little brother. I do have a younger sister, but she stopped being cute ages ago."

Tsing shot Farley a bewildered look, then sought Torio's gaze. "I'm seventeen. Almost."

An ordinary sort of fact, but it slipped under Torio's guard like a dagger. This boy might have been his boy. Jaw set, Torio snagged the last chair, sat across from them, and gently touched Tsing's dirty, bruised arm.

Long ears slowly lifted.

Farley beamed. "Me and Torio are travel partners. If you stick with me, that means sticking with him, too. We're going to see the world. Every part of it."

Tsing asked, "I am … intruding?"

"No, dear boy," Torio warmly assured. "Though you may come to regret Farley carrying you off. He's a reckless one."

"I have reason to be glad of it," he murmured.

"*Sixteen*," interjected Artor. "That's why you haven't any rings."

Tsing blushed. "My covey was making a present of me to our benefactress. We're islanders, but we have close ties to the Snowmantle Cloister."

Artor looked stunned. "You're a Wentletrap."

"Y-yes. You know about our covey?"

"Your brotherhood is famous." With a glance to include Torio and Farley, Artor added, "All the great beauties are Wentletraps. Indeed, this young man is a prince among Pika."

Tsing hung his head.

Farley loudly whispered, "Hey, you're a *prince*?"

"More like … prized," muttered the boy.

Torio ventured, "I thought white fur was the marker for royalty."

"All the greatest beauties have white fur and pink eyes, but it's the eyes that matter most. Tsing has been blessed by Itzel to look upon the world with eyes like the dawn."

From the doorway, Larkin blandly said, "Brothers, is it?"

"Bond-brothers," Farley cheerfully corrected.

Torio hoped it wasn't a bad sign when Larkin turned away without a word, but he was back in a trifling with a jar. "Give proof of your promise in the proscribed fashion. Otherwise, I won't consider the thing done."

Farley's gaze sparkled with an admiration that put the barest of smiles on their good captain's face. Then he turned to Tsing and announced. "It's a family tradition. You've gotta share one of Ulrica's peppers with me."

The tub they'd used to warm Farley was still in his room, wedged between a steamer trunk and the starstone statues, who'd been secured against the storm with both tarps and netting. Larkin and Artor saw to filling the bath while Farley rummaged for spare clothes.

"It's nothing fancy," he warned. "And it'll be a bit too big. But that's how it is with hand-me-downs."

Tsing gripped the opening of his fancy robe thingie, but his voice was steady enough. "I don't mind. Thank you kindly."

So formal. Maybe even princely? But Farley decided to leave the courtesies to Artor. He really *had* always wanted a little brother, and having been on the receiving end of big-brothering all his life, he figured he was thoroughly qualified. Because Carden would have sheltered Tsing and found quiet ways to comfort him. And Ewert would have talked and teased until there was a smile on his face. And he'd already followed Tupp's quietly practical example by listening. And making things right.

"Will these do?" Farley thought the pants might if they were belted.

Tsing offered a doubtful, "Maybe ...?"

Artor wisely said, "*If* you add a notch for his tail."

Without hesitation, Farley reached for the slim dagger in his boot and attacked seams.

Meanwhile, Artor knelt beside Tsing's chair and declared, "Teach me the names of your brothers, and I will mourn with you."

"You understand," murmured Tsing.

For the remainder of the meal, Farley listened closely as Artor calmly asked for details about Tsing's lost brothers. Not just their names. He plied until he was satisfied that he knew something of the essence of each man. What they were good at. Who they were at home. Why they were important to Tsing. Then Artor fit that information into a kind of ... pattern of words. Farley supposed it must be traditional.

The rote had a calming effect on Tsing.

Artor definitely had more experience being a big brother, but Farley wasn't feeling left out. Not with the way Tsing kept reaching for him. They were small touches. The twitch of his sleeve or the bump of shoulders. It was almost like Tsing needed to reassure himself that Farley was really there. So he nudged and tweaked right back. And kept his plate filled. And undid the work of Aurelius's fine tailor by adding comparatively sloppy stitches to the seat of dun-colored pants.

Larkin didn't linger, and Torio also excused himself before Artor hustled Tsing into the bath. Farley stole a peek and was saddened to spy so many bruises on Tsing's pale skin. The Pika caught him looking and held out a hand, silently begging for him to come closer.

Farley dropped to the floor beside the washtub, propping an elbow on its rim. "How long since your last bath?" he asked conversationally.

Tsing stared at his hands before answering. "Four days ...? Perhaps five."

Not long at all. Less than a week ago, this guy had been surrounded by family, sailing toward what probably amounted to a kind of wedding. But any celebrations had been cut short along with the lives of his brothers.

To distract Tsing—and to make it easier to ask certain questions—Farley rambled on about meeting Greysallow and Hespero. Seeking Artor's gaze, Farley said, "Seems to me Pika don't sleep alone."

"Never," assured Artor.

"So ... siblings usually share a bed?"

"Always."

Farley had figured they were headed that way. "How's that going to work, though? We've only got hammocks."

"You'll fit," Artor promised.

"Guess we would, though we'll be snug as nestling Fwan. Did you know they sleep in baskets? I'm totally going to make them for all the nubbins next time I'm home." Farley circled back around to the matter at hand and flicked water at Tsing. "You okay sharing my hammock?"

A mute nod.

It was settled.

Or nearly so.

"He needs rest *now*," Artor said in an undertone.

Tsing muttered, "He is right here, and he is well aware."

"Guess I don't mind lazing around for the rest of the day." Farley sheepishly admitted, "My leg kind of hurts anyway."

Artor promptly dosed him.

Not long after, Farley failed at holding the hammock steady as Tsing—all elbows and knees—jumbled in beside him, which was more *on* him, at least until Artor steadied the swaying bed long enough for the Pika to resituate himself.

"Sorry, sorry," the younger man muttered.

"You've never been in a hammock?" Farley guessed.

"We didn't have them."

With a final flail to get onto his back, Tsing held still. Briefly. Because when Artor let go of the hammock's sides, it curled inward, neatly folding its occupants together.

Now nose-to-nose with the Pika, Farley asked, "Not even aboard your ship?"

"I ... don't know." Tsing wriggled and scowled. "Maybe they had them below deck?"

Farley didn't doubt that the Wentletrap princeling had been ensconced in a fine room with a wide view and a feather bed. "Guess this is kinda humble, compared to what you're used to."

Tsing's gaze lifted and held. "It's not a *cage*."

"Yeah, but ... you gonna be okay?"

"I'll be better if you moved your arm."

Artor lent a hand again, and Farley pulled himself onto his side. This time, when the Ursa let go and the ropes squeezed them snugly, Tsing's head was pillowed on Farley's arm. It was definitely cozy. Even more so when Tsing grabbed Farley's nightshirt with both hands and hid his face against Farley's breastbone.

Asking again if he was okay would have been stupid. He *wasn't*.

Wrapping an arm around him, Farley rested his cheek against hair that was as silken as a rabbit's. Surprised, he moved his hand up to cradle the back of Tsing's head. And pet his hair.

Tsing didn't complain. Only pressed closer.

"Is this good?" Farley whispered, looking to Artor.

"Mmm," was all he got out of Tsing.

The Ursa nodded approvingly and tucked them in, bending to kiss the top of Tsing's head. "Until the sky blushes in the east."

"Until dawnstone stirs beneath its kiss," the Pika whispered back.

A new way to say good night? Jubilee hadn't used these words. At least, Farley didn't think so. He'd been more than a little tipsy when bedtime came around at Day-Peep, so he may have missed the formalities.

It was interesting to consider the Dawnstone Mountain's influence. Thanks to her magic, a whole culture looked forward to mornings. Maybe Frey and Carden should invent some kind of moon festival and invite Flox from the surrounding villages up top. Might be just the thing. Worth mentioning.

The door clicked shut behind Artor, and Farley relaxed into the hush. Had Artor slipped something into that last dose to help him sleep? Or was it the day, wearing him out. He slowly rubbed his nose against Tsing's plush hair and smiled a little. Wouldn't this make a good letter home? Farley couldn't wait to tell everyone about his wedding day.

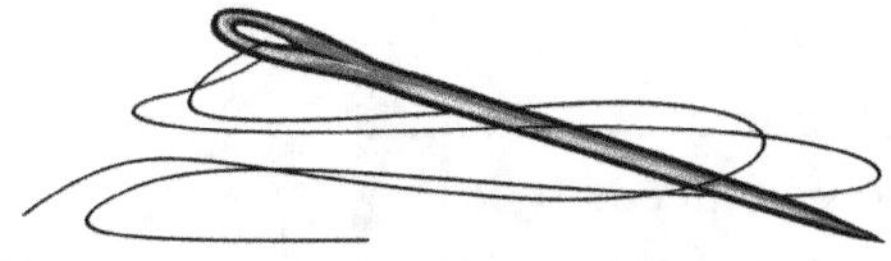

Farley woke to a confusion of sensations—too warm and heart racing. Had he dreamed of drowning again? The sea did seem to be juddering in preparation for another tempest. But ... no. A much smaller storm was trying to drench him.

"Hey," he murmured. "Hey, Tsing. What's wrong? Bad dream?"

The Pika pushed and pulled at him, struggling in his sleep.

"Tsing, you're safe. We got you away," Farley said, keeping his voice low. "No more bad guys."

He mumbled a name that must have belonged to one of the brothers who'd died protecting him.

"Sorry. No. I'm Farley. Remember me?" He pulled one of Tsing's hands up against the curve of his horn. "It's

Farley, the Flox who had enough coin to buy a bride off those Mard creeps."

All at once, Tsing stilled. Then a soft voice asked, "Farley?"

"That's me. I'm right here, yeah?"

Arms wound around him with surprising strength, and Tsing sobbed—harsh, hysterical, and increasingly hoarse. All Farley could do was hold on, patting his back and petting his hair. But then he imagined being in Tsing's place … and what it would be like if he'd had to look on while Carden, Ewert, and Tupper were killed, leaving him bereft of brothers.

He swallowed against the sudden ache in the back of his throat and tried not to dwell on it. But not all the tears were Tsing's anymore. "I'll try to be a good brother," he mumbled. "I know it's not the same, but … I'm here."

Artor's voice rumbled from the direction of his bed. "Pet his ears."

"Isn't that kind of … personal."

"That's why he needs it."

Taking his word for it, he found the base of one long ear, which was laid back against Tsing's head. Farley gave a cautious scratch, then lightly swept his hand over downy fuzz. The world didn't end, nor did the tears abate, so he tried the other ear.

Maybe he wasn't doing it right?

Farley tried tugging a little harder, running his thumb along the inside of the ear while his palm pet the outside. That finally got a reaction, interrupting the sobs with a hiccupping mumble. So he kept on, first one ear, then the other. Rubbing at the edges and gently pulling.

Tsing's crying tapered off, and there was a great deal of hitching and shuddering sighs. He was calming. That had to be good, so Farley didn't stop.

In the dark, Farley could tell when Tsing lifted his face

and squirmed up to brush a clumsy, slightly sticky kiss to Farley's stubble. Gratitude.

So he stayed the course, offering comfort in Pika fashion while Tsing wiped his nose on Farley's front, snuffled around until he found a dry patch, and lapsed into deeper breathing. Asleep.

Farley left off long enough to pat around for their blanket, which had slid off. "Artor?" he whispered.

A low grunt. A creak of ropes.

The Ursa shuffled over, fished their blanket from the floor, and tossed it over them. "Well done," he decreed. "He's had his cry, and it did him good. Don't let him go."

"Couldn't if I wanted to," Farley softly replied. "He's got me wrapped."

"Let him. He'll need this kind of comforting. At least for a while."

"Not a problem. Brothers are for backup."

Artor's fingers found the top of Farley's head and gently tousled his hair.

Farley whispered, "Until the sky blushes in the east ...?"

With a low hum, Artor returned to his hammock before answering in mellow tones. "Until dawnstone stirs beneath its kiss."

13

Basq City

Farley wasn't sure if the land ahead of them was truly blue or if the color was a trick of the light. The Basq port was an indistinct shimmer in the middle distance. A mirage, Torio called it, caused be the haze blanketing the seaside city that stood below the Freshstone Mountain.

"Isn't it strange for a mountain that wants sweet water to be trapped between the sea and a desert?" asked Farley.

Tsing ventured, "Maybe the area wasn't always desert? Lands change. Isn't the Basq city very old?"

"The oldest." Farley squinted into the distance. "Is that ...? Hey, Torio! Isn't that her?"

Leaving his perch on upper deck, Torio joined them at the rail. "Nerida," he supplied for Tsing's benefit. "She's known as the First Mountain, and she has been tended by Keepers the longest. In ancient times, she was considered a goddess, and over the course of a thousand and one years, her worshippers gave her form. Or so the story goes."

"How is that possible? I mean, I saw sketches in Frey's books," Farley muttered. "Even knowing what to expect, I still can't believe my eyes. They carved the whole mountain."

"Nerida qualifies as the largest statue in the world."

A blue mountain rose above the Basq capital—smooth and symmetrical, unencumbered by foothills. Probably because ancient stoneworkers had chiseled them away. As they glided toward port, details became increasingly clear ... and boggling. The Blue Mountain had been transformed into a twining monster. Coil upon coil, she wound upward like a landbound steelfin looming possessively over the city built within the shelter of the final, tapering curve of her tail.

"Will she move?" Tsing asked in awed tones. "You said blue statues can move if they get wet."

"Nerida's devotees gave her shape, but she cannot stir," assured Torio.

Farley boasted, "Dessa is the only mountain on the move."

With a faint smile, Torio said, "Last time I was here, there was some excitement over recent excavations. Over the years, Nerida's quarries have burrowed deep and deeper, and the farther they search, the stronger the magic. Teegay, her current keeper, believes they have yet to uncover Nerida's true heart."

"Can we visit?" asked Farley.

"We will. Teegay is a reasonable man, and though he sent me away, it was only because he thought others would be better able to help me." Torio quietly added, "I'd like to introduce Dessa to him."

"Oh, yeah? Where's he from?"

"Keeper Teegay Caterwaul is Clow. Upon hearing Nerida's call as a boy, he crossed the Expanse with a group of journeymen, and he's been in Meridian ever since." Torio indicated the land beyond Nerida. "This place couldn't be more different from the jungles to the east. Beyond the city walls is the Expanse, a wide, arid swath of land. It appears empty, but only because you can't see beneath the surface. Most of Meridian is underground. I'll show you around. The undercity is worth seeing."

Just then, Tsing gasped and pointed.

Farley leaned closer and looked. "What? Did you see another one of those rays?"

"It was ... a lady?" Tsing huddled close to Farley, eyes wide. "She smiled at me."

"Ah," said Torio, tipping back his hat. "This, too, is part of Meridian."

The water below was uncommonly clear, and Farley leaned out as they passed over columns, statues, and rock formations riddled with the same kind of niches he'd seen at Day-Peep. There were corals and gardens and the flicker of passing fish, all in improbably bright colors. Then Farley spied the coiling body and billowing hair of a mermaid.

"Whoa!" He nearly pitched into the water, trying to see. "Hey, that *wasn't* Livia!"

More mermaids came briefly into focus, their faces upturned as they paused in their activities to watch the *Moontide* sail overhead.

"Meridian includes a substantial underwater city."

"That's freshstone down there," Farley realized aloud. He could feel the pull of potent magic.

"Nerida extends even to here," said Torio. "Many believe her to be both the oldest and the largest of the magical mountains."

Farley's gaze flipped between the city below and the approaching port. "Was the city always there, and it got flooded? Or was it built by the mermaids?"

"A bit of both, I should think. It's only natural for the men of Basq to want to impress their womenfolk. All Basq cities hug the shore, for they are wed to the sea."

For several moments, Farley was staggered by his own ignorance. "You mean to tell me that both Phineas and Nerine are Basq?" They were the two statues who guarded the Harrow's courtyard back home.

"Naturally." Torio's eyes were sparkling. "Basq boys are

born with two legs and tame the land. Basq girls are born with tails and tend the sea."

"But how do they ...?" Farley stopped there, swallowing the question.

Torio answered anyhow. "They meet where the waves touch the shore, and their differences blur in pleasant ways. I understand it's a seasonal thing, having to do with tides. If we're still here when the wind and waves call them together, we will very politely be asked to leave. Basq don't like prying eyes any more than Flox do."

At the docks, Farley quickly realized that he was out of his depth. Again. "What language is this?"

Larkin spared him a glance. "They speak Coloq. It was Livia's first language."

There was a subtle boast there, and Farley acknowledged it. "First, but not last?"

"Aye."

"Is she around somewhere?"

The Pred's smile fell away. "Nay. That wouldn't be appropriate."

Larkin looked completely relaxed, which increased Farley's conviction that he was anything but. More cautiously, he asked, "Why are you here? It's not a job, is it?"

"Nay. I was summoned. We were summoned."

"You and Livia? How come?"

"Probably another round of quivering outrage and pointless rants about the inappropriate nature of our union. But I could not stay away." Clawed fingers drummed Larkin's thigh. "Basq women return to these waters to give birth."

Farley's jaw slowly dropped. "Livia's expecting another baby?"

"Hmm." The distracted sound was definitely an affirmative. "Scandals multiply, since it's the wrong season for babies."

"Because Pred aren't ruled by the tides ...?"

Larkin snorted.

Farley clapped his shoulder. "Congratulations. When will you hear?"

"A messenger already came and went. I'm supposed to report to the Circle of Twelve an hour before sunset for a public hearing."

"Is that how Basq handle birth announcements?"

"I'm not expecting *them* to congratulate me. I've been universally vilified, so it'll be more of a verdict."

"Just because you're Pred?"

Larkin bared his fangs before explaining, "Basq are a little like Pika. Most babies born are boys, so girls are treasured ... nay, they're essentially worshipped. Taking Livia for myself wasn't simply scandalous. It's sacrilege."

Torio strolled up, and he'd clearly overheard the last bit. "I'm surprised the Basq allowed you to live, given their famed jealousy where sea wives are concerned."

"I was half a world away before the truth came out." Larkin gazed pensively out over the water. "The men wanted my head, but the women were pleased ... and their opinion holds greater weight."

"What did you do to appease the ladies ...? Ah! *Daughters.*" Torio laughed. "Are they counting on you for an entire generation of fierce, golden-eyed daughters?"

Larkin rubbed the back of his neck. "Livia's mother and grandmother came after me, and aye ... in their eyes, I'm naught but breeding stock. Should Livia bear another daughter, they'll acknowledge me as a husband."

"What if the baby's a boy?" asked Farley.

"I'll ask for him."

Torio cautioned, "That's not how they do things ...."

"I know," Larkin snapped. "I'm aware. But how could I leave a son behind, knowing he might be demeaned for my choices?"

Farley asked, "What are your daughters like?"

"I have not met them."

"Why not?"

"Tradition." Larkin stiffly said, "No male is permitted to look upon an unattached female until she is ready to take a husband and prospects are called to the shore."

Farley was stricken. He knew how closeknit the Harrows were. It must be hard on Larkin not to be able to know his own daughters. Maybe he was *hoping* for a son?

Torio spoke up. "Your mother has a claim. Given half a chance, Ulrica would demand her maternal rights and make certain your daughters know to be proud of the Harrow half of their heritage."

Larkin's gaze turned inward, and he softly said, "Aye. Perhaps. Aye."

"So we get a verdict *today*." Farley doubted Torio had overheard that part, so he cheerfully tattled on the Pred. "I couldn't tell Livia was expecting, not that I was looking really closely or anything. But there'll be a baby soon, and there'll be a meeting later. We've gotta be there. Larkin will need backup."

The Pred groused and growled over the fuss they made. But he also looked grateful.

Larkin strode toward the Circle of Twelve with his head held high, mostly ignoring his insistent entourage. Fully half the crew of the *Moontide* had decided to attend the meeting. While not heavily armed, they weren't *unarmed*. If today's verdict imperiled Larkin's life, the Basq handing it down might think twice about acting upon it.

He could understand their agitation. Most Basq males never coiled with a lady lover, and even those who became husbands-in-name waited half a lifetime to meet their sea wife. And then, only briefly. None of these men cared that he and Livia had formed a mutual attachment. All they saw was a Pred and his conquest. An intruder and a thief. And an unrepentant one, at that.

Before they even reached the appointed place, a buzz had begun. *Twins*, they said, over and again. *Daughters with eyes like foreign gold.*

Old news. But perhaps they were merely marking him. Larkin kept his annoyance in check and walked on, ignoring the uneasy hisses and wary stares.

"What are they saying?" Farley asked peevishly.

Torio casually said, "About what you'd expect. But it won't matter. Larkin has triumphed over the lot of them."

Larkin frowned. Had he missed something? Surely the Grif wasn't more versed in Coloq than he was. He tried to pick out individual threads of conversation, but they'd entered the Circle, and voices hummed on all sides.

A delegation of men in formal robes crowded together on the low stage at the center of a sweeping amphitheater. Their heads were together in hushed conference, but they noted his approach and sent out a representative.

"Larkin Rakefang?" inquired a wizened man with a prim attitude and a pen poised over a tablet.

"Larkin Harrow," he corrected, since Livia had agreed that he should carry his father's name.

"Ohhh? Ah. A moment." He pursed his lips and made

a note. "Mm-hmm. Now, then. You are a father again. Though you can hardly have missed the news. All of Meridian is abuzz."

He shook his head. "No one spoke to me about Livia's child."

"They are speaking around you and about you. Even now." He twirled his writing implement to indicate the still-gathering crowd. "Larkin Harrow, you are an irregular sort of husband, but extravagant in your generosity. *Some* have the sense to be grateful."

"The child?" he pressed.

"Children," the old man softly corrected. And in honestly awed tones, "Your blessing has doubled and doubled again. Four daughters have been added to the sea, and by all accounts, they are as strong as they are lovely."

Larkin's astonishment faded into concern. His lady had been so tired after the birth of their first daughters. "And Livia?"

The man seemed surprised to be asked. "I am unworthy to fathom those depths. You would know better than any, good sir."

He glanced seaward.

Smiling, the old man murmured, "You would *know* if something were amiss, so trust that all is well."

"Aye."

"Now, then. The council must do what they must do." Angling his head toward the stage, he quietly added, "Apologies, good sir. They do not have the sense to be grateful."

"Your name?" Larkin asked.

The old man squared his shoulders. "Phandil roon Sellinia, head scribe for the uppercity."

"And a man of sense." Placing a raised palm under his heart, Larkin inclined his head. "Livia and I are grateful."

With a slow blink, Phandil inquired, "Will she know my name?"

"Certainly. Next we talk."

The old man's cheeks went quite pink, and he bowed low before waving to the stage. "Go up, good sir, and receive your due."

"My ... my friends?" The *Moontide*'s crew stood in orderly ranks, and many Basq had retreated to give them space.

"Are welcome," Phandil assured. "I will stand with them and serve as translator, should the need arise. Now, then. Go."

Larkin climbed the stairs, which seemed to trigger the start of some ceremony. The robed men sang something ancient enough to be incomprehensible, and by the chorus's end, the crowded amphitheater had fallen silent.

After a brief exchange with Phandil, who then moved to stand between Torio and Farley, a grim old Basq took center stage and lifted both arms. "Larkin Harrow, the Matriarchy grant you a name, a house, and a lineage among our people—First Husband to Livia pell Ellnoria. Though you be *foreign* ...."

There was the faintest of sneers behind the word.

"... will you honor our ways and accept your duty?"

"I will."

The man practically spat the words, but he answered, "So be it." Then he half-turned and nodded brusquely to someone behind him.

A young man stepped forward, nervous and possibly nearsighted, given the spectacles perched on his nose. A weanling child dozed against his shoulder. Cradling the little boy protectively, this fellow faced the crowd and raised a clear voice. "Phillit roon Nerissa is freely given to Livia pell Ellnoria." And to Larkin, "Tend him well."

Larkin's gaze darted between the man and the child. "Given?" he asked.

"Yes." And more softly, "This is a great honor. You must take him into your care before the men of this city."

Despite the lack of explanations, Larkin held out his hands.

The baby's minder took a pleading tone, repeating, "Tend him well."

No stranger to youngsters, Larkin propped the Basq child against his shoulder. He didn't wake, which was a mercy. As a general rule, Pred inspired tears and an excess of squalling. Still confused by this turn of events, Larkin muttered, "You're giving him to me?"

A single nod.

"Why?"

"To establish Livia's house."

"I see." So there was no way to politely refuse. Larkin frowned. "Are there customary words or deeds to make fast my pledge to this child?"

The quailing young man looked relieved. "Nothing set. Say or do what you will."

"Aye." Larkin turned to face the gathering. "I am Larkin roon Ulrica, a seafaring Harrow with the pride of a Pred. I welcome this child in the Basq tradition ... but also in the tradition of my people."

For reasons that were hard to quantify, Larkin's gaze slid briefly to Farley, whose smile held no trace of mockery. Whatever Phandil had told him made him look both pleased and proud. The idiot Flox flashed a sequence of hunter's hand signs that basically meant, *Go in. Go hard. I have your back.*

Taking a deep breath, Larkin committed himself. "A new branch is added to our tree. May he grow straight and strong. A new star shines in our sky. May he add glory to the name we bestow." Larkin swallowed hard and finished, "Phillit roon Nerissa is safe in my keeping. I will tend him well."

"You. What's your name?" asked Larkin.

Even though the crowd was dispersing, the young man who'd handed off Phillit still hovered nearby, clutching a bulky satchel. He edged forward, answering, "Pheldan ... sir. You ... umm. You understand a young one's needs?"

"Well enough." Larkin frowned and amended, "Only children of my own race. There are probably differences with Basq."

Pheldan laughed shakily and fished in his bag, bringing out a squat bottle. "For his scales."

Larkin hung his head. "Right. Scales. How often?"

"Daily. Usually after an evening bath."

He nodded and asked, "What does he eat?"

Edging closer, Pheldan said, "Mashed fruit. Soft grains. Do you have rhesha milk?"

Larkin didn't even know what that was.

He didn't bother hiding his ignorance, and this time, it was the Basq man who hung his head. "No, of course not," he mumbled. "Of course there would be many differences."

Backing up to their scanty introduction, Larkin asked, "Are you part of his mother's household? Nerissa's, was it?"

"Me? Oh, my, no. I'm ... I was never ...." His flush deepened. "No house claims me. I'm the servant of all, and it's only by fleeting good fortune that I was chosen to see to Phillit's care until your arrival."

Farley, who'd kept Phandil back to translate for him and Tsing, piped up. "Doesn't everyone get a family?"

The old scribe patted the Flox's hand. "Only the most beautiful boys are given into the seaside households."

To Larkin's amusement, this seemed to confuse Farley. "You're *not* beautiful? Tsing, don't you think Pheldan's handsome?"

"I'm quite commonplace," Pheldan assured. "Not a charmer like this boy. I was passed over during a first and a second culling."

Torio lightly cuffed Farley's shoulder. "You're asking very personal questions."

"How else will I understand? Hey, it's really different where I come from. And it's different everywhere else I've been." Looking between Phandil and Pheldan, he added, "I can understand wanting to stand out, even when you don't."

Lifting a hand, Torio asked, "Is the baby old enough to travel?"

Pheldan looked stricken. "You're leaving?"

"Aye. My obligations will take me away. But they will also bring me back."

"When?" he asked weakly.

"Eventually." Larkin studied the young man's face. "You have no other obligations?"

"No."

"So I could hire you?"

The old scribe raised a hand. "That is not our way. I'm sure you didn't mean to insult young Pheldan. Hmm. Mmm. Given your new role, it would be possible to adjust Livia's registry. If that is the good sir's wish."

Pheldan gaped as if the old guy had taken leave of his senses.

Larkin chose his words carefully. "How could I retain Pheldan's services while respecting your traditions?"

"You ... you can't!" Pheldan looked increasingly flustered.

"Are you afraid of me?"

"No! Well, yes. A little. Yes, I am." He bumbled to a stop, then urgently explained, "You'd have to add me to your household."

Finally. They were getting somewhere. "And how do I do that?"

Pheldan found the wherewithal to gape further.

Larkin turned to the old man. "Have I suggested something inappropriate?"

"This thing you offer? Hmm. Any man among us would consider it a great boon." With a nudge and wink for Farley, he added in Terse, "A traveler leaves the commonplace behind."

"Have you enough courage for this?" Larkin checked. "I won't force you."

"You don't understand. I would be your … your dahna."

"I don't know that term." Larkin looked to Phandil.

The old scribe wafted a hand, wholly unconcerned. "Pheldan would manage your household."

"Like a steward? Not a *slave*," Larkin checked. "I have no interest in robbing a man of his freedoms."

"A dignified role. You elevate him," Phandil assured.

Larkin knew the old man was being coy, but he didn't care. He needed help if he was going to be raising a Basq child in a way that wouldn't alienate him from his own people. So he appealed to Pheldan again. "There are many things I don't know. About your customs. About your physiognomy."

The young man offered a slow nod.

"Am I unfit to have a … what was the word? Dahna?"

"I really couldn't say," Pheldan murmured.

Larkin rubbed the back of his neck, then suggested, "Stay with us for the duration of our stay in your city. If you cannot abide me, we will part ways amicably. If you can see a way forward as a member of my household, then pack whatever you need, and you'll sail with us."

To his dismay, Pheldan dropped to his knees, bowing low and covering his face.

"Is he afraid?" Larkin ventured.

"Humbled," the old man said, his gaze soft. "Tend to him. Others will not look any more favorably on his elevation than they did yours."

Larkin could only offer a reprise of his earlier vow. "I will tend him well."

As soon as the Basq baby woke, he grabbed a fistful of Larkin's hair and shoved it in his mouth. He'd just spotted his new papa's pearl earrings when Farley butted in. "Hey, little guy! Come to your Uncle Far!"

Larkin yielded the child, and Farley grinned lopsidedly at the way Phillit's startled gaze turned into a gummy smile. Cradling him close, he strolled over to one of the nearby columns and slid to a seat on the ground. Tsing stayed with him, crowding close to see.

"Do you like babies?" asked Farley, slipping a finger into Phillit's sturdy grip.

"I have two younger brothers. They were about this age when they came to us, but that was years ago."

"So you're a big brother!"

"I am." Tsing turned the question around. "You like little ones?"

"Flox have big families, so I do my share of baby-holding."

Farley might know babies, but Basq were totally new to him. He smoothed his thumb over supple scales in shades of green and traced the long, sharp point of one ear. The eyes that blinked up at him were a deep, dark green with flashes of lighter color fanning away from pupils that were long and narrow.

"You have nubs," Farley announced, rubbing at the double-row of ivory bumps that decorated the top of Phillit's head. They were more elongated than Flox nubs, and he found more of the smooth ridges chasing down Phillit's spine, disappearing under the soft cloth of a thick diaper.

Tsing made a soft clicking sound with his tongue and

ran his knuckles along the scales on Phillit's forehead. The little one's lids drooped, and with a contented gurgle, he leaned into the touch. "He likes it!" the Pika whispered.

"He sure does." With a sidelong look, Farley said, "You know, if you told Larkin where to look for that island you came from, he'd probably take you there."

Tsing only hummed in a vague way.

"You could see your other brothers. We could explain what happened."

He looked up then. "No. Please."

Farley frowned. "You can stay with us, of course. I only meant …. Look. I go with Torio and Dessa, and we plan to travel absolutely everywhere, but … we'll still go back to my hometown sometimes. To visit."

"To go back would only lead to my being groomed and re-outfitted, to be delivered to our benefactress."

"You … don't want to go?"

Tsing repeated, "No. Please."

"I'll back you up." And boosting Phillit into the Pika's arms, he cheerfully said, "All right, little guy. Better get to know your Uncle Tsing, too."

Tsing was waggling his ears just out of the baby's reach when Larkin stalked over and dropped to a seat beside Farley. It looked like he was trying to outrun Torio, whose eyebrows were doing the thing that meant he was worried.

"Four daughters *and* a fosterling? Take my advice, young man," said the Grif. "Write home before the news grows any more complicated."

Farley said, "You can tell Tupp I counted all of Phillit's fingers and toes. And nubs. Which probably means that Phineas has horns of some kind under his turban."

Larkin merely grunted.

"How big will the nubs get? All the Basq I've seen have some kind of headwrap, so I can't tell." And catching Pheldan's eye, he beckoned him closer. "Hey, mister house-steward guy, can I see what's under your turban? Or is there some kind of sacred reason you cover your head."

Pheldan hung back.

Artor gestured for him to join the group. "You're welcome here. These men are as good as kin to Larkin."

It was probably a sign of Larkin's discombobulation that he didn't protest their claim on him.

With a shy glance all around, Pheldan murmured something in Coloq.

Farley caught on. "You don't speak Terse? Torio, help us! Ask about his hat thingie for me."

"Does your first question for this young man have to be something potentially rude?" Torio sat, and it sounded to Farley like the man was apologizing for him.

Farley waved both hands at the Basq. "Hey, Pheldan. Nice ta meetcha. I'm Farley." Repeating his name, he thumped his chest, then pointed between his head and Pheldan's turban. He mimed taking it off, and asked, "Can I see your horns?"

Pheldan shot a worried look at Torio, who must have translated some part of Farley's question. He answered in careful tones.

The Grif chuckled and said, "There's no great mystery as to why these gentlemen cover their heads. It's to keep the sun off."

And to Farley's great satisfaction, Pheldan undid a knot and began unwrapping. Most of the Basq he'd seen walking around dressed the same, in loose pants they tucked into their boots ... and with long, open vests over bare chests. Skin tone ranged from warm golds and rich tans to a gray-blue that brought Oxus to mind. And wherever there were scales, more colors came into play. The variety was intriguing.

Pheldan peeled away the last length of his turban and tipped his head to one side, holding Farley's gaze without a trace of self-consciousness. Something in his smile suggested that he was amused by Farley's fascination. His skin was a tawny sort of tan, and his scales were in similarly warm shades, ranging from honey gold to nut brown. Ivory horns rose above his head in a double row of sawtooth curves, with an additional row of smaller spikes alongside.

"Oh, wow. That's ...!" Farley got up on his knees, craning to see.

Pheldan turned his head obligingly, and his smile deepened into dimples.

"Hey, is he curious about us?"

Torio's brows arched. "If he is, *he*'s been too polite to say so."

"Ask! It's only fair. Tsing and I don't mind. Do we?"

"Indeed, no," said the Pika, who'd passed Phillit along to Uncle Artor. "Will you tell him that his eyes are captivating?"

"He knows he's fascinated you. It's plain on your faces." But Torio spoke again in Coloq, and Pheldan murmured his answer.

"If you're set on further exploration, Pheldan very sensibly suggests waiting for a more private setting. And permission from the head of his household."

Farley glanced around. "Isn't it a good thing for people to see that we're getting along?"

"He seems more relieved than anything ... that you've welcomed Phillit so warmly."

Turning to Larkin, Farley said, "Can you believe they gave you a baby?"

With a decidedly harried expression, Larkin countered, "Can you believe I have nearly as many daughters as my father has sons?"

Rather than be miffed that Larkin had left him out of his reckoning—again—Farley switched to Verit and quietly said, "It's not easy to outdo someone as amazing as Aurelius. You should be proud. I know he will be."

Larkin beckoned for the baby, wanting to make his own inspection. Phillit immediately grabbed two handfuls of loose hair and yanked. "Taking on a Pred, are you? Brave brat."

Farley jumped up, untangled tiny fists, then did a creditable job of twisting Larkin's hair into a hunter's topknot.

Phillit's gurgling response was almost a purr, and he wriggled up until his mouth collided with Larkin's chin, which he gummed.

"Not shy with his affections," Larkin muttered.

Farley snickered and passed him a handkerchief.

"So am I raising him to bond with one of my daughters?"

Pheldan stared at him blankly, and Larkin sighed. He'd asked in Verit, which was only useful if Farley could answer. The Flox did look grateful to be included in the discussion. Larkin repeated the question in Coloq.

The Basq opened his mouth, then closed it, seemingly as confused by Larkin's question as if it *had* been in Verit. Finally, he ventured, "Your esteemed daughters will do their own choosing when their turn comes to establish a seaside house."

"So I'm fostering a child as part of my duty to the city?"

Pheldan began to look worried again. "Phillit roon Nerissa was selected. He was freely given to Livia pell Ellnoria."

Larkin glanced at Torio, hoping for some clue as to what he'd missed. "Do I need to get that scribe back here?"

"Nooo." Torio crouched before him and switched to Verit. "How much did you know of Basq culture before you … eloped?"

"All I knew was the language. When she followed me away from here, I thought it was because we'd become friends." Larkin gestured helplessly. "My education about Meridian focused on stone lore connected to the Blue Mountain."

"And Livia has never mentioned lifespan?"

He shook his head.

Torio puffed out his cheeks and begged, "Courage, my good captain." Then he turned to Pheldan and asked, "What is the usual lifespan of a Basq man?"

"Seventy is a full life. Some do see eighty."

"And the ladies? How many years does a Basq woman enjoy?"

"Who can say for certain? Our memories are comparatively short, and we did not always have scribes like Phandil. His mentor's mentor was the first of our order, so the registries begin ... two centuries ago? Though each seaside house holds to an oral tradition. One of Phandil's most important duties is to hear their recitations and to set them down."

Larkin was having difficulty. "Hundreds of years?"

"Many do say thousands."

Torio softly asked, "Do you see why these good men might think they've encountered a goddess?"

Struggling for something to say, Larkin admitted, "There's so much I don't know. Perhaps you can teach me alongside my son."

Pheldan held up both hands. "He *isn't* your son. Phillit is second."

"Second ...?" And with a sudden clarity, he growled, "Second *husband*?"

The Basq quailed, but he managed to insist, "A great honor. A good beginning."

Before Larkin could fully bare his fangs, Torio delivered a smart cuff and sternly ordered, "Curb that instinct. Walk with me, Captain."

Farley swooped in to take Phillit, and Larkin grabbed Torio's offered hand, allowing the man to pull him up, then aside.

Only after they were several paces from the others did Torio face him. "Say it, then. Have it out."

In hissing undertones, Larkin seethed. "They expect me to raise a rival? To play surrogate to my successor? To ... to give Livia to another?"

"Terrifying, isn't it?" asked Torio, exuding a frustrating calm.

"Don't insult me. I'm not *afraid*. I'm ... they've ... how can they ...? Torio, they want me to live alongside my own replacement." He flung an arm at the Basq baby. "I'd sooner kill him than let him take what's mine."

"Not so. You wouldn't. You won't."

"I want to!" Larkin insisted. "She's my wife! *Mine*."

"She's a sea-wife, and it's your honor to be her First Husband. Don't trivialize an entire culture's way of life simply because you weren't raised to it."

Larkin did bare his fangs then. "You don't understand!"

"Don't I?" A new and dangerous light sparked in the Grif's eyes. "Look at the brother you no longer disdain, the winsome idiot who's even now worming his way into Phillit's heart. He's a guileless man whom I willingly choose to live alongside. Not that *I* have much choice either."

"What does Farley have to do with anything?"

"Dessa called him just as surely as she called me. He is *my* successor, and one day, he will be first in my mountain's affections." Torio's unflinching gaze dared him to argue. "A man who heeds a mountain's call is not so different from that of a husband who is called by the sea."

Larkin lapsed into a silence that was mostly stubborn.

He grumbled, "Nobody told me."

"Would it have mattered?"

Memories flooded back to him. Of unruly tides and a lost oar and a moonlit sandbar. Of curiosity and cautious friendship, of good intentions and burgeoning instincts. Of outrage and accusations and an honest attachment that had swept him away and carried him still.

Setting his hand over Torio's heart, Larkin said, "Nay. I'd take nothing back."

Torio covered his hand. "Prove your naysayers wrong. Tend that little boy as you pledged you would. Raise him to be the man Livia will need when the time comes for her to carry on without you."

Every instinct rebelled.

Torio visibly saddened.

"Are you done with me?" Larkin all but snarled.

"No. I'll stay, and I'll take the brunt of your displeasure. Better me, who has seen this face before, than an innocent child and a steward whose trust still hangs in the balance."

It was petty to nitpick, but Larkin sneered, "*Before*? I think not."

"You're wrong, lad. The resemblance is uncanny. You are very like your grandsire."

Larkin's wrath cooled faster than quenched steel. "I hated my grandsire."

"So did I. He hurt Farley." Easing closer, Torio begged, "Don't hurt Phillit."

"Nay. I will not." Gaze lowering, he quietly repeated, "Are you done?"

"No. I'll stay." Gently pressing his hand over Larkin's thudding heart, Torio said, "You may rely upon me, Larkin Harrow."

"I'm not ready for this," he admitted.

Torio offered a little half-smile and countered, "Neither are you alone."

Farley stole glances in Larkin's and Torio's direction. The Pred looked mad enough to tear into something, but the Grif had him cornered. Nobody was going for weapons, so that was a plus. The shifts were gradual, and Farley was surprised to recognize the postures. Was Torio doing that on purpose? Yeah. Probably. He was acting like Aurelius, slipping into the role of a parent. At least ... a Pred parent.

"I didn't even know Torio could *do* that," he said.

Tsing hummed and followed his gaze. "What's he doing?"

"Acting like a father."

"Why is that so strange?" Tsing pointed out, "Your Pred captain has accepted his authority. Doesn't that mean they have a guiding bond?"

Farley tried to think how to explain. "Torio's never acted like *my* parent."

Tsing searched his face. "Are you envious?"

"Nope, it's not that. I just ... I'm surprised ...? He was my master when I was a kid, but he let me get away with everything."

"He neglected you?" Tsing reached for his hand, all sympathy.

"Nothing like that, either." Farley grinned. "I was kind of a handful, but Torio never tried to handle me. He always took responsibility for whatever trouble I got into. He covered for me. Made excuses. Apologized when I wouldn't. Then turned me loose."

"He gave you freedom."

Farley slowly nodded. "Because it's all *he* wanted."

"You were the same."

"Yeah, we've got that in common." Farley watched Torio

set his hand over Larkin's heart and speak softly. Acting like the father Larkin missed … wanted … probably even needed. "I'm glad he never tried to take charge. I would have hated it."

Tsing's tone turned teasing. "Then Torio is a wise guide."

Farley was still trying to decide if the Grif had been parenting him on the sly when Artor ambled over with Phillit. "Your expertise is required, Farley."

"What's the problem?"

The Ursa transferred the baby into his arms before saying, "Phillit is in need of a diaper change."

"You're an expert on brothering in two cultures. Why aren't you volunteering for the job?"

Artor simply smiled in a knowing way.

"Do I want to know?"

"More like … you *need* to know."

Farley snorted. "I've change loads of diapers. Hey, Pheldan."

The Basq man snapped to attention.

"Any chance you have diapers in that bag of yours?" Without translators, Farley resorted to pointing at the satchel, then Phillit's padded rump, wrinkling his nose. "Time for a change."

Pheldan quickly hurried forward, arms open.

"I've got him," Farley assured. "I was just telling Tsing that I've been minding babies for years."

With some reluctance, the Basq brought out the necessary items.

This was familiar territory. "Some stuff is the same, no matter where you go," Farley said cheerfully. "Isn't that right, Phillit?"

The baby cooperated with a bubbling smile, cute as anything.

Pheldan still hovered, murmuring a question that none of them could understand.

"You can trust me, okay? I've got nephews and nieces

and cousins and ... umm ... huh. Is this ...?" Farley cleared his throat, all confidence gone. "Okay, this is different than I'm used to."

Tsing leaned in for a look. "What's wrong?"

"Not sure anything's *wrong* exactly. Maybe this is normal for Basq ...?"

"Hmm?" The Pika shot him a curious look. "You've never seen ...?"

"Uhh ... nope."

"Ohhh. Let me then." Tsing shouldered into position, saying, "This is the same as Pika, but with scales instead of fur."

Farley ventured, "No kidding?"

Tsing's lips twitched into the beginnings of an incredulous smile. "We've changed in the same room more than once. You never noticed?"

He was a little shocked, which only went to show that despite being far from home, Farley hadn't left behind all of his upbringing. Turning his back or averting his eyes was a normal sort of courtesy. Farley grumbled, "Just show me what to do."

Phillit was all fresh by the time Larkin stalked back their way, still talking to Torio in Verit undertones. "Nay. I don't want to ...!"

"They'll have records. Longer ones. Ancient ones," Torio countered. "Teegay can answer your questions about the Basq from another outsider's perspective."

"I'm not seeking the council of strangers!"

"Who *will* you turn to? Your father? Your uncle?" challenged Torio.

Larkin's gaze found Farley's, then strayed to the little boy in his arms. His jaw worked as he visibly calmed himself. Heaving a deep breath, he muttered, "Aye. I'll consider it."

Torio touched his shoulder. "I'll send word. Arrange for a private meeting."

The Pred grunted.

He didn't look so good.

Farley decided he needed distracting. "Didja know Basq boys stow their rigging different than us?"

Larkin's brow furrowed.

Torio groaned, "*Farley* ...!"

From where he loitered—still within earshot—Artor's deep, rolling laughter worked like magic, banishing tension and bringing the six of them closer for a brief lesson in sweeping cultural differences ... and minor anatomical ones.

14

Blue Mountain

Larkin wasn't quite ready to reclaim Phillit, so he left him in Farley's keeping and rounded on Pheldan, asking, "Is there somewhere along the shore we can go? A beach? Preferably quiet."

"Certainly. Yes."

"Lead the way."

The Basq man bowed low and murmured, "As you say."

The rest trailed after, leaving him to walk beside Pheldan, which soon grew awkward for Larkin. Although the man seemed content in his subservient silence, Larkin had never liked lording over people. Cooperation was more his style. Shipmates pulled together.

"Will you try again to explain your role in my household?"

Pheldan clutched the strap of his bag with both hands. "I haven't yet agreed ...?"

"Aye, *if* you choose to stay on with Phillit. I'm not rushing the matter. But while you're with us, I would appreciate your insight. Guide me."

"I would be your dahna."

That word again. "Can you give me examples? Something practical. What tasks would I fulfill compared to those that would fall to you?"

"It is not for me to tell you how to order your household."

Larkin sighed. "Pheldan, I need something more than vague terms and oblique deference if I'm going to do this. I'm *asking* you to manage my home. If I'm not pleased with anything, I'll tell you why so we can find a compromise."

Pheldan looked half-ready to run. "But I'm only ...!"

"Yes. You're the only one here. My one ally in Meridian. I'll be relying on you." Larkin wasn't sure how to put the fellow more at ease. He gruffly added, "Friendship isn't beyond me, if such a thing would please you."

Pheldan stopped, looking ready to argue. But then he closed his mouth, dropped to his knees, and hid his face.

Not this again. "*Please* don't do that."

Farley called, "Hey, Larkin! What're you doing? Why's Pheldan back to groveling?"

"Wish I knew," he muttered.

Torio stepped in, touching Pheldan's shoulder. "Formalities make Larkin uncomfortable. Is it too soon to grant him an inner room in your heart? None of us would be shocked if you made yourself at home with him ... or with us."

Artor and Larkin both offered a hand, and they pulled the Basq to his feet.

Again, they walked on, and as before, the rest of them lagged behind. Farley even had the audacity to make a shooing motion with his free hand. Once more stranded in silence, Larkin tried changing the subject. "Later on, is there someplace I can go to hunt? I would find it ... therapeutic. Even celebratory, given the day's events."

"There are deer in the Expanse. Small herds running wild."

"Fair game?"

"Yes. Though difficult for a lone hunter."

"Don't underestimate me." And with less aloofness, "Several of my crew are capable huntsmen. We'll form a party. You're welcome to join us."

"Oh, no. I have no experience with such things."

"Do you fear new experiences?" Larkin inquired softly.

Pheldan wavered, but he answered in a steady voice. "Don't underestimate me, either."

Extending his hand *may* have been a challenge. To Larkin's relief, the other man accepted the clasp without any sign of fear.

"Dan."

Larkin shook his head. "What ...?"

"My name," Pheldan said determinedly. "My friends call me Dan."

His surprise must have shown because the Basq's lips curled into a small smile. "Friendship isn't beyond me, either. I will try. For Phillit's sake."

It wasn't really all that different from what Larkin was doing. Trying. For Livia's sake.

Dan's attitude was still too polite for Larkin's tastes when they arrived at a quiet strip of sheltered shoreline. Gracious houses with blue tile roofs had been built well back from the water's edge, but nobody else was on the beach. That suggested this was one of the private beaches, and it worried Larkin. "Guests are permitted here?"

"No. Never."

He balled his fists and asked, "Then why did you bring us? It's sure to cause trouble."

"No ...?" The Basq indicated one of the houses, which practically glowed, so fresh was its white paint. "You are within your rights. This is yours."

"I have a house?"

The Basq gestured between him and Phillit, who was still in Farley's arms. "Livia pell Ellnoria has a house, which is newly established for the comfort of her husbands and for the continuation of her line."

Larkin muttered, "Nobody mentioned property."

"What's he saying?" asked Farley. "Why're you scowling?"

"This property. It's mine." He gruffly translated for the rest, too.

"Guess they were being literal when they said that stuff about Livia's house." Farley angled his head toward it. "Want to have a look around?"

"Nay." What was he supposed to do with a house? Switching to Coloq, he announced, "I meant to bathe."

"There are ample facilities inside," Dan assured.

"In the sea. I just thought ... the child and I." Larkin shrugged. "Don't Basq like sea bathing?"

Dan edged closer, voice lowering. "Boyish dares often lead to the water's edge. The pull of the waves his both hypnotic and ... and erotic, but we mostly abstain." Waving back toward the city, he added, "There are underground pools where rest and relaxation are permitted."

Larkin's brows drew together. "I thought your people loved the sea."

"It is our very heart."

"Then why do you *abstain* from it?"

He seemed momentarily at a loss. Finally, Dan ventured, "Respect?"

With growing incredulity, Larkin said, "You don't even know how to swim."

"No!"

"We could teach you ...?"

The man looked shocked. But his gaze darted toward the water, and there was yearning there.

Larkin made up his mind. "I'll teach you myself."

"Not here," Dan whispered, eyes downcast. "I couldn't possibly."

"Nay. Once we're well away from Basq waters. Today, you'll probably only get your toes wet. Unless Farley's dares make you forget yourself." He quietly added, "None of us will criticize. Least of all me. I swim with Livia every chance I get."

Dan looked stunned.

Larkin took him by the elbow and guided him toward the water.

Farley, who'd temporarily foisted Phillit on Torio, had already stripped to his undershorts. "Come on, Larkin! It's warm!"

With half an eye on Dan, Larkin stripped out of his shirt and shed boots and breeches. The whole time, the Basq stood transfixed by the wavelets lapping just shy of his shoes. Only when a scattering of water droplets pulled his attention up did the man see that Farley was knee-deep in forbidden territory.

Crouching before Pheldan in order to roll up the man's pant legs, Larkin asked, "As my dahna, can I insist you join me in the shallows?"

"I've never heard of such a thing."

"But it's not forbidden," Larkin surmised.

"Nooo. It's unheard of," Dan countered, cheeks reddening.

Larkin was enjoying himself. Maybe that made him as cruel as his grandsire. Father had always said he'd inherited his mother's vicious streak. Perhaps he was a meddler as well?

"I won't force you. But I'm inviting you to sit with me while Phillit and I get acquainted."

"If you insist."

"I do. Bring me the baby?"

Larkin strolled to the water's edge, taking a seat on the wet sand, close enough so that each lazy wave flowed up and around him, carrying a froth of seafoam. It wasn't deep enough to be dangerous for a little one. Nor should it have been terribly exciting for anyone bigger than Phillit. Yet when the first wave swirled around Dan's ankles the man gasped.

"Hand him to me so you can sit," Larkin calmly directed. "I want to watch you with him."

"Watch me? Why?"

"You clearly care about Phillit."

"I *do*!"

"Then show me how Basq tend their young. I can learn what's expected of me by observing you."

Dan murmured, "I could do that anywhere. Must it be here?"

"Nay, it can wait." Larkin gruffly added, "Just because I've given you an opening doesn't mean you have to take it."

The Basq looked up and down the empty shoreline, then wilted to a seat at Larkin's side. When the next wave reached him, his low laugh was followed by a breathless oath.

While the man came to terms with his own scandalous behavior, Larkin grudgingly faced his future. The moment he made eye contact with Phillit, the boy smiled, showing off four tiny teeth. This was going to take a new kind of courage. And application. Larkin stripped Phillit down so he could play in the water. Bathing was bonding. He was really only sitting with the child, but it was a start.

Phillit stayed close and kept reaching for Larkin's hair, yanking at tendrils that were straying from his knot. "Enough, little one," he growled. "It's only hair."

"Perhaps he misses his mother," murmured Dan.

Larkin caught on. "Males don't have hair."

"True."

"I'm not even remotely feminine."

Dan's dimples made a brief appearance. "You are not. But Phillit may yet hold memories of closeness and comfort."

With a sigh, Larkin loosed the knot and let his hair fall

around his face. The little boy claimed a fistful and crooned, laying his head against Larkin's chest. Trusting little thing. Larkin picked him up and asked, "If I'm neither father nor uncle, what is he meant to call me?"

"Pasha." Pheldan kept his gaze lowered. "He will call you pasha."

A new word. Normally, Larkin liked learning new words.

He studied the little boy's scales, wondering at their color. Yellow-green at their heart, other shades deepened toward a rich seaweed green along the edge. Given the choice, did Livia prefer greens to browns? Dan's scales were brown, and he thought his looks lacking. Was Larkin ugly by Basq standards. He'd never felt so with Livia. Finally, he asked, "What makes Phillit a beautiful boy and you ... less so?"

"Coloring." Dan stole a peek at him, quickly looking away. "Personality."

Larkin wasn't used to trying to differentiate one Basq from another. He wondered if he could even pick Dan out of a crowd. "Look at me," he ordered, setting his mind toward memorizing the lines of his face and the patterns on his scales.

Dan squirmed under the scrutiny. Was he blushing?

"If your women favor green scales, why are so many of you brown?"

The man cleared his throat and whispered, "I once heard that many of the sea wives are brown."

"Livia's scales are green."

"O-ohh." Dan's fluster intensified. "Sometimes, boys are chosen for the color of their eyes rather than the gradient of their scales."

"And yours aren't prized?"

A fleeting glance. "Mine are nothing special."

"Look at me," Larkin repeated.

Dan did, but his gaze immediately skittered sideways.

Concerned, Larkin asked, "Are you distressed? Is it the water?"

The young man nodded, then shook his head. "This is *all* ... very ... too much for someone like me. I'm ... if I were to ...." Eyes tight-shut, he whispered an oath. "I didn't realize at first. I'm sure I'll adjust ...?"

"Can you manage a little longer? Then we'll return to my ship. That may affect your decision." Larkin said, "I'm afraid it would be close quarters."

"I've never had much."

Larkin frowned. "You'll alert me to your needs, though. For you and for Phillit."

Dan only nodded.

Deciding not to press for more, Larkin gave his attention to Phillit, murmuring to him in a mixture of Terse and Verit. Though he kept his tone light, lest he frighten the boy, he confessed his surprise, his anger, and his confusion. "What am I supposed to do with you?"

Phillit listened, his fingers still tangled in Larkin's loose hair.

"We're kin, after a fashion. My oath is given, and I'll adhere to it, but ... I need time." And because it was true, Larkin gruffly added, "It would help if you slipped under my guard."

"What did you say to him?" Dan asked.

He took his time deciding how much to say. "Phillit belongs to Livia, and I will respect her choice, though it galls me." Echoing Dan's own words, he added, "I'm sure I'll adjust. To that end, I was asking the lad if he wants to be mine, too."

The Basq reached across to caress the top of Phillit's head. "Your second already clings to you. He will love his pasha. How could he not?"

"Take him," Larkin urged. "Show me."

Dan tried, but Phillit's fingers remained tangled in

Larkin's hair.

Unwilling to hurt the boy, Larkin said, "You'll have to do it."

"Do ... what?"

"Loosen his fingers so I can pull free." Larkin wiggled the fingers of his free hand. "I don't want to accidentally gouge him."

"Oh. Yes. I see." And yet Dan made no move to help.

"Is there a problem?"

The man's eyes were especially wide behind the lenses of his glasses. "I'll just ... loosen his fingers."

Rolling onto his knees, Dan coaxed and scolded Phillit by turns while working a finger into one tight little fist. Larkin helped by tickling the boy, whose giggles drew Farley and Tsing. Torio also drifted over, a faint smile on his face. He served as translator, sparing Larkin the necessity, and Dan managed to extricate him from Phillit's grasp. Which should have been the end of it. Except Larkin wasn't so distracted by Farley's ribbing that he missed the rapt expression on Dan's face as he let the abused lock of hair slowly slip through his fingers.

So *that* was it.

He'd blundered straight into yet another Basq taboo. Although Larkin hadn't planned for any of this, Father might have praised him for using such a mercenary strategy. Lure a young male to the seam between land and sea, coax him into the water, and invite him to touch his hair.

Deep-seated instincts were at play, just like that first time with Livia. Larkin doubted the man *could* leave his side now, and he wasn't sure how to apologize.

Dan didn't give him the chance. He switched to one of the promised lessons in Basq culture. "Saltwater baths are a luxury in Meridian. Those who indulge let the sun and wind dry their skin, and then soft brushes are used to sweep away any salt lodged along ridges or between scales. After that, a hot oil massage is traditional."

Torio translated.

Farley asked questions.

Torio diplomatically paraphrased them.

Tsing took the baby.

Artor came to sit with Larkin.

And when Dan next sought Larkin's waiting gaze, the Basq blushed so deeply, his scales changed color. Just a little. Just enough.

Certain as the stars by which sailors navigated, their course was set. Pheldan *would* agree.

Larkin had gained a dahna.

Farley thought it was a shame not to check out Larkin's new seaside mansion, but the *Moontide* was the only home the Pred was interested in returning to. He'd insisted on carrying Phillit himself, though he did it with a grim sort of resolve. Pheldan had to lengthen his stride and even add a little jogging step to keep up. At first, Farley thought he was still worried about leaving Phillit in a Pred's care, but the longer the two had their heads together, the less likely that seemed.

Pheldan was mostly respectful, occasionally flustered, and maybe a little in awe of Larkin. Farley guessed the guy would be staying on. "You suppose we'll need to make room for one more in my cabin?"

Artor said, "I wouldn't mind."

"What about Phillit," asked Tsing. "Won't Larkin want his baby close?"

"Definitely." Farley knew that much about Pred families. "Wonder if I should weave a Fwan basket for his cradle. String it up like a hammock, and the *Moontide* can rock him to sleep."

"You could do that?"

"With the right materials." Which he should buy now if it was going to happen. "Where do you suppose I'd get enough rope?"

Artor gestured ahead. "Dockside ...?"

"Or you could unravel a hammock." Tsing leaned into his side. "Could we have one, too? Maybe then Larkin would let us mind the baby sometimes?"

"I'd like that." Farley pivoted to walk backward. "Hey, Torio! Can you ask some of these merchants where we can get rope? I need a bunch. Gotta get the ship ready for a baby."

"Planning to put him on a leash?"

Farley was halfway through an explanation of his plans when Larkin's hunting signal rang out. He jogged ahead. "What's up?"

"We're stopping in here for supplies. Carry whatever Dan needs."

"Figures the first time you want me, it's for drudge work." But Farley grinned at Pheldan and asked, "What are we shopping for?"

Larkin said, "Phillit's needs."

"So ... baby food and diapers? Stuff like that?" Farley quickly added, "Can I get rope to weave him a bed?"

Larkin's gaze turned inward, and he conferred with Pheldan in Coloq. Somewhere midway through the conversation, things grew awkward. Larkin rubbed at the back of his neck, and Pheldan looked ready to drop to the ground again.

Farley hooked his arm to hold him up. "Pheldan and Phillit can bunk with me, if you want."

"I ... thought to clear one of the smaller storerooms." Larkin sighed and asked, "How much rope? And what weight?"

They split up, with Artor accompanying Larkin toward the docks. Torio stayed, which meant they'd be able to talk to Pheldan. Farley blurted, "How come Larkin called you Dan?"

"A nickname," Torio translated. "You may also shorten his name, if you wish."

Upon entering a building with a freshstone tile roof, Dan greeted the proprietor and strode confidently between narrow aisles. Farley peered curiously at bins of produce and shelves holding tins and jars. Most of it was familiar enough. He'd seen similar stuff back on Far Continent.

In the back corner, an entire section was given over to bottles. Some of it was definitely liquor, but Dan skipped wines and cordials in favor of small, curvy bottles filled with a thick, white liquid.

"Is it milk?" Farley asked, searching Dan's face.

The man glanced between him and Torio. "Rhesha."

Torio traded a few words, then explained, "This is rhesha milk, which is somehow culled from plants. It's a primary source of nourishment for their little boys."

Dan called to the proprietor, holding up all ten fingers, then crossing his palm with four fingers.

The other man laughed like he'd made a joke.

Calm and clear, Dan repeated his order, before gesturing to Farley, Torio, and Tsing. Whatever he said sobered the other Basq, who brought out an abacus and muttered as he flicked beads.

"Forty cases," Torio said in an undertone.

Farley only saw a dozen stacked under the shelves. Curious, he hefted one to his shoulder. It clinked softly, which meant it wasn't packed well enough for rough seas. Also, it was *heavy*. "I know I'm here to lug stuff, but this is ridiculous. I'll need the handcart. And extra padding."

"Use the diapers?" suggested Tsing.

"Dan is arranging for delivery. They'll load a wagon in the undercity and deliver it straight to the *Moontide*."

Without hesitation, the Basq selected other tinned goods, jars of dried fruit, and whole bolts of cloth. The pile on the counter was beginning to teeter by the time Larkin returned with Phillit in his arms. Dan hurried forward, talking fast, and to Farley's amusement, the Pred was dragged to an array of bottles, which he proceeded to sniff, one after another.

"The oil," Torio relayed. "For their scales. Dan wants to make sure their 'head of the household' approves of the scent."

Farley sidled up to Larkin. "Do they smell nice?"

The man thrust a bottle under his nose, and Farley caught a whiff of smoke and pine. Intrigued, he poked through the shelves in their wake.

"Planning to oil your curls?" asked Torio.

"Is that a thing?"

"In some places. The Drom perfume their hair with oils similar to these."

Soon Farley and Tsing weren't sniffing to be curious. They were shopping for a scent with as much seriousness as Larkin and Dan. Farley found a spicy one that reminded him of Aurelius, but he settled on something bright with the scent of lemons. Tsing took longer to choose. Finally, he showed Farley a slender pink bottle that smelled like a garden of flowers.

Farley turned to Larkin, hoping the Pred would handle the dicker. Instead, the man plucked two more of each of their chosen bottles from the shelf, handed them over, and said, "Add them to the pile. At this point, I won't miss the coin."

"But ... the cost," Farley quietly protested.

"If you feel indebted, you can take a turn laundering diapers. I won't ask it of the crew."

"But it's okay for me, since I'm family ...?"

Larkin grumbled, "You'll have to work hard to distinguish

yourself from among Phillit's other uncles, honorary and otherwise."

Farley crowded close to whisper, "Are you glad? Even a little?"

"Nay."

"Need backup?"

"Aye."

"Is it all right if *I'm* glad?"

Larkin bent to speak in Farley's ear. "If you're a rival for the lad's affection, I might make more of an effort to win him over. Put me to shame, bleater."

Farley laughed. "Deal."

A messenger came for Torio from Nerida's keeper, inviting them onto his mountain. Or more properly, *into* the Freshstone Mountain, since the only way in was through Meridian's undercity.

Farley trailed after Torio, Dessa's arm through his. "I thought it would be darker," he admitted. "Morven's deep galleries don't catch any light at all, but we're what ... three levels down already?"

Dessa peered upward, and the light from scores of skylights reflected off her cheeks in a scattering of bright circles and squares.

"Careful," he warned, pulling her hood forward.

She offered an apologetic smile and ducked her head. *"A Keeper wants to meet me."*

"I guess this guy was good to Torio the last time you guys were here. He trusts Keeper Caterwaul."

"I don't remember," she admitted peevishly.

"It was a long while back. You were ... younger, I guess? Just a baby, really."

"I was a block."

"Yep. So it makes sense you don't remember much." They came to a wide bridge, and Farley craned his neck to see past its stone balustrade. "Oh, hey. I think this is a river!"

"Fresh water for freshstone."

"You can tell it's not sea water? I mean, *I* can because of the scent, but how can you tell?"

"Nerida boasts."

"She's talking to you?"

After a lengthy pause, Dessa quietly replied, *"It is more of a lecture."*

Farley frowned. "Is she scolding?"

"No. She is pleased, and I am welcome. I think she wants a ... guiding bond?"

"Like a Pika mentor. That's really nice of her." He patted her hand and lapsed into silence, not wanting to interrupt her tour.

Nerida was so different from Morven. Her keeper didn't live up top like Frey. Instead, she called her craftsmen downward. The air had cooled significantly ever since they'd entered through the seaward gates. A series of waterwheels powered windmill-sized fans, which kept a steady breeze blowing across this level's orderly blocks of buildings. It really was a city, with open markets, shops, eateries. Homes were stacked one on top of the other, creating a blue maze of rooves, bridges, ladders, and stairs.

It looked like a great place to play hide-and-hunt, but he'd have preferred exploring that first level. The whole place had been given over to gardens. Based on the way things worked on Far Continent, Farley would have expected the Basq city to be full of fishermen. Instead, they were farmers who'd found creative ways to make tender crops flourish in an unforgivingly hot climate.

Did Drom have underground cities?

Did the Basq grow heat-loving melons?

Torio was walking up ahead with Dan since they knew the way. Larkin ambled in their wake, Phillit in his arms. Tsing and Artor brought up the rear. As a group, they stood out. *Everyone* else was Basq. The men they passed seemed to know all about what had happened earlier in the Circle of Twelve. Some of them looked suspicious ... or even envious. Still, they offered Larkin grudging nods, which seemed to be his due as the head of a seaside household. That part wasn't so bad. But Farley didn't like how often they traded worried looks and whispered behind their hands.

He might not speak Coloq, but he recognized Phillit's name.

They were acting like one of their own had been placed in the hands of a monster. And Farley wasn't going to stand for it.

Pred had the power to intimidate by reputation alone, but Larkin was very aware that he was one man in the midst of a mob. He kept his head high and his feelings in check. What hadn't occurred to him was that he should also be keeping Farley on a tight rein.

"Hey! You with the sneer! I can guess what you just said!"

Heads turned as the people nearest them fell silent.

"I don't know your words, but I've heard them all before." Farley seemed to be trying to meet every eye. "Only fools haggle for more worries."

Larkin fought for an even tone. "What are you bleating

about, Farley?"

The Flox spread his hands wide. "They're spreading lies and fear! Tell them, Dan!"

Pheldan looked to Larkin. "What did he say?"

"He's attempting to defend me. Leave him."

"No. He is within his rights." And with a fleeting touch to Larkin's arm, he started toward Farley just as Torio rushed to take Dessa by her shoulders. The Grif's attitude carried too much urgency for it to be fear of discovery.

Farley looked stricken. "Sorry, Dessa sweet. It's all right. Nobody's in danger."

"These are a peaceful people," Torio added. "Let me talk to them."

"I only wanted them to listen." And turning to Dan, Farley exclaimed, "Larkin's a good man."

Larkin hadn't ever seen this side of Farley. Even facing off against the Mard, he'd been frustratingly cheerful. Like he hadn't the sense to realize he was in danger. But the Flox stood his ground with unprecedented seriousness. He was calling out a whole city, demanding their respect. For him.

Farley, Torio, and Dan conferred briefly, and then the Basq spoke up. "Our guest has a complaint against us. Patience, and I will speak on his behalf."

To Larkin's surprise, the Basq didn't disperse. Whether duty or curiosity or some tradition held them there, they remained. Indeed, more gathered until they were thoroughly surrounded.

Artor came to stand behind him, making himself a shield.

Tsing pushed himself against Larkin's side and lifted a resolute gaze. It was difficult to tell if the Pika was trying to make him seem more approachable ... or if he was blocking Larkin from drawing a weapon. With their safety in mind, Larkin scanned the area for defensible positions and likely escape routes. That's when he spied someone watching from a footbridge that spanned the road. A rugged Clow leaned against a column, wholly unconcerned as he listened in with the attitude of an eavesdropper. Their gazes met just as Dan raised his voice.

"Larkin roon Ulrica is First Husband of Livia pell Ellnoria, and Phillit roon Nerissa is in his care. This Harrow is Pred, yet I could speak at length about his devotion to the sea, his gentleness toward his second, and the generosity with which he has provided for our needs. I have no complaints, yet Larkin's brother raises one against you. Farley Meadowsweet's outcry was this—*Larkin is a good man*. Do you doubt it? Before you further slander my onayr, please listen to Torio Kite, a friend to Keeper Caterwaul, who knows our tongue and will translate for Farley."

A murmur rippled through the crowd at Dan's use of *onayr*. Yet another new term. Contextually, Larkin could only assume it was the counterpart to dahna. His gaze skipped back to the Clow, who had to be Nerida's Keeper. Would he step in?

Then Farley challenged the lot of them. "You're worried for Phillit because Larkin's Pred? Show's how much you know. You should envy the kid!"

Larkin stifled a groan.

Artor chuckled and quietly asked, "How faithful is Torio's translation?"

"Nearly verbatim." This was mortifying. He hoped it never got back to Father.

Farley waited for Torio to finish before thumping his chest. "My foster father is Pred, and so's my brother's bond-brother. So I know. If you mess with a Pred, you're an idiot. But if you mess with *me*, you're dead. Because I'm under a Pred's protection."

Torio translated with a sardonic smile on his face, then inclined his head, inviting Farley to continue.

He did.

"This kid will see the world. Phillit will learn from every

culture on every continent, and Larkin'll probably teach him every language there is. Phillit will be the best hunter, the smartest haggler, and a decent basket-weaver. If he has stone affinity, he'll have a Keeper's support, and even if he doesn't, he'll have scads of cradle guardians and even more uncles and aunts and cousins and friends."

Torio stepped in again, and Farley's gaze swept the crowd, fearlessly meeting gazes while he waited for the meaning of his words to reach their audience. Expressions shifted—startled, conflicted, thoughtful.

Farley stepped right up to Larkin and offered a tight smile. "Gimme Phillit for a sec."

He yielded the lad. Which any Pred would recognize as a show of complete trust. Larkin had little doubt Farley knew it.

"Don't you dare think that just because Larkin could take you all on—and win—that he doesn't understand family. Or that he can't respect your culture. Don'tcha get it? Larkin won't take a thing away from Phillit. Larkin will give him the world. And I'll help. Because I'm the world's greatest uncle."

This time, when Torio finished relaying Farley's words, tentative laughter rippled through the gathering.

Farley kissed Phillit's forehead, whispered in his ear, then turned and tossed him back to Larkin. Like any Pred would.

Larkin caught the lad and softly grumbled, "Do you have anything to say on your own behalf?"

Phillit blinked up at him, gurgled a spate of nonsense, then rested his head on Larkin's shoulder before stuffing a finger in his mouth.

Farley rubbed his nose to cover his grin.

Torio took over. "Captain Larkin Harrow has been called a thief in my hearing, for he has taken a wife from your waters. But is he not twice sire to twin daughters? There are already four new ladies whose houses your next generations will build. Who knows what the future may hold?"

The Grif certainly knew how to make his voice carry.

"Consider this. Any sons you foster into Livia's house will return to you well-traveled, well-learned, and well-equipped to serve all Basq. Will you not need translators, merchants, sailors, hunters, and diplomats? Make room for Larkin Harrow in your city, and he will enrich it."

Farley was used to walking through Freydolf's door whenever he pleased, so he was more than a little intrigued that there were protocols to follow before they could meet Keeper Caterwaul. One of the man's apprentices, a Drom who knew Verit, led them through a series of rooms that held displays.

"Nerida may be vast, but biggest is not always best." The woman flashed a wide smile and added, "*This* room is one of my personal favorites."

They stepped into a world of cradle guardians. Thousands of miniatures, lovingly detailed, lined shelves and tiered stands. In some ways, it was a grander version of Frey's seaside cave, but in others, the whole thing fell flat. "Hey. How come these are all made from dull stone?"

Her smile widened. "It is said that nothing goes to waste in Nerida's galleries. Every resource, every leftover, and every individual brings value to our community. This room is a celebration of scraps. Every journeyman and apprentice who trains here adds a token in gratitude for what they have learned."

"Where's yours?" asked Farley.

"That would be telling." She laughed and explained, "If you know me, you will know my work. That is part of the lesson of this room. See if you can uncover the lesson in the next!"

She led them into another chamber. This one held a fortune in songstone, and Farley was immediately drawn to the central piece, which reminded him a little of Pollim and Eullia. Only in this version, the Keet was a woman. She seemed to be standing in a forest of some kind, because roots twisted across her pedestal, and there were mushrooms, pinecones, and small birds half-hidden by a sweep of ferns. With one hand over her heart, she sang toward the sky, seemingly unaware of her audience. The four-armed Furl crouched on a stylized cloud above and behind her.

"Think she knows he's there?" Farley whispered to Tsing.

The Pika considered the figures. "I think she sings for him, but she doesn't yet realize she succeeded. He waits in order to hear more."

"Must be quite the song."

"I've heard that Keet have lovely singing voices."

Farley slowly circled the pair, admiring the detail. "The only Keet I've met so far are stone guardians, but we're aiming for the Songstone Mountain next. We'll get our chance."

Artor offered a gruff oath. The Ursa had backed into the corner, and he sank to his knees to touch the floor. Only then did Farley notice that the native stone had been painstakingly inset with a tracery of small songstone leaves, their polished surfaces shining against the blue. It was lovely.

"He's smitten," Farley whispered.

But Tsing's attention had locked onto something else.

"He looks a little like you."

"Huh? Where?"

The sculpture was a smaller piece but incredibly detailed. An armored man with a helm on his head lifted his sword in a valiant display. Farley could almost hear his battle cry. But the wild part was ... the guy was astride a rampant dragon who looked a whole lot like Thrall. But ... the scale was different. Everyone who lived atop Morven could have hidden among her coils, none the wiser. This dragon was big, but nowhere near as enormous. A saddle and harnesses added to the impression that this was a truer representation of a dragon's relative size.

"Hey, is this a real thing?" he called, not taking his eyes from the small rider, whose helm was either decorated with curling horns or ... he might actually be Flox. "Like *really* real, like steelfin and mermaids?"

"Yes."

Farley swung around at the unfamiliar voice.

"Or so the stories go," added the Clow, who arched his brows as if awaiting further questions.

"You're Keeper?"

"Teegay Caterwaul," he acknowledged.

The man's skin was a warm brown that contrasted in interesting ways with the rich gold of his hair and the fur of the triangular ears set neatly against the shaved sides of his head. Most intriguing were the spots that decorated his temples, shoulders, and upper arms. The same gold as his hair, they looked like leafing, as if Keeper Caterwaul had been gilded for a festival. And his eyes were as gold as any Harrow's.

"Well, hi. I'm Farley." And turning back to the sculpture, Farley asked, "Where do you find dragons like this? Are they here on First Continent?"

"They're a creature from ancient lore, but some do say they exist ... in a hidden place."

"Why hide?"

"There are as many reasons as rooms in the undercity, and we're always adding more." With a faint smile, the Keeper said, "I think you're missing the point of this one."

"This room?" Farley snapped to attention, focus sharpening. He loved puzzles. "Starting with the obvious, it's all songstone."

Torio strolled to his side. "More to the point?" he prompted.

The answer hit Farley like a swell upon the sea. "These are all carved from the same block!"

"True." Crooking his fingers, Keeper Caterwaul led the way to a small, lidded dish resting in a niche. "Have a look."

Farley took it and peeped inside. There were maybe three handfuls of chippings. Nothing special.

The Clow said, "This display is counted as Keeper Phellis's masterpiece. It's the first of its kind, but not the last. Many sculptors have taken up the same challenge over the years, so you can visit many rooms like this one."

Torio indicated the dish. "Nerida's keepers are known for their unique patience and ingenuity. They're exceptional stewards of limited resources."

"And we are rewarded for our efforts with an inexhaustible resource." Teegay Caterwaul radiated pride. "We have yet to plumb Nerida's depths, and none has ever laid a hand upon her heart. She is reserved, yet she gives unreservedly."

Torio lifted a finger. "One would *only* call Nerida reserved if they've never seen her on a rainy day."

Caterwaul cracked a wider smile. "You're fortunate in your timing. We've been laboring under a drought all season, parched and patient. But this morning, Nerida began singing of drumming raindrops to the north. A storm is set to sweep down the coast ... and send my mountain into raptures."

Farley looked to Torio. "You've seen it before?"

"I have. We really are fortunate, but ... be prepared to be dazzled."

The Keeper spoke up. "This young man shares your affinity?"

"And my mountain. Dessa called him."

Farley gave a little finger twirl and cheerfully added, "She's behind you."

The Clow's eyes widened, and he glanced over his shoulder. Then he executed a graceful pivot, offered Dessa his arm, and brought her into their circle. "I beg your pardon, Mistress Mountain. Shall we explore the next rooms together?"

To Farley's amusement, Dessa inclined her head, but then she slipped free and returned to Torio's side. The Grif showed admirable poise when she fitted herself against him, but his cheeks did go a little pink.

Keeper Caterwaul's smile widened even more, revealing fangs. "As it should be, lady. As it should be."

"If I may interrupt?" Larkin bowed respectfully and said, "Dan tells me that I can access the hunting grounds from nearby. While the rest of you tour these galleries, may I take a group into the Expanse?"

"Are you trying to avoid me, Mister Harrow?" asked Caterwaul.

"I meant no disrespect."

The Keeper shook his head. "You'll have your hunt, and I'll even applaud your success. But first you'll endure the same tour that every guest must take. It's one of our little rules."

Larkin merely said, "Of course."

Farley hadn't realized they were all conversing in Terse until Larkin bent his head to translate for Dan, who looked ready to drop to his knees over the honor of it all. Or something. Thankfully, Larkin curtailed him by placing Phillit in his arms and steering him forward with a firm grip on his upper arm.

All things considered, the two of them were getting

along quite well. It was almost funny. Because it meant that Farley was *still* at the bottom of the pecking order.

"I want to tear something to pieces," muttered Larkin.

Dan hesitated before asking, "Is that how Pred hunt?"

"Nay. Well, some do. I prefer a clean kill." And since he wanted to be understood, he went further. "They gave me Phillit, but they will not let me see my own daughters." It may have come out with a whine.

"Pred keep their sons *and* daughters?"

"We do."

"Do you feel ... wronged?" Dan asked in an undertone.

Larkin grudgingly conceded, "Nay. But I *am* frustrated by something even Livia considers a necessity. Do you think ... if I had a son ...?"

Dan frowned. "If he is beautiful, he would be given into another seaside household."

"I have no claim?"

"Livia does. Phillit was not simply taken from his mother. He was freely given by Sellinia."

That gave Larkin pause. "Did Sellinia know about me? That her son was going into a Pred's hands?"

"Who am I to know such things?" But Dan quietly added, "The sea wives want daughters."

"And *don't* want their sons?"

The Basq opened his mouth, closed it firmly, and simply shrugged.

"I want my sons."

Dan searched his face, then nodded. "If Livia gives you sons, they will be loved and guided by their pasha."

This was a welcome revelation. It would seem his new

dahna knew the answers to questions Larkin hadn't even realized he could ask. At the earliest opportunity, he would speak to Livia about the future of any sons they might have together.

As they trailed after Keeper Caterwaul and the rest, Dan ventured, "How do Pred fathers interact with their daughters?"

Larkin thought the question strange, then realized why it wasn't. "Girls and boys grow up alongside each other. Some lore is handed down from father to son and from mother to daughter, but … my mother was my primary guide. I shared her passion for languages."

"How strange. I cannot even …." He sorted out his thoughts, and confessed, "It sounds idyllic."

With a short laugh, Larkin said, "You might revise your opinion once you meet my mother."

Dan's eyes widened. "Is such a thing possible?"

"Aye. Gather your courage, friend. You'll need it."

"Harrow."

Larkin's gaze jumped around before snapping to Keeper Caterwaul's face. He wasn't used to his new surname yet, and with his thoughts lingering on his parents, he'd half-expected his father to somehow be there. Such a thing wasn't totally impossible. Aurelius *did* still travel on Uncle Freydolf's behalf.

But no, the Keeper was only beckoning to him. Dismissing a fleeting pang of loss, Larkin obliged, steering Dan his way.

"Through here." The Clow pressed a flower, which tripped a latch, and an ornately carved panel swung inward, allowing passage. His gaze drifted to Dan before he asked, "How much privacy do you want for our chat, Mister Harrow?"

Dan immediately lowered his gaze.

Larkin kept his hold on the Basq's arm. "He's my dahna."

Turning his back, Caterwaul drawled, "Aren't you a

fortunate fellow."

When Dan relaxed, it rankled that Larkin wasn't sure why. And for the life of him, he couldn't work out which of them the Clow meant. Was *he* the fortunate one? Or did he mean Dan?

Stairs spiraled down into darkness, but Caterwaul paused long enough to flick a match and touch the wicks of three beveled glass lanterns that scattered tiny rainbows like prismatic sparkflies. Something tugged him from behind, and Larkin glanced back. Dan had him by the shirt. "Something amiss?"

"Sorry. It's um ...." His gaze skittered to the blackness beyond the stair rail.

"Heights?"

Dan shook his head, nodded, but shook his head again. "Depths."

He looked so uneasy, Larkin asked, "Want me to take Phillit?"

"Would you?" His voice was high and tight.

Well, now. If Farley had been the one clinging to him, Larkin's blade would be bare, and a sneer would accompany his insult. But he couldn't imagine calling Dan a *milk-faced weanling* for this. And Larkin couldn't decide if that made Farley special ... or his new dahna special. Or perhaps Larkin was making allowances for Dan in the same way his father did to the Meadowsweet family.

Larkin beckoned for Phillit, and when the exchange was made, Dan's hand returned to grip Larkin's shirt. With a sigh, he called, "Keeper. Take this for me."

The Clow glided back to take Larkin's lantern.

"Give me yours," he directed.

Dan surrendered his light, mumbling apologies.

"I'm the only one who owes apologies. Not much further, young friend," promised Keeper Caterwaul.

"Hold my belt," murmured Larkin. And so they continued.

True to the Keeper's word, it wasn't far. Another swinging

panel opened into a spacious room that seemed too bright to be this far underground. Polished blue stone reflected the illumination of dozens of lanterns, each fitted with frosted glass that diffused the light. Larkin immediately noted the change underfoot, for the room had wood flooring. Old and thick and riddled with dings and divots, it had clearly seen many years of use.

Larkin asked, "Is this your workshop?"

"One of them, yes." Caterwaul walked to a dressed block of redstone and touched it as if in greeting. In Coloq, so Dan could follow the conversation, he asked, "May I be blunt?"

"Aye."

"Torio asked me to speak with you."

Larkin grunted.

Eyebrows lifting, the Clow said, "You've become a husband of the sea. Few would have believed that one of their ladies would ever call an outsider."

"Torio compared my call to his."

Caterwaul nodded briskly. "A mountain calls whom she will. And it seems the same could be said of the sea and her beauties."

"I was a man of the sea before I ever met Livia."

"Such a surly glare." Instead of being intimidated, the Keeper smiled. "You gave me that same look before clambering onto my lap and pulling my ears."

Larkin stiffened. "What ...?"

"You were such a serious child. Perhaps three or four years old. Demanded I speak to you in my native language."

"I know I've been here but ... I don't recall."

"In his last letter, Aurelius asked me to do whatever I could for you. Let me." Inclining his head to Dan, he included him in his question. "Is there anything I can offer."

"Answers ... perhaps?" Larkin looked to Dan.

The Basq cleared his throat. "Meridian's written records only go back two centuries, and oral tradition is difficult to substantiate. Perhaps Nerida's records are more ... robust?"

Caterwaul warned, "Most of our information revolves around stonecrafting. Remarks about the Basq city are largely incidental. But Nerida called more than eight hundred Keepers before me, and some were Basq. Are we not part of the same community? Ask."

Dan offered his hands to take Phillit, but Larkin's hold tightened. Was he using the babe as a shield? He kept it simple. "Do you know how long a Basq female lives?"

"Not as long as mountains, but beyond several generations of their male counterparts."

"But surely not forever. Nothing lives forever."

The Keeper's ears quivered, as if hearing another voice. "That would be like saying something made from stone is not alive."

Larkin didn't like talking in circles. "So ... these Basq are magic?"

"Facts. I can tell you that none of the established houses have ever stood empty, and they are *old*."

"This is true," Dan quietly interjected.

Caterwaul acknowledged him with a nod. "I can tell you that this is the oldest of the Twelve. Pardon me, the Thirteen. And one of the early keepers was Basq and a husband himself. Many of his statues, including his masterpiece, were dedicated to his sea wife, Marinnia."

Larkin went still. This was a name he knew. Indeed, he knew the loveliness of her face and the keen edge of her tongue, for she'd been furious with him for making a conquest of her granddaughter.

"An early Keeper?" he managed. "How long ago was this mention of Marinnia?"

Caterwaul was studying his face as he absently reached for a thick pad of paper. Larkin had little doubt that the man was sketching him. Perhaps he should commission a statue for Livia to remember him by? Nay.

That was leaving things to the wrong person. Far better that he live alongside her in such a way that she never, ever forgot him.

"How long, sir?"

"Hmm?" The Clow answered distractedly. "Keeper Phond managed wisely and well during the decades when Nerida's serpentine form was first planned."

Charcoal whispered across the page.

Larkin traded a look with Dan, then patiently repeated, "How long, sir?"

"Well, now, let me think. Yes. That would have been ... six thousand years ago."

15

Tests of Courage

There was no way Farley was going to visit a mountain that had been carved into the world's largest sculpture and not climb her. Torio was surprisingly easy to convince that scaling the giant serpent was worth the effort, and both Artor and Tsing were glad to agree with Farley's plan. Only Larkin begged off, wanting to make preparations for his trek into the Expanse with his people.

"What if the rains come while you're in the middle of nowhere?" asked Farley.

Larkin said, "We'll take shelter."

"But you'll miss the magic!"

"I'm a dullard. The effects would be lost on me."

"You can't see the magic, but you can see the statues. And Teegay said there are displays that past keepers created especially for rainy days!"

"I don't smell rain yet. I think we have time."

"Oh, right. You should go. Isn't this how Pred dads celebrate the birth of a kid?" When Larkin grunted, Farley added, "Save me a haunch?"

Something glittered in Larkin's eyes, and it didn't bode well for any of the critters currently wandering in his chosen hunting grounds. "We shall feast."

Farley guessed they'd each be having fun in their own way. "Want us to take Phillit?"

"Aye. Artor already has Dan's bag and the rhesha milk."

"Is the little guy gonna be okay in this heat?" The afternoon was getting on, and though Torio had assured him that summers here were *much* hotter, standing between sun and stone meant getting baked.

"Ask Dan."

So they backtracked to where the rest of the group had gathered in the shade. Artor sat on the ground, legs outstretched, and he beckoned for Larkin to hand down the baby.

Farley *meant* to ask Dan about Phillit, but he was distracted by a new development. The Basq was wrapping Tsing's head in a turban, right over his ears, which were pressed down and back so their length fell behind Tsing's shoulders. "Doesn't that hurt your ears?"

Tsing replied, "Not at all. In the Cloisters, it's good manners to fold. This is considered ... *demure*." He pouted up at Farley, adding, "And it's better than the alternative. I burn and ... and freckle!"

Farley checked, "Freckles are bad?"

"Bucks have been rejected for spottiness."

"Oh. So you *do* still want those cloistered ladies to accept you?"

"Nooo." Tsing's pale lashes fluttered. "No. I don't need *them*."

"Then why not raise a crop of freckles?"

The Pika fidgeted on his seat, then mumbled, "Because then I'd be spotty."

"Okay, okay. I get it."

Torio asked Dan something, and the man responded. With a nod, Torio relayed, "Some of the apothecaries will have Pika-made medicines. We should check for sun creams before setting sail. And possibly a brimmed hat with proper ear holes."

Tsing mumbled his thanks.

Farley plunked down beside him, done teasing. "Hey, Dan? Can I have one, too? A turban, I mean?"

After a quick exchange, Torio relayed, "He didn't bring any other headscarves."

"We could wrap him in diapers," suggested Larkin.

"Couldn't I buy some cloths? I really want to try."

"It would be a sensible way to hide your horns," Torio pointed out. "Should any further need arise."

Dan asked something then, and both Torio and Larkin seemed to be catching him up, then Dan smiled into Farley's eyes and gestured to his own head. His next question was definitely an offer.

"He'll loan you his," said Larkin. "And stop at an apothecary on our way back to the *Moontide*."

"Hey, that'd be great! Thanks!"

With deft twists and tucks, Dan began, then backtracked, muttering to himself.

"What's wrong?" he whispered to Tsing.

"You're kind of ... lumpy. It's the horns." A minute later, he reported, "Dan's working around them now. It's much better."

When Dan stepped back, Farley carefully patted at his head. The cloth had been wound around and under his horns, so that the fullness of the cloth was mostly where it belonged, on the crown of his head. Tsing fiddled with the drape of the trailing end, which had been left loose to protect the back of his neck.

Farley asked, "Well? Do I look Basq-ish?"

"With tiny round ears and a big blue eyes?" Tsing teased.

"You can't pass as Basq, but the headgear does give you a certain ... dignity," said Torio.

He thanked Dan again, and the man murmured something.

Larkin immediately clammed up, but Torio was only too happy to translate. "Anything for his onayr's brother."

It took a moment to process the new word. "Larkin's a what now?"

The Pred grumbled and stalked off, calling for Dan to follow, leaving the explanation to Torio.

"I gather that it's a respectful form of address for the head of a seaside household. In Verit, the best translations for onayr and dahna would probably be … master and steward. Pheldan will manage Larkin's household."

Farley gazed after them. "That's it then. He's coming with us."

Torio hummed an affirmative. "I think Larkin's invitation represents a considerable step up in Basq society."

"I think Dan wants to have adventures."

"Travel does seem to appeal to him." The Grif nodded toward Artor. "And there's Phillit to consider."

Farley swore under his breath. "I forgot to ask if it's too hot for little Basq boys."

"He'll be fine," assured Artor, who levered himself up. "I'll make certain of it."

So they started along the uphill road that curled to the top of the Freshstone Mountain. It wasn't terribly steep, which must have been good for the workers and their wagons. At this rate, surmounting Nerida would be little more than a leisurely stroll. Not at all what Farley was after. So he pointed to the swell of the coiled scales on the uphill side of the road and announced, "I'm going this way."

Tsing shot him a look of disbelief. "You mean … climb?"

"I wanted to *climb* a mountain. So yeah … I'm gonna climb. What do you say?"

The Pika studied the vast serpent and came to the same conclusion Farley had. "The way it's carved, it wouldn't be too hard."

"Easy as climbing a ladder." Farley raised his brows at Torio. "Want to?"

The Grif patted his side. "Still recovering. I'll walk with Dessa and Artor."

"No, I'll climb, too," announced Dessa. She slipped out of her feathered cloak and passed it to Torio. *"I'll make sure Farley doesn't crack."*

"Fine by me. Come on, Dessa! Let's see the view from the top!"

Farley leaned contentedly into Dessa, pleased that his fancy new turban acted a little like a pillow, cushioning his head against her shoulder.

"Come here with us," he urged, beckoning to Tsing.

The Pika was still out of breath from the climb and too stubborn to admit it.

"Tell him my lap is soft, even if I am stone."

Farley said, "She's offering her lap. You don't want to disappoint a lady, do you?"

Tsing slowly inclined his head. "Does she really want me?"

"I'm not teasing. This time." He held out a hand. "You won't be too heavy, and ... I think she's curious. You are, aren't you, Dessa sweet?"

"Jubilee liked me, but this one never comes close. Is he afraid of me?"

"Uh-oh. Now she's calling your courage into question." Farley quietly asked, "Are you afraid of her?"

"No!" Tsing hurriedly dropped to one knee before Dessa and offered his hand. "But I'm not used to grand ladies. I never met one before, and my readying ... well. I don't know what I'm supposed to do."

"Sisters aren't all that different from brothers. You let *me* hold you. Dessa wants to hold you, too."

Tsing scooted forward, and Dessa grabbed hold, pulling him onto her lap. She pressed his head against her opposite shoulder and favored Farley with a smug smile. *"I have tamed him."*

Farley laughed. "Relax, Tsing. She's pleased by her acquisition. Rest."

"I want to know things. Ask for me, Farley?"

"Sure thing. What did you want to know about Tsing?"

"Freydolf often worked with Dapple, and it might be Carden's favorite stone. But it's freckled. Does Tsing hate it?"

He relayed the question.

Tsing fumbled through an awkward explanation that ended in an admission that he didn't even know what Dapple was.

"It's one of the other magical stones. All dabs and speckles. We can probably find some in the galleries later. Carden—he's the oldest brother—likes it well enough, so there was talk of sending him to Last Continent, mostly to see if Kasumi was calling him."

"Oh. I didn't know." The Pika wriggled to get more comfortable, then whispered, "Where do I put my hand?"

"Right here." Farley grabbed hold.

Dessa looped her arm around him, and Tsing mumbled, "Feels real."

"Yep. That's how it is with living stone." Farley asked, "Any other questions, Dessa?"

"Does he love you? I can't tell. With Jubilee it was easier, but ... he had affinity."

That sparked Farley's curiosity. "Can you tell how other people with affinity feel? Like that Drom apprentice? Or Keeper Caterwaul?"

"Yes. Always."

"You mean ... you can tell if someone has affinity, just by

being near them?" Farley asked, amazed.

"*Yes ...? Why are you surprised?*"

"I didn't know!"

"*Oh. Well, I do. And now you know.*"

Tsing asked, "What did she want to know?"

"She wanted to know if you love me."

The Pika seemed baffled. "It's only natural."

"Well, yeah. But some things are easier for her to understand than others. So we talk it out and try to explain. It's interesting, seeing the world through a mountain's eyes."

Tsing peeped up at Dessa through his lashes. "How do you see if you're made of stone?"

Her lips curved upward. "*You see when you wake. It was the same for me. Now, I always see because I never sleep.*"

Farley was in familiar territory here, since they'd talked about a stone's senses before. "Near as we can figure, Dessa was aware of her surroundings, and she could hear things before Frey gave her shape. But once she was stirring, she could also see. And she has a sense of touch. And she told me that she can tell how certain people feel, so long as they have affinity." He realized something and smiled. "Doesn't that mean you've always known how Torio feels?"

"*Yes. But also ... no? Feelings can be simple. But they can also be hard to understand.*"

"Yep. People can be really complicated. But I'm as simple as they come."

Dessa gently patted his turban and said, "*Usually.*"

"Only usually, huh? When am I not simple?"

She had an answer ready. "*When you have to say goodbye.*"

"What do *you* think?" asked Farley.

Torio studied the smudged sky to the north. "I think Nerida is a better judge than I. If she says rain is coming, then it will come."

"It's still a while off, though. What happens if the storm gets here after dark?"

"You know how Morven is on cloudy nights?"

Farley grimaced. "That bad?"

"Oh, much worse. Nerida and all her get are a thirsty lot. If they're held in check until day-peep, we'll not get a wink of sleep."

Tsing asked, "The magic only works at daytime?"

"There's two conditions for stirring the blue stuff. It's gotta be between sunup and sundown, and some part of the statue's gotta be wet with fresh water."

Then to Torio's amusement, Farley launched into one of the teaching songs. He had a good singing voice, but the most impressive part was that he was translating on the fly so Tsing could follow along. The rhymes were lost, but the tune was catchy enough. Soon, they were singing together, arm-in-arm as the strolled down the summit road.

When they circled around so that they were once again facing north, Farley pointed out across the Expanse. "I thought those were colonnades, but something's glittering on top. They're aqueducts, aren't they?"

"They are."

"Why send water out into all that nothingness?"

"While it's not as verdant as your homeland, the Expanse isn't truly empty. In fact, by this time tomorrow, if the rains water that plain, it will be awash in flowers—orange and purple and gold."

Farley radiated eagerness. "All of it? I wanna see!"

Torio went on. "The Basq keep domesticated animals. Most of those aqueducts lead to manmade watering holes for their herds. But they do hunt. Not with the same drive as Pred, but they ride out after those wild deer whenever the city is preparing for a feast day."

"When's the next party?"

"When the tides are right for meeting upon the shore." Torio fluttered his fingers in the general direction. "For instance, at winter's end, the men of the city will go to collect any unclaimed baby boys that are left there."

Farley's brows drew together. "You make it sound like picking up seashells on the beach."

"I doubt it's that haphazard."

"I kinda wish I could see for myself," Farley muttered. "Hey. How good do you suppose the view is from Larkin's new place."

Torio considered that. "If Livia were to have a son … Harrow might talk his way into the right to be here."

"Yeah, Aurelius probably could. Same goes for Ulrica, if it's more girls."

"Then your patience may be rewarded. Eventually. Let's leave it at that."

Mercifully, Farley changed his line of questioning. "Where's the best place to watch the rain?"

For the rest of the way down the winding road, Torio offered options ranging from a zoo and a dance circle to stone gardens and a series of interconnected wading pools. True to form, Farley wanted to do everything, but Torio reminded him that Nerida's many courtyards would be jammed with revelers.

In the end, Farley asked Artor to decide. "It's probably your only chance, so you should fit in all the things you want to see while we're here. I'll be back. Probably lots of times."

That offer led them back into Nerida's galleries.

Their Drom guide from earlier was still giving tours to guests, and she was pleased to learn that mosaic floors held a special fascination for Artor. "We have several mosaic masterworks that you must visit, but first, there are twenty different repeating patterns that are part of the Blue Mountain's teaching traditions. They are essential!"

Torio chuckled at the way Artor lit up over the prospect.

Predictably, Farley said, "As much fun as that'll be for an actual journeyman, what would you recommend to someone who doesn't want to spend the rest of the day staring at floors?"

She rattled off several points of interest, and Farley voted for the undercity market. "I should have enough coin for turban cloth, yeah?"

"Certainly." Torio thought to add, "If you happen to spot something on a grander scale, I can handle the barter and loan you the coin."

Farley flashed him a sheepish look. "We need another job or two. My purse is flat."

"Perhaps Teegay can arrange for an odd job or two. There's always inventory to grade."

"Are we staying that long?"

"I didn't get the sense that they're running us out of town. And we're in no particular rush to return to Morven. She'll be snow-stuck until spring."

Farley stood there for a moment, looking mildly surprised. "That made me feel kind of ... impatient. Once we left, I didn't think I'd ever want to go back."

"We can come and go as we please, seas and seasons allowing."

"Okay. Sounds good." And hooking arms with Tsing, he headed off in the direction of the market.

At his side, Dessa said, *"Farley* does *want to go home?"*

Torio made a flip-flop gesture with his hand. "I think it would be truer to say that having seen the homes of so many others, Farley wants to show off his own."

Farley was mostly lost in thought when Tsing jerked him to a stop. "Wait. Farley, I want to see what they're doing."

"Something going on? Which stall?"

"Not a stall. Over there. See the tables?"

Tsing's ears strained toward a kind of courtyard that had been carved out in the midst of crowded stalls. From that direction, Farley could hear the faint click and clack of stones.

"You like games?" Usually, Tsing went along with whatever Farley wanted to do. This was the first time he'd asserted himself.

"I'm good at games."

"Oh, yeah?" Farley steered them toward the clustered tables. "What kinds of games did you play with your brothers?"

The Pika happily rattled off the names of half a dozen games that were a mystery to Farley. But it was pretty great when Tsing suddenly grabbed his hand and took the lead. Like ... Farley was seeing his bond-brother's true face for the first time.

Tsing was used to being in charge. Or at the very least, he was used to getting his way. And even though they were in a brand new setting, Tsing acted like he was in familiar territory. He towed Farley from table to table, where men placed stone tiles in patterns. Farley couldn't even begin to fathom the rules, but it was definitely a strategy game.

The hexagonal tiles were nothing like the tall playing pieces for Pinnacles. Finally, Farley spoke up. "What's this game called?"

The two old guys playing looked up, then goggled at them.

Farley tried the question again in a couple more languages, but the two Basq only muttered together in undertones. Spinning on his heel, Farley scanned the crowd for a familiar flutter of feathers. He waved urgently, and Torio made his way over. Alone.

"Where's Dessa?"

"Nerida invited her to go deeper into the galleries. I think they're trading secrets." Torio nodded toward the game underway. "You're interested in learning Changing Seas?"

"I am!" Tsing bounced up on his toes. "Will you ask for me? What do the different patterns on the tiles represent?"

Holding up a finger, Torio spoke to the men, who quickly shed their wariness in favor of asking several questions of their own. They offered upraised palms to be pressed in a customary Basq offer of peace, and they exchanged names. Then, the old guys scuttled their game while Tsing dragged over extra chairs from an empty table.

Then a lesson began, with Torio serving as translator.

"This game allows men to hold sway over the sea. The pieces have symbols representing different actions, and knowing which to play and where and when ... they say no man has ever played the same game twice."

One of the Basq men set out the tiles, which were solid stone and inset with a contrasting color. His were blue with white markings, and his partner's were the reverse—white with blue markings. The hexagons fit neatly together. Farley recalled Carden's grumbling over beadwork in the loft at Frey's. This set of game pieces represented hours of careful work.

Tsing touched pieces and gave their names as Torio had translated them. "Ripple. Swell. Wave. Calm. Spout. Whirlpool. Wait, what was this one again?"

"Tidal Wave," supplied Torio.

More pieces forced the play inside boundaries. Reef. Kelp. Cove. Shore. Tidal Pool.

And there were pieces that imposed temporary changes in the balance of power. High tide. Low tide.

Farley was keeping up okay, but then the Basq brought out pieces that had even more special rules. School. Steelfin. Writher. Goddess.

They set up pieces for a teaching game, and Tsing volunteered to go first.

Farley nudged Torio. "It's really nice of them to show us how to play."

"This isn't all out of the kindness of their hearts." Torio's smile was wry. "They're merchants, and they sell sets of these stones. They can tell by Tsing's enthusiasm that we represent a sale."

So this was a haggle? Wily old guys. Farley laughed and slouched lower in his chair. "So do you play?"

"A little. And poorly. Pinnacles has more straight-forward goals."

"Would Aurelius like this?"

But before Torio could offer an opinion, Tsing turned to him with another question. Farley tried to follow along while Torio translated. He'd probably end up as Tsing's opponent, but strategy games had always been more Torio's and Aurelius's thing. Farley was okay with trying stuff and seeing how it went, which wasn't really planning.

One of the old guys must have noticed his flagging attention, because he gestured at Farley, then called for Torio to hear him out.

"He says there's a three-player version of the game. Adding another set of tiles complicates the balance of power ... but also allows two less-experienced players to team up against a master of the game."

To Farley, it sounded like they guy wanted to sell another set of tiles.

Torio arched his brows and said, "The two who go up against the Changing Seas together are traditionally called *onayr* and *dahna*."

"Well, now we *gotta* get three sets. I wonder if Dan plays."

The old guy beamed as he stood, beckoning for Farley to follow him over to a stall that was clearly dedicated to the game. Most of the hexagonal gaming pieces were blue, yet freshstone could vary a lot, from a pale, powdery blue to a deep indigo. But Farley's interest sparked when he spied other colors. The pale green of songstone. Dawnstone's pink. "Do they come in all twelve colors?"

After another exchange, Torio reported, "At tournaments, the highlight of the day is a twelve-man melee. All very cutthroat. It's nicknamed Churning Seas."

"Sounds like it'd appeal to a Pred."

"Shall we take the lot?"

"Kinda have to, don't we?"

With a low laugh, Torio turned to the Basq to give him the good news. And that's when something else caught Farley's attention. Well, Nestor tipped him off. There was a whole lot of magic bouncing around inside a magical mountain, but freshstone was fairly reserved when it wasn't wet. Farley wasn't having trouble tuning it out. So he didn't notice the stealthy bursts of magic until the little black snake biffed Farley's chin.

A statue was skulking through the market.

Hardly a surprise. Guardian statues could do all sorts of things, from carrying heavy stuff to carrying messages. Freshstone statues were a respected part of the community in Meridian. Tupp would have loved it.

The surprising thing about this statue was the way sly strands of magic were linking it to Torio. And not in that cute, attention-getting way of a friendly statue. Farley would swear on the edge of his blades that this thing was stalking the Grif.

Larkin and his crew caused a stir as they strode through the undercity, bound for the only gate that led out onto the Expanse. Dan had needed to stop by his lodgings, which had been spare enough to startle Larkin. This young man had nothing. Or next to it. Once he'd rewrapped his head in a fresh turban—the only other one he owned—and changed from worn slippers into sturdier boots, Larkin ordered him to bundle up whatever he wished to keep, then went to settle his account.

Dan had obeyed, but he hadn't thanked him for it. Indeed, he'd flashed an actual temper before turning to the boarding house manager in order to apologize and explain why he'd be leaving. Several other young men poked their noses out, and the common room grew crowded.

They asked after Phillit, exclaimed over Larkin's daughters, and begged for news of the adventures to come. As one after another these young men offered to press palms with a Pred in an offer of peace, Larkin's conscience twinged.

Artor had needed rescue, and so had Tsing. But he wasn't snatching Dan from any kind of squalor or depredation. Larkin had been irked by what little the man could claim, only to find him surrounded by a community of similarly knowledgeable and progressive young men. Old Phandil's many apprentices. The friends his dahna had mentioned. The ones who called him Dan.

"You can write and send parcels," Larkin had gruffly offered. "And ... we'll return from time to time."

Welcome news, apparently.

And ... every last man of them had congratulated him. Then scurried to find enough glasses to toast the happy occasion. Not because Dan had become a dahna. But because it wasn't every day that a man became a father.

Here and now, Larkin intended to mark the day in his own way.

He would hunt for Livia. He would hunt for his daughters. And ... he would hunt for his dahna. Because for Pred, the strongest bonds were always forged by blood and by feasting.

Larkin eyed the Basq and conceded that the boots were an improvement. Dan's only other visible addition was a sizeable canteen slung across his body. "Where is your weapon?"

"I don't own one." Dan showed him an etched metal tag and stiffly retorted, "I am not without resource. I won't slow you down."

The purpose for the tag became clear when Dan spoke to the gate guards, a couple of boys barely into their teens. They gawked at Larkin and his crew, then shyly offered to carry bags if they could watch. Dan smiled as he scolded them for trying to abandon their post, and they wheedled for stories upon his return. Then the boys hefted the lid from a cistern and carefully drew a dipper of water. Waving for them to follow, they led the way into a long hall lined with the makings of a substantial stone cavalry. Ponies, horses, oxen, and donkeys waited alongside more whimsical mounts, like a saddled wolf and a tortoise with seating for six under an elaborate sunshade.

"We may be out past dark," Dan muttered worriedly.

The boys exchanged a glance, looked both ways, then handed Dan a match tin. With a much more furtive stride, they moved into an alley where all the statues were redstone. Larkin eyed these with appreciation. They all appeared to be fire-eaters.

Dan wavered over the impromptu offer of what had to be an upgrade.

Larkin eased to his side and slipped him a purse. It wasn't his only purse, but it wasn't his lightest one, either. "Do as you see fit, dahna. A hunting party should be properly supplied."

It took him a few moments, but Dan's fingers closed over the coins.

Not long after, he rode out astride a bear who pulled a long cart that was supplied with water skins, ground mats, corded wood and kindling, and a rented tripod and cookpot. Larkin noted a case of liquor and casually asked, "No food?"

Dan asked, "Was I wrong? I thought that might be … insulting."

Larkin said, "You understand perfectly. Well done."

Larkin set an easy pace, following the blue stone aqueduct out into the barrens. It would have been so much faster to reach the hunting grounds from the sea, but that route wasn't even considered by the Basq. It belonged to the sea wives. So they walked.

The Expanse wasn't truly barren. Unlike the featureless sands that surrounded the Drom capital back on New Continent, this terrain showed numerous signs of life. Spindly shrubs and tough grasses grew thick enough to support herds of domesticated animals. Mostly goats and deer, but Larkin noticed a few horses and oxen browsing in their midst.

Herders called greetings, which Dan answered cheerfully enough.

"They know you?"

"Before Phillit, I came out here weekly in order to collect reports and confirm headcounts."

"You counted goats?"

"I ... yes. Is that so strange?"

"I pictured you locked up in some sort of archive all day and all night."

"Head Scribe Phandil likes for us to explore our aptitudes. I've done many jobs since my appointment to his staff. While some *don't* want to leave the undercity, I like to see the sky and hear the sea and ... this scent. Nothing in the undercity compares to wind-scent."

No wonder Phandil had been so eager to forward this man. Travel would probably suit him.

"Aye, the air smells of the sea here. But in other places, other lands, the wind carries very different scents." He wondered what Dan would think of the heavy, wet stillness of the tropics. "When lazy breezes drift across the river in Prahkreet, they are so thick with the scent of flowers, you can taste them."

Dan gazed half-lidded into the distance, as if he were trying to imagine such a thing. Finally, he shook his head. "We're fortunate those clouds haven't yet sent storm winds reaching for us. In the Expanse, grit can scour."

"May the winds favor the hunter."

That earned him a sidelong look. "Is that a Pred saying?"

"One of the gentler ones."

"What would be an *ungentle* saying?"

"Fare better than your prey, and feast upon them. Wear home their blood as a trophy."

"You don't really wear blood ...?"

"Oh, aye. Usually right after we feast upon the beast's heart with ready fangs."

Dan's expression went blank.

"Are you squeamish?" asked Larkin.

"I have no idea. I suppose we'll find out."

Beyond the herds, the aqueduct continued between seemingly haphazard heaps of blue boulders. Scrub grew more thickly on their north sides, and the crew inadvertently flushed out a pair of does. Larkin watched as they sprang away, then moved toward the sound of splashing water.

Around the next jumble of stones, the aqueduct split in two directions, one branch continuing north while the other swung east. At the divide, water spilled into a shallow pool below. The leak was clearly intentional, and the pool was shielded from prevailing winds by what had once been a low wall, now overgrown into a thickly tangled hedge that served as both wind break and shade. The soil all around the pool was thick with tracks.

"How many of these pools are there?" he asked.

"After the troughs we just passed, there are eleven other wild pools like this one. Though in summer, the three farthest get little more than a trickle." Dan pointed along the eastern branch. "This one splits twice more, carrying water into sheltered places."

"Doesn't anyone protest the loss of water to the city?"

Dan laughed. "Would any who live within Nerida's coils be so wasteful? We spill the water from every sink and washtub and bathing pool into the Expanse."

Larkin frowned. "This isn't potable?"

"If thirsty enough, a man might be glad for a mouthful of bathwater. But I doubt it tastes nice."

"What of soap?" Larkin didn't see any residue.

"Have you never visited the bathing pools? We clean ourselves before soaking in hot water. And our fullers use fine sand and strong backs to launder our clothes."

"What of waste?"

"Disposed to the south, away from any habitation." Dan seemed amused. "Are Pred also interested in the sluicing of excrement?"

"Nay, though I shall have to plan for the sluicing of diapers. Remind me to purchase another washtub."

"A cauldron, please." Dan smiled faintly. "I prefer both

my drinking water and my diapers to be clean."

"So be it." Larkin glanced around at his crew, who were already taking measure of the tracks. They were rather pointedly not-looking, and he doubted any of them knew more than a few phrases of Coloq. Probably a mercy, since he didn't really want to be teased for chatting about diapers, of all things. "Do you know the path of the aqueducts? Including their splits?"

"Yes."

Casting about for a stick and finding nothing suitable, he drew his dagger and indicated the mud. "Draw a map for us."

Dan may not have been skilled with a weapon, but he cut a very serviceable map into the mud. Larkin took in the lay of the land, considered the lowering sun, and handed down his orders. His men slipped away, no doubt eager to show off. It wasn't often that Larkin left matters in their hands.

"Our hunt begins there." Indicating a cluster of boulders, he added, "Leave the bear, lest he spook our prey."

So saying, Larkin stripped to the waist, knotted his hair, and checked his blades.

Dan shouldered a water skin and mutely followed.

When they reached the stones, Larkin asked, "Do I need to roust out anything with venomous tendencies?"

"Our snakes are small constrictors, only a danger to mice and sleepy lizards. Spiders can be trouble, but they don't range by day." Dan said, "I wouldn't recommend thrusting your arm into any holes."

"Are there no larger predators?"

"There are." Dan pointed up. "By day, we're at the edge of fell eagle territory, and by night, we're troubled by fisher owls. Either is capable of carrying off a goat ... or a child. In the city, we discourage them with banners and canopies, but out here, we're ever under their eyes and ever near a strike."

Larkin squinted into the sky. "You should have said something sooner."

"I apologize."

"Nay. We have no small persons in our party. But I do like to know when I've entered another predator's hunting grounds."

From their new vantage, Larkin could better see the path of the aqueduct and the low thickets that marked the locations of additional pools.

"I don't see them," Dan remarked.

"They'll wait for twilight."

So they sat upon the blue stone to watch the sun evade the coming clouds by dropping below them. Larkin had nothing to say. Not yet. And Dan held his peace until the sun was gone. Then, he whispered, "Is this really how Pred hunt?"

Larkin kept his voice low. "Patience is part of bringing down prey."

"This isn't what I imagined. At all."

"Usually, I would track my quarry and bring it down, but today my goal is different. *Our* goal." Larkin pivoted to face the east, and his gaze sharpened. Rolling into a crouch, he murmured, "There. Do you see?"

"They're returning."

"And not emptyhanded. Look there." They'd fanned out, and they were driving several deer before them. Larkin crept to the edge of the boulder and drew his blades. "This day, our quarry comes to us."

Dan edged closer.

"My men work well together. I've known most of them since I was a boy." He spared Dan a glance. "My father preferred to sail as a family, bringing us and Mother along. So he favored crewmen with similar leanings. Fathers and sons. Siblings. Cousins. Always families. It didn't matter where they were from, so long as they were capable and courteous."

"A household on the move," Dan whispered.

"Aye. Some were my mentors. Some were my play-mates. We've hunted together just as long as we've sailed together. Blood and salt and trust bind us." Larkin readied his daggers as the patter of hooves gained in strength. "Community is important to Basq. Torio told me you might worry, and I don't want that. Not when I can end your fears with one flash of my blade. Watch me. Watch them. Sailing with us on the *Moontide* might mean losing your place in Meridian, but you'll find a new place. With us."

Then the deer were there, and Larkin was upon them.

"Scuse me! Sorry about that! Hey, let me by? Thanks!" Farley was usually on the other end of a game of hide-and-hunt, but the chase was on. When he'd walked in the direction of the statue who'd definitely been creeping up on Torio, the thing had bolted into shadows.

He'd followed—how could he not—but catching up wasn't going so well. The workday must have ended for most of the underground city, and the streets were full of people walking or shopping or standing around to chat.

"Coming through! Just need to ...! Oh, for ... sorry 'bout that. Is this yours?"

A group of boys gaped at him when he tried to return their ball.

"Hiya. I'm Farley. Didja see that statue? Has to be some kind of crystal. Not sure of the color, but it was about this high ...?" He put his hand at the level of his knees.

"Skittered past you a few seconds ago. Had to be flashy. All I could really tell is that it's on four feet."

Understanding lit their eyes, and they began chatting amongst themselves. Not helpful. But one word was being repeated.

"Kressee?" he checked. "What does that mean?"

And finally, one of the boys pointed toward a nearby alley. "Yeah, I know. That's good, kid. You're my kind of helpful." He clapped his hands and promised, "I owe you one ... if we ever meet again. Gotta run!"

As Farley worked his way through the crowd, he could have sworn the kid shouted ... *Caterwaul*? If the Keeper was involved, then this might be okay. Like maybe he'd asked one of his statues to guard Torio ...? It did kinda sound like something Frey might do. But there was no way to know for sure, so Farley wasn't giving up.

Tracking a statue would probably be impossible for a typical hunter, but this thing wasn't going to be able to elude *him*. Outrun him? Sure. But Farley had gotten a good look at its magic, and it hadn't outpaced him by *that* much. He'd catch up to it sooner than later. Well, by dawn at the latest. Nighttime guardians had to return to their pedestals before sunup.

"Is Farley in danger?"

"Not at all, Dessa sweet. Just playing a game of chase with a little sparkle monster."

"There's a monster?"

"Okay, poor choice of words. No monsters. Nothing misbegotten about this statue. But I want a closer look, so I'm playing catch-up."

"You are playing?"

"Yep. Definitely playing." He took a corner and caught the glint of lanternlight against faceted stone. He was eager for a closer look, especially since Frey didn't often work with crystal. It was used for accents and in displays, but ... Farley had never seen a crystal guardian.

"Torio is concerned."

"Well, yeah. I ran off without saying anything." Pausing at the head of a stairway, Farley worked to catch his breath. "I'm headed down next. Pretty sure I'll end up lost. Or possibly with Caterwaul. Actually, yeah. That's a good place to look for me."

"Nerida is amused."

"What'd I do to warrant a smile?"

"You found Kressee."

"So it's a name? Gotcha. Yeah, I'm on Kressee's trail. Any idea what kind of critter I'm after?"

Dessa paused, then answered, *"She is 'all kinds of trouble.' But also beloved. Maybe she is like you?"*

Farley started down the stairs. "I dunno, Dessa sweet. What's that Pred saying? Too close can cut."

"I don't understand."

"Mmm. It's like ... you get along really well with Morven, and Nerida befriended you, too. And maybe it's partly because you're all mountains. But what if we get to the Songstone Mountain, and Shiri doesn't like you ... even though you have a lot in common. Some people don't get along because they're too similar."

"I will be disliked?" Dessa sounded uncertain.

"Not really sure. My point was ... I think *I'm* disliked. By Kressee. Even though I get along fine with most statues. Not as good as Tupp, mind. But better than most."

"Turn to the right."

Farley drew up short at the foot of the stairs. "Why? She went the other way."

Nerida likes you.

"And she wants to help? Nice! Tell her thanks." He jogged along the righthand passage.

More softly, Dessa said, *"Nerida likes you, but you are mine."*

"All yours, mountain mine."

In mollified tones, Dessa said, *"I can share. I already shared you with many people, and you are always finding more. But you understand. You love me."*

"Always will." He had to wonder what she and Nerida had been talking about. "Hang on. Dead end."

"There is a panel."

It took a few moments to find and trip the latch, then Farley found himself on the narrow landing of a winding staircase. There was a whole lot of stone somewhere below. Descending at a skip, he asked, "Where am I headed."

"Teegay's workshop. He is there. He is working."

"He knows I'm coming?"

"No. But he needs you."

"For what?"

"Nerida says ... you are like the rain."

Not the kind of answer he was looking for, but ... well, it had to be something hoped for ... even needed. "Good enough for me."

Farley noticed that the longer he descended, the more Nerida's ambient magic coaxed for his attention. It was easy to see why early Keepers had decided to delve further down. Anyone with affinity had to be able to tell that the magic was gaining in this direction.

Other types of stones danced in the periphery of his awareness, and ... yep, there was that crystal guardian again. Opening the door at the bottom of the stairs, he strode into a well-lit room. Definitely a Keeper's own workshop, given the superlative quality of the blocks.

Caterwaul turned from a long table strewn with books and sketches, a letter in his hand. His gaze darted briefly to the door, as if expecting someone else to be following. "Farley Meadowsweet ...? Did Larkin show you the way?"

"Nope. I followed *her*."

Half-hidden by the Keeper's boots, a glittering crystal feline skulked. Kressee was nearly clear, though Farley could see streaks of pale blues and greens in her depths. And her maker had given her eyes of pale blue freshstone. The stone wasn't bound to her the way Freydolf would have done, but as ornamentation, it gave weight to her baleful gaze. And ... it looked nice, too.

"She led you here?" Caterwaul dropped to one knee and stroked sparkling fur. "No, I don't think so."

"I tracked her." Farley quickly amended, "With a little help from Nerida."

"You can hear my mountain?"

"Nope. But Dessa's been passing along messages." He nodded at Kressee. "Didja know your tree-cat was stalking Torio."

"Kressee," the man groaned.

She planted wide paws on his leg and stretched up to rub her cheeks against his. With all its facets, her fur looked like it would cut, but the Clow's big hands ruffled and rumpled, proving she'd be soft to the touch.

"Is she yours?" Farley checked. Their bond was strong, but not as solid as the ones Frey formed with his creations.

"She's not my handiwork, but she was given to me by my predecessor. Master Bissik made and marked Kressee, and my hands were upon her the moment she stirred." The Clow's expression gentled. "She's a jealous thing, always in a snit when another statue demands my attention. Or ... another Keeper."

Farley moved closer and crouched. "Of course she adores you. She was made for you. Not another statue in this room has a bond to rival the one that connects the two of you."

Caterwaul said, "In a way, Kressee will belong to every future Keeper, because Master Bissik bound her directly to the mountain. However, it's generally agreed that his gift marked me as successor, so my apprentices spoil Kressee. Her favor is considered a sign of Nerida's."

"But you are first and best ...?"

"So it would seem. Therefore, any time I spend with Torio is a terrible injustice."

Farley offered his fingertips to the feline. "Don't you worry about Torio. Him and me are wanderers. Gone before you know it. Jobs to do. Adventures to have."

The Keeper's expression slowly shifted into something decidedly speculative. "*Jobs.* Aurelius's last letter touted your capabilities as a hunter of stone."

"Yeah. We mostly go after the Misbegotten." Brightening at the prospect of fresh work, he asked, "Have you got a statue even more troublesome than Kressee?"

"Not ... quite." Caterwaul stood and plucked up the letter he'd been looking at earlier. He began to pace with it.

Seizing his chance, Farley tried to coax the tree-cat closer.

Her posture was still warning him off, but then she slowly stretched out a paw. He held very still, wondering if Master Bissik had given his creation claws. If so, they were velveted, for all she did was bat at Nestor. But then the little snake slipped out of Farley's collar and twined up her foreleg, settling like a collar around her neck.

Kressee's eyes widened, and she sprang backward, going into a whirling, leaping dance as she tried to shake free. It was dazzling. And kind of funny, too. Farley called, "Come here, Kressee. I'll get him off you."

He'd finally coaxed the gorgeous guardian into a full sprawl across his lap when Caterwaul broke his silence. "I do have a problem, and statues are involved. You can track them? You and Torio both?"

"Yeah. We're suited because of our affinity. And Larkin is suited because ... well, he's in it for the hunt."

Caterwaul began slowly. "There is a man of questionable reputation in Bellicose, a territory that lies to the north, along the coast. He's a Tisk lord, and people say that no one can oppose him, even when he oversteps the bounds of civility or legality. My merchants have been bypassing his vicinity for years, in large part because Lord Roth is a collector. If something takes his fancy, he takes it."

"He steals from people?"

The Clow bared his fangs. "It's said he even steals people."

"So ... *he's* the Misbegotten?" Farley shook his head. "I don't think hunting people is something we can do."

He lifted the letter. "One of my clients recently came to me in dismay. The statue I'd created as a companion for his wife was stolen, pedestal and all, during the night. No trace. No trail. But he followed his suspicions to Bellicose. While he couldn't confirm that his own statue was there, this letter says that Lord Roth's estate is thick with statuary. If my good friend's stone guardian is there, could you find her? Get to her?" Caterwaul solemnly asked, "Could I pay you to *rescue* a statue?"

16

Bellicose

Farley spent most of the night at Torio's side, sitting on the roof of a gazebo, watching lightning flicker along the edges of oncoming clouds, and squinting against answering bursts of anticipatory magic. "The rain'll get here before sunrise."

"Yes."

"Wind's picking up."

"Yes."

"Want to find better shelter?"

The Grif simply said, "No."

Which suited Farley fine. They'd have a prime view of daybreak over the courtyard Artor had chosen, one of the smaller ones that featured intricate displays of flora and fauna. Its transformation wouldn't be flashy, but stuff didn't have to be. Artor was across the way, swaying on a bench-swing under the shelter of another gazebo. Phillit sprawled against his chest, and Tsing draped across his lap, sound asleep.

Farley ventured, "Anything bothering you?"

The question clearly surprised the man. "Nothing's amiss."

He thrust out his hand, sure that Torio was holding something back.

With a wry smile, the Grif made a sweeping gesture, indicating the courtyard. Then he reached for Farley's hand and slowly spelled out, D – E – S – S – A / I – S / S – O / S – M – A – L – L.

Farley shook his head.

Torio shrugged. M – Y / F – A – U – L – T.

They'd been through this before. If not for Torio, Dessa would have been lost forever. Yes, taking her had meant that some underwater mountain in the middle of an inhospitable sea had lost its magic, but … so what? It was better she was here and happy. Farley wasn't sure why Torio still wrestled with guilty feelings. It wasn't as if Dessa would've ever had courtyards or galleries.

H – A – P – P – I – E – R / H – E – R – E, he argued. N – E – E – D – S / U – S.

Torio gave a small nod, but he was still brooding.

Maybe it had been a mistake to suggest watching the storm roll in. Sky-watching made Torio nostalgic, and he seemed to have more than his fair share of unhappy memories.

The wind picked up, still hot despite how late it was. Actually, it was early, now. He could see a little, so dawn *was* approaching. He could almost feel it since the magic in the surrounding stone was straining eastward, like it could hasten the sun into the sky just by wanting it there. "An hour or so?" he guessed.

"At most," agreed Torio.

Gaze drifting toward the north, Farley asked, "You think Larkin's okay?"

The Pred hadn't checked in since leaving for his hunt the previous afternoon. Of course, he could have gone back to the *Moontide*, but … for some reason, Farley had figured that Larkin would come find them, if only to brag.

"It would be insulting to think otherwise," Torio pointed out.

"Well, yeah."

"I did expect him to return ahead of the rain."

"I can smell it."

Torio hummed. "That's the scent of wet ground in the Expanse. Any minute now."

Farley could faintly hear it. The hiss of rain on stone. "Don't tell him."

"Hmm?"

"Don't tell Larkin I was worried. He'll take it wrong."

Clamping a hand over his hat at another flutter of wind, Torio angled his head toward the courtyard entrance and promised, "Your secret is safe, as is our captain."

"He found us?" Farley didn't see him.

"I left word."

And then Larkin leapt lightly onto the gazebo roof and turned, presumably to reach for Dan. But then came a bundle of some sort. Then a shirtless Dan was up and over the edge, crawling up the roof tiles. Farley thought the man looked a little rattled, but it was hard to say if it was the hunt or the heights.

"You found us," was all Farley managed as a greeting. He was too busy ogling the bloody smears on Larkin's skin.

He casually thrust the bundle against Farley's chest. "Your haunch."

Trying to hide how touched he was, Farley nodded at Dan. "Did you really paint him with the blood of your prey?"

Fangs flashed. "He isn't squeamish."

"Good thing. So ... did the two of you feast upon the heart of your prey?"

"It's traditional."

"Hey, what do you say?" Farley patted the wrapped haunch. "Will you share this with me?"

Larkin's brows lifted. "That would also be traditional."

"Look there," murmured Torio.

On the opposite end of their courtyard, torches guttered and doused, and stone darkened in a straight line that pushed closer. For a moment, Farley could see the rain wavering like a curtain, but then it washed over them, drumming straight down over his hat with enough force to bend the brim.

It did nothing to block his view of what mattered most.

"Whoa." Nerida and her children might not be able to move yet, but they *knew* they were wet. Pent up magic was still potent.

"Can you hear her laugh?" Dessa's voice held wonderment. *"Can you hear her sing?"*

"No, but I can *see*. Actually, it's like I *can't* see for all the sparks and swirls. And the sun's not even up yet."

"She knows. She waits, but she is happy."

"Does that make you happy?"

"I'm not sure. I don't sleep as she must, so it's not the same. I ... I don't need more blood ... do I? Would that make me happy?"

Farley shot a quick look at Torio, who was frowning. "No, no. Once was good. Once was plenty."

"Oh."

"Dessa?"

Her voice was so soft, but he could always hear her fine. Like he wasn't hearing with his ears, but with his heart. *"I want to laugh and sing. I want sparks and swirls."*

Farley kept his tone light despite the stunned expression on Torio's face. "Come find me, Dessa sweet. I'll dance with you in the rain and teach you a new song. One that will make you laugh."

"I will find you. I can always find you." She sounded pleased to be asked.

"I'll look for a quiet corner. It'll be just you and me and Torio."

She didn't answer. Which probably meant she was satisfied.

Torio snatched his hand and practically scratched a question into his palm. J – E – A – L – O – U – S?

Could mountains compare? Dessa wanted to be like Nerida on some level, but ... she hadn't asked for spacious courtyards or ranks of statues. And she hadn't exactly asked for blood, either. Not really.

Pulling Torio's rain-wet palm close, Farley carefully traced his reply. S – H – E / W – A – N – T – S / T – O / B – E / H – A – P – P – Y. He confidently added, "We can give her that. Easy."

Torio relaxed.

But now they needed someplace to go. Gesturing to Dan, who was hugging his knees and smiling serenely as the rain washed the blood from his scales, Farley said, "Ask Dan about quiet corners, and let's get there before the sun's up."

While Torio applied for insider information, Farley leaned across to prod Larkin's shoulder.

A hand caught his wrist before he could connect. Larkin gruffly chided, "Use words. *Much* safer."

He smiled and scooted closer, not wanting to have to shout his news over the sound of rain.

Larkin snorted in a resigned way but didn't shove Farley back.

"We got a job from Keeper Caterwaul," Farley announced, studying the Pred's face. "And it's going to be dangerous."

Farley wasn't disappointed.

Golden eyes took on a shine.

"Ready to hunt again?"

Larkin answered, "Aye. Always."

Larkin ushered Dan up the gangway, puzzling through options on where to put the man. It didn't seem quite right to string up a hammock for him in crew quarters, though he doubted the Basq would complain. A private room would be more appropriate, so one of the smaller storage rooms should do. Even a closet wouldn't be much smaller than Dan's room back at the boarding house.

Stymied, Larkin simply asked. "Would you prefer private quarters or a place with the crew?"

Dan quietly admitted, "I ... couldn't say."

Examples. He needed more information. So Larkin ran lightly down a set of stairs and pulled open one of the storage cupboards near the galley. It was nearly empty, which might have made it ideal for stowing the rhesha milk. "Here, for instance. We could clear it for you."

"Where will Phillit be?"

"Good question." Larkin frowned. "Maybe this is best, then? Phillit is too young for a hammock. Unless ... did you want to see the crew quarters before making up your mind?"

Dan stood there, eyes downcast.

With a creeping sense of inevitability, Larkin asked, "Is there something I should know?"

"You should keep Phillit close."

"Aye, I can do that. Pred are the same in that regard, but ... would you prefer he stay with you?"

"I would ... that is ...." Gaze still averted, Dan said, "A rug upon the floor would suffice, but do not turn me out. I couldn't bear the shame."

This was an unexpected twist. Larkin wasn't sure what to do, because in this, Pred were not the same. "I'm not accustomed to sharing. Pred keep to themselves, since we do not trust easily."

"Do not put me out," Dan whispered.

Larkin tried again. "Nobody here would know any different. You need not adhere to tradition."

The man swayed in place, but he didn't argue.

"Come, you barely slept last night. You need a bath and a bed. Farley shares quarters with Artor and Tsing, and they still have the bath. They have Phillit, too. Perhaps you can show them what Phillit needs ...?"

Dan trailed after him in a heavy silence.

Larkin was almost glad to see Farley when the younger man opened the door to his quarters. He practically dragged Dan inside, eagerly pointing out this and that, chattering on as if the man could understand him. Then again, nothing in Farley's realm needed much in the way of translation. Except perhaps the stone lionesses. They gave Dan a start.

Tsing had Phillit, who was fresh from the washtub. The Pika was crooning over how fine the little boy's scales looked with oil shining upon them.

"Did we do it right?" Farley asked.

"No idea. Ask Dan. Or better yet, have him demonstrate." Larkin switched to Coloq. "Have your bath. Then get sleep."

Dan paused, caught with his hands deep in black fur, and glanced uncertainly at the nearest hammock.

Larkin made up his mind. "Farley. Once he's cleaned up, put him in my bed. He and Phillit will be quartered with me."

"Sure." Farley didn't even bat an eye. "Might take me a few days to figure out that Fwan basket-bed thingie, but Phillit should be fine if you guys keep him between you."

He managed a nod.

Farley eased closer. "You need sleep, too."

"Aye. Once I have a clearer idea of your plans."

"Nope."

Larkin wearily dragged his hand through his hair. "And why not?"

Farley took another step, like he was daring Larkin to slip a dagger between his ribs. But there wasn't any sauce to his smile. If anything, he looked frazzled. "Tsing's the *only* one who got any sleep last night, and ... Torio's trying to talk to Dessa, and ... how come Dan looks close to tears? Can't you at least stick your feet in the washtub with him? He's family, yeah? Welcome him *properly*."

"I *did*." Larkin tried for a superior tone. "It's your turn."

His expression wavered from surprise into something ... warm, but Farley didn't belabor the matter. Just lapsed into an easy smile and said, "Sure. Happy to."

A few days later, Torio strolled off the *Moontide* in search of information. He'd visited Bellicose before, but not this particular port. As they'd moved up the coast, the landscape had changed to include sparse trees and sprawling fields. The dockside buildings were modest, and the shops were the typical mix of merchants and crafters. Nothing gave him any inkling that these people were under the local lord's thumb.

This wasn't the Tisk homeland, but there were a fair number of their race going about. Still, Torio spotted other Grif, as well as Keet, Oxus, Clow, and even a couple of Hund. Again, nothing untoward.

So he aimed for The Brooding Dragon, a respectable-looking tavern, and ordered a meal and a mug of the local ale. He chatted with the Tisk taverner about ordinary things before making his first foray into local gossip. "Someone mentioned a Tisk ... mayor? Is he a fair man?"

The man's smile had a wry twist. "You won't find a soul who'll speak ill of Lord Roth. You never know who's listening ... and what'll get back to him."

Torio glanced around the dining room, which was mostly empty. "That's rather ominous. But ... you're plainspoken on the matter ...?"

Tapping the counter, the Tisk said, "I do his lordship a service by making sure newcomers understand how things are done around here. So what's your line of business?"

"Oh, I'm a merchant. I deal in magical stone."

"That's no good. I recommend you resupply your ship and move along."

Torio frowned. "There's no stone market here? That's unusual."

"It's a friendly warning, sir. Bring your wares ashore, and you'll lose them quicker than you can sell them. That goes double if you have wives or daughters. Just turn around. Move along."

"What about skilled workmen? I have journeymen on my crew," Torio improvised. "Would anyone hereabouts be interested in mosaic floors?"

The Tisk pursed his lips. "Are they Grif like you?"

"Why do you ask?"

"Grif are as common as copper in a poor man's purse. No offense." Leaning closer and lowering his voice, the taverner said, "Lord Roth fancies rare things. He might invite you in if you want to flaunt your wares or your skills, but if he takes a liking, you won't be leaving. Simple as that."

"I'm a wanderer. Not looking to settle." Torio drained the contents of his mug and slid two additional coins across the counter before making his way out the door and along a side street, where he chose a small tea shop.

Two inquiries later, and he decided that the risk of drawing the wrong kind of attention was too great. He retreated toward the docks and hoped that Larkin's reconnoiter of the Tisk lord's estate didn't cause any unforeseen problems. Because Lord Roth collected novelties. A Pred would probably appeal to a man who liked to intimidate people.

"Are you with Farley, Dessa?"

"I did promise." And more warmly, *"I'm holding a baby. Hamish holds babies."*

"He does indeed."

"Why are you worried? Do your cracks hurt? Should I come carry you?"

"No, thank you," he replied more crisply than he intended. "Wait with Farley. Please."

"Why are you worried?" she repeated.

With a furtive glance over his shoulder, Torio muttered, "Because *I* may be common as coppers, but this is probably the worst place in the entire world for *you* to be."

Farley listened with a growing sense of confusion. Finally, he blurted, "And people just let him get away with it?"

Larkin gazed at him in mild exasperation. "Did you yield your horn willingly, Floxling?"

"No, but ... we stopped him."

"Did you? Or did someone stronger come to your defense?"

"Well ... okay, I see your point, but ...!"

"Let's be clear," Larkin cut in. "Our job is to find Keeper Caterwaul's missing statue and carry her off. *Not* to impose Flox sensibilities on a Tisk lord's territory."

"She's like me." Tsing lay a hand upon Farley's arm. "You'll rescue her, and she'll be glad. Focus on the captive, not the captors."

Farley was beginning to be embarrassed. "I get it, okay."

Helping Tsing hadn't stopped the Mard, and retrieving this statue wouldn't change how one Tisk lord ruled. But he felt bad for all the people who must be living in fear of their own leader.

Larkin resumed. "Lord Roth's collecting habits don't stop with statues. He conscripts or retains the many men who guard his estate. They're big, and they're armed. I can understand why they might be intimidating, but they're largely for show."

"Meaning they're no match for a Pred?" Farley guessed.

"None whatsoever."

Torio said, "I was warned by no less than three well-meaning citizens to hide my daughters and sons. Apparently, pretty girls and comely boys are snapped up as servants. Lord Roth likes to be surrounded by beautiful things. So I thought ... why not beautiful floors?"

Artor said, "I'll do anything to help. Of course."

"But there's no guarantee Lord Roth is in the market for a new floor or two." Larkin drummed his fingers against his leg. "Wouldn't your starstone pair be a surer way to gain entrance?"

Farley was horrified. "You want to give him Pollim and Eullia?"

"I'm bringing up possible approaches," Larkin countered. "We need a plan."

Torio pointed out, "They may be more of a hinderance than a help. Starstone can only move by night, and the freshstone lady can only move by day."

"Aye." Larkin frowned. "But could they carry her?"

"That's possible, yes. I'd been working under the assumption that she'd need to be able to walk out."

Tsing, whose hand still rested on Farley's arm, tightened his grip.

"You wanted to say something?" Farley invited.

"If I may?"

Torio waved for him to speak, and Larkin sat back with an expression of aggrieved patience.

"Farley is the one who will find the statue. He has the means and the magic."

"So does Torio," Larkin pointed out.

"But Lord Roth collects beautiful boys, and Tisk are enamored of cloudstriders."

Torio sat a little straighter. "He could apply for a position as houseboy?"

"No. That would take too long." Tsing's smile was superior. "You will dangle two rare opportunities before the greedy lord. A cloudstrider with golden curls and a pink-eyed princeling. Are we not irresistible?"

"Farley is novelty enough," argued Torio. "There's no reason to risk you, too. Not after everything you've been through."

"I can be a distraction."

Artor hummed in a worried way.

Torio glanced at Larkin, as if for help. The Pred eyed them both critically. "How does it work, though ...? A Grif walks up to the door with a spare boy or two? What's to stop them from coshing Torio in order to take possession of two attractive new houseboys?"

"Future acquisitions," Tsing said confidently.

"I don't follow."

"Torio won't be a Grif, and he won't be alone. Pardon me, friend." Tsing slipped behind Artor and set his hands across his eyes, fingers parted so he could look through. With a smile that twisted, Tsing said, "No one will think it suspicious if a group of Mard have flesh to trade."

Farley worked lather into his shaving brush and swiped his cheek.

"You remove the hairs from your face every morning," remarked Tsing.

"And you stand there watching me every morning," Farley returned, reaching for the blade in his shaving kit. "I gotta do this, or I'd look like the world's youngest grandfather."

"I'd like to see you bearded."

"Too bad. I'm never gonna be a granddad. But my brothers look enough like me, you'll get the general idea once their nubbins start pairing off." Farley paused. "It's been more'n two years already. Might be a few nubbins I've never met. They'll need to know their Uncle Far."

"And ... they'll want to meet me."

"They'll adore their Uncle Tsing," he promised. "You, too, Phillit."

The little boy curled against the Pika's shoulder, calm and sleepy after finishing his bottle of rhesha milk. Behind them, Larkin was applying oil to Dan's back. Ever since his tumble into the sea, Farley's cabin had been doubling as their washroom. He didn't mind. No ... he *liked* it. He'd finally regained something of home. Aurelius would have called this ... *morning ablutions*.

"You'll bring him, won't you ... Uncle Lar?"

"Don't shorten my name."

"Uncle Larkin, then. But don't blame me if Quin and Arni clip it. Or Hanley, since he mostly copies everything they do. Hewey's manners are better, but he might be too busy playing with rocks to notice he's got extra uncles."

Tsing asked, "Does your family also speak Terse?"

"The youngsters do. Ulrica started them early." Farley turned to ask, "Larkin, can you ask Dan if he wants to learn Verit along with Tsing?"

The Pred gave him a flat look. "I don't want him speaking with a Floxish accent."

Farley snorted. "Pretty sure he'll have a Coloq accent, no matter which one of us is doing the teaching. Just ask him."

Larkin did, and Dan brightened.

Pleased, Farley turned back to the mirror and finished his shave. Larkin stole up behind him and patted his smooth cheeks, then dragged his palms along his jaw, smearing him with the remnants of Dan's oil.

"Hey! Whad'ja do that for?"

"Adding luster. Mmm. We should oil those frizzy curls of yours. You'll look more like a prized pet that way." Pointing to Tsing, Larkin asked, "Are you versed in face paints and powders?"

"Naturally!"

"I'll explain to Dan. Go with him into the shops. Choose what we'll need."

Tsing radiated pleasure. "Leave it to me."

Once they were away, Larkin sighed and pointed to a stool. "Sit."

"You're going to put oil in my hair?" Farley asked skeptically. "Won't that be ... soppy?"

"Hardly. I may not bother with this sort of thing, but that doesn't mean I wasn't thoroughly instructed. Father invested a great deal of time and effort into personal grooming."

An understatement.

"Where's that oil you bought? It should suffice."

So Farley retrieved one of the little yellow bottles and dropped to a seat across from Artor, who was adding the finishing touches to one of the three masks he'd spent half the night creating from strips of cloth, pulped paper, paste, and paint.

"You're good at this."

"Masks are part of an old Ursa custom. I used to make them with my mother for the interval festivals." Artor's smile was nostalgic. "Ours were prettier and invited the arrival of good omens. Let's hope these grant you good fortune."

Like the Mard masks they'd seen in Turncove, these were designed to intimidate.

Monstrous eyes.

Gaping beak.

Snarling teeth.

Turning to look up at Larkin, Farley asked, "What if they know about Mard killing all the males?"

"Then we'll be sly, double-dealing Mard who are keeping the odd male in order to line our own pockets, tradition notwithstanding." He flicked Farley's horn. "Face forward. I'm doing this by section."

"It's going to take forever, isn't it?"

"Patience is part of the hunt."

Artor calmly added, "This will be worth the wait. It's a lovely effect."

"No way. Really?" Farley tried to turn again, only to be dealt a sterner knock. "At least bring me the mirror."

"Nay," decreed Larkin, who sounded really cheerful when he repeated, "Patience."

"Are you afraid?" Farley locked his fingers with Tsing's as they followed Torio and Artor through Lord Roth's front door. Larkin, who'd insisted on having a part in the proceedings, brought up the rear.

"No. This will work," the Pika murmured. "He'll take us, and he'll want to keep us. And that'll get us closer to the blue lady."

If that was all Tsing was worried about, then he'd be fine. Farley gave his hand a quick squeeze and tried to let go. Tsing didn't let him, and his ears went kind of pink. So maybe he *was* a little nervous about what they'd face. Farley guessed it was just about right for two people in their predicament.

Hand-in-hand, they strolled into a house with rooms as big as galleries and nearly as full of statuary. Along the way, he spotted statues representing eight of the Twelve. Some were passable enough in an artistic way, but there was very little life to them. Had some unscrupulous merchant passed these off as true guardian stones? Or had Lord Roth snatched up statues indiscriminately?

Those possessed of magic pulsed with a dim, sleepy awareness. But many more were carved from dull rock. The Tisk lord's collection might impress dullards, but anyone with even a hint of affinity would recognize these as the handiwork of beginners, wrought from practice blocks.

"Do these statues need rescue, too?" whispered Tsing.

"No," Farley admitted. "None of these are even marked, so they're not aware."

"Will that make it easier to find the blue lady?"

"Yeah. Oh, hey. I think those are some of the fancy lord's houseboys."

Two teens in pale green tunics pressed against the wall as they passed. One was Grif, and the other was Keet.

Farley offered a small wave. "My first Keet!"

Eyes wide, the boys waved back, traded a look, then grinned.

More servants—or maybe slaves—stopped to gawk.

Coulda been the masks. But it could have been him and Tsing. The Pika had been so excited to do things with his new kit of pearly powders and tinted gloss. Farley knew what makeup was. Flox women didn't go in for the stuff, but Ulrica did. It had been common in both Pred and Grif territories, but Farley was a little fuzzy on what was normal for Pika males, especially since he'd tried so hard not to look at them. But Tsing? He'd cooed while smoothing on creams and wielded little brushes with the confidence of a warrior.

In the end, Farley barely recognized himself, what with his every curl smoothed and oiled and shining like actual gold ... and his cheeks shimmering with golden dust. Tsing looked similarly ethereal, but all in silvers and pinks.

"You could stand to cower more," Larkin muttered.

"I don't see why." Farley beamed. "You'll get a better price if I'm smiling."

"We look like pampered companions." Tsing glanced up at Larkin. "If you seem to regret parting with us, his estimation of our value may rise."

Under the edge of his mask, Larkin's lips quirked. "Aye, lad. I'll look properly mournful over your impending sale."

Torio hushed them, then, and they entered a room filled with low couches and more servants dressed in green. Judging by the banners draping the walls, green was either Lord Roth's favorite color or some kind of family heraldry. This room sparked Farley's interest more than the statues because bookshelves lined the walls, and several servants lounged about reading.

Okay, that was unexpected.

At a desk as big as the table in Melina's bakery, a Tisk with spectacles perched on the end of his nose mumbled over the contents of a letter. Papers and ledgers were stacked to either side of his chair, and he seemed totally immersed in his business. Again, Farley had to realign the scene against his expectations. Aurelius did this kind of work all the time. He often groused about how much paperwork was involved in management.

It looked boring.

More to the point, it didn't look especially *bad*.

Farley had been braced for something more sinister. Like

the slavers who'd killed Tsing's brothers. Like the ruthless Pred who sometimes still crept into his dreams, making them nightmares.

This guy looked like an overworked clerk. And there were two Tisk children playing with their cradle guardians under his desk. Was he their father?

Lord Roth looked up, and his eyes narrowed at the trio of masked men. Farley kind of approved of his attitude. He wouldn't have wanted any Mard in his house either.

But then the Tisk noticed Farley and Tsing, and his expression morphed into wonderment. Leaping to his feet, he offered a tumble of greetings in three of the major trade languages. "Hello! Peace and patience! Welcome to my home! This is an unforeseen pleasure ... gentlemen?"

Torio struck an indolent pose and proceeded in Terse. "You're interested. Good. That simplifies matters."

"Skies and scales! When my men passed along your inquiry, I had my suspicions, but ... skies and scales!" Lord Roth hurried forward, but Artor stepped into his path. "They're authentic?"

"What's the harm? See for yourself," Torio invited.

And then the Tisk was reaching for them with hands that trembled slightly. Not a good haggler, this man. Anyone could see the want in his eyes. It made Farley feel like ... well, like just another statue.

"You'll come work for me, won't you, boys?"

Farley tried to look appropriately awed. "Hello, sir."

Lord Roth toyed with Farley's hair, then ran a finger along the side of his face.

"Straight out of legends! Where did you capture him? Fables say that cloudstriders make their homes in heights unreachable by mortal men." He went on without really expecting an answer. "He certainly looks like a celestial being. Eyes as blue as the heavens. Remarkable!"

Maybe Tisk were as bad as Pika about personal space,

and he should be giving the guy the benefit of the doubt. But Farley didn't like the look or feel of him, and he trusted that instinct. It wasn't easy to keep smiling.

Larkin growled menacingly.

Lord Roth shot him a startled look that turned to annoyance, but he did take a step back.

Torio warned, "The bounder, we … ahh … emancipated him from a remote island. Only speaks Tauke, but our golden boy knows enough to get by. That's why they come as a set. One speaking for the other and such. And they take comfort in each other's company, if you catch my meaning."

Tsing slipped his arms around Farley's waist and leaned into him, but his smile was all for the Tisk.

The man breathed deeply and exhaled on a sigh. "So this is a Pika."

"A prince among his people," Torio assured. He'd mostly dropped the act. No need to sell this guy on anything.

Lord Roth dragged his gaze away to ask Torio, "Are the rumors true?"

"Never had the pleasure?" Torio's teasing tone had the barest of edges. "He currently favors the cloudstrider, but a patient man could win him over."

Farley bent to whisper into Tsing's ear, needing to reinforce the notion that he was a necessary part of the deal. But all he said was, "I don't like this guy much, but the green hair is interesting."

Tsing did something shy with his ears and fluttered his lashes.

The Tisk guy went all … smitten.

According to plan.

Farley looped his arms around Tsing and tried not to glare.

Gaze fixed upon Tsing's face, Lord Roth asked, "How much?"

Torio named a ridiculous amount. Enough to cover the cost of two more blocks of magical stone.

To Farley's amazement, the Tisk simply murmured, "We have a deal."

Torio and Artor followed the man to his desk, and there was much clinking and counting of coins. Meanwhile, Tsing made a show of clinging to Larkin. The Pred pet his hair, then dropped to one knee to bid his 'fond farewells.' Lord Roth kept shooting them looks from across the room.

"That went well enough," Larkin murmured.

"Should I be worried about that?" Farley asked.

"Nay. This job will be done before dawn, and you'll be gone."

"A lot can happen between now and then," Farley pointed out.

Larkin lifted Tsing's hand as if to kiss it. "Torio smoothed the path. Walk it confidently. And cling to one another. Tenaciously."

"I will, but ...." Tsing whispered, "Don't leave me behind."

To Farley's surprise, Larkin answered with both surprising warmth ... and an inflection that brought his father immediately to mind.

"Perish the thought."

To Farley's relief, nobody tried to pull him and Tsing apart. Judging by the number of soft looks the Pika was gaining from other servants, everyone was quite prepared to dote on the princeling their master had paid a small fortune to possess.

"Do as you're told, and you'll be fine," said the Tisk woman who took charge of them.

As they passed through less ornate sections of the house, Farley saw more servants in the household's signature green. Most were Tisk, but he spied representatives of other races whose home territories were on First Continent.

Farley asked, "What sort of jobs will I have to do?"

"New boys usually start with serving meals," she said briskly. "Once he's bored with you, you'll move on to something else. A household this size needs many hands. If you have any special skills, let Lessolani know. She'll sort out something."

"Lessolani ... is she Lady Roth?"

The Tisk woman shot him an incredulous look, then shook her head. She all but pushed them through a door, repeating, "Do as you're told, and you'll be fine."

Lessolani turned out to be an Oxus woman with dark eyes and a slow smile. "Usually, I have to clean up the newcomers to make them presentable, but you're *resplendent*." She served them cups of cold water and crisp rounds of toast spread with a paste that might have been made from beans ... or nuts. Her questions were simple, and she was the first person in the house who asked for their names. It still irked Farley that Lord Roth hadn't bothered to ask.

Once she was satisfied that they'd refreshed themselves, Lessolani said, "Come along. I'll show you where things are, and then you can help me choose flowers."

She was aimable, and Farley felt comfortable asking questions. "Is this a good place?"

"We lack for nothing here," she replied mildly.

Farley asked, "Do you want to be here?"

Her steady gaze gave nothing away. "You'll get used to the way things are."

His concern for her must have shown. She rested a big, warm hand on his shoulder and said, "He likes for us to smile. He'll try to make you happy."

Farley dared to press, "What makes you happy?"

"I'll show you." And through a door off the kitchen, she led the way into a garden full of flowers.

"All the Oxus I ever met loved flowers."

"We need some for the tables tonight." Lessolani had him follow her around and hold the flowers she snipped. Then, she wove a crown of pink and white blossoms, which she carefully set on Tsing's head. "Tell me, Farley. What makes you happy?"

"He does. I'll be fine with whatever, so long as we can stay together."

"And ... can you ask him for me? What can I do for Tsing?"

Farley didn't know a jot of the old Pika language, but he figured Verit was safe. Tsing wouldn't under-stand either, so it didn't matter *what* he said. "Dessa sweet? Let Torio know that we're safe. The other servants are nice, and the jobs they're giving are easy."

"He promised me you are safe."

"Be patient. I'll be home in the morning." Farley waited for Tsing to answer.

His bond-brother searched his face, smiled impishly, and went up on tiptoe to kiss the corner of his mouth.

Farley laughed. "We're the same, I guess. I make him happy, too."

"I'll place you together." Lessolani poked a couple of fragrant blooms into Farley's hair. "Your duties begin tonight. For the most part, your only job is to not spill any of the dishes you carry to the table. Are you skittish around living statues?"

"Nope. I like them."

"Some of them serve alongside us. Treat them as you would any other person."

Farley liked her enough to hope she really *was* happy.

The sun set long before the evening meal was served, and it didn't take Farley long to figure out why dinner was so late. Lord Roth's collection included four starstone statues, who moved through the candlelit dining room. A starstone Basq statue stood to one side with a wine bottle in his hands, waiting for the lord to call for more drink. A matched pair of Fwan statues twirled through a graceful dance, providing entertainment. The fourth statue was a bear who was clearly a favorite of the children. Farley thought she'd been made to mind youngsters, since she kept checking on those in her charge. She even trundled over and thrust her nose into Farley's palm.

"Good work," he whispered, giving her a pat.

Tsing returned from delivering a bowl of fruit to the head table and leaned into Farley's side. "Did you find the blue lady?"

"I know where to look. She's somewhere above us. On another floor."

"The house has four stories."

Farley hadn't noticed. "After everyone turns in, we'll search."

"What if we're not free to roam?"

"We planned for what we could." Farley peered around. "It doesn't seem like they're going to lock us up or anything."

Tsing nibbled at his lower lip. "But will they leave us *alone*?"

Farley followed his gaze to where Lord Roth watched them over the rim of his goblet. "Don't mind him. We'll be gone tomorrow."

"What about tonight?"

"Tonight's our chance, remember? Nothing to worry about."

Tsing had been right to worry. When Lessolani showed them to a room for the night, Farley balked on the threshold. "This is our room?"

"For now."

The room was fancy, with a fire banked on a hearth and candles softly flickering upon the mantle. Tall mirrors multiplied the view of a low bed that was half hidden by swaths of sheer cloth.

Farley ventured, "Can't be insect netting. There's no windows."

Lessolani set a steaming pitcher on the washstand and set out two nightshirts. "Wash. Change. Sleep."

Tsing pointed to the only other furnishings in the room—a deep chair and a low table where a goblet waited.

Her smile was apologetic. "Lord Roth may pay a visit."

"Why?"

"He likes to ... admire his things." She softly added, "He only looks. Usually."

When she excused herself, the door clicked softly, but there was no sound of a lock. An advantage that would come to nothing if the Tisk lord dropped by.

In silence, they got ready for bed. The nightshirts were short and silky, and the bedsheets were equally fine. "Guess this is a nice break from the hammock," Farley remarked.

"Mmm." Even with room to spread out, Tsing pressed as

close as ever.

"It'll be fine," Farley soothed. "Better than fine, since our statue is on this same floor."

"How soon before we go check."

"A while, I think. We need to wait and see if Roth shows up."

Tsing promised, "I'll try to stay awake."

Farley knew better. He watched the fire as he petted Tsing's ears. Minutes later, the Pika was breathing deeply. "Third floor, a windowless interior room to the left of the main stairs," he quietly reported. "Our statue is also on this floor."

Dessa said, *"We're nearby."*

"Don't come charging in. Tsing and I are expecting company."

"I'll know if you're frightened. I'll know if you're hurt."

"I'm clean and fed and comfortable, and Tsing's right here with me. Fell asleep as soon as I tucked him in, same as always."

"Larkin knows. Larkin will hunt."

"Nothing to hunt, Dessa sweet. He just wants to show off."

She didn't answer.

Farley watched the fire burn low, and he let his attention stray to the threads of magic that drifted through the vicinity. There were statues above, but most were on the main floor. Those were probably the starstone guardians from earlier. But he was also picking up on hints of redstone, moonstone, and titian jade on the move. The rest weren't stirring. Or couldn't stir.

He caught himself dozing and pulled Tsing closer as he opened his eyes ... then going still. Lord Roth sat in the chair, a glass of amber liquid in one hand.

"Don't be afraid," he soothed. "I didn't mean to wake you."

Farley glanced around. As far as he could tell, the Tisk was the only other person in the room. "Hi. Why are you here? Is this your room?"

"All the rooms are mine." Candlelight flickered across the glass of his spectacles. "I must confess, this is one of my favorites. Are you comfortable? You certainly look comfortable. Do you always sleep with your princeling?"

"Yeah, since he's Pika. My brother would be lonely otherwise."

"He likes to be touched?"

Farley frowned. "He's mine."

"On the contrary, he's mine." The Tisk took a slow sip of his drink, then gestured with his goblet. "Both of you are. Tell me, cloudstrider, do you remember the sky you came from?"

"Not sure," Farley hedged. "Sometimes, people will tell stories that sound familiar. And sometimes, people—especially Tisk like you, sir—say I stepped out of a story."

Lord Roth propped his chin on his fist. "Do you know the stories of your kind?"

"Next to none ... sir. Will you tell me one?"

"All right, lad." Taking another swallow of liquor, he began, "It's long been said that Basq are the dragons of the sea, and Furl are the dragons of the sky. But *Tisk* are the dragons who rule over territories. Like me."

"Sounds important."

Lord Roth beamed and launched into a detailed account of how he'd struggled and strived and prevailed over all opposition in order to rule over this territory. Farley had hoped for more about cloudstriders, but he didn't feel like interrupting the droning man. As the hero of his own fable, Roth was a patron of the arts, a protector of his people, and a lover of beautiful things.

Farley would have liked to point out that people were not things, but he pretended to drift off instead. Maybe without an audience, the Tisk would go away.

He did ramble to a stop, and Farley could hear him lingering over his drink. He tried to think serene thoughts instead of being unsettled that some stranger wanted to watch him sleep.

Eventually, the glass clinked softly as it was set down, and the Tisk lord's shadow fell across the bed. Farley was ready to leap to Tsing's defense, no matter the consequences. But then fingers brushed lightly through Farley's hair before coming to rest upon his horn.

"Your kind are said to be the best bait for luring sky dragons." Lord Roth's voice was mellow with liquor and weighted by greed. "Shall we find out if my investment can net me an even greater rarity?"

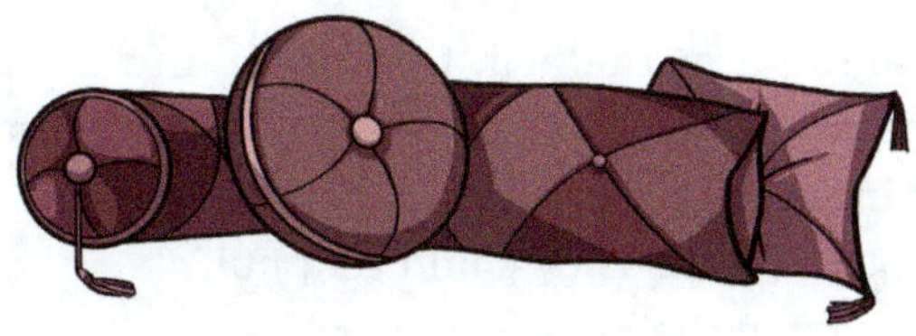

Farley woke to Nestor nipping his thumb and knew Larkin had arrived. He had no idea what time it was since the fire had burned out and Lord Roth had snuffed the candles.

"Nestor's with me," he mumbled for Dessa's sake, then gave Tsing's shoulder a shake.

They untangled themselves, and Farley put his feet on the floor. Almost immediately, a draft caressed his ankles, and he relaxed. The hand at his throat made him smile.

"I'll have you know that counts as affection," Farley murmured. "A Harrow is a Harrow is a Harrow."

Larkin leaned close and breathed, "Bring the sleepyhead princeling."

"Any guards?"

"None currently conscious."

"So ... you guys found her?"

But the Pred was already gone.

Farley gave Tsing another shake, and this time his bond-brother pulled himself up. "M'sorry. Fell 'sleep."

"Ready to go home?"

Cloth rustled and Tsing sounded more awake. "Are Char and Nyx here? I can't see anything."

"Right here." Farley extended his hand, and Char nosed it. "You go on ahead to where Dessa's waiting. I'll follow."

Tsing fumbled his way onto the lioness's back and wrapped his arms around her neck.

She slipped away without a sound, and Farley murmured, "Char has Tsing."

"I'll keep him safe."

"Thank you, Dessa sweet."

He bent to grab the bundle of clothes and boots he'd left at the foot of the bed, then stole into the hall, where Larkin stood with Pollim and Eullia before a door. The Pred pointed to it with his dagger.

"Yeah. In there. They could tell, huh?"

Larkin tried the door. Unlocked.

Farley followed them into what appeared to be a bathing chamber. Moonlight filtered through high windows, showing a sunken tub, the stove for heating water, and gleaming pipes that led to a spigot. Beside all that was a freshstone Clow standing upon a low pedestal.

At Larkin's signal, Eullia stepped forward and lifted the lady, bracing her with all four of his arms. As soon as he walked toward the door, Pollim bent to collect her pedestal. Larkin tossed an impatient hand sign and followed. Farley had to jog to keep up.

"Get aboard Nyx and go," Larkin ordered, as if Farley didn't remember the plan.

"Hold up," he countered. "We've attracted someone's attention."

The starstone Basq who'd been waiting on tables earlier glided along the hallway toward them. Eullia and Pollim stopped, and Farley hurried forward. Larkin growled a warning, but Farley waved it aside. "Hi, again. We came to get this lady. She wants to go home to her family. We'll take her there."

Offering an upraised palm, the Basq statue inclined his head.

Farley matched his offer of peace and couldn't help but ask, "Did you want to leave?"

He received a genial smile and a single headshake.

Larkin got everyone moving again. Farley swung a leg over Nyx's back and bent low over the bundle of clothes to hold it in place. But before signaling for the lioness to run, he searched the starstone Basq's face and whispered, "Thank you." Because really, the stone guardian was doing his job, looking after the members of this household. Including him and Tsing and the kidnapped blue lady. "Be brave and do your best."

17

Thousand Bells Road

Torio sat with legs stretched and ankles crossed as he watched Larkin working with Artor. Since Papaver Pass, the good captain had been trying the man with different weapons, and he'd finally settled on a cumbersome old greatsword. There was little doubt the Ursa had the necessary strength for such a weapon, and his superior reach would give him a considerable advantage against most adversaries.

Larkin came over and crouched beside Torio's chair. "Well ...?"

"It suits him. Where did you come by the thing?"

"It belonged to my uncle, Flaygore Harrow, who inherited it from Bram Flaygore, his grandsire ... and namesake. Not sure he liked either legacy."

"A family heirloom."

Larkin flapped a hand dismissively. "It's deucedly old-fashioned, but it's tough as a battleax. If Artor swings true, it'll cleave stone."

They watched the Ursa go through the training exercise Larkin had outlined.

Artor approached these lessons with the same focus and

tenacity he showed while toiling over intricate floor tiles.

"Given time, he might be useful," Larkin said diplomatically.

"Especially if your parents take him under their wing."

"Aye. Mother was more famous for thrown blades and for the saber dance, but she handled a greatsword with frightening grace."

"Artor's true calling is to stone."

Larkin conceded the point with a grunt, but pointed out, "Uncle is useless with weapons. If he takes on an apprentice who can defend him, all the better."

A few swings later, and Torio cleared his throat. "Better correct that now."

"Aye." Larkin stood, calling Artor to a halt. Beckoning for the blade, he slowly demonstrated the correct motion.

Artor muttered something, and Larkin missed a beat. He peered around, again showed the proper way to swing the weapon, then mimicked the way Artor had been pulling short. The extension needed to be correct, or the greatsword would be more of a hindrance than a help.

The weapon traded hands, and Artor proved he could be taught.

But also that ... something else was getting in the way of success.

Larkin explained.

Artor listened.

But then Artor said something that made Larkin turn to Torio with a look that pleaded for help.

Rising, Torio joined them. "What seems to be the trouble?"

Larkin couldn't have looked more baffled. "He says ... he's afraid to hurt someone."

"How very un-Pred-like," Torio said with a smile. "Artor, there's room out here, and the others know better than to step into your swing."

"What about Char and Nyx?" he ventured. "They like to

steal up on me, and I wouldn't hear them coming. Or ... even Dessa."

"They were sculpted by a Pred, and they spent many weeks lounging in courtyards while small people endured lessons in every conceivable fighting style." Torio tapped the sword with a talon. "Their knowledge of this blade likely exceeds your own."

Artor didn't look convinced.

Torio turned to Larkin. "Perhaps if we wrapped the blade ...?"

Larkin caught on. "Aye. I'll fetch bandages ...."

"It's not much of a sword if it can't slice through cloth," Artor flatly pointed out.

With a laugh, Torio said, "Sheathed, then?"

"Nay ... the balance!"

Artor ran a finger along the grip and tentatively spoke. "These colors. They're a bad omen."

Larkin frowned. "Given this blade's history, I'm not really surprised." With all seriousness, he asked, "Is there a countermeasure?"

"You've encountered Ursa omens before?" asked Torio.

"Aye. We spent many summers on Last Continent, and our vacation home is in Ursa territory." Seeking Artor's gaze, he asked, "Is there a charm that would ease your mind?"

"Something yellow."

"Give me a moment." Larkin hurried away, disappearing into his cabin and emerging a minute later with his hands full and Dan in tow. Showing three different items of clothing, the Pred asked, "Which of these is the right color?"

Artor tentatively chose. "This ...?"

With a grunt, Larkin sat upon the deck and used a blade to slit the garment down the center. With more quick slashes, he reduced the cloth to narrow strips.

"I'm sorry. Your things," Artor mumbled, joining them

on the planks.

"Have you noticed my wearing an abundance of yellow?" Larkin inquired wryly. "These are things my father foisted on me at one time or another. To *set off my eyes*."

Torio smiled. It was the sort of thing Harrow would do.

Larkin knotted one of the yellow strips to a flat ring and spoke to Dan again. Then began a three-way, bilingual conversation about cord-weaving that didn't require Torio's arbitration, so he meandered back to his chair.

Since their little heist, things were going smoothly.

He was on the mend, and that had improved Dessa's mood.

Farley had wangled a superlative block of freshstone out of Teegay Caterwaul, then used the coin Lord Roth had used to buy him and Tsing in order to secure two sweet-natured smaller stones from Meridian's stone markets—one crystal, one dawnstone.

Tsing was pestering for language lessons at every other turn, clearly anxious to make a good impression on Farley's family ... *his* family.

And as the Grif stretched out his legs and recrossed his ankles, he noted that the sinking sun had turned much of the sky to gold. A good omen, surely.

Four more days brought them to Verge, a vibrant coastal city that was the main port for both Keet and Clow territories. Of course, being the closest port to the Songstone Mountain didn't mean they were anywhere near it. Unlike Nerida, Shiri wasn't along the shore, so Farley was readying his carriage.

Tsing laughed softly and pushed at the stallion who was lipping one of his ears. "Which one is this?"

"Coquet." The Pika's blank look had Farley mentally scrambling to sort out what the stallion's name would be in Terse. Back when Jubilee was getting introductions, it'd gone more smoothly since they both spoke Verit.

"So you're a flirt," Tsing accused, stroking Coquet's glossy neck. Then he confided, "So am I."

Farley snorted. Tsing wasn't a flirt. Not really. Not like Jubilee.

His hands stilled, and he frowned up at Rexus for several long moments before moving on to harness Hillock, then Blaze. But Farley's thoughts nagged at him.

Tsing startled him by flinging both arms around his neck. "Where have you gone? Why are you sad?"

Farley smiled into his bond-brother's upturned face. Tsing might not be a flirt, but he sure was sensitive to moods. "I'm not sad. Not really."

"I know when a brother needs my embrace. See? Here I am."

Hugging Tsing back, Farley admitted, "I just realized something. I miss my friend."

"Isn't that normal?"

"Not for me ...? I guess I don't really ... I dunno. I don't think I dwell on the past. It's more fun to keep moving forward."

"But you miss your friend. Which friend?" Tsing's ears tipped sideways, at an angle that Farley now knew meant he was teasing. "You make friends of every stranger."

"I've mentioned Jubilee, yeah?"

"Nooo." Tsing's ears slowly lifted. "That's *interesting*!"

"Huh?"

"People hide their treasures."

Farley snorted. "I'm not hiding anything."

Tsing nodded. "You don't. Not a thing."

He frowned and repeated, "I'm not hiding anything."

"I know." The Pika happily added, "It makes you easy to love. And easy to beat in games of Changing Seas."

Farley's plans met a hitch when he found out that all the Oxus on board were taking leave so they could visit Prahkreet, which lay farther to the east. "I wasn't even thinking. I assumed one of them could take care of my chickens."

Torio showed him on a map. "Since our trip to the Songstone Mountain will take several weeks, they'll cut through the jungle here ... straight into familiar territory. They can spend time with their kin, and once we've satisfied your considerable curiosity, Larkin will move the *Moontide* to this port." He pointed to a city at the northeastern point of Far Continent. "From here, at Halcyon, we can either make the trek into Prahkreet ourselves *or* Harrow has an estate overlooking the sea. I suspect our good captain would prefer to stay there."

"Because of Livia ...?"

"I believe he's hoping she'll be able to meet with him there."

"Any chance she'd bring her little girls?"

"Highly unlikely." Torio paused and amended, "Highly irregular. But they have already flouted their share of traditions."

In the end, Farley left his flock in the care of a pair of Selk who turned out to be father and son. Farley didn't know them well at all, in part because he didn't know a scrap of Ortor. But Larkin not only mediated for him, he also suggested checking out the local poultry. Farley was skeptical, but if there really were pink chickens and green pheasants, he'd be haggling hard for hens, eggs, or both.

After that, they found Dan, who'd been spending his

every free moment at the rail. Farley had never seen a guy so in love with the sea and the sky. It was like ... he was basking in every sunbeam and turning his face into every breeze. Dan made breathing look like an act of worship, just because there was salt in the air.

"Ready for the next adventure?" Farley asked in Verit.

Dan, who was trying to immerse himself in Larkin's native language, dimpled. "Aye. I want to adventure."

They took extra care unloading the carriage and checking harnesses, and Larkin insisted on walking the team through the city, Artor ambling along at his side. It was slow going because the streets were narrow and crowded.

Farley was only chafing a little over not being able to stop and look. The plan was to go directly through the heart of the city, then catch the road to the Songstone Mountain. They'd explore Verge on their way back through, after visiting Shiri.

Even though Larkin had the lead team in hand, Farley rode up top. Better view.

An opinion shared by Tsing, Dan, and Torio, who was acting as tour guide. Four across was a little crowded, but the inside of the carriage was full to bursting with Dessa and the lionesses hidden away.

"This section is mostly occupied by Keet. Note the architecture?" Torio indicated a house that looked more like a stone tower topped by a prickle of spires. At every level, curving balconies were overrun by plants, and from every direction came the scent of flowers and the gentle ringing of chimes. "Clow homes are also tall, but only because they're built in trees. They live on the outskirts of Verge, among the branches of ancient trees. In this way, they form a protective ... hmm." He trailed off.

Farley followed his line of sight.

A group of Grif acrobats were leaping and tumbling on a stage that had been rolled onto the edge of a market square.

Bright costumes and cheery music had drawn a crowd. Farley would have liked to join it, but Larkin didn't slow.

"Do you know them?" Farley asked.

"I know only that they are Grif. It's not my sister's troupe."

"But you thought it might be ...?"

Torio admitted, "Quilleria has a similar set-up. A traveling stage and minstrels. And the last I heard, they were somewhere on this continent."

"So we *could* run into them?"

"I'm not sure you fully grasp the enormity of First Continent."

"Even a slim copper can buy bread."

A saying that took so long to explain to Tsing and then to Dan, they made it all the way through Verge and onto Thousand Bells Road.

Farley had never seen such a road.

Wide enough for four carriages to travel abreast, it was paved in gray stone that was mottled here and there with green. From his seat, Farley couldn't tell if the rock itself changed color or if the increasingly dense overhanging foliage had encouraged moss. They were barely out of the city when the jungle closed in, surrounding them in a dense, green tunnel.

"At least it's shaded?" Farley remarked.

"No more breezes off the sea," Tsing complained, his ears flicking to dislodge a whining insect.

Dan asked something, and Torio nodded. "Bells. Yes. Thousand Bells Road is a good name. Although I suspect Ten Thousand Bells Road would be more accurate. Their sound is supposed to warn away wild animals." He lapsed into Coloq to give the man a more thorough explanation.

Up among the branches, Farley spotted metal tubes hanging in clusters. And yeah, there were bells. Some were so crusty, Farley had to wonder if they even rang anymore. But intermittent notes sounded on all sides.

"Can't feel the breeze, but the branches are moving enough to stir up a little music."

"Imagine this road on a windy day," said Tsing.

Torio said, "In this part of the world, cloudbursts come through at very regular intervals, and they're heavy enough to shake the trees. The Cantl word for these bells literally means 'rain bells.'"

They were still at a walk. Farley called, "Come up, and we can get along faster."

"Nay, not until we've paid our courtesies," replied Larkin.

Torio said, "The bells are one deterrent, and here is another. They keep the road safe from bandit and predator alike."

"A shop?" Farley asked.

"The first of many wayside shops and watering stations. Each is run by a family of Clow who lives alongside the road. They patrol this part of the jungle, making it safe for travelers."

"Who show their gratitude by being good customers?" Farley guessed.

"We're under no obligation to spend our coin, and they don't charge for water. This is their hospitality." Torio sounded proud. "Thousand Bells Road is utterly unique, the only safe road on all of First Continent. Everywhere else, travelers must form caravans and hire guards."

Larkin led the horses into a clearing where sunlight pooled around a low building with thatching that looked like heaped fronds. It wasn't as tidy as the reed thatching Farley had grown up with, but he had little doubt it'd shed water. Other features caught his eye. Long troughs for watering animals. Tables under a rain shelter. Netting to ward off bugs.

The Pred chose the furthest edge and arched his brows. "Now would be a good time to ... rearrange."

Torio leapt down and opened the carriage door. Without

a sound, Char and Nyx slipped into the jungle's shadows.

Setting the brake, Farley jumped to the ground and offered to take Phillit from Dan. The man wasn't at all comfortable tossing the baby in Pred fashion, so Tsing slid down to the wheel and served as middleman in the transfer.

"Come with your Uncle Far. Let's take a little look around. Because something smells nice."

Dan caught up and offered, "May I take Phillit?"

"Your Verit's solid, but nope. It's my turn. Rest. Drink. Wash." He indicated the shop. "Adventure."

"Thank you," he murmured, his hand briefly resting on Farley's shoulder.

Tsing lifted aside the netting that swathed the entrance to what amounted to a fruit stand, and they ducked through. Farley stepped right up to the counter and addressed the woman, trying out his very limited Brohg. "Good day to you. I'm Farley, and these are my friends. I want to know more ...." He ran up against a gap in his vocabulary and sighed. Waving at the array of produce, he searched for a word that might do. "New. Umm ... mysterious."

She grinned broadly and reeled off something, but she spoke so fast, he was lost.

"Again?" he begged.

Her gaze went from Phillit to Dan to Tsing, then back to Farley. "I am Velda, and you are welcome." She spoke much more slowly, and her smile included them all. "This is new for you? Good. I will give you your first taste of Clow hospitality."

Velda bustled them to a table, and a boy brought them cups. His hair and spots were the same reddish brown as the woman's, and Farley asked, "She is your mother?"

Which earned him a shy smile and a quick nod.

"This is my brother."

The boy shook his head and said something that Farley

was pretty sure meant he was using the wrong word. The Clow boy showed open palms to Tsing and said, "Pika." Dan received the same gesture. "Basq. But ... *you*, honored guest?"

"I'm Farley, and I'm Flox. And we really *are* brothers. In a way, Dan is family, too." He checked the door. "Torio or Larkin can explain once they come inside. Sorry. I don't know much Brohg."

Velda came to sit with them, a low basket in one hand. She'd gone through the shop and chosen one of each of the kinds of fruit on display. Dan murmured with pleasure, so he knew at least some of them, but it was all new to Farley. Then Velda proceeded to slice into the first fruit, distributing pieces while she taught their names in Brohg. There were tiny fruit with rinds like melons, and there were berries and something like a grape, except they were light yellow and perfectly round.

Soon, Farley figured out that she was referring to all of them by an endearment. "Taste this, my lovelies," and "So sweet, my lovelies." And Phillit got his own nickname. "My little wee love."

Tall bowls with heavy bottoms arrived, filled with steaming soup, and Farley started guiltily. The better part of an hour had passed, and he'd given no thought to Torio or his team or paying for all this food. He fumbled for his coin purse, muttering apologies, but Velda only laughed.

"No, no, my lovely. Your other brothers are there, with my husband. Was there ever such a family?"

At a table on the other side of the shop's enclosure, Torio, Larkin, and Artor chatted with a Clow man. They'd been served the same bowls of soup, and a half-empty plate of sliced fruit sat at the center of their table.

"Didn't even hear them come in." Farley dearly wanted to know if Larkin had actually claimed him. "Surprised Torio didn't come over to translate for us."

Tsing asked, "Do we really need the help?"

To Velda, Farley said, "Those two speak Brohg."

She countered, "The Grif speaks Cantl. One must be born in treetops to speak Brohg."

Which required translation.

Torio bowed his head. "With apologies, dear woman. You are entirely correct." And to Farley and Tsing, "Brohg is a dialect of Cantl, which is the language of the Keet. The same, yet different ... and the Clow take pride in the distinctions."

Farley was intrigued. "Hey, Larkin! Does that mean you can't actually speak Brohg?"

"I can." And he addressed himself to the couple, spinning out what sounded like a grand announcement. Their hosts laughed and clapped and fetched him a frothing tankard.

"Hey, what'd you say? How come they're so impressed?"

"That woman. Leave it to Ulrica ..." was all Torio managed before giving himself up to laughter. And signaling for a tankard of his own.

"What ...?" Farley demanded.

Larkin said, "Rest assured, my accent is flawless. These good people are impressed because—according to their own declaration—Brohg is my birthright."

Retracing the conversation, Farley frowned. "You were born in a tree?"

"Aye."

"How'd you manage that?"

"Mother went into labor during a tree-cat hunt deep in Clow territory. The host clan escorted her up into their family home, where I was born."

Farley could believe it. He could almost see it. And then he was laughing, too.

Before leaving that first wayside, Farley dragged Larkin over to haggle with Velda, and coin traded hands. There'd be root balls and cuttings waiting when they made their way back through. Farley kissed his fingertips and flung his arms wide in a show of Floxish gratitude. "The trade is good; may our next be better still!"

It sounded even grander when Larkin said it in Brohg.

"They won't grow well on Home Continent," Larkin cautioned. "Winter would kill them."

"What about an indoor garden, like the ones in Meridian?"

Larkin paused. "Aye. They use similar methods on Last Continent, overwintering their plants in caves."

"So I'm onto something? Good." Farley's mind raced. "Hey, could I plant them somewhere at your dad's place in Halcyon? Then I can transplant or take cuttings whenever Tupp gets things arranged on Morven."

"You think your brother will build you an indoor garden?"

"I think he'd do it for Frey and everyone else who lives up top. He'll decide it's worth it, especially if your mom likes the idea. Which she will. You should see how she fusses in the grove."

"Aye." And again, "Aye. Father would certainly give you permission to potter in his garden."

"What about household servants or whatever? Is someone who's living there gonna protest a bleater mucking about in their garden?"

"Nay." Larkin turned to leave, but Farley still caught his next words. "I'll back you up."

New shops came into view at regular intervals, and there always seemed to be something worth a closer look. The smell of grilling meat. The tuning of a bard's instrument. A climbing vine with vivid flowers. A chance to ride tame elephants. So Farley would rein in the team and make time for an extra adventure.

"There's a saying," Torio said, with a decided twinkle in his eyes. "The hospitality of Clow both shortens and lengthens the journey."

Farley sheepishly admitted, "At this rate, it'll take us three weeks to get to the Songstone Mountain."

"Five," countered Torio. "But we'll lack for nothing along the way."

"Are there places we can stay over?"

"Many inns. And many more Clow who would willingly open their homes."

"I feel a little guilty, keeping Larkin from his ship."

"He would be a good deal grumpier if his wife wasn't otherwise engaged with family matters." Torio softly added, "He's relaxed. I think he's enjoying Dan's discoveries nearly as much as I'm enjoying yours."

"What about you, Dessa sweet?"

"We are the only ones for miles and miles," she answered. *"It's empty. Almost like walking under the sea."*

"No other statues?" Farley checked. "Is it lonely?"

Dessa took her time replying. *"No statues. No threats."*

Farley wondered if he should point out that the Misbegotten weren't the only dangers in the world.

He glanced at Torio, who shook his head.

"This is a safe road," Farley promised. "Are you restless? Did you want to walk with the lionesses?"

"I will not wander. That's for Char and Nyx to do." She softly added, *"If I'm close, no one can crack you."*

Farley didn't want to disappoint her, but he couldn't help offering a small protest. "You love me *because* I'm adventurous ... remember?"

She didn't answer, but he could kinda, almost, sorta tell that she was happy. And that was good enough for him.

They were nearing another set of structures when Tsing's ears snapped upright. "Hear that?" he asked.

Farley glanced around, ears straining.

"The chimes. Up ahead." Eyes widening, Tsing looked to Torio. "Is it ...? It must be the rain!"

"Ah. It is getting to be that time. Farley, this one's an inn, which is perfect for waiting out the downpour. If there's room, drive the team straight under that shelter. It's meant for wagons and carriages."

With a flip of the reins, Farley encouraged the stallions to pick up their hooves. He could hear it now, a frantic jangling coming from further south along the road. As they rolled into the inn's yard, he looked up, catching a glimpse of the sky. Swirling clouds were sinking their way, trailing streamers of mist.

They rolled to a stop under a long shed with open sides, right as the rain hit it with a hiss and rattle in the thatching. Farley hopped down and walked to the far edge, putting his hand out into the rain. It wasn't like any kind of rain he'd ever seen. "I've said it's pouring before, but ... this. This is unbelievable. It's like a waterfall."

"We may as well stay the night here," Larkin decided. "I'll speak to the innkeeper about rooms."

"I'll help you with the horses," offered Artor.

With Torio and Tsing pitching in, the stallions were soon out of harness and rubbed and praised for a good day's work. Larkin returned from the inn with a sturdy old Clow who clucked admiringly over Farley's horses. He showed Farley where to find feed, then went right down the line, murmuring in low Brohg while he ran his hands over them, even going so far as to check their hooves.

Farley arched his brow at Larkin, who said, "There are

pests that sometimes latch onto animals. He'll show you what to watch for."

Rexus and Coquet were clear, but Hillock had picked up a clinging bug, and they combed a big spider out of Blaze's mane. Satisfied, the Clow next pulled netting into place around horses and carriage.

"To keep off insects?" Farley reasoned aloud.

"Them, too," said Torio. "But it's mostly for the bats."

"Don't bats eat harmful insects?"

"Not these bats." With a thin smile, the Grif said, "Inns like this are a necessity. Many jungle predators are nocturnal."

All thoughts of bloodthirsty creatures faded once they made the short dash to the inn's front door. The inside was an interesting combination of a high, raftered ceiling and low windows. Lanterns cast a warm glow over an assembly of mismatched tables and chairs. A savory, smoky scent drew Farley's attention to a netting-draped porch at the opposite side of the building, where a couple of Clow were turning skewers of meat over a long, narrow grill. But between him and them was a feature that he'd completely missed in the haste of their arrival.

The inn was built around a tree.

A staircase was fitted and braced right up against actual bark, and it spiraled up and away. Farley elbowed Larkin, who retaliated with a pinch. "Tell me I'll be sleeping in a tree tonight," he begged.

"Aye. You'll be sleeping in a tree tonight."

The rain kept up, and more people sought shelter, crowding in and ordering food and drink that Farley hadn't realized was on the menu. Torio went to negotiate with the kitchen, and plates soon arrived with a sampling of various dishes.

Tsing brought out stones for Changing Seas, and soon he, Dan, and Farley were absorbed in a three-way game.

At the next table, Larkin sat with Phillit on his lap, feeding him slivers of fruit. The little boy was "talking," a string of untranslatable baby noises. Larkin encouraged him by murmuring replies into one tiny, pointed ear, and Farley caught just enough to gather that Phillit's lessons in Verit had begun.

"This," he sighed.

His bond-brother dragged his attention from his strategies to ask, "What?"

"This. I like this."

Tsing's gaze went to the contents of the plate, and he looked doubtful. "Really? Are you sure? I think it's a stuffed and roasted frog."

"Oh, that one's okay, but I mean this. Us. Today." He caught Dan's eye and waved to the room. "The sky is a waterfall. The jungle is all around. The flavors are new. This game doesn't care that we're from three different continents and speak three different languages. And tonight, our beds will be in a tree. It's like ... the perfect day."

Dan peered around the crowded room, murmured something in Coloq, then nodded. "I like this adventure," he offered in Verit.

Not to be outdone, Tsing made his own observation in Verit. "We are perfect."

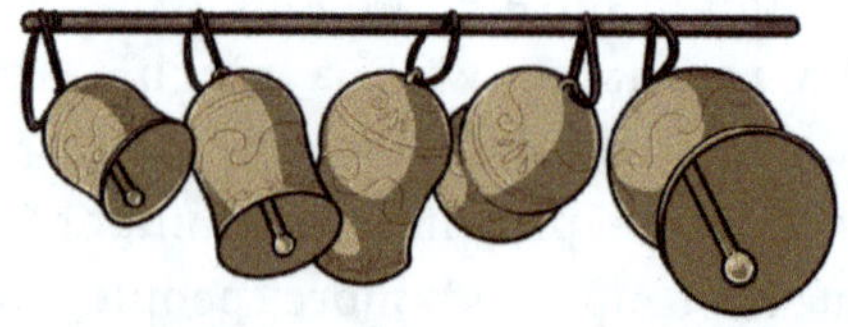

They set out again shortly after sunup, and Farley had every intention of getting further down the road. But excuses to stop were easy to come by.

Every wayside shop had its own specialty, not to be missed.

With the heat, the horses needed rest and water.

Bells rang warnings, and they'd rush to find shelter

from the rain.

Nights came early, and who knew when the next inn might appear.

So days passed, and with each, Farley felt a little richer for the experiences they held. His purse was lighter, though. He'd spoken for more potted shrubs, vines, and cuttings, including a spindly twig that might someday be the biggest tree on Morven's southern slopes. Maybe Tupp's great, great grandchildren would build homes in its branches and open a roadside shop in its shade.

They'd wiled away two weeks and were well into their third when Dessa alerted them to a change.

"*There is stone. There are statues.*" She later added, "*This mountain likes to sing.*"

"So we're close?" Farley asked.

Torio hummed. "Not as close as we are to the next twenty or so distractions."

Tsing sweetly asked, "Three more days?"

"Perhaps four. This close to Chime Winds, the shops are larger and more lavish."

Farley was afraid they might be right, but he wasn't about to let on. "I wonder why Morven isn't surrounded by a city. Most of the other ones are, yeah?"

Torio hummed. "Your villages are prosperous enough, but the Flox have only expanded away from Morven. Not toward her."

"We don't have a capital city, either."

"Neither do Grif. Although we have royalty. Technically, Chime Winds *isn't* the Keet capital. It's their royal city."

The shops *were* getting larger, and they were more crowded. "I'm seeing a lot of feathers."

"Customers from the city," explained Torio. "They take daytrips on the Thousand Bells Road to enjoy Clow hospitality."

So at the next stop, he and Torio called to Nyx and Char,

who slipped back into hiding with Dessa.

Larkin recommended letting the horses pick up their heels and bypassing the remaining Clow shops in favor of reaching Chime Winds. When Torio seconded him, Farley conceded. "Are we going straight to Shiri?"

"Aye, we're expected. The Keeper of the Songstone Mountain is a Tisk named Anka Thuen. Her husband acts as her secretary, and he's been in communication with both me and my father. I sent him word of our plans before leaving Far Continent." Larkin's gaze settled on Tsing then. "I should probably mention ... he's the son of Shiri's previous Keeper."

Interesting, but not terribly informative. Farley held up thumb and forefinger. "You left out some tiny details. Like why that matters."

"Keeper Thuen's husband and children are all Pika."

At Farley's side, Tsing gasped.

18

City of Chimes

Magic flitted in Farley's periphery as they neared the end of Thousand Bells Road. Slowly, the jungle receded. Well, not completely. Because the Keet had welcomed greenery into their city. Tall buildings and spreading trees created a lush maze through Shiri's foothills.

In the jungle, Farley had been impressed by stuff he'd never seen outside of the Statuary. Birds with fanning tail feathers. Butterflies bigger than his hand. Hooting calls that turned out to be monkeys.

In Chime Winds, all those new things had been flipped, because the people were the ones with bright feathers, and they dressed like butterflies. Plus, they kept tiny pet monkeys on ribbon leashes. From the carriage seat, he and Tsing and Dan gawked while Torio did his best to elucidate.

And the citizens of Chime Winds all turned and gawked right back.

Farley's black carriage and team didn't fit their city's mood at all.

Everyone and everything was cast in soft colors, as if a rainbow had descended. Farley searched for the right words to explain it to Tupp, who was interested in far-off places even if he never did want to leave home. Chime Winds was ... well, it was pretty. But in an especially elegant way. And there was a feeling to it. Joyful. Gentle.

"The whole city is singing," Tsing whispered.

"How do all the different noises not clash?" Farley muttered back.

True to its name, chimes were everywhere. They passed under a bridge that had an entire carillon of bells set into its trestles. Another had pipes that Torio swore sang in perfect harmony when the wind was just right.

"Are all the people here Keet?" asked Tsing.

"In this part of the city, yes. Nearer to the Keep is the stonecrafters' district, and you'll find representatives of most races there."

Dan asked something, diverting Torio's attention, and Farley gazed around, trying to memorize the scene. Only ... he realized that Tsing was especially quiet. And tense. Farley put his elbows on his knees, leaning low to catch the Pika's downcast gaze. "Hey," he said softly. "This place is amazing, yeah?"

Tsing's smile was quick and gone. And not especially genuine.

Farley tried again. "Need something?"

His bond-brother tensed.

Now he was confused. "Tsing?"

"It's ... nothing."

But it wasn't. Rather than argue, Farley eased an arm around the Pika's back, inviting him closer. Tsing pressed close but kept quiet. Unsure what else to do, Farley let the matter slide. Tsing would speak up when he was ready.

By now, Farley was noticing certain trends. Keet men and women both wore robes that left their shoulders bare. Jewelry seemed popular, especially arm bands. And a startling number of people were carrying the sorts of cases that were used for instruments.

Farley had seen plenty of Keet statues, including Pollim, but stone feathers couldn't emulate the array of color on display around him. Plumage incorporated two, three, and even four colors, and there was a sheen to it. He really wanted a closer look.

"Turn here," directed Larkin. "Cross the bridge, then look for any open hitching post. We'll need a guide before we can go further. I'll have a runner carry a message into the Keep. Let them know we've arrived."

Farley had no trouble, and while they waited to hear back, their group drifted toward a large gazebo where a group of men and women with wind instruments were putting on a concert. Just ... in the middle of everything, adding to the city's music.

A response didn't take long to arrive.

From a wide gate with doors painted songstone green, a Pika half-jogged, half-walked. The man swiveled, spied their group, and waved an arm. He reminded Farley a little of Greysallow. His hair and fur were the same sort of blended gray.

Before the Pika could launch into whatever greeting he drew breath for, Tsing broke from the rest of them, hurling himself at the man. The kiss that came next clearly took the older man by surprise. Farley knew from his etiquette lessons that this was one of the more ... well, it was an enthusiastic kiss. Jubilee had called it *heartfelt*.

Larkin looked shocked, and Artor groaned.

Torio moved to intercede. "Tsing. Dear boy, I don't think Tourmaline can ...."

Farley was hurrying forward, too, so he heard when the gray Pika pulled back and softly said, "I apologize, young buck, if my kiss falls short in any regard. You see, I was born here, among the Keet, so I never learned all the customs that are part of my father's heritage."

Tsing tried to push away, ears as pink as he cheeks, but Tourmaline pulled him into a snug embrace.

"I did have a *real* Pika for a tutor, though that was years ago now. Because when my father answered Shiri's call, he came to this place with a few friends—a small brotherhood of journeymen—since Pika cannot be alone for long. Are you the only one in your party?"

A small nod.

Farley spoke up. "Tsing's family died, but he has me. He has us."

Tourmaline's gaze went soft. "Let me try again, Tsing."

The kiss was an offer of comfort more than anything, and when it ended, Tsing's cheeks were wet. He hid his face against Tourmaline's shoulder, and the older man began petting his hair, then his ears. Tsing just kinda melted ... and clung there.

Farley felt sick.

Sure, Tsing had him, but he needed more.

Artor moved to Farley's side and put an arm around his shoulders.

"Am I a terrible brother?" Farley whispered.

"No."

"He wants another Pika, though." It was so obvious now, watching him.

Tourmaline was saying, "My siblings and my sons will be delighted to meet you. Probably plague you with questions. And quite possibly try to woo you away from your friends." With this, he addressed the rest of them. "Hello, my name is Tourmaline. Welcome to the Songstone Mountain. You'll be staying with us in the Keep. Larkin, it's been years. And Torio Kite! According to the letters we received from Aurelius Harrow, your long journey finally met with success."

"Thank you for permitting my return."

The man raised a hand. "I hope you'll forgive Anka's

treatment back then. Your stone's cacophony fouled Shiri's mood, and ... well. My wife is the protective sort."

"Dessa's presence hasn't caused any trouble?"

Tourmaline's gaze went straight to the carriage. "Freydolf has all our respect for bringing something so lovely from out of that storm."

Farley blurted, "You can see magic?"

"Not see, but ... sense. Farley Meadowsweet, I presume? Your reputation precedes you."

That sounded suspicious. "Oh, yeah? What did Aurelius say?"

Tourmaline's ears drooped. "I apologize. That was so vague. I'm referring to your skills where the Misbegotten are concerned. When we first heard from Aurelius and later, when Larkin's letter from Verge confirmed your intention to visit, we were delighted. *Relieved*."

Farley caught on. "You need us to hunt something down?"

"We have ... let us say ... a problem child. And yes, it would be best if they were stopped."

When Tourmaline released Tsing, the young Pika moved to rejoin Farley, who opened his arms. "Hey," he murmured. The poor guy looked heartbroken. So Farley pulled him in and rocked back and forth, the way he would have done if he was goofing off to cheer up one of his nieces or nephews.

His intent must have carried through, because he felt a puff of laughter against his neck.

Farley guessed he hadn't lost his touch.

Scooping up his bond-brother, he manfully toted him in wake of the rest. With a sidelong look, Farley said, "I'm not

Pika, but you know I love you, right?"

Tsing wrinkled his nose and kind of batted at him with the tips of his ears. That was a new trick.

"I can kinda guess what happened. I mean ... he looks like the home you've been missing."

"Yes."

"And ... I'm not the home you need ...?"

"You are!" protested Tsing. "But when I saw him, I suddenly wanted everything back."

Farley adjusted his hold and marched on. "So does he kiss with a Cantl accent?"

"Mmm. His heart wasn't in it."

"I should hope not. He has a wife."

"Oh! Yes." Tsing tentatively asked, "Will she be upset?"

"Not really sure. I mean, you were just saying *hello.*"

Tsing guiltily ducked his head.

"Oh, boy." Farley tried not to laugh. "Maybe it's a good thing your intentions didn't translate."

"I'm so embarrassed."

"I think Tourmaline didn't want you to be. He seems nice."

"Mmm."

"Hey, you *do* remember that Artor is fluent in ... well, I assume kisses and all that. Since he coached me a bit when we first entered Pika territory."

Tsing's ears lifted, then went all cockeyed. "You've kissed Artor?"

"Nooo, that's not what I meant. Back then, I didn't even know better than to make direct eye contact."

"Yes. You *are* a bold one."

"Oh, whoops. I've been looking at you straight-on this whole time."

"It was confusing at first, but I'm used to it now." And with a small squirm, he added, "I must be heavy."

"You *are.* Another minute, and I'll be forced to stagger."

With an exasperated sniff, Tsing rapped his shoulder

and demanded, "Put me down."

Farley did, but he kept the Pika trapped in the circle of his arms. "I need to know what you need, even if it's embarrassing to talk about. Or if not me, confide in Artor or Torio. Maybe even Larkin. You could work out a—what'd you call it—a guiding bond with one of them."

Tsing looked after their group. Larkin was back to leading the team, and they weren't exactly rushing. They'd have no trouble catching up.

With a pout, the Pika said, "I wish I could speak to Dan. I think *he* would understand."

"Well, if you both work on your Verit, I think ... hey. How come *Dan*?"

"Because." Tsing's smile turned impish. "We stow our rigging the same way."

"And that's important?"

"Essential."

"If you say so." Farley angled his head toward the others. "Ready?"

"Nooo. But yes." And more quietly, "Thank you, Farley."

Hand-in-hand, they entered the Keep.

Torio fell in step with Artor. "Do you have much experience with songstone?"

"Hardly any. Ketik didn't deal in the rarer stones."

"It's certainly not rare here." He pivoted and pointed, wanting to make sure Artor got a look at the reverse side of the arched gate they'd just passed through. The whole thing had been carved with an intricate scene. "Behold, Shiri's most famous masterpiece. Not the most potent stone … but remarkable for its exquisite detail."

An enormous dragon coiled amidst stylized clouds, its four viciously-clawed hands fanning out as they framed the lovely figure of a Keet woman who stood at the top of the archway, her hands set in the sign for peace, her face turned toward the looming dragon as she sang.

"Another story from Keet lore?" Artor guessed.

"Quite famous. In fact, when I was a boy, our troupe used to put on a play, reenacting Moneta's tale. While a crowd-pleaser, I dreaded every performance." Waving at the heroine, he admitted, "I was cast in the title role and forced to wear a dress."

"I thought you mentioned a sister. Couldn't she have stepped in and saved you?"

"Father knew she couldn't pull off the sweet and innocent act." Dropping into a conspiratorial tone, he said, "Quilleria has always been more of a dragon."

Artor pointed out, "Dragons are protectors."

"A popular theme as guardians go. Have I mentioned that Morven's first masterpiece is also a dragon? Quite formidable."

Beyond the next courtyard, Tourmaline led them through a set of double doors, carriage and all.

Torio spoke up. "I'm grateful for the consideration, but won't this cause a stir?"

"Not really. Any time we take delivery of a large stone, it's carted along this same route, which leads directly to the Keeper's private workshop. People will assume this is another one of my little gifts for Anka."

And so Dessa was delivered in fine style to Keeper Thuen's doorstep.

"You're very quiet," Torio murmured as he handed Dessa down from the carriage.

"I've been listening. There's so much to hear."

"Do you like music?" He'd never thought to ask before.

"I like it when you hum."

"Do I?"

"Only sometimes. Not often. But when you do ... I like it."

"Farley sings."

"Farley does," she said, sounding thoroughly pleased over this detail. She rested her fingertips over his heart and added, *"Humming accompanies your happiness, so it's very ... satisfying."*

"You want me to be happy?"

"I want to make *you happy."*

"An interesting distinction."

"You are mine," she reminded before sweeping through the door.

Their group filed into a sizeable storeroom for magical stone. Blocks bore the wax seals of other mountains' Keepers. Indeed, two columns of moonstone showed documentation in Aurelius Harrow's own hand of the grades he and Farley had assigned.

"Nice!" exclaimed Farley, who jogged up a ramp to the room's second tier. "Why doesn't Frey have a set-up like this? Wait 'til I tell Carden!"

Torio spared a glance for the pair of burly fire-eaters—currently still—who flanked the door they'd entered, poised to help with the shifting of rock.

"This way, please," called Tourmaline, who was already at the top of a different ramp. "Things are more comfortable through here. Please, be welcome in our home."

"You live in the Keeper's workshop?" Farley asked, jumping down and grabbing Tsing's hand before going to Tourmaline. "So does Frey. Him and my brother both did, at least up until Tupp got married. Oh, wow! Hey, little guy!"

A child collided with Tourmaline's leg and clung there, peering up at Farley. He looked to be five or six, a perfect replica of his father, save for the color of his hair and fur.

Torio had known, of course, as had Larkin. But Tsing was visibly taken aback ... and taken. He sank to his knees before Tourmaline and held out his hands to the little boy.

"This is Evensong, our youngest," the Pika said with an indulgent smile. And to the boy, "Here's a new friend. Go ahead, Evie. Show him your new pet."

From the front pocket of the apron he wore over his other clothes, the boy lifted a wriggling songstone monkey with a ribbon leash. It was a tiny thing, just right for small hands, and it connected the child to its maker with a fiercely protective magical bond. Torio didn't intend to find out if Anka had given it teeth.

Torio only half-listened to Tourmaline, who was showing Larkin a letter, presumably from Aurelius. Apparently, an order was being placed on Frey's behalf, and so they'd carry home a sizeable chunk of songstone. Another personal guardian in the works. Something about another baby on the way.

They lapsed into an initial dicker, during which Larkin offered their services to assess any of the Keep's blocks with the new system ... in partial payment for Frey's hoped-for stone. Torio had heard it all before, so his attention returned to Tsing, who'd already won over Tourmaline's little one. He and the boy were almost nose-to-nose, and they were shyly petting each other's hair.

Like his mother, Evie's was a dark, rich green.

Evie was equally fascinated by Tsing's pale fluff.

Once things had progressed to ear petting, Farley must have decided it was his turn. Dropping to a seat beside Tsing, he said, "Hiya, Evie. I'm Farley. Guess what! My brother has a moonstone monkey. Does yours get into mischief, too?"

The boy couldn't have noticed Farley earlier, because his eyes rounded, and he lapsed into excited Cantl.

"Whoa, whoa, there. Switch back to Terse for us. I'm

still learning your language."

With a pitying look and a cautious pat to golden curls, Evie confided, "I like stories about cloudstriders. Do you have a dragon?"

"You're, like, the third or fourth person to mistake me for a cloudstrider. I'm Flox. My people come from New Continent. I grew up—mostways—on Morven, the Moonlit Mountain."

"This is a mountain, too."

"One of the prettiest I ever saw," Farley said easily. "Your mom's Keeper?"

"Yes. She made this for me. And lots of others, too."

"My brother's Morven's Keeper. He's a Meadowsweet like me. And Tsing here is also my brother."

Evie's ears tilted sideways in confusion. But then they popped back up, and he said, "Okay. You know what? Mum's Tisk, so I know. It's okay not to match."

Tsing's smile trembled. "Yes, little buck. You can be a good match without matching."

Just then, Tourmaline's oldest boy strolled in, offering a warm greeting.

"Terse, please," directed his father. And to the room at large, "This is Verdal, who'll serve as your guide while you're in Chime Winds."

The young man had a charming smile, a Cantl accent, and a protective streak not unlike his mother's, given how closely he was eyeing Farley and Tsing. But he did go around the room to bow over the hands of everyone else—Dessa included—before sitting on the floor behind his baby brother.

Farley introduced himself as he always did, utterly certain of his welcome.

Tsing was noticeably less enthusiastic, but ... ah. Not for lack of interest. He really needed to ask if Larkin would consider adding a few Pika to the crew. They thrived best in community.

But then Tourmaline was corralling them even further inside, and he closed and locked the big double doors behind them. "Only a precaution," he assured. "Anka has taken the apprentices into her confidence on the matter, and they're doing their best, but we'd prefer to keep this from the journeymen. They gossip, and ... panic creates a sour note. If Shiri goes into one of her furies ... well. We'd very much prefer to take care of this quietly."

While they found seats around a large table where three more green-haired Pika were setting a meal, Farley slipped briefly to Torio's side. "Furies?"

"Some mountains are more temperamental than others." In partial answer, Torio caught his hand and pressed it to his ribs, which were still tender. "Depending on the nature of the threat."

Which suggested something sobering.

This mountain's Keeper might be in danger.

Tourmaline reappeared, firmly steering Anka Thuen. She was a petite woman with long green hair pulled back so that her pointed ears showed. Silvery, slit-pupiled eyes sought him, then bounced to Dessa for several long moments before ranging over the rest of their party. Finally, she looked to her husband. "I don't even know where to begin."

"The soup, I think. And I'll introduce you."

"I won't remember their names," she grumbled.

"Such things fall to me, but let's err on the side of courtesy." He drew out the chair at the head of the table. "Come, now, Anka love. These gentlemen are the ones Aurelius and Ulrica bragged about. They hunt Misbegotten."

"Ulrica's letter?" Her expression changed—avid, urgent, and then ... sheepish. She grimly held Torio's gaze, then bowed at the waist, her long braid slapping the edge of the table. "Torio Kite, Keeper of the Heartstone Mountain, I apologize for my behavior when you came to us before."

Sweeping into his own bow, Torio matched her courtesy for courtesy. "At that time, neither of us understood the import of what I'd found. This reunion is welcome. Doubly so if we can be of use to you."

Anka straightened and propped a hand on her hip. "Ulrica wrote to me about you and your 'lamentably incorrigible business partner.'"

"Hey!" exclaimed Farley, a laugh underlying his protest.

She went right on. "Given the viciousness of her descriptions, she's clearly very fond of you both. And she praised Dessa's hunting skills alongside those of her own daughter."

"A compliment not lightly given," Torio said.

"Good for you, Dessa!" added Farley.

"This is nice. You should compliment me more." She smiled up at him, her hand once more settling over his heart.

"I'll see what I can do," he murmured in the vicinity of her ear.

When he looked back up, Anka was staring at him with the oddest expression on her face. Then she elbowed Tourmaline. "Skies and scales, Ulrica was *right!*"

By the end of the meal, Anka had nicknamed the lot of them "Dessa's Menagerie," as if *she* was the reason they were together. Farley figured he deserved way more credit than he was getting, but Dessa was so obviously pleased by the idea that he kept quiet. But not as quiet as Tsing.

Tipping a little more of the fizzy, citrusy drink that'd come with dinner into his bond-brother's glass, Farley softly asked, "Are you done being flustered yet?"

"Hush."

"Well, I'm glad to know Tisk aren't all bad. Anka's vanquished my bad first impression."

"Mmm."

"Verdal has all kinds of affinity. Heaps of potential, isn't that right, Dessa sweet?"

She looked their way, studied the green-haired Pika, then said, *"Very like his mother, although I don't think Shiri will call him."*

"Does another mountain want him?" he guessed.

Heads turned. He'd interrupted the others. "Sorry. I was talking to Dessa. Go on."

"Him *who*? And which mountain wants him?" demanded Anka.

Farley held up his hands. "Maybe I shouldn't have, not without asking first, but I wanted to know what Dessa thought of you, Verdal. She thinks your affinity is like your mom's, but that Shiri isn't likely to call you."

Verdal sat a little straighter, then glanced at his parents. "I don't think that's a secret."

"But how did Dessa know?" Anka pressed.

"Oh, yeah." Farley sought Torio's gaze. "We should probably add highly accurate affinity testing to our list of services."

Torio blinked. "Since when?"

"It came up while I was ... uhh ... a houseboy. Slipped my mind until now."

Conversation took that tangent for a while, with Torio relaying Dessa's answers to a slew of questions from both Anka and Tourmaline.

Meanwhile, Farley waved for Verdal's attention. "You're a sculptor?"

"Born to it, I suppose. All of us boys learned the craft from the cradle."

"Can I see something you've made?"

Verdal snorted. "Look around. Mum kept our assignments practical. This room is full of early efforts. They're embarrassing, but ... they also show our progress."

Farley tried to evaluate carved borders, stone serving bowls, and assorted small statues, but it wasn't easy. All four brothers had contributed over the years, and the skill level was all over the place. "Any of your work stirring?"

"Sure. The two stone movers in the next room are mine."

"The fire-eaters? Those are *great*. So you work with redstone?"

"Not exclusively." Verdal's ears dipped like he was embarrassed to brag. "I've been in close contact with every variety of magical stone. Well, twelve of them. And they all respond favorably."

"Ever heard of Graven?"

"Of course! Master Platt's masterpiece is the stuff of legends. I'd love to try something similar, but ...." He shot an uneasy look toward his mother. "There's a temporary ban on bonding different varieties of stone, especially unsupervised."

Farley was quite sure Verdal hadn't yet realized he was in the middle of a haggle, but Tsing had. The Pika's eyes were round with worry. With a wink, Farley brought out Nestor and sent him slithering across the table toward Verdal, who's breath hitched.

"Nestor's mine. He's the first Heartstone sculpture ever to stir." Farley said, "Go ahead. Pick him up. Then you really will have been in close contact with all the magical stones."

Verdal was all wonderment and pleasure. "Aren't you a beauty?"

At Farley's side, Tsing trembled.

"Frey specializes in bonding different stones. On Morven, we have a bunch of guardians that stir both by day and by night. Brownstone and titian jade. Freshstone and starstone. Sunstone and moonstone. He makes it look easy."

Without a word, Verdal begged for more details.

Farley loved getting the upper hand in a haggle. He casually asked, "Ever think of becoming a journeyman?"

By his stunned expression, it was plain that Verdal *hadn't* considered it. But he was now.

While the young man stroked black scales and weighed possibilities, Farley nudged Tsing and whispered, "Pleased with me?"

"I'm in awe."

"Just the way I like it."

At the other end of the table, Verdal's younger brothers bounced up to help their father clear dishes and bring out pots of fragrant tea. After that, Anka ushered the three youngest boys out, leaving them in the care of a freshstone minder. The mood quickly shifted, and Farley settled back to listen.

Tourmaline began. "One of our journeymen was trying to work out the knack of binding the magic of two stones in a single statue. It's not an easy thing, and something went ... well, *partially* wrong. The statue stirred, and she seemed to be faring well. But soon, a couple of our apprentices spoke up, saying they'd noticed something ... off."

Anka jumped in. "It wasn't anything blatant. I took a look myself, and I couldn't find any substantive reason for concern. The mark and the magic sang a true note. But ... that was by day."

"More apprentices came to us in the days that followed. Those with the strongest magical affinity described the issue as ... a sour note in an otherwise sweet melody." Tourmaline nodded to Verdal. "Isn't that how you put it?"

"Yes. But how do you tell another sculptor that their work sets your teeth on edge?" He lowered his gaze and slowly stroked Nestor. "I wish I'd found a way, though."

"I'm Keeper. The duty was mine." Anka rubbed at her

temple. "We're careful about such things, and the decision was made. But before we could move her into one of the safe rooms, she abandoned her pedestal and fled."

Torio shook his head. "A statue *always* returns to their pedestal."

"She found and stole a portion of her block. Somehow, she's making it work as a touchstone." Anka bared fangs. "I've never seen it before, but ... there hasn't been a Misbegotten in Chime Winds for four generations."

Torio asked, "This statue is endangering people?"

"Yes. At first, it seemed like mischief." Tourmaline drew a steadying breath. "She was intended to serve as a laundress, and during the day, she performed her duties with a smile. But after dark, she would pace and wring her hands. Then, she began looking for things to wash. We had some very disgruntled journeymen report that she tried to steal the clothes they were wearing."

"Statues are strong. There were bruises. A broken wrist," added Anka.

Tourmaline nodded. "They struggled to get away, and so ... this was a couple of weeks ago now ...."

"Sixteen days," Verdal grimly interjected.

"Yes, well. She changed her methods. People couldn't struggle or get away if they were dead." Tourmaline stared fixedly at the table, his jaw working. "Her victims have all been drowned, and their freshly laundered clothes are found nearby, neatly left to dry. Three people have died."

"So far," whispered Verdal.

Torio asked, "What about the sculptor who made her? Usually, they hold *some* sway over their creation."

Anka looked miserable. "He was her first victim."

"Ah. What stones were used?"

"Songstone set with starstone." She touched her throat. "He gave her a necklace, very delicate, like a cascade of tiny pearls."

"Her form?"

"Keet." Anka sighed. "As you can imagine, there are dozens—no, *hundreds*—of songstone guardians ranging through Chime Winds, and the vast majority of them are styled as Keet."

"So she doesn't stand out."

Farley finally spoke up. "Doesn't Shiri know where she is?"

"Mountains—*our* mountains—aren't people, even if they do have personalities. Wait, that sounds wrong. Maybe it's better to say that we aren't equal to them. Shiri is vast, and in some ways, that makes her above such things. Aloof. But she's also aware of *more* things, like ... the whole city. Peoples' emotions affect her mood, so we work directly with the royal family to ensure that the people of Chime Winds are cared for and content."

"So you don't talk to Shiri?" Farley tried to remember if Frey had ever mentioned conversations with Morven.

"I understand what she needs. I know when she's stirred up, and I can usually figure out why. But ... to converse with her the way you do with Dessa? I can't even imagine it." A speculative glint shone in her eyes. "Maybe you really *are* a cloudstrider."

"The laundress, Anka love," said Tourmaline, calling her back to the subject at hand. "After dark, we have our apprentices fanned out through the city, but she's proven difficult—and dangerous—to corner."

"Wouldn't a songstone statue moving after sunset draw attention?" asked Torio.

"Definitely! But we're in cooperation with the queen. There's a curfew in place from sunset to sunrise, a time of prayer and preparation for a brand new holy day. It's kept moods bright and people safe."

"Our citizens are safe," Anka said grimly. "But my apprentices are not."

"You did well. The hunting grounds are prepared," said

Larkin, sounding wholly unconcerned. "Call your people to safety and send us out instead."

Anka passed a hand over her face. "Thank you. That would be ... *thank you.*"

Tourmaline said, "Mercifully, the rainy season has begun. We've been blessing every overcast night."

Torio asked, "Where does she go to catch starlight in the evening? High places are best for that, but potentially difficult to navigate. Rooftops, balconies, bridges. Squares and courtyards would leave her more vulnerable to discovery, especially on cloudy nights."

"We thought of all that, too," Anka said wearily. "We focused on likely places, but all our searches have come up empty. I think she must leave the city."

"But she comes back," interjected Verdal.

"Anybody thought to put out a basket of laundry. Sorta ... bait?" asked Farley.

"Yes," Anka sighed. "The second victim tried that."

Farley winced.

Larkin asked, "What about open areas outside the city—fields, parks, meadows, clearings? I remember exploring them."

"Yes, of course," said Tourmaline. "I'll provide a map."

"Are there any other pieces of her block I can ... oh, wait. She left her pedestal behind." Farley asked, "Can I see it? That'd be a big help."

"Go with Verdal. He'll take you around."

Anka pursed her lips, and she looked like she wanted to say a lot. But all she managed was a gruff, "Be careful, Verdy."

Farley laughed at Verdal's expression when Dessa picked up the laundress's pedestal like it was nothing more than a platter of fruit and followed Torio back out of the storeroom.

"Our quarters?" Larkin asked.

"Your usual suite. Do you remember ...?"

"Aye. I won't take you from your pleasures." Larkin lengthened his stride until he caught up to Torio, then pointed the way.

Nyx had gone up on her hind legs, casually pinning Verdal to the wall, and he was lavishing her with the attention she demanded ... while also worshipping Freydolf from afar. "She *purrs*!" he whispered. "I can feel it! Can you feel this? I'm not imagining ... no, I'm quite sure ...! How did he manage? I've never ...!"

"Is it really that unusual?" Farley couldn't recall Kressee purring, but Rimbles certainly did.

"I have to try it! I have a bit of brownstone that's been coaxing for my attention. I could turn it into a little feline."

This guy. Definitely a sculptor. Farley asked, "The Harrows were here enough to have a usual room?"

"Every winter when I was little. I'm closer in age to Hadwin, but Larkin was always bored. We'd explore together. There were a *lot* of games of hide-and-hunt in the galleries."

"Come on, Nyx. He can pet you later. I want to get back to Tsing."

She swiped Verdal's cheek with a smooth tongue, dropped to all fours and padded away.

"Did she just lick me?"

"Yeah. Guess she's decided she likes you."

"But ...!" Verdal's hands went through several positions, and his brows knit. "I can't see how ...! How did Freydolf design a working mouth?"

"Oh, you know. Magic," Farley said breezily. "Say, I've been wondering for a while now. What's that around your neck? I mean, I know it's songstone. And stirring."

Diverted, Verdal pressed a hand over the front of his shirt. "You really can see magic?"

"Yeah. Me and Torio both."

"What's it look like?"

"Mmm. Bright. Kind of sparkly, I guess. But every type of stone has its own way of shining. And I can tell where the connections are. That one has a link to your mom, since she marked it. Aaand, it's linked *really* strongly to you, which means it looks to you. Somehow."

Verdal pulled a necklace out from under his shirt. A tiny dragon, intricately carved so that its long, ribbon-like body doubled back on itself, twisting to catch and hold the cord on which it hung. "See these holes? It's a kind of whistle."

"Does it move?"

"No, but ... she did bind him to me." Verdal smiled sheepishly. "His name is Toot."

Magic sparked around the dragon in response, like he was happy to be called. "I'm guessing you were just a little guy?"

"Yes. He was a talisman against nightmares. A dragon guardian to chase away bad dreams."

"My brother has a key that needs moonlight to stir. It's not a *typical* guardian, but Keepers can get amazingly creative when something—or someone—is important to them."

They arrived in the Harrow's usual suite.

Everyone else had already made themselves comfortable. Tsing had nestled against Dan, who was coaxing Phillit toward sleep. Artor and Torio had begun a game of Pinnacles at a tiny table for two, and Larkin leaned against the frame of an open balcony door, watching rain pummel the city.

"Where's Dessa?" Farley could tell she was no longer inside the Keeper's household, but somewhere below it.

Torio said, "Acquainting herself with this mountain. She was curious about Shiri."

Farley crossed to Larkin. "The daily downpour?"

"Aye."

"Will it linger? Give us a cloudy night?"

Verdal joined them. "Difficult to say, but this time of year, the clouds can and often do stay."

Farley cuffed Larkin's shoulder. "Well, leader? This is familiar territory for you. How do we approach this hunt?"

"I don't see any point in going over the same ground that Anka's people have been searching for the last several days."

With a nod, Verdal said, "Outside the city, then?"

"Aye." Larkin cuffed Farley's shoulder. Vengeful thing. "How close do you have to be in order to tell if we're headed in the right direction."

"I mean, you've been with me. I've gotta be close by before I can even get a read on what kind of stone we're tracking."

"And there's no way to get a direction?"

"Like a compass? Nope. That's now how my affinity works."

Crossing to the table where a map was spread, Larkin touched several points that lay outside the city walls. "Covering this much ground would take several nights, and we have no way of knowing if she changes her hideaway. Better to split up."

Farley could appreciate the practicality, but would Dessa? "Dessa can sense magic, and she knows what Char and Nyx can see. To a lesser degree, so can Nestor."

"Two teams, then. We'll make an initial foray tonight, see if we can pick up her trail."

Torio came over, and Larkin assigned three areas to him. "The botanical garden, the riverside park, and this section of farmland."

"I'll be with Dessa," said Torio. "And she'll insist Farley keep the lionesses."

"Aye. And you'll bring Artor. Just in case we need a healer."

The Ursa accepted this with a nod.

"What about me?" asked Tsing.

Farley wavered.

Larkin didn't. "Nay. You'll be safer here. Verdal can tuck you in with Evensong."

It was neatly calculated. Tsing offered a token pout, but he didn't argue.

Catching Farley's eye, Larkin said, "There's an amphitheater built into a high valley. It overlooks the city. And beyond it, a series of linked meadows. They're only used for their midsummer festival, so our prey may have retreated there."

Verdal said, "You can leave as soon as curfew goes into effect. Sunset."

"A Keet woman with a pearl necklace," Larkin said. "Locate her. That's all. Don't risk anything further."

Farley answered for all of them. "Aye, leader. We're agreed."

"Back in Bellicose," Larkin began thoughtfully. "You and Tsing rode the lionesses."

Farley cracked a smile. "They're not as spacious as Graven, but sure. They can carry a rider if it's needed."

"You *ride* Graven?" And with doubled incredulity, "You ride *Graven*?"

"Well ... Tupp does. But he's let me tag along before."

Larkin shook his head, returning to the matter at hand. "If the lionesses are willing, we could range farther, faster."

Farley called Nyx over and demonstrated. Staying astride meant tucking up his legs and lying low. "It's not easy for long rides, but it works great for a quick getaway."

With his larger frame, Larkin had more trouble, even when Char adjusted her shape slightly to accommodate Pred bulk. "Nay. Unless she'd allow a harness?"

"You mean like the one you use with Livia?"

"Aye. Hold on." He went out, and when he returned, he held a length of rope. Then he sat before Char and explained his plan, finishing, "With your permission ...?"

She bumped his forehead with her nose.

While he fussed with knots, Nyx went over to watch. Farley asked, "If it works, do I get one?"

"Aye."

"Maybe we should commission saddles for you girls." Both felines turned their heads to stare at him. "Something with feathers at the ruff, so you match the rest of us ... yeah?"

Larkin's lips quirked. "They like the idea."

"*I* know. But how'd *you* know."

He stopped knotting long enough to stroke stone fur. "They're purring."

Once the sun set and the city's curfew was soundly in place, Tourmaline and Verdal swung wide the Keep's outer doors, and a dozen or so apprentices flanked the way, hands outstretched. Larkin and Torio were familiar with this custom, so Farley and Artor followed their lead, linking their fingers with each sculptor in turn.

Anka's apprentices looked troubled, shaken, and exhausted by their nights on patrol. They offered wan thanks. It was plain to Farley that they were desperate for this to work, for them to be the solution.

One young woman bitterly whispered, "End this. End her."

One guy's chin wobbled so bad, Farley pulled him into a hug. Tourmaline had to come take over so Farley could go.

The city streets were empty, but not in any kind of ominous way. There were lights in every window. Rehearsals were underway—singers, dancers, instrumentalists. Laughter and the occasional patter of applause kept the mood light. The people of Chime Winds were safe, and Shiri was saved from a perilous mood swing.

At a crossroads, the two teams parted company.

"Want to go to this big festival they're planning?" Farley asked as he settled into Nyx's harnesses.

Larkin glanced his way. "Wouldn't miss it."

"Really?"

"I like it here. So did my parents." He gestured at the surrounding city. "We were here every winter since it was a favorite of Mother's. Because of Anka."

"I could see them getting on."

"Anka's strong. And ... I think they sympathized with each other because they both had sons."

"And both wanted daughters?"

Larkin huffed. "Mother bemoaned her surfeit of sons often enough. But she found her own way. Claimed your sister."

"She's your sister, too, you know."

"Oh, aye. Father made that clear." Ropes creaked as he lay low over Char's shoulder. "And more than half of Anka's apprentices are women. Although that's due to Shiri's influence as well. She likes a sweet singing voice. Ready?"

"Let's run!"

Farley clung to Nyx as she skimmed along roads and over bridges. They were past the city's fringes and into the trees at speeds that rivaled his carriage on an open road. "The harness works great. I think you could go even faster," he coaxed.

Nyx obliged.

Judging by Larkin's low oath, Char kept pace.

Farley grinned at him.

With a roll of his eyes, the Pred growled, "*Focus.*"

Oh, right.

He was catching fleeting hints of magic, but he'd been having too much fun to pay them much mind. Reluctantly, he asked Nyx to slow so he could sort through his impressions. Lots of songstone, all of it still and therefore not their quarry. Clouds were stealing up on the moon, but the sky had been clear at sunset, and the moon was on the rise. Starstone and moonstone statues should be stirring. Titian jade, too.

"Anything?"

"Up ahead. Starstone guardians. And sleeping songstone."

"That'll be the amphitheater."

To be safe, they dismounted and stole up on it from behind.

The amphitheater was huge, with benches rising in concentric circles from the central stage. Along the outer edge, a double colonnade of wide arches and sturdy columns supported twisting vines. Stone guardians had been arranged in pairs. He and Larkin watched for a while as white statues danced around their silent green partners.

"She's not here."

"Aye." Larkin stepped out of hiding, a scowl on his face. "I suppose this would have been too easy."

While Farley worked his way back into Nyx's harnesses, something passed over the moon, bringing his attention to the sky. "Well, that's weird," he remarked.

Mist seemed to be trickling toward them. Creeping through the greenery, swirling uphill, twisting through the tops of trees that were lower on the slope. Moonlight briefly made it luminous, but then it closed over and around them, muffling everything in a cool fog.

"Silent as statues. So ... is this normal?"

"I've seen it before. Let's try climbing above it."

"Sure." And to Nyx, "Chase the open sky so we can see what we're doing."

She sprang forward, and it didn't take long for her to outdistance the mist. Farley hunkered down and urged her on.

Larkin caught up right when they spilled out into one of the big meadows Farley remembered from the map. They were halfway across it before he could get a word out. "Slow down, sweetheart. Oh, wow. *Look* at this place!" He slid from Nyx's back and bent to brush his fingers across petals. He was knee deep in flowers. "Did you know this was here?"

"Aye. They're the royal flower." He spared a glance for the mist which was already catching up with them. "They're blue."

"Can we come back during the day? I want to show Tsing."

"Aye. Dan would appreciate it as well. Anything?"

"It's really quiet. Wouldn't that be a problem for songstone? Even if she's stirring all night, she'd still need something to wake her once the sun's up."

Larkin raised a warning finger. "Do you hear that?"

Farley strained his ears. "Which way?"

The Pred pointed ... and then vanished behind a billow of mist.

Blind, Farley asked, "What did you think you heard?"

"A bell. Small and high."

Bringing his hands to his ears, Farley listened and ... yes. There was a tiny, wistful ping. "You think she brought her own bell?"

"Redstone guardians can procure their own fire," Larkin pointed out.

"I don't sense a statue. Probably too far, though."

Just then, the surrounding mists swirled oddly, and Farley found himself ducking. "Hey," he called softly.

"What's up with the wind?"

"Not sure." Larkin sounded grumpy.

It had almost felt like something passed overhead. Farley ventured, "What were those huge, predatory owls back in Basq territory called?"

"Fisher owls."

"Yeah, them. Think they're here, too?"

"I don't know if their territory extends this far."

There was another rush, and it sent eddies through the mist. For a moment, Farley saw the stars, but the stuff closed over them again. It gave him a chill. "Hey, Larkin? How big do those bats get. The ones the Clow warned about."

"Did you see one?"

"I saw *something*."

"Move toward me," Larkin ordered, all business.

With a hand tangled in Nyx's fur so she could guide him, Farley walked to where Larkin stood, blades out, poised for attack.

"Get astride. I want to move."

Farley fumbled into his harnesses.

Larkin swung a leg over Char's back and addressed her. "We need overhead cover. A large tree with low branches. Can you find one?"

Both lionesses turned downhill.

"Good. Quietly, now. And slow," directed Larkin. "And avoid any statues."

They slunk from the meadow and into the surrounding thicket of tropical foliage. Farley was as good as blind. All he could do was push branches away from his face whenever Nyx walked through them. Then he was close enough to see Larkin, who stood beside a smug Char. She was sharpening her claws on the bark of an enormous tree.

"Up," Larkin ordered.

"You're treeing me?"

The Pred reinforced his order by burying a dagger into

the trunk. "Use this."

Farley swallowed back a smart remark about fathers and sons, put his boot on the offered foothold, and climbed. He found a serviceable branch and sat. Slow minutes passed, and the surrounding leaves began to drip. Finally, he whispered, "Anything?"

"Nay." Larkin had to be standing at the foot of the tree.

"It's not the laundress," Farley offered.

"Aye, but it's not nothing."

They stayed still. They stayed quiet.

Finally, Larkin called, "Come down. We'll retreat for tonight. Try again tomorrow."

It felt like giving up. But for once, Farley was glad to.

Farley dragged off his boots, shed his clothes, and dropped onto the bed beside Tsing. His bond-brother didn't stir. Neither did the two littlest Thuen boys, who were snuggled up on either side of him. Tired as Farley was, he took a moment to appreciate how happy Tsing looked. But only a moment, because sleep needed to happen.

And then someone was there.

And somehow, it was morning.

He kept his eyes closed, hoping their hosts wouldn't mind if he stayed in bed for a few more hours. Last night had been long and fruitless and ... weird. He wanted to put off thinking about it. At least for a while. Then he registered the distinctive magic in Verdal's dragon flute. With a sigh, he opened one eye and offered a rusty, "Hiya."

"Father wants to know if you want sleep or food?"

"Sleep."

"Mmm. Good choice."

Farley opened his other eye and squinted. Verdal looked a whole lot like Frey. Well, no. He looked *nothing* like Frey, but he looked like a sculptor who'd been chipping at stone all night long. Scooting over to make room, he held out a hand. "Come to bed, sculptor."

Verdal placed a tiny, perfect tree-cat on Farley's palm. "See if you can talk him into cooperating with my plans."

"This little guy's gonna purr?"

"That's my hope."

"I'd love to help, but my brother's the one who can sweet-talk stone."

Verdal sank to the edge of the mattress. "I can talk to a rock all day, but it's not like they're capable of conversation."

"Maybe not with you." Farley shifted around so he was more comfortable and closed his eyes again. "Tupp can hear them. Rocks, I mean. They mostly bend over backwards to make him look amazing. Really frustrating."

"Wait. Your brother can hear stone?"

"Mm-hmm. Seems like it must be a rare affinity. Frey and Aurelius looked into it, but they never turned up any records about Keepers with the knack." Farley patted the mattress. "Seriously. Lie down before you keel over."

"Farley," Verdal said.

"Mm-hmm?"

"If they couldn't find a record, it's only because they weren't reading the right kinds of books."

"That's a keen observation right there. Can't wait until you point it out to Aurelius."

"*Farley.*"

Reluctantly, he opened his eyes. And made Verdal pay by dragging him down and tossing the edge of a blanket over him. "Sleep," he grumbled. "We both need it."

"Your brother's affinity. It's beyond rare. It's a cloud-strider trait."

"Huh?"

"Those born with ears to hear were *prized*."

"By who?"

"By dragons." Verdal's eyes were dark gray, like his dad's. "Maybe you look like a cloudstrider because you're descended from them."

"Back up. I want to hear the part about dragons. What's stone affinity have to do with dragons."

"In the stories, there are always tests to find the rare child who can listen to stone and understand what it wants."

Farley frowned. "That's Tupp. My brother. He hears them. Thinks like them. Speaks for them."

"Just like in the stories. And that's why they'd want him."

"Who'd want Tupp?"

"The dragons."

"What for?" he asked suspiciously.

"To hear them. To speak for them. To ride them."

For several long moments, Farley fitted pieces together. And once he had, he was miffed by the injustice of it all. "Figures," he grumbled. "Tupp has all the luck."

19

Banner Blue

Larkin tracked down Torio. "Farley didn't stir with the sun, and I haven't the heart to wake Verdal to get at him. Be my eyes?"

"Verdal?" asked the bemused Grif.

"See for yourself."

Larkin trailed after him to the sleeping alcove that had been claimed by Farley and Tsing. The latter was sitting on the floor, leaning against the bed with Evie on his lap. They were paging through a picture book, conversing in low voices lest they wake their respective brothers.

In the middle of the mattress, the two men slept as snug as if they were in a hammock, Verdal tucked under Farley's chin.

"*Another* smitten Pika?" Torio drawled.

"Merely a tired one," Larkin countered. "Sculptors are always working themselves to exhaustion."

"Oh, he's smitten." Tourmaline joined them in the doorway. "But not by Farley in particular. It's Freydolf Meadowsweet he's pining for. Came to Anka and me last night, wondering if we'd grant him journeyman status."

Larkin hummed. "If you can spare him, I can guarantee

safe passage to Morven."

"Thank you." Tourmaline's gaze drifted to the bed. "The timing's good. When Kimmis died, it hit him hard. They were good friends."

"One of the victims?"

"Kimmis was the journeyman who made and marked Pearl. That's what he called her. The laundress." He cleared his throat. "Hadwin is there now, isn't he? Another familiar face on Morven. And it helps Anka, knowing our boy would be going to Ulrica."

"Aye, Mother would watch over him. Whether he wants it or not."

"Then I'll consider the matter settled. By the time you're ready to move along, I'll have Verdal's references prepared. Now, please. I interrupted. What did you need Keeper Kite's eyes for ...?"

"I want to find a certain bell."

Torio's eyebrows shot up. "In a city bedecked in bells of every size and shape?"

"This one was alone, in a high meadow. Farley and I weren't close enough to tell if it was someone's harmless castoff ... or if it belonged to a furtive statue. I would rest easier knowing which." With a decidedly awkward expression, he added, "And ... Dan would probably appreciate the view. Tsing?"

The lad's eyes lifted to his, wistful and wary.

"Come along," Larkin invited.

He fidgeted and frowned.

"Yes, we can all go," Tourmaline said gently. "What do you say, Evie. Shall we show Tsing Moneta's Meadow?"

The little boy hastily agreed, but Tsing still hedged. "I would need a sunhat."

"Is that all?" asked Tourmaline, offering Tsing a hand up, then turning it into a fatherly embrace. "I'll be counting on you, too, Tsing. Verdal and I weren't raised in a covey, so there's a lot we don't understand."

Tsing leaned back in order to search the man's face. "Be glad. You're free."

Tourmaline shot a startled look Larkin's way.

He chose a diplomatic tone. "Tsing is in a position to know. You *should* be glad. And ... you shouldn't let any of your other sons travel without proper escort. Preferably mine."

"Noted." Tourmaline pet Tsing's hair, and asked, "Are you free, now, too?"

The teen leaned into him and mumbled, "Thanks to Farley."

As it happened, hats with ear holes came in all sizes in the Thuen household, and Tsing was soon outfitted for their outing. Tourmaline arranged for an open carriage pulled by a pair of sturdy songstone ponies. They climbed to the meadow in fine style, and there was no finer tour guide than Tourmaline.

Larkin occasionally caught a glimpse of Char and Nyx slipping through the thick foliage alongside the road, but only because he was watching for them. He was fairly certain Dessa was also on the move, if only to keep a middling distance between Torio and Farley.

Torio touched his arm and asked, "Tell me what happened last night."

"I wish I knew." He thought back. "Visibility was poor, thanks to the night fog, but I would swear there was something above us. It felt large."

Ears angled their way, Tourmaline said, "Maybe it was a dragon."

Larkin snorted. "I'm not a boy you can tease with tales of sky castles and dragon riders."

The man cheerfully rejoined, "Just because the stories are old doesn't mean they cannot be true. Are you not yourself wed to a sea-wife, Larkin Harrow?"

"How ...?"

"I speak Coloq as well as the next Basq." With a significant nod toward Dan, he smugly added, "Your dahna is a delightful young man. If not for your house-bond, I'd hire him away from you."

Larkin's eyes narrowed. "As you say, he looks to me."

Tourmaline laughed. "He'll manage you well enough, but to think ... he could have managed a whole mountain."

"Do *not* tell Anka. She'll get word to mother before I can, and my life would be forfeit," growled Larkin.

"I'll look forward to Ulrica's letter on the subject and pretend to be thoroughly astonished."

"But what's this about dragons?" asked Torio.

Larkin shot him a grateful look for changing the subject.

Tourmaline smiled knowingly but veered to the new topic. "Dragons are loved and feared by all Keet ... or have you not noticed they have a place in nearly every mural and carving on the city's walls? According to most histories, the first queen of Chime Winds was a Keet who attracted the interest of a dragon. She won his heart with her songs."

Smoothly switching to Coloq, he brought Dan into the conversation.

"So ... they were like the Basq?" asked Tsing.

Larkin hesitated over this leap. "How so?"

"They met on the edges of their worlds. But instead of the seam between land and sea, they met in a place between land and sky."

"Well put," said Tourmaline. "They met on a mountain-top, which is as close as any of us can get to the sky ... without help."

"Is that where the sky castles and dragon riders come in?" asked Torio.

"Not for this particular story. Moneta's tale is a romance, and the one who made her the first queen of her people was her dragon." Turning to look back over the city, Tourmaline pointed. "From here, you can see that Shiri has two peaks. Against one stands the royal residence, and against the other, the Keep. This is why some say that Shiri has two hearts. His and hers. Forever united."

As the carriage rounded the curve of the amphitheater and crested the additional rise that would bring them into Moneta's Meadow, Larkin covertly watched Dan's face. The man never hid his emotions, and it was surprisingly entertaining to be the force behind each change.

Dan's jaw dropped, and he exhaled on a soft, "Ohhh."

Tourmaline guided the carriage straight into the meadow, so they were wading through a sea of sky blue flowers. It was a stunning sight.

"Flowers? Look how many flowers!" Tsing leaned way over the side, reaching to pluck one. He presented it to Dan and spoke the Verit word for *blue*.

Dan twirled the bloom between his fingers, and Phillit grabbed for it with pudgy hands. Tsing laughed and picked more, presenting them to Evie, who cheerfully assured Phillit that they were good to eat. So everyone had a taste.

"This is the royal flower, and it's also the royal color," Tourmaline said. "Blue as the banners that fly over the royal residence and upon all official buildings. This often comes as a surprise to visitors. Since most records of Moneta's story are carved into songstone, she's understandably associated with the color green. But it's believed that her feathers were blue."

While Tourmaline paused to translate for Dan's sake, Torio beckoned to Larkin. "Which direction was your bell?"

He checked the position of the amphitheater and eyed the

treeline, looking for the big one in which they'd sheltered. "That way."

Torio gazed off that way, his eyes slightly out of focus.

Tourmaline switched back to Terse. "There are countless versions of Moneta's story, and so people tend to believe the one they like best. For instance, some cast a Basq or a Tisk in the role of the First Queen's dragon. But in the Keep's oldest records, he was neither a dragon of the sea nor a dragon of the land, but another race entirely. Sky dragons! It's said that his scales were a most remarkable blue, which allowed him to pass unnoticed through a cloudless sky."

Larkin said, "I find that difficult to believe."

"Ah, but it makes a good story," countered Tourmaline.

Dan spoke again, asking, "If I'm considered a sea dragon and your wife and her people are counted as land dragons, what race are the sky dragons? Do the records say?"

Tourmaline looked surprised. "Didn't I say? They're called the Furl."

Torio held up his hand. "My apologies, Tourmaline, but could you direct the ponies that way? My lionesses have found something."

"Quiet, please." Larkin crouched on his seat, poised to leap.

Everyone went still, so that the only sounds were the swish of flowers parting around them and the musical scrape of Larkin's daggers as he drew them. Then finally, so faintly, a distant *ting* reached them. Tourmaline's ears twitched toward it, and he adjusted the ponies' course.

Torio broke the silence. "The statue isn't here, but I believe she's left her touchstone behind. Stop, Tourmaline. Wait here while Larkin and I look for the block. Perhaps you could tell the others another story to pass the time?"

Larkin wondered at Torio's caution.

The Grif softly called, "Nyx, guard the carriage. Char, make certain we're not ambushed."

Waiting until they were out of earshot of the rest, Larkin

muttered, "What do you expect to find?"

"You knew Dessa uses the lionesses to extend her awareness? It's a way of seeing. I'm not sure how it works, but ... she says Char found someone sleeping here."

"Another death?"

"Probably."

Larkin took the lead, and they quickly found the single chime that had been looped over a branch. Below it rested an uneven section of songstone that showed a smooth side from a clean break. It had likely been knocked from the laundress's block in the early stages of shaping.

"I hear water," Larkin murmured.

Torio's heart sank.

An established path led into the trees, probably a game trail or possibly a shortcut used during festivals, because it led to a freshwater spring. They found the clothing first. Loose blue pants. Sleeveless white robe. Striped apron. Socks, one with a hole worn through at the toe. That little detail made it harder, somehow.

"He died last night?" Torio asked.

"Aye, I think so." Larkin grimly retrieved the apron and spread it over the body. "She'll return here?"

"Yes." Torio's expression went blank. "Wait."

The Grif picked his way around the spring, then followed the trickle of a stream as it led downhill, back toward the city. It wasn't easy going, nor were they the first to pass through this way. Broken and bent greenery released fragrant sap. Larkin was about to ask where they were going when the first soft *ping* reached his ears.

Then Dessa was there, beckoning.

To another chunk of songstone.

To another lonely bell.

"She gave herself options? Is that even possible?" Larkin asked incredulously.

"She did. Dessa says this is the second one she found.

And that Shiri has complained about three more bells whose sound is *unpleasant* to her."

When Torio took Farley aside and explained what they'd found, he was honestly glad to have slept through the whole ordeal. "Tourmaline knew him?"

"One of the journeymen, an older gentleman who's been cobbling new paths in the botanical garden. When he didn't return to work after yesterday's lunch break, his coworkers mentioned it to the foreman, but ... well. It would have been too late by then."

Farley's mind raced. "But ... I thought she was only dangerous after dark."

"This suggests otherwise."

Later, at the dinner table, with Anka's children in the mix, the conversation stayed on brighter things. Farley wanted to hear all about the flowers, and Artor asked for more details about the tradition that Shiri had not only two peaks, but two hearts. Farley perked up a little when the Furl were mentioned.

"Like Pollim and Eullia," he said.

"*Their* story is a little different," said Tourmaline. "But in the sense that a Keet and a Furl overcame their differences to become friends? Yes."

Farley was stuck on one detail. "So are the Furl dragons? Or people? The stories keep switching them around."

Anka shook her head. "My people are associated with dragons, in much the same way Tourmaline's are associated with rabbits ... and the Keet with birds. It's probably figurative."

"So ... Furl can fly? In all the art I've seen, they're standing in the clouds."

"And they supposedly have sky castles," said Larkin.

"And four arms," added Verdal.

Tourmaline said, "The most reasonable explanation is that they were an ancient race that lived so high in the mountains that their homes were often lost in clouds. So that when they descended into the valleys where the Keet lived, they were depicted as coming down from the clouds."

"Pick your favorite explanation," suggested Anka. "One is as good as another."

If Shiri's own Keeper didn't know, Farley supposed nobody ever would.

After dinner, Torio proposed a slightly different tactic for the evening's hunt. "Farley, have Verdal guide you through the city. Two of those *unpleasant* bells that Dessa mentioned are nearby. Verdal checked, and he thinks there are six or seven large pieces missing from her maker's room. Eight at most. Tonight, we'll gather up all those stones. Then we'll set out her pedestal and stand watch. With no place else to return to ... it should draw her out."

"Worth a try, yeah?"

Torio said, "Larkin and I will take the lionesses. We'll need their speed to cover ground."

Farley asked, "What about you, Dessa sweet?"

"I will protect Artor."

"Artor will follow us in a cart." Torio nodded at Larkin. "To collect the stones we need to ferry back to the Keep."

"So it's just me and Verdal?"

Torio said, "In this instance, I wouldn't discount Nestor's usefulness."

"I can guide him. A little. And I can hear you. Always."

"All right. Let's get to work." And because Tsing looked equal parts unhappy and uneasy, Farley hung back in order to wrap him up in his arms. "Don't wait up, but ... save me a place, little brother.”

Tsing mumbled, “Why must *I* stay back? Artor is going.”

“When we get to Morven, there will be two more lionesses waiting. When you have a guardian of your own, we can ride together. And ... well, I think you’ll need to learn how to walk.”

“I can *walk*,” he protested.

“Trust me, Pred have different rules for walking. The minute we get home, you’ll have bells on your ankles and a rain of peas around your ears.”

“Peas ...?”

“Better peas than pebbles. But you’re smart. You’ll catch on quick. Or ... we *could* start your lessons early.”

“Tomorrow?”

“It’s a promise.” And with a quick tweak to one drooping ear, Farley hurried after the rest.

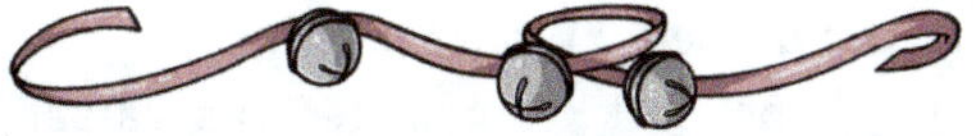

Farley strolled along moonlit streets with Verdal. “Ever consider going with a statue escort, like those two stone-movers you made? I mean, they’re hardly subtle, but safer ...?”

“The apprentices who patrolled with stone guardians never saw her, and those who didn’t never saw her coming,” Verdal said in subdued tones. “Mother decided that it wasn’t worth the risk to draw her out if it meant dying. Even though it probably hindered our search.”

“Mmm, yeah. Hey, you okay?”

“No.”

Out of habit, Farley reached for his hand.

Verdal startled and stopped walking, then carefully pulled away. “I don’t need ....”

“Oh, right. Sorry. If anyone should know better, it’s me. Really. I mean .... Okay, you *know* Aurelius and Ulrica, so you’ll understand. They took in my baby sister. Sweet little Flox girl, all golden ringlets and big blue eyes. At a glance, you'd think Aggie's your typical cute, sweet, harmless girl. Right up until her dagger is tickling the underside of your chin."

With a crooked smile, Verdal admitted, "I've been at the point of Ulrica's dagger before."

"Exactly!" Farley grinned. "Aggie looks Flox, but she thinks and acts and lives like a Pred. So ... again, I'm sorry. Just because you look like your Pika grandpa doesn't mean I should expect you to understand an offer of comfort that's completely foreign to you. It was ... impulse, I guess?"

"I'm not offended. You surprised me. Among Keet ... well. I was surprised, that's all. Honestly, I wouldn't mind learning more about my Pika heritage."

"Well, sure. But not from me. I'd probably kiss with a Flox accent."

Verdal's ears dipped. "What?"

"Nevermind me. Ask Tsing. He was raised to it. Or maybe ask Artor to teach you *no*, first. That's where I started. Very important."

"Uh ... huh."

Farley paused at a street corner, trying to decide which way to go. "You're definitely the most reserved Pika I ever met."

"Most people say I'm overly familiar."

"Could be in your nature. I mean, my family thinks I'm ... oh, hold up, now." Nestor had nudged his chin, turning his head to guide his line of sight. "I think we've got the next one."

Verdal followed his gaze and angled his ears. "Did you hear a bell?"

"Well, no. I'm not even sure why the laundress would hang one in a place like this. She wouldn't *need* a bell here, would she? Plenty of music in the squares." Farley focused, winnowing out the hint of songstone they'd been searching for since sunset. Yep, there it was. "You know, this is kind of the same. We're surrounded by songstone, but I can still tell her block from all the rest. Even stones have their own aspirations, their own voices."

"*That* I understand full well."

Nestor suddenly clamped onto Farley's ear, and he jerked in surprise. "Ow! Hey!"

Magic from Pearl's block was coming from somewhere above, up among the bridges that connected the second-level shops. But from across the wide square, a swell of kindred magic reached for him. It was the same, yet very different. *This* songstone was stirring.

"Umm ... Farley ...?" Verdal grabbed his arm.

"I see her."

Misbegotten could feel perfectly normal. The stone vibrant and sure. But more often, the statue's magic took on a restless, confused energy. Like the stone guardian knew something was wrong, yet they couldn't stop their own momentum.

"Oh, I don't like this one," Farley murmured, slowly backing up and pulling Verdal with him into a deeper patch of shadow. "Maybe she didn't see us?"

A willowy figure glided forward, moonlight gleaming against the high polish for which songstone was famous. Her gaze swept the empty square, then fixed on their position. Picking up her skirts, she hurried forward on bare feet, a sweet smile on her face.

Tension choked Verdal's voice. "What do we do?"

Farley said, "Dessa sweet? I'm being approached by a lovely songstone lady with a pearl necklace, and frankly ... she makes me nervous."

"*Coming!*"

"Help is on the way." Farley grimly added, "In the meantime, let's be elusive."

Games of hide-and-hunt entered strange territory when there were statues involved. They moved without a sound and with surprising speed. And if they were adhering to some inherent purpose, they were impossible to dissuade, let alone out-pace.

"Say ... Verdal," panted Farley. "Sacrifice your shirt for a good cause?"

"You think that would work?" It was a mild protest, but the Pika was already peeling off his tunic.

"The lady loves to launder. And ... we need to get around her."

"Sorry. I wasn't thinking ahead." Verdal handed over the shirt.

"Yeah, yeah. We'll be okay. Probably." Farley stood, balled cloth, and threw high. The tunic unrolled midflight, fluttering to the ground, and ... she stopped. The opening was small, but he and Verdal were through it before she straightened, shaking out the tunic and checking it over. "I can't believe that worked!"

"You said it would!" Verdal gasped out.

"Well, I was *hoping*. Okay. No more dead ends, yeah? If she corners us again, we could lose more than your pants."

"Shouldn't it be *your* shirt that's next to go?" They rounded a corner, and Verdal pointed the way. They dashed along a colonnade that was reassuringly wide.

"I really like this shirt."

Stopping in an alley, they worked to catch their breath.

"What about your ax? Can't you throw *that* at her?" Verdant puffed and wheezed. "You specialize in Misbegotten, don't you? Isn't she the kind of prey you usually hunt?"

"Not alone," Farley grumbled. "My affinity is top notch for tracking, but ... we're more of a ... coordinated-effort hunting group."

Verdal indicated another intersection. "That way will get us to the night gate. It's not far."

"We can lead her out. Regroup." Farley peeked back around the corner and swore. "She's fixating a whole lot more than I like. Any chance she knows you?"

"Her maker was my friend." Verdal pushed off the wall and jogged on. "I was there when Kimmis marked Pearl. I ... I chose her name."

"She remembers." Farley was beginning to be very worried. "Dessa? We're doing our best, but I don't think Verdal can keep this up much longer."

"The lionesses are close. They'll bring you to me."

Two shadows swung into view ahead, and Farley whooped. "There's my girls!"

"She's here." Verdal's ears were totally limp, and he tugged at them as he backed away from the songstone laundress.

"And we're practically gone," Farley assured.

Char and Nyx skidded to a silent stop on either side of them, their harnesses hanging empty. "Did Torio and Larkin send you for us? Careful, now, Char. Verdal's probably never ridden someone as fast as you before." With a firm hand, he guided the Pika onto the lioness's back, fitting his boots into looped rope. "Can you manage?"

"Not much choice." Verdal clung to the handholds. "Hurry."

"Calm down. Look at Pearl. She's hanging back." Farley beckoned to Nyx and settled onto her back. "She's right to be wary. Dessa, are you sure? With the lionesses, I could probably take her."

"Do not risk a crack. Come to me." And then, *"Torio agrees."*

"Not gonna argue."

Nyx and Char sprang away,

Pearl picked up the loose ends of her robe and chased after them.

"She's really well-made," Farley remarked to Verdal, who rode so close beside him, their knees nearly touched. "Not every statue can express what's beneath the folds of fabric. Or stuff like bone structure beneath fur."

"Her maker was a master. Or so we thought."

"Even a master can make a mistake."

Verdal bowed his head.

Farley kind of really wanted to plunk the man down between Tupp and Frey. They'd know what to say. And probably what not to say. "I'll get you to them," he promised.

"The rest of your coordinated-effort hunting group?"

"Sure thing. Trust us."

Char dropped back so Nyx could go first through a gate that stood open. They veered uphill, along the same road they'd traveled the previous night. Dessa was ahead, but higher up. Their bond wasn't stretched over-much, and its brightness promised help and home. Everything would be fine.

The lionesses ignored the road, cutting cross-country toward the amphitheater. Farley soon spied the borrowed cart, which was parked alongside the double row of columns. Torio and Larkin stepped into the open, weapons ready. The laundress followed, but she ran in a wide arc, keeping him and Verdal between her and Dessa. Smart statue.

When Char and Nyx stopped beneath the trellises, Larkin barked, "Climb!"

Verdal struggled with the harnesses. Farley needed to get him free and steady him to his feet. The starstone dancers looked on with concern, and like true guardians, they formed a line between the oncoming Misbegotten and her targets.

"Up," Farley urged, pushing Verdal toward the closest

trellis. "You'll be out of reach."

Shaking hands grabbed hold, but Verdal faltered. Farley got him moving, then pushed a shoulder under the man's rump, forcing him to climb faster.

"This is nothing," Farley said cheerfully. "We'll have you scaling the *Moontide*'s rigging before long."

Verdal swore. Then apologized for swearing. But he did manage to surmount the vine-draped colonnade, crawling to a clear patch of stone and huddling there.

Farley stood and leapt lightly over the man, then straddled the stoneworks in front of him. It was wide enough to be secure and high enough to keep them safe. "This is a good, sound structure. Best thing's to keep your eyes up. Come on, Verdal. Look at me."

Gray eyes lifted, and they were glaring.

"You did great. Not bad for a first adventure. Look, the others have her surrounded. It's basically over. Congratulations! You helped protect your hometown."

Verdal followed his gaze.

Swinging a leg over so he wouldn't have to twist, Farley watched Dessa and the lionesses close in, cutting off Pearl's escape routes. Torio's black, double-handled blade glinted dangerously, and Larkin prowled closer, weapons ready.

Their expressions were so serious. Times like this, there was a weight to the responsibility.

Farley said, "Some stuff can't be fixed. So it has to be stopped."

Verdal's ears slowly lifted. "He was so proud of her. He was so happy."

He simply nodded. As far as Farley could tell, sculptures only ever stirred because their creators found them and shaped them and loved them and called them. But some still found a bad ending.

"It'll be a clean break," Farley promised.

Suddenly, Verdal's ears swiveled, and he was looking up, eyes wide.

Dessa's scream came next, a soul-rattling cry that might have been his name and might have been a warning, but it came too late for Farley to react. Claws closed around him and jerked him from his perch, pulling him higher. The amphitheater fell away with staggering speed. And the distance? It was already starting to hurt.

Scales. They rippled and gleamed in the moonlight.

Two sets of forelimbs. Total dragon trait.

Needle-like claws and teeth. Just like Thrall back home.

But ... how were they flying? No wings beat the air. If anything, this dragon was slipping along like a snake, long body twirling higher.

Farley's gaze tracked further.

Harnesses. And not the mishmash of rope harnessing that he and Larkin were using to ride the lionesses. This dragon was properly saddled, and there was a rider.

Farley had enough presence of mind to resheathe his dagger. The last thing he needed at this height was to give his captor any reason to let go. The drop would kill him. Of course, so would the climb.

"Hey, mister!" Farley called. "Is your dragon blue?"

"Blue as banner flowers!" The rider leaned his way and grinned. "I'm glad we were in time. That was a dangerous situation, lad. So which of the lofts dropped you? Not for that mere bit of a scrape, I hope."

It took a moment to register that he was referring to Farley's horn. And that he was speaking in Verit. And that the accent held echoes of home.

"Hey ... mister? How come you're Flox?" And perhaps more importantly, "Are you trying to save me? Because you're going to kill me if you fly much higher. Kind of bound to that stone, you know?"

"I'm sorry to hear that, lad. Take us lower, Realm. Nice and easy."

There was a sudden weightlessness that sent Farley's stomach into his throat. He loved it.

"Let's make you more comfortable, shall we?"

The dragon's second set of hands came around Farley, carefully cradling him while lifting him toward the man in the saddle. He extended a hand and a push and pull later, and Farley felt much more secure. The rider turned enough to guide a harness around him ... and to meet his gaze. "Realm didn't nick you, did he?"

"No! No, I'm fine. Well, *better*. Now that we're lower." And because he hadn't done it in forever, he leaned forward enough to tap the man's curling horns. With more awe than enthusiasm, he added, "I'm Farley. And we're on a dragon. Hey, mister. Are you a cloudstrider?"

The man ignored the question and posed one of his own. "You can hear her, can't you?"

"You mean Dessa?" It was getting more and more difficult to tune her out. "Yeah, of course. She's furious with you. And me. Again."

"Oh, I know it." He stuck a finger in one ear and grimaced. "Never encountered the like. Most statues have tamer attitudes."

"*You* can hear her?"

He arched his brows. "I'm a cloudstrider, lad. Last in

my loft. The way she's carrying on, even a dullard would be clapping hands to ears. Maybe you could get her to ease off? Assuming you're on good terms."

"Yeah, I'm ... hers. Dessa's not a statue, though. She's a mountain. The thirteenth."

The man scratched at the stubble on his jawline, "That's an interesting perspective. Very ... landbound."

Farley really wished he had more light to see by. The man shaved, but the fanning lines around his eyes suggested that he was an agemate of Farley's grandparents. And his long, pale curls weren't shorn. It was hard to say if he'd been born silver or gone that way with age. He was Flox. *Had* to be. And yet he didn't adhere to the same customs as those on New Continent.

The very idea fascinated Farley.

"Maybe you could put in that good word *now*," he prompted. "I won't risk Realm if she's going to rampage."

"Dessa," Farley called. "I'm on my way back. You can tell, can't you?"

"That beast took *you!"*

"I'm fine. I promise."

"I will crack it," she vowed.

"Don't say that, Dessa sweet." And more softly, "He can hear you."

"No one will take Farley from me!"

"I'm not taken. Barely even borrowed."

They were getting near enough to the amphitheater for Farley to tell what was going on, and it was a mess. The lionesses had scrabbled up onto the colonnade and looked ready to leap after him, which was risky at that height. If they landed wrong, they'd be risking a fatal break. And Torio had joined Verdal, leaving Larkin to face the laundress alone, effectively erasing their advantage. Pearl could escape again. Or maybe even overpower Larkin. Was he ... was he favoring his arm?

"Dessa!" Farley hollered. "Call back Char and Nyx. Larkin needs their help more than I do!"

Torio's shout seemed to reinforce his plea, and the lionesses slipped back to the ground and bowled over the songstone laundress. Larkin stalked over to deliver a fatal strike, then glared Farley's way.

His hand sign demanded, *report*.

Farley returned an *all well*.

Artor hurried to Larkin, so the Pred really must have been injured. But Farley dragged his attention back to the cloudstrider. "I have so many questions."

"Unfortunately, I'm not free to give many answers."

"But ...! People keep saying all kinds of things, mistaking me for a cloudstrider and contradicting each other about dragons. You ... both of you .... You're the truth. I want to know it."

"And what difference would it make? Your knowing?" His smile had an apologetic twist. "Rather, consider what your knowing would mean for *us*. We've worked hard to fade from memory, and I risked everything for ... well, for nothing."

"I'll keep your secret. It's just ... you're Flox. And you ride a dragon. And your dragon flies."

"I can tell you mean well, lad, but ... you have no idea what you're talking about. And it needs to stay that way. I'll let you down. We'll be on our way. And if you and your companions really can keep a secret, that'll be the end of it."

"Your name, at least?" Farley begged.

"Aren't you a relentless one?" He offered a hand. "Nice to meet you, Farley Landbound. I'm Cantor. Cantor Brightstream."

"And ... your dragon is Realm?"

"That's his name. Whether or not he's mine is a matter of differing opinion." Withdrawing his hand, Cantor turned his back dismissively. "We're low enough now. The drop won't harm you."

Farley stubbornly kept his seat. "What you said before. About being the last ...? Could you tell I have an affinity?"

He waved a hand, but he did answer. "It's rare to find someone who can hear stone."

"It's not me who can do that."

"You obviously can. Or did you think I'd miss the fact that you were conversing with that statue."

"Dessa's a mountain. The only reason I can hear her is because she called me. My affinity's different. I can see magic."

"Ah. Well, no loss then. Unless you have a passel of nubbins who can impress me during an affinity test."

"I don't. But my brothers do." Farley blurted, "Tupp's always been able to hear, and he thinks Hewey's the same."

Cantor turned, interest clearly kindled.

And then Dessa tore him from the saddle, threw him to the ground, and fell upon him. She'd already landed two blows before Farley managed to free himself from the bucking, wailing dragon. "No! Dessa, don't! You can't!"

There was blood.

He could smell it.

Larkin barreled into Dessa, pinning her arms to her sides, but she writhed free, readying her scythe-like arms for another slash. Black stone and blood. The combination fizzed so much, Farley had to squint, but he got between her and Cantor. "Stop, Dessa! He never hurt me! You gotta stop!"

"Took you! Took you! Took you from me!" she raged. *"I will protect Farley!"*

All Farley could see in his mind's eye was the frenzy with which she turned the stone griffins who attacked Torio to rubble. If this continued ...!

"Dessa! Dessa, listen. You mustn't kill!" A sob slipped

out, but he said what he had to. "I don't want you to become something we have to hunt."

Her fury wavered. *"I'm not Misbegotten. I'm a masterpiece."*

Torio reached them then, joining Farley in barring Dessa from her prey. His voice was rough when he demanded, "Did Farley call for help?"

Dessa looked between them, sullen in her silence.

"Did Farley tell you he was all right?"

"I did. I told her I was fine. That they were bringing me back."

"You need to *listen*!" exclaimed Torio. "How many times did the young master prove the importance of listening? He was the first to listen to you!"

Behind them, Artor dropped to his knees and briskly called for Larkin to bring a light.

Dessa argued on. "He *should listen! I told him no. He took Farley anyhow!*"

Torio's voice shook. "Do you understand what you've done?"

"I protected Farley. He's safe!"

"No, Dessa. You may have killed a man." Torio looked sick.

"He might have cracked Farley."

"He *might* have ...!" Torio's shoulders dropped. "Oh, Dessa. You don't understand, do you? Not really."

"Why are you sad ...?" Dessa's tone had a desperate edge to it. *"I protected Farley. I'll protect you, too."*

"This wasn't protection. You misunderstood, and you lashed out, and a man is bleeding to death on the ground, and you don't even understand why this saddens me."

"Torio should be happy."

"Pinions and pinfeathers, woman. I am the furthest thing from happy. I am *un*happy."

Dessa took a step back, and her blades dwindled back into hands. *"I defended my home."*

"No."

"I was brave! I did my best!"

"NO! This wasn't brave. You were afraid. And you call *this* your best?" Torio's voice cracked. "Since when would any creation of Freydolf Meadowsweet's aspire to violence, bloodshed, and murder?"

Dessa whirled to apply to Farley, begging him to take her side.

He couldn't, and it hurt.

Farley could feel her turmoil, sense her heartache. She was near-frantic, and he tried to stifle a lurking fear. If she felt they were betraying her, would she crack or break or ... warp? But Dessa chose a different course.

Stepping back, she lifted trembling hands and folded them over her heart. Then she lowered her gaze and went still. Her clothing stopped moving. Her hair and the details on her clothing reverted to Frey's original design.

Farley swayed in place. This ... all of this. Was it his fault?

"Dessa?" Torio whispered, trying to take her by the shoulders. But she was no longer pliant, and his talons clicked against her surface. He snatched back his hands.

Their mountain. The Heartstone Mountain. Dessa.

She was still a masterpiece. But all the life had gone out of her.

20

Blundering Onward

Suddenly, it was too quiet. And not simply because Dessa wouldn't answer Torio. Oh, right. The dragon. Cantor's dragon had been so noisy up until a moment ago. Calling and crying. Farley looked up and around, but he couldn't see Realm anywhere. Had he fled?

"Farley!" Artor snapped. "I need you *here*."

He swung around. In the circle of lanternlight, a shirtless Artor beckoned with a bloody hand.

Larkin's blade flashed as he slashed through the Ursa's tunic. The ripping noise felt too loud in all the sudden quiet, but ... on some level, it registered as a good sign. Dead men didn't need bandages.

"*Farley*!" Artor repeated.

"Pull yourself together, Meadowsweet. We have need of your particular skills." Larkin was keeping an even tone. The diplomatic kind that meant trouble. "Come here by us. Now."

"Yeah. Here." He sank to his knees beside Cantor, who was breathing, but in pained gasps. What was Farley supposed to do? "Need me to go for help?"

"Nay." Larkin angled his head toward the cloudstrider.

"He's asking for you."

"Farley Landbound." Cantor licked his lips and tried for a smile. "Do you truly have kin with the right sort of affinity?"

"Yeah. A brother. A nephew."

"Seems I need a favor. Maybe two. Could be more." Cantor sucked in a breath over something Artor did, and when he coughed weakly, blood flecked his lips. "Just until I'm back on my feet."

Farley made the hand sign for a haggle. The old guy huffed a laugh and called him a brat, which was probably justified under the circumstances.

"Hide him for me."

"Realm? Uhh ... well, sure. I could probably figure something out, but ... he's kind of enormous."

Cantor said, "Look again."

Larkin made a subtle hand sign.

Artor lifted his chin.

Farley turned his head.

"Come'ere, lad." Cantor beckoned with a twitch of his fingers. "That little scuffle wasn't much of anything. See? These gentlemen have already forgiven our blunder."

A boy in his early teens edged into the circle of lanternlight, crawling on all fours. Well, it was actually all sixes since he had two sets of arms. He had some Basq features, like the pointed ears and that same series of small, curving horns atop his head. But instead of patches of scales here and there, they covered Realm's body in an iridescent blue that shifted and shone with his every move.

"Get on with it," Larkin silkily urged.

Farley was honestly stumped. "With what?"

Artor murmured, "Be fair, Larkin. He doesn't do it consciously."

Still baffled, Farley extended his hand in silent invitation.

Realm's eyes were the same stunning blue as his scales. His gaze bored into Farley, like he was searching for something. Then he just ... gave up. The intense look retreated, and there was only sadness as Realm pushed past Farley to get to Cantor. He huddled at the man's side, holding his hand and watching every move Artor and Larkin made.

"Farley Landbound," rasped Cantor. "Meet Realm. My son."

Two Months Later ...

Farley didn't normally garden by lanternlight. Of course, up until now, Farley'd never had so much trouble sleeping. So he turned soil and unbundled root balls and pretended that keeping busy kept him from brooding.

He didn't hear Larkin coming.

Wouldn't have turned even if he had.

Annoying the man was still somewhere on his list of priorities.

"Come with me."

Farley looked, if only because Larkin's tone was strange. It wasn't like a Pred to coax.

Offering a hand up, Larkin repeated, "I want you with me. You owe it."

"Owe you?" He rubbed dirt-caked hands together and shook his head. "Since when am I in your debt? Go away, Larkin. I'm busy."

In a blink, the man was in his face. "You bleated endlessly about brotherhood, but when I come to you for backup, you deny me?"

"Oh." Farley quietly resheathed his dagger. "Well, sure. When you put it that way."

Larkin grabbed hold to get Farley on his feet, and he didn't let go. Just started walking. The situation was somewhere between being led by the hand and being dragged along.

Out of the walled back garden.

Past a deep veranda with its aviary.

Around the freshstone wading pool.

They'd been at Aurelius's place in Halcyon for more than a week, having inched their way back up the Thousand Bells Road with three extra carriages. Larkin had rather pointedly secured one of those carriages for Farley's many purchases, which the Pred insisted they collect. Farley had tried to tell him he didn't care anymore, but the man wouldn't let the coin go to waste.

He'd shaken a detailed record under Farley's nose. Every single haggle, every slim copper—accounted for. Then Larkin had turned the list over to Dan, who'd immediately requested a translation. And a ledger. Those two had been doing okay as master and steward, but they were ten times more formidable as merchant and cleric. Aurelius was going to be so smug. The family business was in good hands.

All the way to Halcyon, Farley's borrowed carriage steadily filled with slips and saplings, eggs and peeps, and—at Larkin's insistence—ropes and reeds. To further busy Farley's hands. To pass a long, empty winter without Dessa.

"What's going on?" Farley asked.

Larkin still had him by the wrist, and his pace suggested some measure of urgency.

Along the path through the lemon grove.

Past the stable and carriage house.

Onto the cobbled road that ran down to the pier.

Farley could see the *Moontide* from here, moored in Aurelius's private cove. Farley's carriage was safely aboard, with Dessa inside—swathed and bundled and crated and silent.

Because they'd taught her to hunt, even praised her for her skill.

Then reprimanded her for putting their lives above someone else's.

Because of a terrible mistake with consequences that were still unfolding.

And because somewhere deep down, *they* were afraid, too. Of something that might happen. Of a future in which Dessa found her way to a bad ending. Farley never would have thought it possible. Until Dessa's idea of protecting had adapted to include killing.

Farley really, *really* wished spring would come and un-strand them from this shore. Maybe then, he could start moving forward again. And Frey could coax Dessa out of hiding, and Tupp could make her understand. Because Farley thought she did, deep down. Because she was Frey's. And because she was theirs.

When his boots sank into fine sand, Farley dug in his heels and repeated, "What's going on, Larkin?"

The man stopped, too, but he didn't turn. "I have need of your particular skills."

"You're kidding, right?"

"Nay."

He'd been half-sure Larkin was making fun of him the last time he'd said that. The Pred couldn't *really* think that being friendly took skill. Farley tried pulling free.

Larkin didn't let go. But he did turn, and ... his guard was down—rare and raw and just the tiniest bit rebellious. Like he was daring Farley to make fun.

And with that, Farley knew. Looking past him, he whispered, "Why are we going down to the water?"

"She's there."

Was he ... shaking? Farley stood a little straighter. "Livia's here?"

Larkin grunted an affirmative. Then revealed, "She's not alone."

"Your girls?"

"Aye. I caught sight from my balcony. Even though it's early, even in the moonlight, I could tell." Larkin's hold tightened. "My daughters are here."

So Livia had pulled off the impossible ... or at least the improbable.

"Okay, I'm impressed. She's definitely my favorite mermaid sister." Farley gave Larkin's shoulder a poke. "Hey. Not to call your courage into question or anything, but why'd you run to the back garden instead of straight into the cove?"

"Because ...." Larkin took him by the shoulders, glaring even as he fumbled for an excuse. "I would be ... outnumbered."

This was a big deal, so Farley treated it like it was nothing. "Gotcha. I mean, four girls. That is a lot of fangs to surrender all in one go, yeah?"

Larkin huffed. And swore. And sighed.

Farley pointed out, "You're great with kids. Look at Phillit."

"This is different."

"Maybe so." And searching Larkin's face, he asked, "I can really be there? What about Dan?"

"He'll get his turn." And finally letting go, Larkin grumbled, "Dan will probably expire on the sand from the honor of it all and need *me* for backup. So you're first. Lend credence to your boast, Meadowsweet. Prove that you're the world's best uncle."

Farley was having the hardest time hiding his grin when he went up on tiptoe, right up under Larkin's guard, and whispered, "Race ya!"

He bolted.

Larkin bested.

And when Farley caught up, Larkin was already hip-deep in dark water with a baby in each arm and tear tracks shining on his cheeks.

"Hey, no fair." Farley tossed aside his boots before wading in. "Save some for me."

Livia laughed and announced, "Farley is your papa's brother. By Pred tradition, this makes him your uncle."

Like it was true. *And* she said it in Verit.

Because she'd taught her girls their father's language.

No wonder Larkin was getting all emotional.

"I'm your uncle by Flox tradition, too," Farley boasted. "I'm your Uncle Far. Nice ta meetcha!"

Two little girls who looked to be six or seven were watching him from amidst their mother's coils. Waiting for their turn with their papa.

"Need a hand?" Farley offered.

"Aye." Larkin sloshed over and placed a baby mermaid in Farley's arms.

And it was pure magic. Literally. He could see it softly sparkling. Different from stone magic, but no less real. It reminded him of Realm. "Hey, sweetheart," he said, smiling into wide eyes. She looked a whole lot like Quinny when he'd been her age. Except for all the scales, of course. Her long, finned tail wrapped snugly around his arm.

Larkin gruffly announced, "Her name is Livinnia. And this is Rurrica."

Farley accepted the second baby, who giggled squeakily and quickly wrapped his other arm in silken scales. "Hey, am I doing this right, Livia? I won't hurt them or anything?"

With a ripple of serpentine coils, she came to his side,

and he sat in the shallows, attention still fixed on the babies. "You're fine," murmured Livia.

Like Phillit, the girls had pointed ears and spots where their skin was decorated by scales. But instead of nubs, these babies had thick shocks of dark hair. He wished there was more light to see by. He was curious about colors.

"This is amazing. Back home, when babies come, we count fingers and toes. But with Basq girls, I guess it's fingers and fins."

Livia laughed. "They're prefect. Nobody could deny it. Not even grandmother."

"You know, I like you even more than before, and you were already one of my favorite people, what with the whole life-saving thing." Farley watched Larkin haul one of the older girls into his arms. "You know the Pred saying? Little girls wear their father's fangs on a ribbon. He'd do anything for them, you know."

"I know." She laughed softly when Larkin knelt to speak to the other girl, only to have both of his daughters capture him in their coils, toppling him onto his rump. "I tell them stories. They've wanted to meet their Papa for so long."

"Was the trip dangerous?"

She said, "It was ... worth the risk."

"Yeah. Guess he agrees."

Livia radiated pride and pleasure as her daughters petted Larkin's hair and played with his claws and plagued him with questions.

"This means so much," Farley whispered.

"I know," she repeated.

He left them to it, content to sit in the warm water and cuddle baby mermaids until the sky began to lighten. Now, he could see colors. Larkin's older girls had the same dark brown hair as their father, and that brought out a strong resemblance to Ulrica. But the babies? Yeah. Totally inherited Aurelius's auburn hair, which looked very nice alongside green scales.

Eventually, Larkin crawled over to Farley. He brushed his knuckles against Rurrica's cheek, then Livinnia's, but he didn't move to take them. "I'll go get Pheldan now. I want Livia to know him."

"She'll *love* him," Farley predicted. "Umm ... anybody else?"

Larkin traded a long look with Livia. "We'll see. Aye, perhaps. But Dan next."

The Pred stood, stole a swift kiss from his wife, then jogged toward the house.

Farley said, "Hey, little misses? Do I get to learn your names, too?"

They swarmed over, and without a trace of shyness, they introduced themselves. Aurelia and Fortuna. He smiled wider, beckoned them closer, and asked, "Want me to teach you how to spit water between your teeth?"

Two Months Later ...

"It's done." Artor kept his voice low, but Farley still startled. "Do you want to take a look?"

He roused himself enough to mumble, "Yeah. Of course. That was fast."

"You've been asleep for nearly two hours."

"Oh. Well. Late night." He patted Phillit's padded bottom and asked, "Trade with me?"

Artor lifted the baby from his sprawl across Farley's chest. "You took a turn on the watch again?"

"Yep."

"I could give you something to help you sleep."

"I'd rather not." Sleep wasn't hard to come by, but his dreams were hard to take. It had been easier to hide his sleepless nights at Aurelius's estate, where they'd had bedrooms to spare.

Farley rolled out of the hammock while Artor tucked Phillit into the Fwan-inspired cradle that Farley had woven for him and strung up in the corner. They'd all puttered around with small projects. Artor had spent much of their time in Halcyon finishing the floor in Larkin's cabin. Farley had asked for his floor to be next ... *after* one other small addition to his home.

Walking into the passage, Farley turned, looked up, and reached. Evening and morning stones. "Day in and day out," he said, touching the matched blocks of titian jade and dawnstone now set into the wood over his door, holding up his hopes for a happy home.

Artor had done a beautiful job with the shaping and fitting. The stones were so sure they belonged there, happy with their lot, doing their best, blessing what amounted to Farley's doorstep.

"Say, Dessa. Did I tell you what I learned from those Fwan?" He talked to her now, as often as he thought of something to share. "Life is sober. Life is sweet."

She didn't answer, but he and Torio were sure that even if their words weren't reaching her, their feelings did. They'd keep trying, and they'd bring her back out of hiding. And then they'd listen to each other for as long as it took to understand.

"Satisfied?" asked Artor.

"It's perfect. And I made up my mind about the floor." Farley fished in his pocket and withdrew a solitary songstone bead. "I want you to use this."

The Ursa took it between thumb and forefinger. "And ...?"

"I'll leave the rest up to you. But ... I want that bead to

be happy. Make sure of it, and I'll be satisfied."

Artor hesitated. "That's it?"

"Yep."

"You don't want to ... pick a pattern or anything?"

"Nope."

"May I ask ... why *this* bead? Is it special?"

"I found that bead in the market stalls on the day we met. I figure that makes it a good omen."

A smile bloomed on Artor's face. "And I can do *anything* I want?"

"Sure."

"Could I try a scene? The mosaic masterworks at Nerida were exquisite, and I've been wanting to try something similar ever since."

"Sure. Seems like something you'd enjoy."

"It might take me a while." Artor held his gaze. "I'd probably have to stay on. Longer than expected. In order to see it through."

"Weren't you excited to get to Morven?"

"I am. Truly, I am. But ... I think I'd like to travel some more. Visit other mountains." He shrugged and shyly added, "I know it's not what we'd planned ...."

"Stay," Farley urged. "For as long as you want, *stay*."

Artor gazed around their room, and Farley could practically see the man forming plans. But then the Ursa turned to him, and this time, his gaze was that of a healer. "Go up on the deck. Fresh air. Sunshine. And see if Cantor needs anything?"

So Farley gave the touchstones over his door another caress, then went to find their convalescent.

Cantor Brightstream wasn't really one to sit still. In fact, Artor had threatened more than once to tie him to the second chair they'd added to the deck beside Torio's. The old man was very ... interested. In everything. And usually in hands-on ways.

Outside, Farley quickly scanned the masts. "Good news, Dessa sweet. We don't have to pull Cantor out of the rigging today. Well ... *yet* today."

Tsing and Dan and Verdal had taken seats on the planks around Cantor's chair, and a language lesson of sorts was underway. Now that the ship was bound for New Continent, everyone wanted to be more conversant in Verit. The surprising gateway through their assorted language barriers had been Artor's ability to communicate with his hands. Verit, Terse, Coloq, and Cantl might all have a different word for *sky*, but the gesture for it in Artor's silent language was the same for all of them.

Larkin, always keen where languages were concerned, was obsessed. He never talked anymore without accompanying verbal instructions with signed ones. The whole crew was catching on, and Farley couldn't have been more pleased.

Tupp would be impressed.

Chelle would love it.

And ... advantages. This one counted, and he wanted as many as he could scrape together if he was going to keep his promise to Cantor.

"Need anything?" Farley asked. "Artor wants to know."

Cantor reached for the crutch he still needed, might *always* need. "I'll have a word with him. You never can be too careful. Lend me a hand?"

Baffled, Farley offered to pull the old man to his feet.

Instead, Cantor caught his hand and traced three letters onto his palm. **T – R – Y.**

"Who wants to play Pinnacles?" Tsing asked brightly. But the hand sign he made was for *mast*.

Verdal said, "I should get back to work. Cradle guardians don't sculpt themselves." But his hands signed *climb*.

Dan asked, "Is Phillit asleep in his basket? Good boy." And with a faint smile, he proved he'd also been learning

Pred hunting signals. *Go in. Go hard.*

Despite their words, nobody moved. Instead, they watched him expectantly.

"I'll just ... get a bit of exercise, shall I?" Farley bent and stretched, limbering muscles that hadn't been used in a while.

"There are steelfin nearby," Cantor said in an undertone. "The lad's skittish."

"Stubborn, but not stupid. Oh, well. Wish me luck."

Tsing bounced up to kiss Farley's cheek and whisper, "Bring him home."

They'd all been worried about Realm, who'd thus far fled from all of Farley's invitations. The poor kid was desperate to get close to Cantor, yet he'd been thwarted at every turn. From a distance, he'd followed his foster father from Chime Winds to Halcyon, and now onto the open sea, where steelfins weren't the only thing that made the Furl nervous.

Farley doubted Realm was actually afraid of him. More likely, the dragon was afraid to get his hopes up. The affinity for hearing stone must *really* be rare if Farley's claim was too good to be true.

Halfway up the ropes, Farley caught the briefest flutter of blue. Realm was hard to spot in the open, since his scales vanished into a clear sky. But up here, his whiskers were always giving him away. Because Harrow sails were red.

And there was that teensy hint of magic, which Farley had yet to admit he could see. Mostly because Torio hadn't brought it up. But also because Realm would probably hate knowing that his camouflage was useless against the Flox he'd been trying so hard to avoid.

Sails strained against the ropes that held them fast.

Wind that tasted of salt pushed Farley's curls off his face.

Sunlight sparkled like magic across the surface of the sea.

And for once, there was someone to share the view.

"Do you like it?"

Farley worked his way closer to the basket he'd woven, then pulled himself through the circular opening halfway up its side. Larkin's crew had helped him secure it here, high on the foremast, just above the sail. Thanks to Farley, the *Moontide* had both a crow's nest and a dragon's nest. Provided they could get Realm to use it.

"It's made from good rope. Sturdy. Safe."

No response.

"And I did try to make it comfortable."

Still nothing.

Farley guessed he'd better state it more plainly. Climbing back up to the nest's entrance, he hooked his arms over the edge and found himself nose-to-snout with Realm. "There you are! Good. You should take a look inside. It's yours. What do you think? More pillows?"

The dragon was wrapped around the basket. He probably could have crushed it in his coils. Farley slid back into the shallow bowl of its bed, and when he checked over his shoulder, Realm was a boy again, crouched in the entrance. He used all four arms to control his descent into the jumble of blankets and pillows.

Farley flopped onto his back, hands folded behind his head while he waited to see what'd happen next.

The dragon crawled closer, testing a pillow and touching a blanket in passing. Then he reached for Farley, and long fingers slipped around his throat.

His heart leapt, but he held still. Retaliation had always been a possibility in his mind, but Cantor had asserted— again and again—that Realm wouldn't hurt a soul. Farley sure hoped not.

"Are you angry with me?"

Realm's gaze held silent messages.

"I won't give up, you know. May as well give me a chance."

The hand withdrew, and the Furl sat with his legs crossed.

Farley sat up and faced him, hands folded, mouth shut.

Because he'd said his piece before. What they were all waiting on was Realm's answer. By rights, they should've needed Cantor to mediate for them. Nobody else could hear the dragon or speak for him. Except ... Farley knew this kid's magic. And he knew how often Realm had been loitering in the rigging. In fact, Farley had chosen *this* spot for lashing the dragon's nest because it was Realm's usual perch.

A single finger slowly extended, pointing.

"Farley," he cheerfully supplied. He made the sign for his name. "Like this."

Realm lived up to every expectation by repeating the motion. Then calmly, deliberately, he formed words in the language everyone aboard ship had learned. *"Farley is foolish."*

He laughed. "How long have you been wanting to say that to my face?"

Realm flung his arms wide, his expression one of pure exasperation.

"I know. I get that more than you'd think. Want me to apologize again? It won't change anything. I meant it the first time."

"Where is my one?"

"On the Gray Mountain. It's a long way from here, but that's our bearing."

Realm leaned forward, beckoning with all his hands.

"What?"

Insistent gestures.

Farley caught on. He repeated himself, this time accompanying his words with sign language. "The Gray Mountain. We're going to my brother's mountain. My kin have a cloudstrider's affinity."

Realm pointed again, then smoothly signed, *"Give me my cloudstrider."*

"You know, I've been thinking. Tupp will probably be able to hear you, but he's *also* bound to a mountain.

Morven has him knotted up good and tight."

Realm looked stricken.

"Hang on, I wasn't done. I only mean it'll probably have to be Hewey. My nephew. Hewett Meadowsweet. He'd be ... hang on, let me think. Hewey would be five now, going on six. Still just a little guy."

The Furl's gaze dropped, and his hands insisted. *"Give me my cloudstrider."*

"He's not mine to give. We'll go see him. Cantor can explain everything to Ewert ... and ...."

But Realm hadn't finished signing. Gaze up and urgent, he repeated himself. *"Give me my cloudstrider. He will speak for me, and I will speak for her."*

Farley missed a beat. Then another. He hadn't even realized he'd entered into a haggle. Nor that—for once—he didn't have the upper hand.

"Speak for her?" he whispered. "Who do you mean?"

"Your one. Your mountain."

"Dessa?" He showed him the sign for her name. "You can hear Dessa?"

"Yes. That. Her. Dessa." Gesturing toward his ears with an expression of pure disgruntlement, he complained, *"She will not stop calling."*

THIS ENDS BOOK 1

Thank you for purchasing *Farley*. I do hope the tale was to your liking. If so, I shall borrow from Flox tradition and say,

"THE TRADE IS GOOD; MAY OUR NEXT BE BETTER STILL."

C. J. MILBRANDT has always believed in miracles, especially small ones. A lifelong bookworm with a love for fairy tales, far-off lands, and fantasy worlds, CJ began spinning adventures of her own. Her family-friendly stories mingle humor and whimsy with a dash of danger and a touch of magic. Follow your curiosity to CJMilbrand.com, where you'll find more stories and story art. CJ's books are also on GoodReads, and you can further support her storytelling on Patreon.

ALSO BY C. J. MILBRANDT
GALLERIES OF STONE

Meadowsweet
Harrow
Rakefang

THE JOURNEYS WILL CONTINUE ...

Hadwin

JOURNEYMEN OF STONE - BOOK TWO

C. J. MILBRANDT

9 781631 230912